Praise for *The House of Impossible Beauties*

'An exceptional first novel... The writing is erotically luscious, lyrically intense, forthrightly in your face, and pitch-perfect in the dialog... A grittily gorgeous work for readers who don't go for cozies.'

Library Journal

'Intimate and dazzling...a novel full of desire and suspense and heartbreak.'
Margot Livesey, author of *The Flight of Gemma Hardy*

'A marvellously serious, deep, artful, humane read. I'm really knocked out by this... [Cassara] managed to put actual, living, breathing human beings on the page... There's so much downright gorgeous prose here, so many beautifully and *precisely* observed images, subjects, emotions. Beautiful because *true*.'

Paul Harding, Pulitzer Prize-winning author of *Tinkers*

'Some debut novels are much anticipated... Others seem to come out of nowhere. Who knew Joseph Cassara's *The House of Impossible Beauties* would be that good?'

Publishers Weekly

'It is a tragic book, a lyrical book, a defiant book, and ultimately a loving book... Cassara clearly has deep love for every character who struts across these pages.'

Rowan Hisayo Buchanan, author of *Harmless Like You*

'Cassara has done a superb job of reimagining a world that will be foreign and even exotic to many readers, while creating fully developed characters to populate it. The tone is singularly apposite... A compassionate story, which is altogether moving and unforgettable.'

Booklist

'Fierce, tender, and heartbreaking.'

Kirkus

THE
HOUSE
OF
IMPOSSIBLE
BEAUTIES

JOSEPH CASSARA

ONEWORLD

A Oneworld Book

First published in Great Britain & Australia by Oneworld Publications, 2018

ISBN 978-1-78607-314-3 (hardback)
ISBN 978-1-78607-315-0 (export paperback)
ISBN 978-1-78607-316-7 (eBook)

Printed and bound in Great Britain by Clays Ltd, St Ives plc
Designed by Michelle Crowe
Glitter texture by KannaA/Shutterstock, Inc.

Oneworld Publications
10 Bloomsbury Street
London WC1B 3SR
England

Stay up to date with the latest books,
special offers, and exclusive content from
Oneworld with our monthly newsletter

Sign up on our website
oneworld-publications.com

For my family

In sorrow, seek happiness.

—Dostoevsky, *The Brothers Karamazov*

i need to know their names
those women i would have walked with
jauntily the way men go in groups
swinging their arms, and the ones
those sweating women whom i would have joined
after a hard game to chew the fat
what would we have called each other laughing
joking into our beer? where are my gangs,
my teams, my mislaid sisters?
all the women who could have known me,
where in the world are their names?

—Lucille Clifton, "the lost women"

AUTHOR'S NOTE

Though some of the characters who appear in this novel are based on historical figures, and many of the places described—such as the Christopher Street Piers, Sally's, The Saint, Paradise Garage— were important places during the decades covered, it is important to note that this narrative is fiction. The portraits of the characters who appear in this story, along with the events and journeys covered, should not be taken as a historical record. I believe that the role of the novelist is to search for poetic and narrative truth, and it is my sincere hope that this novel is a representation of such an effort.

THE HOUSE OF IMPOSSIBLE BEAUTIES

PART ONE

MOTHER HOOD/ SISTER HOOD

(1976–1984)

Perhaps home is not a place but simply an irrevocable condition.

—James Baldwin, *Giovanni's Room*

MOTHERHOOD

(1976–1981)

ANGEL

1980

Girrrl—

Before there was Dorian and before there was Hector, there was 1980—the year that things began to change. Diana Ross was pumping on the radio, Angel was sixteen years young and already she felt she was being turned upside down, inside out, boy oh boy, everything was turning around-around. If the seventies were the decade of disco, then the eighties would be what?—the beginning of a new era?—the decade of the sequin? It was the time that Angel the he became Angel the she—even if it was only something felt within the deepest layers of her soul, she knew that it was there, underneath the skin and the bone, as thin as a sheet of silver foil.

It's not that she felt trapped in her boy body. She felt as libre as a paloma on a humid summer night, flying up and around the project buildings of Da Boogie Down. How good it felt to say she!—because she didn't need to *be* a woman as much as she needed to have the *air* of a woman. So when her mother and brother, Miguel, were out of the house to run the weekly errands, Angel would take off her jeans and shave her legs. She stood there naked in front of Mami's vanity. She tucked her stuff back—up and away with a piece of duct tape—and closed her legs so that they crossed like an *X*.

Her skin was so smooth, her body so lean. But then there was her face. She knew she wasn't nobody's conception of cute, pero maybe when she got older she could cover it up with makeup. She could put on fake lashes, tweeze her brows, and put liner on her lips to make them look more plump. Years later, she'd think back on those nights and wonder what in Christ she was thinking being all tacky-tacky like that. Pero in the moment, it all felt right and she—for the first time that day—felt beautiful.

She took out the crumpled picture of Bette Davis that she hid inside her science textbook. She loved Bette Davis because she loved her sass. On summer nights, she sneaked down to the midnight showings of Bette's flicks in the Village and Chelsea multiplexes. She loved the drama of it all. She had picked up smoking because Bette Davis made it look so classy. Then eventually she found herself hooked to the damn things.

Miguel, who was only two years younger than Angel, had a stash of Newports hidden under his bed, so she took one and watched in the silver reflejo of the mirror as the smoke curled out of her lips. She walked to the bathtub and finished smoking while lounging in the water.

Once the cig was done, she dipped the end of it into the water, got out, and dried herself down. She always feared that Mami and Miguel would arrive home earlier than expected. (Ay, Dios mío, the Pathmark was closed down, Mami would say, but I forgot my wallet on top of the counter, and what the fuck are you wearing?) What would Angel say then? Caught red-handed, smooth-legged, in her mother's silk kimono that was so long, it looked like she was a tree made of flowing silk.

She imagined it would go something like this: Mami would cry and smack her with the broom, scream the Apostles' Creed, and threaten to call the santera lady to cleanse Angel with chicken blood and soothing tree oils, or some mierda like that. Miguel would watch, too stoned para decir nothing. And as this fantasy-nightmare played in Angel's mind, she practiced the lines from *What Ever Happened to Baby Jane* in the mirror:

—You wouldn't be doing these awful things to me if I weren't still in this body.
—But you *are*, Angel! [mouthing to the mirror, pointing a finger at her reflection as the bath water got swallowed by the drain] You *are* in that body!

* * *

She met Jaime one day when she was gliding around St. Mark's looking for an outfit that would pop. Jaime worked behind the sales counter even though he looked so bored at it—the kind of guy who seemed to have stumbled into fashion because he was beautiful. But it was his boredom that looked mad cute, like it was some kind of accessory that he was working. He had a fitted light-denim jacket and black pants that were so tight, Angel got a peek at his bulge.

Pero Jaime didn't give her no time of day. He just sold her the glitter nail polish she wanted with that same blank look of boredom. As she walked toward the door, she could feel his presence walking right behind her. She thought of what she could do: side-glance at a pair of black leather pants to ask the price (she was too flaca to make them pass), or drop the nail polish on the floor (and risk breaking the damn bottle?!), or just turn around and say, The weather today is crazy, ain't it (but girl, her stomach was in *knots*, and besides, the weather was perfectly natural), so she didn't do or say nada. And it was for the best, because homeboy was just looking to take a drag on his cigs, not nothing more, not nothing less.

He became Angel's recurring daydream. In these fantasies, Jaime and Angel were never in the same spot. In one, they're on a dance floor and nobody stands between them. Blondie is on blast. Even though she can't hear the music, she can feel it and knows that it is so. In another, they're at the Botanical Garden next to some flowers she never knew the names of. In yet another, they're on the subway platform at Grand Central watching a tourist scream at a rat. And the same thing happens in each one: that is to say, nothing. Nothing happens: they make uninterrupted eye contact, the kind of eye contact that feels like it is penetrating warmth into her body, but Angel can't think of anything to say. They stare and stare and Angel knows she gotta say *something* to fill the silence, and because she's daydreaming, it's almost like she can feel the words dangling from the tips of her fingers, but they can never travel to the tip of her tongue and come out of her mouth.

Nothing changed in her fantasies, nothing ever changed, day after day, night after night, except what she was wearing. Sometimes a tight silver-lamé onesie, or leather chaps (that one gave her cold sweats when she woke!), or another time it was just a simple little black dress or pair of jeans. She'd want to tell him that he was cute, that her body longed for his, but nothing would come out of her mouth, and then she would force herself to wake.

A month later, she decided that she had to go back to the store to throwdown. And by throwdown, she didn't mean nothing violent or wack. By throwdown, she meant, ask for his number. When she arrived, however, he wasn't at the counter. In his place, there was a chica as pale as costume pearls. She was wearing black lipstick, black pants, black eyeliner. Angel watched as she leaned against the counter and glanced back at Angel, probably to calculate if Angel was worth helping. The girl gave Angel a once-over, then went back to her nails.

"Pardon me," Angel said. "Can I ask you something?"

The girl didn't look up from the ferociousness of her nail filing. Angel asked again.

"I heard you," the girl said. "I heard you the first time."

Angel did not appreciate the tone or the attitude. "Well," Angel said. "Can I ask you then?"

The girl gave her a long set of eyes. "I suppose," the girl said, planting the nail file down on the counter as if she were in pain.

Angel explained that she was there the month before to buy, well, it didn't matter what she bought, but she was helped by this dude. She didn't mention the bored face or the cigarettes or the dreams she had of making awkward, uninterrupted eye contact while wearing nothing but silver lamé. Instead, she described the way his chin pointed just so, the way his eyebrows were groomed, and how his hair went just a tad over his ears, like some cover model for *Christopher Street* magazine that Angel had once seen with the caption: INTERVIEW WITH THE BUTCHEST MAN ALIVE.

"Oh, you mean Jaime?" the girl said. She rolled her eyes and Angel wanted to pry those eyelids open with her fingernails. "Of course you would be looking for Jaime. I should've known. Every little queen south of Fourteenth is looking for Jaime."

"Well I got news for you," Angel said, the sass in her voice unintended until it actually came out. "Do I look like one of those Fourteenth Street hippies? Girl, I am from Da Boogie Down Bronx. Just look at this style."

It was true that Angel shouldn't have given off any other aura than that of the Bronx, and maybe if that girl wasn't rolling her eyes up to the back of her head every time Angel spoke, she would've seen Angel's cute white T-shirt and Yankees cap. Angel's style that day was giving vibrations of the little flaco Boricua boy that Angel's body inhabited. Only in those dark moments at night, when she was alone at home, would she allow herself to indulge in her feminine beauty.

The girl blew a giant gum bubble. A pink ball against black makeup. Angel watched as the bubble grew bigger and bigger and hit the tip of her nose. Then it popped. As she reeled the deflated gum back into her mouth, Angel saw the black lipstick smudged on the gum.

"Ugh," the girl said, like it was a statement. "The Bronx."

"Yeah," Angel said. "What of it?"

"What a shithole."

* * *

As it turned out, Jaime was on his lunch break. Angel should have figured that out, and even though the girl clearly wanted Angel out of her nose hairs, Angel stayed and pretended to finger through the racks of clothes that were too punk rock for her to ever pull off. When Jaime returned with a McDonald's soda cup in his hand, the girl raised her eyes, popped her gum, and said, "Jaime, baby, you got another visitor."

The girl punched out and left without any goodbye. They were alone in the store and Angel was fishing for something to say. She settled on asking him what he got at Mickey D's.

"That's the question you're gonna ask me?" Jaime said. He was smirking at her from where he stood at the back of the store, near the dressing room that was really nothing more than a side alcove with a red curtain as a door. "I remember you," he said.

Angel was too nerviosa to ask something else, or dish out her usual dose of sass that she usually flung when someone was short with her. "Yeah," she said. "I just wanted to know."

Then, just like in her dreams, they stood at opposite ends of the store, alone, giving each other long eye contact in total silence. At least in the comfort of her fantasyland, she could startle herself awake, but she knew that now, since this was a real-life moment, she couldn't do none of that. His eyes scanned her up and down and she felt naked under the heat of his attention. "Come over here," he said. "There's something I want you to do."

Her heart raced as she walked over to the dressing room. Once they were inside together, Jaime pulled the curtain shut. Angel wanted to ask what would happen if a customer came in, but she knew better than to say anything. They both faced the mirror, which was an eight-foot ordeal leaned against the wall in all its hand-smudged glory. She loved that Jaime and the girl hadn't even bothered to clean the glass that day, as if there was no point to cleaning a surface that would be smudged again.

Jaime sat down on the stool and told her to undress. When she was finally naked, nipples tight with excitement, Jaime said he'd be right back and swooshed around the curtain. He returned with a tight silver dress, size who-knows-how-small, but it fit Angel's figure like plastic wrap over a plate of chuletas: tight but giving. She slipped it on and when she finally stared at herself in the mirror, then at Jaime staring at her through the mirror, she raised her arms to the side like she was about to launch into flight. Head back, mouth open, she closed her eyes and laughed. *Free,* she thought, *totally free*.

It was the kind of freedom you felt when someone was looking at you and finally saw what others couldn't see because it had been bottled away for so long. Angel had walked into that store in boy clothes, and there was Jaime, who had seen her and knew. How Jaime had known that Angel was the type of maricón to wear a dress, Angel didn't know.

When she turned around to face him, she saw his eyes devouring her. She felt it—like she had an invisible hook attached to her body and she was going to reel him in, until he was closer, closer, closer.

"Turn around," he told her, grabbing her shoulders in order to swivel her body back around. "I wanna do something to you, you slut."

She faced the mirror as he bent her body down enough so that he could pull the bottom of the dress above her hips. He bit her right nalga, then he slapped her ass. She wasn't expecting it, as if it were a sheet of glass about to smash into a concrete slab. The next morning, she would look at the bite mark in the mirror and think about how it looked like an itty-bitty bear trap had closed in on her, but then, when the bell at the front of the store jingled, Jaime stopped slapping her ass. He told her not to make a sound, and then he left her there all alone.

* * *

The next weekend, Jaime told her to wear the silver dress and meet him at The Saint, where he worked as a bouncer. It was a side gig, he told her, so he could treat himself to some booze and blow every now and then. She was faithful to Jaime's request: she wore the silver. Once she stepped outside, she was dressed like a woman for the first time outside the confines of her bedroom.

She took a jar of Vaseline, smeared it all over her face, and dabbed the rest on the bits of skin that were still exposed once she had the dress on. Then she doused herself in a bottle of glitter like she was shining brighter than a quinceañera dress. The goal was for her to embody silver in all its element—head to toe, didn't matter if it was radiating off her skin or the fabric—*she* was silver.

"Girl, what is this, what is going *on*?" Jaime said when Angel arrived. His fingers buzzed around her, snapping here and there. She loved the way his triceps bulged whenever his arms moved. He was the kind of man who looked so lean in his clothes, even his muscles came as a surprise.

Behind her, a group of five denim-clad muscle-gods stood with crossed arms until they flashed their membership cards and Jaime waved them in.

"What?" Angel said. "You don't like?"

"Oh, honey, I love me some glitter," Jaime said. "But you took it way over the line."

"What line!" She snapped her fingers once, then got closer to his face so she could whisper, "You know I don't give no care about some line."

"Ay, mi Angel," he said. "Whatchoo think this is—Baby's First Ballet Recital? You ever heard that saying, 'Too much of a good thing'?"

"No," she said, trying to make sure she didn't cry in front of him. She knew that Jaime was right. She looked like a glitter factory exploded and she was caught in the center of it all. "But if it's a good thing," she wanted to know, "how can you ever have too much of it?"

"Honey," Jaime said. "Look, it don't matter. Next time, use enough glitter to *accentuate*, not distract." He placed his hand on Angel's culo and guided her through the door. "Come see me later," he said and winked.

The Saint was off the hook. Shirtless chulos in leather pants, feather headdresses, crystal-encrusted nipple tassels, a man dressed like an Egyptian pharaoh pushed up against the side wall getting a blow job from not one but two boys dressed like Cleopatra. (There were normal guys too, in jeans and tight tees, but it was the locas that caught Angel's eye.) A man in a neon-yellow thong walked over to Angel and grabbed her ass, smiled at her, and gave her a plastic cup filled with bubbling white wine and a strawberry slice that floated to the top. "On the house," the chulo said before giving her an air-kiss. "The next one ain't free though."

The theme, Angel noticed from the posters that were taped to the golden theater doors was HISTORY, emphasis on the HIS. A shame that Jaime had not informed her of the theme (think of the possibilities!), although she thought she could always throw down the claim that glitter was timeless, and therefore, fit the *essence* of the theme.

Time passed not in minutes, but in drinks and the men who bought them for her. The Long Island from the club kid in the green spandex bodysuit, the Manhattan from the daddy in the blazer, the Bloody Mary (really?—it was one in the morning) from the muscular Italian guy with the gold-chain crucifix that he told her was for bumping coke straight from the baggie.

When she was drunk enough to feel everything spinning, she leaned her head back. The dome ceiling was designed like a fucking planetarium. There was a chandelier of sorts with dozens of multi-colored lights projecting stars onto the dome in a dizzying jodienda. Angel could feel the booze tingling in her brain and buzzing with each pulse of her heart to the tips of her toes. Her chin, she was sure of it, was numb.

She turned around to search for Jaime, but everyone looked the same. Each man, almost identical to the last, with the exception of his outfit. She looked out again, through the sea of muscled bodies gleaming with sweat, and there he was, twirling around in his white tank and black jeans. But who the hell was next to him? Jaime was dancing with some boy dressed in a white toga. The garb was clipped together at the shoulder with a golden olive-branch brooch. Angel took the celery stalk garnish out of the plastic cup and took a mean bite. She lit a cigarette and threw the Bloody Mary down to the floor. The liquid splashed at her ankles.

Smoking with one hand, chewing celery with la otra, she walked up to White Toga Bitch, finished eating the celery, and placed her free hand on Jaime's crotch. And she squeezed. Squeezed like his balls were an orange and she was making Sunday morning juice, fresh for church. "Who is this?" Angel said to Jaime, but White Toga Bitch beat Jaime to it.

"Who the fuck are you?" White Toga Bitch screamed above the music.

"What?" Angel screamed back. "Who the fuck are *you*? You're dancing with my man, girlfriend."

"And what are you gonna do about it?"

Angel thought about ripping the olive branch out, for starters, so that the toga would fall to the floor and he'd be left standing there naked. How dare he take that tone with her when she was only asking a question.

White Toga put a hand on Angel's shoulder to push her out of the way, but they were both too drunk for the fight to trip them up.

"Get your hand off me," Angel said. "Or I'll burn you."

"Oh, you're gonna burn me?" White Toga said, unbelieving.

Of course Angel didn't mean it in a *figurative* sense. She wasn't going to burn him with words, or dish out a piece of shade so dim it would melt the tears out of his eyes. Oh no. Angel was going to leave a literal mark. She was drunk, sure, but she was also learning how to be ferocious.

"I'm not gonna ask you again," Angel projected so that the music wouldn't hold back her words. She watched as Jaime watched them, just standing there. And with that, Angel took the tip of her cigarette and dug it into White Toga's arm, on the inside-side of the elbow, where a heroin addict would shoot up. Most sensitive area of the arm. That's why she picked it.

"You fucking bitch," White Toga said, holding rage. "You fucking burned me."

"You sound surprised," Angel said.

"Fine, bitch," he screamed. "You can have his skanky ass." He snapped twice in her face, twirled around, and walked away.

"Damn," Jaime said. "Didn't know you had it in you."

"Like hell you didn't," she said. "And don't pull that shit on me again. I don't need to see you macking it up with other people."

He pulled her close and rubbed his hard dick against her leg. "You turn me on with your feisty spitfire."

Ah, Jaime.

Jaime, with eyes that could melt the pyramids. Jaime, lean muscle fit perfectly in a leather jacket, as if he were the Puerto Rican James Dean. Jaime, the model on The Saint poster—his head thrust back as if in mid-orgasm, with rays of painted rainbows shooting upward. She placed her other hand around his back and on his shoulder blade and pulled him in, and even though she knew that he was a malcriado, a sinvergüenza, an up-to-no-good puto, she didn't care because as the coke and the drinks and the lights swirled around within her, she pressed her body up against his, trying her best to silently communicate everything that she desired.

* * *

If sex was a language, then Jaime knew all the letters, all the words. The next three months she spent in and out of Jaime's bed, in and out of the claw-foot bathtub in the middle of his kitchen. He would make her huevos estrellados as she smoked cigarette after cigarette in the bubble bath, saying, "I'd like to kiss ya, but I just washed ma hair."

She absorbed his sex. All it took was his hand on the inside of her thigh, or a serving of bedroom eyes at the right moment from across the bar, and she was his. And it was good. He taught her how to untwist a bottle of poppers with one hand. He held her other arm against her back as he fucked her. She huffed the poppers until she could feel her face flushing red, begging for him to go harder or deeper.

One day at the end of May, the birds that lived inside Jaime's AC unit were chirping. It sounded like they were trapped and screaming to be freed. She was starting to get the feeling that Jaime wasn't much of a bargain. He was conceited and thoughtless and messy. But it was a problem, of course, because she could tell that Jaime was falling for her—the sex had gone from Intensity So Rough She Couldn't Sit For A Day to Intensity Cariñoso Como La Flor. It wasn't that this set her off, but that she had come to view any trace amount of gentleness with distrust. After all, she thought, what *was* it that he wanted from her other than sex? She couldn't wrap her mind around the possibility that anyone would want something more from her.

She lay there next to him and wondered when he'd wake up so they could get the fucking over with and she could go home. She wondered how many side-boys he had. That is, if he had any.

It had been three years since Angel had fallen in love for the first time. His name was Kevin and he had lived in the same building as Angel before going off to UCLA on a soccer scholarship—one of the only boys in their building who was lucky enough to get out of state for college, or rather, to go to college at all. Angel was thirteen then. Kevin was on the verge of eighteen, had leg muscles harder than ripe aguacates, and was painfully straight. That didn't stop Kevin from inviting Angel over to the apartment when his parents were out of town every other weekend. He poured the rum out of the plastic handle and mixed it with whatever they had at their grasp—jugo de naranja, Sprite, that coconut soda that was so sweet it burned the roof of Angel's mouth.

He fucked her slowly because he said he didn't want to cum too quickly. He was gentle but he kept his eyes closed. When he turned her over, she put her hand on his cheek and said, "Don't you wanna see me?"

"Shh," he said.

When he came, he told Angel to bite his nipple hard enough to make him feel, but not hard enough to draw blood. He pressed the back of her head into his chest and said, "I love you, Ana. Don't ever leave me."

And who the hell was Ana?! Angel had no idea, but she played along because that was easier than bringing it up. Angel's worst fear was that Ana was some girl at the high school who had left him. The loca—who would ever leave a boy like him? So Angel thought that she could be Ana if that was what Kevin wanted. If Kevin wanted to fuck Angel facedown so that her boy parts weren't showing, if Kevin wanted to close his eyes when he came and dream of a blonde girl with long flowy hair and nails that could scratch his back, then that was what Kevin wanted.

When Kevin left, he promised to write, he promised to call, but then nada. More silent than a fly in outer fucking space. She vowed she'd never open herself again. She smoked a cigarette and stared at her body in the mirror, wondering what it was that Kevin didn't find good enough. She cocked her head like Bette and said to her reflection, "I'm still not to be had for the price of a cocktail, like a salted peanut."

Jaime was still asleep and his arm was holding her down, close to his body. She slipped out from under his grasp and went to the cocina. She took out two eggs from the nevera and set a pot to boil. Her plan was to wait until they were perfectly hard-boiled. She would eat breakfast, then she would walk out of the door for good.

She could hear his snores from where she stood, as if someone were strangling him in his dream and he was struggling his best to fight for air. It never bothered her while she was in bed with him (when she was out, she was out cold) but listening was a different story.

When the eggs were done, she cooled them down under running water and cracked the outer shell off. She popped them into her mouth, looked around the apartment, and thought, *What a dump.*

She slipped on her heels and walked out the door to face the sunlight for the first time in lady clothes. *Now* she was a woman, she thought, as she walked out the door and up Avenue A in search of the nearest uptown bus. Now she was a woman, because now she had learned to muster up the courage to walk out that door for the first time in her life.

* * *

When she was outside her building, she called the apartment from a pay phone and Miguel picked up. She told him to meet her in the hallway, just outside the elevator, and when they were finally face-to-face, Miguel gave her a look like, oh shit.

Angel was still wearing the dress from the night before. Her hair was frizzy with sex, and she bet that she probably still smelled like Jaime—the whiskey and Camels and lavender incense that clouded his apartment.

"Shit," Miguel said. "You walk here like that?"

"What do you think?" Angel said. "Course I did."

"Damn lucky nobody beat the shit out of you."

"What you think Mami's gonna say?"

"Shit, pues no sé," Miguel said. "Damn, Angel. Gonna get yourself killed. Whatchoo *thinking*?"

"Hasn't happened yet," Angel said, "so I dunno what to say to you."

"Yet? Whatchoo think—she's been drinking like always," Miguel said, moving his hand up like he was draining a bottle, neck back.

When they entered the apartment, Angel tried her best to keep her head high like she was some Miss Universe runner-up, too proud to cry in front of the audience. *Save the tears for when the doors are closed,* she thought, *just save them.*

"Ma," Miguel said. "Don't flip out, okay?"

Y entonces, they just stood there, where the little hallway met the even smaller cocina, where their mother was preparing the tostones and the little dish of olive oil with mashed garlic chunks. Angel watched her as she looked at the silver dress, at the heels, at the hair mess atop her head. Mami's face went sour. "Ay, m'ijo," she said. "So *that's* where you went? Go fucking change into your right clothes. I pay for you to have jeans and shirts and you go off and dress like a puta?"

Mami placed the glass so gently on the counter that Angel could see the ice cubes sway, but couldn't hear them clink together.

Angel regretted every decision she had made in the last hour. She wished that she could turn back time, crawl back into bed, and stay with Jaime. She had no idea what kind of bullshit was spinning through her mind to make her think that she could walk out the door dressed like that, like a whore. And of course Mami was drinking. Angel could have smacked herself for thinking so selfish—for thinking that just because she had made the decision to walk the streets as a woman, that her mother would be ready to accept that decision right there with her.

"You look like a no-class whore," Mami said. So calm, like she was reading a time slot out of *TV Guide*.

Angel walked to the bedroom to change. He put on a T-shirt and sweatpants and looked at the boy in the mirror. The word *whore* sliced through him. Maybe Mami was right. Maybe he did look like a whore.

He glanced at the silver dress on the floor, as it lay there like a puddle of fabric, and began to cry. He looked at himself in the mirror again—at the face that was too fea to ever be beautiful without makeup or glitter, at the legs that were too flacas to be manly, at the hair that was growing out, but could never be long and luscious like a blonde swimsuit model. He stared at the reflection in the mirror and he saw a boy—a flaco little boy in sweatpants and a dirty T-shirt. He saw a boy who was now wearing his right clothes. He lay on the bed and cried into the pillow.

"No llores," Miguel said. "C'mon, wipe those tears." Angel didn't hear the door open or Miguel walk in. He didn't know how long he'd been all alone. "Don't take this the wrong way," Miguel said. "But you won't look pretty if you're crying all the time."

Angel looked up at him, at that goofy smirk on his face. She smacked the side of his arm gently. "You joking?" she said. "Don't joke with me like that."

"Come on, Angel," he said. "She's drinking. She had a bad day."

"Means tonight's only gonna get worse."

"Maybe, but that don't mean you gotta be a bitch about it and cry. I got your back."

Angel had never loved her younger brother more than right then. She would come back to this moment years later, after everything that happened, and marvel at how *knowing* her brother had been. How understanding. How comfortable in his own body that he could still look at his older brother, who was dressed like a whore in a silver dress, and *understand*.

"Be straight with me though," Angel said. "You stoned right now?"

"Nah," Miguel said. "I'm out of stuff. Why? You want some?"

"No, I don't want some," she said. "I want you to stop with that shit."

Miguel laughed. "Look, I got your back. If you wanna dress like a girl or whatever, that's alright. But I love my weed and you gotta let me love what I love, okay?"

* * *

Angel was standing too close to the pan. Pops of oil jumped up and burned the skin on his arm. He lifted each flattened banana chunk out of the bowl, where they'd been marinating in olive oil and minced garlic, and placed them in the pan so they could sizzle like burning chunks of flesh. When they were crisped just right, he took a fork, stabbed each one, and placed them on a paper towel to soak the oil out. He loved tostones, the way they crunched in his mouth and then settled into their own mushy kind of sweetness. Another droplet of oil burned his arm and he squealed.

"Mira," Mami screamed, "you're standing too close." She grabbed his arm tight to pull him back and away from the stove. "You wanna get burned like that?"

Mami was downing a glass of water now to sober up because Miguel had drained the rest of the rum bottle down the sink when Mami went to the bathroom. Angel looked in the glass and saw the cubes of ice were melting away into little shards of their former selves. Mami's breath stank like a pack of cigs left to curl in a bottle of Don Q.

"I'm fine, Mami," Angel said.

"Yeah," Miguel said from the kitchen table, as if he were backup support. He was doing his algebra homework. "It's no biggie. I get burned all the time when I make tostones."

"Oye, peanut gallery," Mami shouted.

"Why don't you take a seat," Miguel said.

"I'm just telling him to move back so he doesn't get burned."

"Whateva," Miguel said.

Angel admired the way that Miguel was good at algebra problems. There was a kind of beauty to it. One night, when Miguel was balancing an equation, he told Angel about something called equilibrium. He said that in order to solve a problem, you just had to make sure shit was balanced on both sides of the equal sign.

He formed the plátano and moved it from the burning oil.

"Así you're just selling your culo down there with the maricones," Mami said, "as if it was a pussy, is that what you're telling me?"

"Ma!" Miguel said. "Stop it right now."

"¿Y qué?" Mami said, swirling her drink and taking another gentle sip as if it were a fine brandy. "You think I don't know how it is? I wasn't selling nada when I was young because your father was a good man—it's the truth."

Angel added another tostón to the pan and it sizzled as it hit the oil. "I wasn't selling nothing, Ma," Angel said.

"Pues, I didn't raise no mothafucking tonto, tampoco," Mami said. "If you're gonna do it, you better at least do it right and get paid, shiit."

"Ma, I said that's *enough*," Miguel said.

"Cállate, Miguel," Mami said. "No estoy preocupada por ti. At least you got the looks to get a nice girl. Pero that one over there?"

Angel turned around and said as soft as the cotton fabric on her pillow, "Mami, por favor. You're not being very nice."

"That's where you're wrong, Angel," Mami said. "I didn't raise you to be nice. The world ain't nice. You think shit was nice when they pushed your father off this building?"

Mami started drinking more heavily the summer that Papi fell off the roof of their building. When the cops had arrived, Mami had screamed, Don't tell me, don't tell me, which in the months and years afterward had changed to, You'll never understand, my husband was such a good man.

Angel was convinced that it was all her mother's fault. That she had driven him off that roof with her misery. Miguel had said that he thought Papi was too sad to even think about any kind of life. Pero it was Mami who insisted that he had been pushed, and there were some days that Angel entertained the possibility that, just maybe, she was right.

"Nobody pushed him," Angel said. "He fucking jumped so that he could get away from your crazy ass."

Mami slapped Angel so hard, Angel had to catch her balance so she didn't fall into the oil pan. "I am your mother," she said. "Don't you ever talk to me like that. You want to be a woman, then you better learn how it is, my son."

Miguel watched from the table. Angel gave him a look that said, I got this. "You know, Mami," Angel said. "You're totally right. Papi was a good man."

Mami held her head higher and closed her eyes. Her head moved like the bobblehead that Angel and Miguel had got at Yankee Stadium on Angel's ninth birthday—all Papi's idea. The best birthday gift Angel had ever got. Angel refused to believe what Miguel believed: that their father was too depressed to want to live, because then that would mean that Angel was part of the problem, o por lo menos, if Angel wasn't part of the problem, she wasn't part of the solution.

"He was a good man," Angel said, digging deeper. She was searching for the right string of words that would burn Mami so hard. "And it's amazing that he'd ever marry a woman like you."

Mami slammed the glass against the floor and reached her hands out to grab hold. Before Angel knew it, Mami's fingers were around her throat, squeezing mad hard. Angel only had a couple of seconds to think about her options—grab the pan of oil and clock Mami over the head? No, she could never burn her own mother. Kick her with a knee? Tampoco.

Miguel swooped in and carried Mami down the hall. She was screaming sounds that weren't words, as if pain had no vocabulary comprehensible to the human ear. He pushed her into her bedroom, slammed the door shut, and locked the door from the outside.

"Go to bed," Miguel shouted at her door as Mami banged on the other end. "You're drunk, Ma. Bo-rra-cha and you don't wear it good."

Angel turned off the stove and poured the hot oil down the sink. When Miguel walked back into the kitchen, she handed him two tostones that were plopped on a bed of paper towels.

"¿En serio?" Miguel whispered to Angel. "You're gonna bring up Papi when she's fuckin' wasted like that?"

Angel didn't say nothing.

Miguel grabbed her arm and pulled her into the sala. "Okay, listen to me," he said. "Punch me." He puffed up his chest and swagged back and forth on both feet.

"What?" Angel said. "Are you buggin'?"

"Just punch me."

"¿Por que?"

"Mira, Angel," Miguel said. "You gotta learn how to protect yourself. If you wanna be a chica, whatever. I still love you. But I'm not always gonna be there to throw shit down. You gotta learn how to throw a punch. So punch me."

She punched him and her knuckles hit his chest muscles, which were harder than she expected. *How was it,* she thought, *that two brothers could be born so different?* That night, he taught her how to spray a guy straight in the eyes with a can of PAM. He told her to aim her knees at a dude's balls and to really dig in as hard as possible. Because, he said, if she went after a man's junk, they won't fuck with her no more. She readied her second punch, then a third. "You think Papi would love me?" she asked.

"Damn, Angel," he said. "That's quite the fuckin' question."

"Yeah," she said. "I'm just wondering."

She watched as Miguel thought about it, one second, two seconds, three. "Sure," Miguel said, but Angel could hear it in his voice—he wasn't sure at all. Miguel had lingered too long before answering. But she smiled anyway, because she knew that Miguel was lying just to make her feel better about what they both would never—could never—actually know. She readied her fist and punched again, but this time, it landed like a gentle tap over her brother's heart.

THOMAS

1976

He feared that with that name, he would become the type of man who wore plaid button-downs and tucked them into chinos. With a belt.

She would *never.*

* * *

He lived in the Puerto Rican and Italian area of Jersey City. From his classroom windows and the roof of his building, he could see the Manhattan skyline. He liked to imagine that he was Dorothy and New York was his Oz—a place where he could go to become his true self. He'd only have to get across the water that held him back, and all that would take was one PATH train under the river. Then he'd be in Times Square with the businessmen, the hookers, the twenty-five-cent sex shops that promised a good show. He stood looking out at the buildings and thought, *One day*.

When he was eight, nine, ten, he used to stay in the apartment with Nonna while his mother was out with her boyfriend, Antonio. Nonna liked to open the closet door and take out all her wild outfits and drape Thomas in them. He stood against the plain white wall— the only wall without any picture frames—and posed for Nonna's camera. The goal was always to fill up an entire roll of film on the Instamatic with pictures of a certain theme. Nonna's favorite theme was Elizabeth Taylor, which wasn't as much a theme as it was a person. But it worked.

Tonight, he wore Nonna's rabbit-fur coat—the one with the hole in the left armpit that he liked to worm his finger through. He had on a long, red, chunky block-shaped costume necklace, and rings on every finger. "Hand me a cigarette, darling," Thomas said, and even though Nonna didn't smoke and there were no cigarettes in the apartment, besides the fact that no one was giving a ten-year-old a smoke, Nonna laughed until she had to readjust her dentures.

Thomas loved those nights, not just because it was Nonna-Thomas time, but because he didn't have to see his mother and Antonio. He didn't hate his mother. That would be extreme to say. He simply didn't love her the way that he loved Nonna. And sometimes before bed, he would pray that when he woke up, the world would be as it should be—no pain, plenty of food, and Nonna would actually be his real mother.

Then there was Antonio, with his thick Brooklyn accent and the gold ring on his pinky shaped like a lion's head with two small diamonds for eyes. *What a waste of diamonds*, Thomas thought, amazed that it was even possible for diamonds to be wasted.

After dinner, still in the rabbit fur, he and Nonna watched *The Gong Show* because Nonna had the hots for Chuck Barris. "That hair," Nonna said when the camera went to his face and he held the needle microphone to his lips. "I want to run my fingers through that hair."

They sat on the couch and cuddled while they watched, and

Thomas laughed at Nonna's running commentary. "Ma-donna," she loved to say, "what is this singing?"

He sat there, still in his Instamatic photoshoot outfit—swimming in the clothes like a miniature Liz Taylor—clapping so hard whenever Gene Gene the Dancing Machine or The Worms appeared. "Get up!" he screamed at Nonna whenever Gene Gene came out. "We gotta dance-dance-dance!"

They danced, shook it out, moved their hips as if they were doing a never-ending Hula-Hoop race.

Thomas loved to be overdramatic about it, so when the show went to commercial, he put the back of his right hand up to his forehead, looked up, and shrieked as he fainted to the floor. Nonna laughed and bent down to kiss him on the forehead. "Ah, *bello, bello*. You are so delicate," she said. "You have a delicate soul and it's beautiful and you no let nobody tell you wrong."

* * *

His mother decorated the entire apartment with magazine cutouts and postcards of Hawaii. Palm trees, rainbows, water that glittered so hard under the never-ending rays of sunshine, all taped to the walls with flimsy bits of Scotch tape. In the summer months, the air was so humid, the tape would unstick itself from the walls and Thomas would hear, *plop, plop, plop*, as the pictures and postcards fell to the floor. His mother would just tape them back up again. Didn't matter how many yards of tape she had to get through, there would always be more in the drawer.

These pictures were filled with smiling faces and couples that had no relation to Thomas and his family. Most of the people were blond and the wind blew through their hair like mad. Some of them were surfing or suntanning. One couple held hands and walked on the sand. Then there were the ones with no people at all, and those were Thomas's favorite. The volcanoes and fog and trees with roots that looked like they were ballerina feet balancing on top of the mud.

"Antonio is going to take me to Hawaii," his mother said one day as she was taping another magazine page to the wall, "for our honeymoon."

Thomas gave his mother one of the smiles he gave her so often—the kind where his mouth curled up but he showed no teeth. He knew that he would never get to go along on that trip. The world of Hawaii would only be seen through the pictures on the wall. But that was okay, because it meant that he could stay home with Nonna and watch *The Gong Show* and eat tomato salads with slices of mozzarella and tiny bits of oregano.

"What is it with this Hawaii?" Nonna asked. "Hawaii everything. Take these off the walls."

"Antonio and I are going to Hawaii," his mother said.

Thomas watched from the kitchen table and focused on his scrambled eggs.

Nonna laughed. "Antonio said this to you?"

"Yes, we're going to get married," his mother said. "You should know."

"You're getting married?" Nonna said. "He's already married!"

Thomas continued looking down at his eggs and watched out of the corner of his eyes. He had only met Antonio a couple of times, but he knew that his mother had been seeing him for much longer than that. He tried to imagine if Antonio were married, but he didn't know what the signs could be, other than meeting his wife. He had the feeling that he was hearing things that he wasn't supposed to hear, like the nights when Nonna cried in the bathroom alone with the sink water flowing, or when his mother's bed shook and shook until Antonio moaned and it stopped.

"He's going to leave her," his mother said.

"Oh, Isabella," Nonna said, "I no teach you to be so blind."

"Ma che dici?" his mother said. "These things take time."

"Eh, what is time?" Nonna said. "You no tell a woman like me about time."

He was almost done with the eggs, and he swirled the last clumps with his fork. He spread butter on a piece of toast and bit into it.

Earlier that morning, when Thomas woke up, he'd cracked open Nonna's bedroom door. The room was empty but the bed was made. He didn't know it at the time, but she had gotten up early to get eggs at the corner store. So Thomas knocked on his mother's door and walked in. She was lying on her side, running her fingers through her big hair. Even though it was so early, she already had her perfect Sophia Loren Persian Eyes penciled on.

"Really, Bella?" Antonio sighed as he unheld her and plopped back down on his side of the bed.

"What's the matter?" she asked Thomas.

"I'm hungry," he said.

"He's hungry," Antonio echoed.

His mother put her hand on Antonio's chest and told him to shush. "Nonna's getting eggs," she said. "Ant and I will come when the breakfast is ready." Antonio laughed and Thomas walked back out the door.

Now he bit into the last piece of eggs and they felt mushy in his mouth. "And where's your ring, eh?" Nonna asked his mother.

"Love is more than a ring," his mother said, adding more tape to the wall to hold the pictures up.

"Days like this," Nonna said, "I wish your father were still alive to tell you to have sense."

"Well Daddy ain't here."

"Why you no understand," Nonna said, "he will not marry you?"

"Ma che cazzo!" his mother shouted.

"Ma che cazzo is right," Nonna said. "No ring—ha!—*ma che cazzo."*

"Fuck you," his mother said.

The Maui postcard with the orange letters HANA and rich green trees had come untaped on one end. It was lopsided now, dangling off the only remaining piece of tape.

"You have no place to criticize," his mother said. "You work for him too, so I don't want to hear it anymore from you."

Nonna was silent. Thomas walked over to the sink to place his empty plate in as gently as he could. He didn't want to make a sound. He didn't want them to remember that he was standing so close by. He tiptoed down the hallway to his bedroom, lay on his bed, and hugged his pillow.

"Can't you think of your son?" he could hear Nonna saying. "You bring that man into this house," Nonna said, "and what if the police come and find?"

"That won't happen," his mother said. He squeezed the pillow harder, closer to his chest. "You shouldn't bite the—what's the phrase?—you shouldn't bite the finger? The hand?"

"Ha—" Nonna said, "I bite whatever I want to bite. I bite, chew, and spit right out if that man brings the trouble into the house."

* * *

When spring came to New York City, the world felt like a daydream. The trees budded out into cotton candy, people lunched outside, and the ring-a-ding tune of Mister Softee trucks whirled on every other block. And then there was the lake. Nonna's favorite place in the entire world was the lake in the middle of Central Park. When she was in a good mood and the weather was right—no spot of April showers to be seen in the sky—she paid for two round-trip bus tickets from JC to Port Authority.

Nonna rented a boat for them, which meant that he had to strain his tiny arm muscles to row them both.

"*Aspetta,*" she said. "Look there." She pointed her thick fingers—hands that could knead dough, fingers that could pinch cheeks—toward the East Side. Just above the trees, there was a trace of building tops.

Thomas stopped rowing and they stared at the buildings together. Thomas loved how, on a beautiful and clear day, there was a crisp line where the building edges met the sky. Those building tops were the only hint that they were still in the city at all.

Nonna told him that she loved Manhattan more than the other boroughs, and much more than Palermo, because of the buildings.

Manhattan buildings, she said, had expectation and desire. They were aware of their own beauty and power. They wanted to compete with the sky. But not in Palermo. Those buildings, she said, were brown like caca and old and sprayed with bullet holes. She said that holes were sad reminders of the past.

Thomas didn't understand how a hole could be a reminder of anything. Nonna took out two butterscotch candies for them, and after Thomas popped one in his mouth, he continued rowing. They passed a couple that had stopped to kiss. Thomas was worried that the couple's boat would fall over if they didn't pay attention.

When they returned the boat to the dock, his arm muscles were on fire. They walked past the pretty fountain with the angel on top of it, then up to Central Park West. On Seventy-Second Street, Nonna pointed up to a large building. "This is the Dakota," she told Thomas. It looked like a square castle.

One of Nonna's favorite hobbies, that she said made her feel like a real American, was to learn the names of monuments and buildings. The Statue of Liberty was just okay, she said, because everybody knew what that one was. Her face, she said, looked too much like a man.

She was interested in the other places. The Dakota, Thomas guessed, was one of them. There were men at the entry gates dressed in fancy suits. They stood under goblets of fire. "This is where the rich people live," she said. "Like Jonathan Lennon and Yoko Uno."

"Who are they?"

"He sings for the Beatle," she said. "The girls used to love him. Use to throw their panties at him and I say, Ma-donna, what is it with these girls?"

*　*　*

It was a little past four o'clock when there was a pounding at the door. Thomas was sitting at the dining room table working on his science homework—a worksheet that asked him, for the fourth time that year, to place the planets in their correct order. The exercise angered him—it was bullshit, he thought—because the nuns had already taught this to his class last year, and unless there was some kind of cosmic game of musical chairs going on that he was unaware of, the planets were still where they always were.

Nonna popped a saltine into her mouth, gummed it, put in her dentures, and got up from the table to answer the door. The man on the other side sighed when the door opened, and when Thomas glanced up, he saw that it was Vanessa's father, Henry.

Vanessa was in his grade at Our Lady of the Flowers. Not in the same class, because the nuns separated the girls and the boys, but they were in the same year. Vanessa was a nice girl, a bit quiet. She wore her uniform like all the other kids did—braided pigtails, plaid skirt, white collared shirt under a green sweater-vest. The other boys were mad for her. Thomas was mad for her plaid skirt. He liked to imagine he could be better friends with her so they could play dress-up and he could try on the skirt himself.

"Oh, thank god," Henry said. "You're here, Rosaria. I gotta talk with you." Henry's eyes darted around the room and he rubbed his hands together quickly, like he had just washed them and the water wasn't coming off fast enough.

"Henry, Henry," Nonna sang. "You've got yourself caught in a situation, eh?"

"You've got no fucking clue, Rosaria. It's bad." Nonna led him to the table and offered him some saltines and tea. He said he was too nervous to eat a crumb.

Henry was a nice man, from what Thomas could tell. They lived in a small house that was painted sky blue and had a porch with a swing. One day, in the second grade, Thomas had cut himself bad on the playground and Vanessa sat with him and soothed him while the nuns ran to fetch some bandages. "Don't worry, Thomas," Vanessa had said. "My mom is a nurse and whenever I get a cut, she says not to worry because everything will be okay."

"I don't got the money for Tonio," Henry told Nonna. He glanced at Thomas, then at the table, and he slid his fingers through his uncombed hair. When Henry looked at Thomas again, Thomas looked back down at his worksheet like he had been caught. He scribbled the word *Jupiter* next to the largest circle drawing.

"This is no good," Nonna said. She stopped spreading margarine on the cracker and let it sit on the plate. She sighed, "Henry, this is no the first time."

"I know, Rosaria," he said. "I'm so sorry, but we just had to get Vee a new uniform after that Menendez kid vomited all over the place last Friday. Cost me fifty bucks, can you believe that?"

Nonna hummed.

Thomas had learned what the word cunt meant because of Vanessa. Not that Vanessa had said the word. She was far too sweet for that. But it was the boys who had started calling Vanessa a good-for-nothing-little-cunt in the fourth grade.

"What does that mean?" Thomas had asked one of them, Sal, who was the ringleader of the group of self-appointed bad boys.

Sal had laughed at him. "It means she's a nasty bitch," Sal said.

"But Vanessa's so sweet," Thomas said. "She isn't a cunt, don't say that."

"Like you would even know, you fucking fag."

Now Henry put his elbows on the table, hands to his face.

Saturn, Thomas wrote. *Has seven ring groups. They are separated by gaps in space called divisions.*

"But seriously," Nonna said. "Why you put five hundred on the Mets? Do you even know what is this sport?"

"They're gonna bounce, Rosaria," Henry said. "I can feel it."

"You're in a lot of debt," she said. "Don't tell me what you can feel." Nonna put her hand on Henry's shoulder and he started to cry. "I'll tell you what. Let me get the book."

When Nonna left the room, Thomas stared at Henry as he wiped his eyes with a napkin. "Those napkins," Thomas said, "are really rough. I can get you a tissue from the bathroom. Or toilet paper. If you want something softer."

"You're sweet, Tommy," he said, "but I'm fine, thank you."

Nonna came back with her marble composition notebook, the same kind of notebook that Thomas used except Nonna's pages were filled with numbers and dashes, and the book was so full, the cover could barely stay closed. She had to use a rubber band to keep it tight.

"I'll see what I can do," she said. "Maybe if I fudge the last zero, it will look like fifty. Then you can just pay that, good?"

Thomas looked back down at the worksheet. *How many rings does Saturn have?* Henry thanked Nonna. "But you tell no one, eh?" Nonna said.

"Not a soul," Henry said. "You're a lifesaver."

"And for the love of Jesus and his heavenly mother," Nonna said. "Start to think about this game. The Mets are a path straight to hell. The Yankees, sure, they have lower return pay, but at least the odds are better."

"But I can just *feel* the Mets—"

"Eh!" Nonna screamed. She cupped her hands under her chin and cradled them back and forth. "What I just said about this feeling? You want odds or you want safety?"

"Safety."

"Well there is no safety in this game," she said. "I help you this one time, but no more if you continue with the shenanigans."

"Thank you, Rosaria. Thank you so much."

How many rings were there? Was this a trick question? *We don't know how many rings Saturn has. The number could be in the thousands, (maybe?!),* he wrote. Thomas imagined Vanessa sitting at home, wondering the same thing about the rings. Could Vanessa put a finger on a number? Could she say: Yes, there are 2,753 rings circling around Saturn and they all look like blue spaghetti strings, except made of ice crystals. Numbers were weird, he thought. He felt bad for people who believed in the power of numbers to tell them anything about the world. There were too many of them, too many to ever count. It was better that he didn't know how many rings there were—that no one could know—because then there was mystery. And mystery was always a beautiful thing.

ANGEL

1981

There was a write-up in *Christopher Street* magazine that caught Angel's eye about some diva named Dorian Corey. The foto was a black and white: Dorian center stage, dressed in ivory silk georgette, cigarette in hand, and hair as big as Pomeranian fluff. Her mouth was open midlaugh.

Angel trekked down to Collage one night to see Dorian turn one of her shows. Angel was still dressed like the flaco Boricua boy that the world saw her as: a down-low Bronx baby-gay shooting through the underground tubes of the city in jeans and a Yankees cap to that hole-in-the-wall club. Her eyebrows were plucked, but that was it.

The stage took up the entire dance floor. Dorian was dressed like Marie Antoinette that night, lip-syncing to Kim Carnes's "Bette Davis Eyes." Just the song made Angel jones for a bubble bath and a cigarette.

Dorian went all out with three gowns, one atop the other like there wasn't any shame in the world. She had a feather cap big enough to cover a Cadillac, so that when she shed her damask gowns like a lizard shedding its skin, she revealed a sequined body stocking. Two shirtless men with abs and pecs like nobody's business raised her silk organza train up on wooden poles so that the audience was swept under her outfit like a tent. There was a smoke machine and a disco ball and a fake guillotine. Someone even fainted, but not before shrieking. It was fabulousness incarnate, and it was so much for Angel to handle, she wept.

At the end of the show, Angel rushed backstage and opened

Dorian's dressing room door without knocking. Dorian, who must have been in his forties, was there with a handsome man about half his age. Dorian and the man looked at her and blinked at a glacial rate.

"And who are you?" Dorian said.

Angel introduced herself and gushed—she expressed her love, her admiration, her absolute fucking desire to follow in Dorian's steps, if only Dorian could explain how Angel could make it happen.

"Another one," the man said, fanning himself with an old Broadway *Playbill* like a Spanish lady on a summer day.

"Hush, Hector," Dorian said to the man. "I didn't order any tea tonight—iced or hot—I want none of it."

Angel didn't know whether to stay or go, until Dorian looked at her and said, "Alright, baby, but first let a queen get changed. Hector, honey—the wig."

Hector lifted the wig from Dorian's head. It was all white-gray curls, the size of a multitiered wedding cake. "As I was saying," Hector said to Dorian, ignoring Angel completely, "I think Rashida's pulling a fake, and if she ain't pulling a fake, she sure as hell is pulling a stunt on the whole damn group."

"Well, you always knew she was a shady little cunt," Dorian said.

"Oh, you're *such* a bitch," Hector said, "and that's why I love you." He placed a hand on Dorian's shoulder and they both laughed until Dorian coughed. Angel lit a cigarette and leaned against the dressing room door.

"And she smokes!" Dorian said. "Menthols? Be a doll and give mama a smoke?"

Hector put the wig in the closet and when he turned around, Angel could see his eyes scanning her, head to toe.

"Be a doll, darling," Dorian said to Hector. "Let me speak with the damsel."

"You asking me to leave?" Hector crossed his arms.

"You throwing shade, honey?" Dorian said. "Because I'll read your ass all the way to the New York Public Library, fool. Don't be trifling."

* * *

All Angel wanted was someone to look up to. When she turned on her television, or went to the movies, or flipped the pages of a magazine, she never saw anyone that looked like who she was, who she had been, or who she wanted to be. She had left her digits with Dorian and then waited by the phone every night, hoping it would ring. After a week passed, no one had called for her and she began to lose hope. It made her sad, the thought that a drag queen had seen her and decided no.

A week later, Hector rang. He was calling on behalf of Dorian. Leave it to a diva to have someone else do her bidding. Angel's hand shook as she held the receiver to her ear. Hector told her that the first month would just be a trial period. Then if Angel could handle things without getting in the way, she could stay on. "There's no money here though," Hector said, "so don't be coming to Dorian looking for a paycheck."

She whispered into the phone, even though the apartment was empty. She wasn't expecting to get paid. All she wanted was to learn the ins and outs. She wanted to see what it took to be a working woman in the clubs, performing for the crowd.

For three weeks, Angel wasn't allowed to touch the wigs. Only Hector could, and he guarded them like the crown jewels. "If you drop one," Hector said, "and it gets knotty, you will never hear the end of it."

In the fourth week, Dorian wanted to go out on stage as Olivia Newton-John. "There just wasn't a choice," Dorian said while eating a mozzarella stick. The cheese strung from her mouth like a tightrope ready for a high-wire act. Dorian had to reel the cheese in slowly with her tongue. "I'm surprised my neighbor hasn't murdered me yet. I've been belting out 'Summer Nights' in the shower, in the kitchen, in the goddamn hallway, for god knows how long."

"Good thing you can carry a tune," Hector said. "If it was me, the bitches would burn my house down."

"Why?" Angel said. "You can't hold a note?"

"Hold a note?" Hector said. "I'm basically tone deaf."

"He is, darling," Dorian said. "I can confirm. And so now I'm just living *Grease*. I simply need a pink jacket for my performance. I want, I need."

Dorian sent them out on a mission to find the pink jacket by the end of the week. It took them two hours to realize that they had a problem: it was impossible to find the pink jacket in Dorian's size. All three of the Broadway costume places they had checked only went up to double-XL. "Impossible," Hector said, holding the large by its hanger. "She'll look like a salchichón if we try to squeeze her into this."

Angel laughed and told Hector to stop being silly.

"Or what?" Hector said. His neck swayed all playful.

"Or nothing, excuse you," Angel said. She put on the pink jacket in size S. She turned to look at herself in the mirror. "Ay, I don't know. Maybe pink is just a bit too much for me."

"No," Hector said. "It looks fine. But we're not here for you."

She could have sworn he winked at her, but it all happened too quick to know if her mind wasn't making up games. "If you have a sewing machine," she said, "we can get the biggest one they have, cut it down the middle, and tailor in some more fabric."

Hector nodded. He said that he did, indeed, have a sewing machine that had belonged to his abuela. "The issue is," he said, "I don't got the fingers for it."

"I can sew well enough to put it together," she said. "We'll just need to scout out the garment stores. So we just need the jacket to give a little in the back, right? Maybe in the arms, too."

"Right," Hector echoed. "We just need the back to give a lil'-lil'."

* * *

She sat in Hector's cocina—shoes off, toes out—for an hour, working her magic at the sewing machine. She had banished Hector to the sala because he was talking her ear off and she needed to concentrate. She could swear that he was staring at her from where he sat, but she didn't take her eyes off the needle to check. Or else she'd accidentally add a zigzagged line right down the middle of Dorian's jacket. During her monthlong trial run? Absolutely not.

When she was done, she slipped into the jacket. "Penny for your thoughts?" she said, standing before Hector. He was sitting cross-legged on the floor with a yellow pencil and a crossword.

"Only a penny?" he said. She laughed at this. "It looks way too big for you."

"It's not for me," she said, too literal for her own good. "It's for Dorian, you know this already."

"I know, I know. I'm just busting your balls. Give me a twirl?"

She put her hands in the jacket's pockets, bit her lip, and looked to the side. She spun around slowly, gyrating her shoulders.

"My, oh my," he said in a drawl. "I do declare, you look beautiful, Georgia belle."

* * *

Pre-show, on a Saturday night, when Hector ran outside to fetch a pack of Newports, Dorian gave Angel an up-and-down look. "Well don't you look radiant this week. Glowing, really," Dorian said. "You two are fucking, aren't you?"

Angel giggled. "Ay, Dios mío," she said. "No, we aren't doing it. We're just, you know, spending time with each other."

Dorian rolled his eyes. "It's worse than I thought," he said. "He's got you feeling emotions."

"Shh, what if he comes back and hears you?"

"Matchmaker, matchmaker, make me a match," Dorian crooned. "Find me a find, catch me a catch."

* * *

Angel must've been the only girl at the zoo that had the absolute gall to wear a Lurex halter top with matching flared trousers. And it was, like, 90 degrees. The horror: fabric all sticking to her. Even the moscas were sticking to her.

Near the lagoon, Hector told her that flamingos were pink because they ate a lot of shrimp. "So if they were to eat," Angel said, "just for hypothetical's sake, nothing but pineapples, you're telling me they'd be yellow?"

"I got no idea," Hector said. "Why you asking me?"

"Because you're the one making claims," she said.

At the buffalo area, they argued about whether the right way to say it was buffalo, buffala, or buffalos. They couldn't agree, but it sure as hell made them laugh. "What about buffalo mozzarella?" Hector asked.

"A good cheese, indeed," Angel said. "Very tasty. We should make pasta tonight."

When they got to the hippos' tank, there was this fat old hippo mamacita with her baby, just all blubbery and cute. The baby spun and twirled in the water for Angel as she put her hand up to the glass.

Hector was leaning against the wall. "Ay, would you look at this?" she said to him. "I'm having a *connection* over here."

Hector smiled at her. It was as if the hippos could see her body standing there, with her hand on the glass. The mama did another loop-the-loop for her just like her baby did, with that goofy hippo smile, like she was proud of her baby just for doing its own little thing. Hector walked over to stand next to Angel and he placed his hand over hers, and they stood there having a precious moment together.

They walked around until Angel's feet were all blistery. They sat down on a bench near the pretzel stand. "Ay, Dios mío," she said. "I can't believe I was tonta enough to wear kitten heels to the damn zoo."

Hector laughed and put his arm around her. "You want me to rub your little toes?"

"Ay, fó," she said. "Don't be fochi. We're still outside and people are staring at us."

It was true—people were staring at them. Or maybe they were just staring at her. Angel didn't want to give a flying shit what anyone thought. But when it came down to it, she did care. She didn't want people to glare at the way Hector's arm rested on her shoulder. She didn't understand why people had to be so shady. She knew she shouldn't have worn that halter top. Not that day, not that place.

"What're you looking at?" Hector said to a mother who was trying to redirect her toddler from walking over to the bench where they were sitting. "We're not gonna steal your kid if he comes close to us."

The woman's other child was around five or six years old. He was devouring a blue cloud of cotton candy. He pointed a blue-sugar finger at Angel.

"Deja," Angel whispered to Hector. "Dont make a scene. Let them stare if they wanna stare."

* * *

A week later, he brought her to the New York Public Library. The actual, physical location. The main reading room was a large marble cave with old-time chandeliers. She looked up at the big lightbulbs, the pink clouds painted on the ceiling square of blue sky. "It must've taken them lifetimes to do all that molding," he said.

"Damn," she said. "I can't even imagine."

When they walked around the hallways, Angel loved the echo sounds of people's soles and tacones against the floor. He told her that the building was so old, if she wanted to request a book, they'd go back and use a pulley system to get it.

She gave him a side-eye. "A pulley system?" she said. "They don't have anything more up to date?"

He laughed. "Sure, maybe they do in some places," he said. "But I don't know, I find it charming."

She nodded. Yes, it *was* charming.

When they stepped outside to sit on the steps, she missed the smell of the place already. Like vanilla and almonds and a little bit of dust. There was something freeing about being back outside though, with the sun and the wind. She was worried that if she coughed or sneezed, the concentrating people would be up in arms.

"Sometimes I go to the Lincoln Center branch," he said. He bought them both ice-cream sandwiches and they sat on a bench looking up at the skyscrapers. "Like watching dance tapes with the headphones on. Get to seal out the rest of the world for just that moment."

"I love when people dance," she said. "Never seen someone look sad when they're dancing to the right beat."

"Ain't that the truth," he said. "That's what I want to be. A dancer. And a father. And maybe, if I got some money, I'd buy a house somewhere."

The ice cream was melting fast. Even though there were two reasonable-size bites left, she took it all in one. Licked a white drop of vanilla on her thumb. She looked up to see if Hector had saw. He did and now her cheeks were bulging. "What kinda house?" she said through the mouthful.

"Ha!" he said. "At least the nice thing about having no money is that when you dream big, you can dream whatever because it ain't gonna happen anyway. So I think a beach house, with a porch for playing dominoes outside. Or maybe a cabin in the Poconos. Learn to chop some wood, set a fire, make s'mores every night for dessert until you never want to see another marshmallow again in your life."

"A penthouse right on Madison Avenue," she said. "All glass."

"With a marble sauna the size of a bedroom," he said.

"And a driver."

"Yes," he said. "Getting places would be very important. A driver is a must."

* * *

In bed that night, she traced her fingers over his tattoo. It was a slash, like / about the size of a thumb between his hip and armpit. Her head was resting on his shoulder, but she could still see him wince a little as he looked at the ceiling. "Am I hurting you?" she asked. "Like is it hurting when I touch your ink?"

"It's not that," he said. "Just brings back a memory. Got this tattoo with my ex. It's nothing, forget about it."

"Oh."

"I don't like the sound of that oh."

She didn't know why she was reacting this way, like stone cold. She had to have figured that he had exes, but why'd he have to bring it up like that? Her heart was fluttering a little. She sat up and reached for her pack of Newports on the floor near the edge of the bed.

"Getting a tattoo with someone is a big-ass deal," she said. "It's permanent on your body."

"Girlfriend, you know how it is sometimes," he said.

"Do I though?" she said. The nicotine hit her straight after the first inhale. Her mind felt a clearing. "What does that even mean, that I know how it is sometimes."

"I don't know," he said.

She told him that she was surprised she was acting this way. She thought maybe it was a sign she liked him more than she had thought. "And then what happens when you leave me for your ex," she said. She counted in her mind: there had been Kevin, Jaime, some other lesser loves that didn't bear repeating.

"That's not gonna happen," he said.

"Such a smooth talker," she said. He leaned over for a puff on her cigarette. She rolled her eyes and moved her hand over so he could reach his lips to the cig without breaking his neck.

"Tyler doesn't live in New York anymore," he said.

"Did you love him though?" she asked. The cigarette was almost done.

"Of course I did," he said. "But it's not like we only have enough love reserved for one person. It's possible to love multiple people over time. If you ask me, I think that every time you experience love, it feels and looks and sounds different."

Angel nodded and pushed the cig into the glass ashtray. She didn't want to tell Hector that she had never really fallen in love with anyone yet. There had been flings, but nothing that made her want to scream out on the street and announce it to the heavens.

"I don't got any tattoos," she said. She stood up and spun around slowly so he could capture every inch of her body with his eyes. "Maybe one day though."

* * *

At night, before sleep, he'd whisper into the crook of her neck: *C'mon, Angel. All you gotta do is think about it.* He wanted to start a house in the ball scene. He would be the father, she the mother. All Latin. *What if they got nowhere to go? Or nobody?* Just like the morenas at Paradise Garage. And the white queens that trek out to the far reaches of Long Island. *Shit, we don't have cars to go out there joining them.* She liked the idea of it, but she knew it would be a lot of responsibility to be a mother. At least the good kind of mother who knew how to love and appreciate. Not like she was racing to make the same mistakes that her own mother made, so she didn't want to get too excited too fast.

Then Princess Diana got married. Angel was awake at the wee hours of the morning and, like the rest of the world, was peeled to that television like Gay Santa Claus was about to shower the world with diamonds. Hector held her as they sat on the floor of his sala. She watched Diana walk down that aisle in her mega-long train of ivory taffeta and antique lace. She was so overwhelmed by Lady Di's beauty that she cried. She thought of all the hands that sewed the thousands of pearls and sequins, all done with love and admiration, so that Diana could wave to her people.

"See?" Hector said. "Diana is an up-and-coming mother of that house."

"She is," she said. "She will be."

Hector watched the whole procession even though he told her that he thought it was too stiff. They ate their bowls of Cheerios and drank their glasses of OJ and Hector wiped her tears with the edge of his white pajama shirt.

"I got an idea," he said, standing in front of the TV.

"I can't see through you, babe" Angel said. "You're not a ghost."

"I've already seen this story before," he said. "They get married at the end."

Angel rolled her eyes and took their bowls to the sink.

"So my idea is," Hector said, "that we should dress up and go to Saks."

Angel pursed her lips like what for, what are the two of *us* gonna buy on Fifth Avenue, Mr. Pipe Dream?

"For window shopping," he said. "No sé—we could try on shit, have a look-see in the mirrors. You know—the mirrors in Saks are magical."

Angel sat back down on the floor and kicked out her feet so Hector could move out of the way of the TV. "Are they made of crystal?" she asked and Hector laughed.

"No, but wouldn't that be the shit," he said. "No crystal, but they do make you look like pure glamor."

"But the real question is," she said, "do they have dresses with hand-sewn pearls?"

They decided that they needed to dress as proper as possible. Hector searched through his closet to find his suit, an old thing he had got for a wedding a few years ago. He wet his hair and combed it to the side, then doused it in hairspray until it hardened. Angel went the route of simplicity—a zebra-print button-down with chunky green buttons and a white faux-silk foulard tied around her neck for an added ounce of pizzazz.

They took the uptown bus from Hector's apartment in Alphabet City and when they got there, the first floor was *divine*. The rush of people was mostly elegant women and less elegant tourists, all clutching bags of items gobbled up from previous purchases. The perfume spritzer girls looked hungry, the handsome men in suits simply stood in their corners—the clacking of heels, the shine of the lights against the waxed floor. Angel felt dizzy. She felt like she was walking into a Ralph Lauren ad from the pages of *Vogue,* except these people didn't look like they were about to hop on their horse and play a match of polo.

"Holy shit," Hector said. "That woman is wearing a full-on *Saga nishiki* getup, do you *see* her?"

"Yes," Angel said. She saw her alright. "And I want to give her my digits so we can be friends." The woman must've been in her fifties, with the tautest skin Angel had ever seen. She had blue eye shadow, hair that screamed Madison Avenue salon, eyebrows in a permanent state of raised wonder, like the world was constantly throwing her pleasant surprises. She looked like the kind of woman who knew how to hydrate.

And that *Saga nishiki* blazer with golden buttons! Could have been straight out of the Met costume archives. The woman walked right past them and Angel got a whiff of her perfume—surely some kind of floral scent, maybe from Paris, maybe Milan. Somewhere far away from where she was standing.

As Angel looked around, first at Hector, who had stopped at the Guerlain counter to get a tester spritz of some green cologne, then at the other women wearing silk foulards around their neck, suddenly everything felt so wrong. Angel's foulard wasn't Gucci, wasn't Fendi, Dior, or Chanel. It was some polyester piece of shit she got at a cheap boutique downtown. Everything was all wrong. They would be spotted. They would be seen for exactly who they were— two poor Puerto Rican boys who could barely afford a three-course meal in Midtown, let alone any kind of shirt from Saks. When they took the escalator upstairs, she realized that she couldn't even afford the panties. What were they thinking? Who were they trying to fool?

They took the escalator one floor higher. Hector held her hand and guided her to his favorite section: Chanel suits. There was a little boutique section set aside for each designer house. A woman in what must have been a Chanel suit was standing behind a counter, reading from a giant binder. She had a silver pen in her hand, but she wasn't writing anything. To Angel, she looked like a living mannequin, with those white gloves and a long strand of pearls around her neck. She was flaca y elegante, vibrating to the tune of Audrey Hepburn circa 1961.

Hector whispered into Angel's ear. His directions were simple: pick out any suit and he would buy it for her.

"Are you out of your loco, ever-living mind?" she said.

"A new outfit for the mother of our house?" he said.

"With what money?" she said.

"¿Qué dices?" he said. "I work. I get money. Aren't you trying to get in with Dorian and make it into the scene?"

Hector had a point. Dorian was all about acquiring the clothes, not mopping them like some of the other girls. *Most* of the other girls. Dorian's rules were simple: If you can't make it yourself with the fabric from the Garment District, then you gotta buy it. Don't be déclassé and steal, because stolen clothes never looked good or right on nobody.

Angel chose a black-and-white herringbone jacket with an all-white collar and a long, black silk tie that fell down the chest. There was a matching skirt that would hit just below the knees, but she would need to try it on first to see how it looked. She imagined herself with white gloves and a long, *Breakfast at Tiffany's* cigarette holder, standing in front of the Eiffel Tower.

When Angel tried to make eyes with the saleswoman to get a fitting room, she realized that the woman wasn't giving them no focus at all. She must have decided, Angel thought, that they weren't going to buy anything. Angel had been right after all. This saleswoman had seen through them. She had detected that Angel was not the kind of boy who could wear a black-and-white herringbone suit in front of the Eiffel Tower.

Hector grabbed the woman's attention, and she came over to unlock the door. She gave Angel a silent side-glance, eyebrows raised in doubt. It was such a quick look that Angel wasn't even sure that it had happened. Angel felt enraged as she slid off her clothes and put on the Chanel. The woman's doubt made her want the suit even more, so she could wear it and give off fuck-you vibes to all the people who tried to front with her.

She looked in the mirror and felt what she imagined all the brides-to-be in the world feel when they first see their gowns. That sense that this was the outfit that had been preselected by the universe at the very instant she popped out of the birth canal.

She smoothed out the fabric that bunched under her armpits. The herringbone felt soft and supple between her fingers. She put on her sunglasses and waved to an imagined audience of fans. Did she look like Lady Di? *No,* she thought, but she was exuding the same energy.

The problem came at the register. "It's okay," she whispered to Hector. She stood next to him at the counter while he recounted the five C-notes, as if there was some kind of mistake. He didn't have enough cash on him.

"Babe, it's really okay," she said again. "I don't need this." She tried to say the words as softly as possible, as if they were for both Hector and the saleswoman, who really did look sorry that she couldn't sell the Chanel to them. The saleswoman looked almost embarrassed herself, as if they had caught her eating with her hands at a formal gala.

They stepped onto the escalator that would bring them back down to street level. "It's not okay," Hector said. "I wanted to buy this for you."

"I'll just go to the Garment District and make my own," she said. "I'll give you Princess Diana realness any day of the week, with or without Coco Chanel on my side."

As the escalator steps disappeared into the ground, they had to readjust their strides to the ground below them.

He insisted that they not leave empty-handed, so he went to the counter and bought something he could afford. When she held the bottle up to the light, the perfume looked like melted, translucent gold. Chanel No. 5. The glass was thick, unbreakable, with a topper that looked like a giant crystal.

I told you I'd get you Chanel, didn't I?

Angel would replay these words in the back of her mind as the years passed, as everything and everyone passed before her. She didn't know it at the time, as she walked out the door with her small paper bag with the words as elegant as ink on bone—Saks Fifth Avenue—but she would come back to that glass bottle and spritz it on her neck, her wrists, for every funeral she'd ever have to attend. It would become her goal, years later, to never have to reach the end of that bottle. Because she didn't want to think about what it would mean when that unbreakable glass was finally empty.

HECTOR

1978

He met Tyler in dance class. Tyler was this beautiful, muscular faggot-queen that practiced next to Hector at the barre. The man could get into fifth position quicker than anything Hector had ever seen. His allongés made Hector confused about his own desires. He didn't know if what he felt was envy or lust or both wrapped in one.

They practiced next to each other every week. Stretches, hip openers, the gamut. The view from the window was of the brick building right across the way, so Hector's eyes wandered from barre to brick to boy. Of course his eyes did, how could they not? Tyler's body was lean muscle. Gold hoop earring. Moustache.

Their instructor was trained in the Martha Graham method. She was a middle-aged Russian woman named Katya whose footless black tights exposed a series of corns, blisters, and cracked skin. Sometimes Hector's eyes would be drawn to her feet, a warning of the horrors that could happen to the human body. She didn't seem to care though. She wore them, it appeared, like they were a badge of honor for every shock her feet had been made to endure over the years. Hector was careful not to let her catch his wandering eyes, fearing the tongue lashing she would surely deliver. He was supposed to be focusing on his own body.

"Children, now we will move to the center," Katya screamed. "I need to see you harness the core energy within your vaginas—both your physical and metaphorical vaginas—and jeté, jeté, jeté. Harness!"

They tried to harness the power of the vagina. Even the several men in the room, like Hector and Tyler, whose vaginas were merely metaphorical. She told them that she had seen enough of their attempts at whatever it was they were doing. She told them all to sit on the floor, backs straight.

Tyler was to demonstrate the choreography for the class, she said. Of course it would be Tyler. Hector was not jealous about this. He was relieved that he could sit and watch Tyler in motion. All anyone had to do was look at the man dancing and they could see that he had been tapped by something divine. Watching him was like watching time open up into air.

"Now kneel on the floor," Katya instructed Tyler. He knelt on the floor, rolled out his neck and shoulders, and looked straight at Hector. Tyler held his gaze and Hector felt his face flushing red. Katya stomped her foot on the floor and told Tyler to raise his leg close to his chest, then to his head, then beyond his head. The body in deep contraction. "We call this the vaginal cry," she yelled at the class, "for all that she cries to her lover. Her husband. Her child, or her children. I want to see sharp angles. Nothing soft, so help me. Now all of you: harness!"

Tyler remained frozen, leg up above his head. His arches as rounded as a banana. Hector had never seen thicker calf muscles. Simply imagining the amount of core strength that this must've required sent a sharp pain behind Hector's eyeballs.

"We dance for the memories of things we dread to remember,"

Katya said as the rest of the class went into position, raising their legs up, then beyond the head. "We dance for the things we wish to forget."

* * *

The things he wished to never forget, in no particular order: what it meant to grow up on la isla; parents that up and died before he could remember their faces; living all his memory with his abuelitos; listening carefully enough to the coquís chirping into the night; running through the streets of Viejo San Juan up to El Morro, pretending that the castle-fort was all his for the taking; the days when Abuela didn't have to work at the Caribe Hilton and they ate lemon piraguas on the street under the orange-ball sun; Abuelo showing him how he worked the tram cars that connected Viejo San Juan to the rest of things; imagining what it would be like if the cannons were still there to shoot at the ships in the water; the way the blue waves crashed into rock, turning to foam; when he was all alone in the fort's stone alcove and he stood on his tippy toes just like Señora Rodrigues had taught them in ballet class, staring at the golden square of sunlight on the ground, kicking his right leg back, left arm forward, fingers up into an arabesque . . . *Less rigid, niños, don't be so pedestrian; fingers soft, Hector, so that a droplet of water can dangle off the edge. Remember this.*

* * *

They started to arrive early each week so they could do their floor warm-ups together, before the others came. Tyler was working Hector's abs like a bitch on wheels. Making him go from high plank to curling his forehead in so he could reach his knee to his nose. It felt like he was wringing his body out like a sponge. When they did standing barre, sometimes Tyler arched his body in toward Hector. For a quick second, Hector could smell the musk in Tyler's cologne. It would hit him like a wave, and then it would be gone. As if it had not happened at all.

It only took two or three weeks for Tyler to ask Hector out. Hector tried to play it cool, saying, Give me a day to think it over, even though he knew he would say yes. The next day, he dialed Tyler and said yes.

Tyler took him to Saturday Mass at Paradise Garage. It was Hector's first time, so Tyler insisted that they take a cab. Tyler's treat. "It's not Studio Fifty Four," Tyler said. "But at least in a cab, we can pretend to make an arrival."

So they pretended to make their arrival. It was a two-story parking garage with a long line to get in. Tyler told him to wait there in line, he'd go talk to a friend in the know. As Hector waited alone, a middle-aged queen several people downstream was talking loud about her date the night before. "You know it's always an *ordeal* when they're fucking hot, but dumb-dumb-dumb," the queen was saying to a confidante but projecting for all to hear. "And he was a California Republican, so gag me with a spoon already. I told him if he didn't stop talking about the virtues of former Governor Reagan, I'd be forced to manually shut him up by sitting on his face. And he said he didn't see a problem in that, so it was a win-win for everyone if you ask me. I didn't have to hear him blather *and* I got to sit on his face for two hours. It was delicious, I'm sure. Only way I knew he wasn't suffocated and dead was that his tongue wouldn't stop moving."

Hector felt an arm; Tyler was back, dragging him to the entrance. The bouncer nodded, and in they were. The first thing that hit him was the curled smell of alcohol mixed with sweat. The floor was a little sticky. Tyler ushered them through the mob of people to the side tables. It seemed like there was no bar, just the tables with self-service punch bowls. Tyler handed him a clear-plastic cup. They raised them up and cheers'd. Head back, Hector downed the purple punch.

The place was shoulder to shoulder, everyone swaying. And the sound. Like no other sound he had ever heard. The lows punched him straight through the heart. When the bass dropped, the entire garage thumped. Felt like they were all one giant heartbeat, giving the place life, screaming yesss. The DJ played the same deep beat over, like five or six times in a row, and some queen shouted out, "We get it, Larry. We *feel* you." For the jam wasn't just a jam. Now it was the anthem of the night. It had been decided and the dancing merely confirmed it. There was no attitude, just communication. Because they were all happy, dancing and prancing, choosing and cruising. Tyler swayed back and forth in front of him. Hector put his arms around Tyler's waist. Snuck his hand down to grab his ass right in that sweet moment before the beat dropped, when they all knew what was about to come and the anticipation was killing them.

* * *

"Sorry if I shot all over you like some Jackson Pollock canvas," Tyler said immediately after they fucked. The cum was still fresh on Hector's torso when Tyler got up to get him a towel.

"I don't know what you just said," Hector admitted. He grabbed the towel from Tyler and tried his best to wipe off the mess without smearing it into the pelitos on his chest.

Tyler told him to hold on a sec. When he came back in the room, he had a coffee-table art book. The paintings looked like a can of paint took a giant shit on the canvas. But in a beautiful way.

"Pollock was an abstract expressionist," Tyler said. They both sat up in bed as Tyler slowly turned the pages. Each of the paintings looked like a different take on the same theme. Hector wondered what a dance version of one of these paintings would be like. Something intense and energetic. Uncontrollable movements, limbs that thrashed and convulsed.

"You went to college, didn't you?" Hector said.

"I did," Tyler said, sounding guilty about it. "I went to Yale."

"Yeah," Hector said. "You sound like you went to college."

Tyler closed the book and slid it under the bed. Hector pulled the covers over the both of them.

"I graduated last year," Tyler said. "Still figuring things out."

Hector was eighteen. He knew that college wasn't in his future. Even if he wanted to go, where was the money at? He wasn't some Mr. Moneybags.

"Yeah," Hector said. "Me too. Still trying to figure things out."

* * *

He had been poor his entire life. When Abuelo died, after a lifetime of rum and chicharrones, Abuela sold what few things they had and they moved to Nueva York. It was a rinky-dink walk-up on the fifth floor just off Avenue C. Hector was twelve years old, and the first night in the NYC, he missed the sound of the coquís. Manhattan was by no means silent. Eventually he would learn to be lulled to sleep by the sounds of car horns and fire-truck sirens. It would seem to him that there was an emergency happening around every corner that needed attention. But that first week, all he wanted was the sound of the coquís, so he went to the pet store in the East Village and bought a dozen crickets. He poked several holes into a cardboard box, and when he closed his eyes, he pretended that the crickets were frogs singing for him, until one by one, they each died and he became accustomed to the silence.

Abuelita started selling numbers for an Italian bookie from the Bronx. She spent most of her time cooking or being a bochinchera with the other viejas in the neighborhood who had also made the trek from PR. One night, when Hector was scratching some math problems at the kitchen table, the landline rang. It was some cop. Deep voice. He told Hector that his abuela was being held and if he wanted to come get her at the precinct, he could post bail the next morning.

Leave it to Abuela to get her bookie-making ass thrown in jail! Hector couldn't believe that shit. The next morning, he brought the cash and bailed her out. "It was that bitch Montserrata," Abuela said. "I always knew she was a malcriada, going to inform on me like she is no better."

Hector didn't know who Montserrata was, and he didn't want to push any more buttons by asking. He figured she was one of Abuela's "friends." A true bochinchera to the end.

"You don't know what they did to me in there," Abuela said like a case of overdrama.

He told her to sit down on the sofa, he would make her some soothing tea. The box said words like calming, chamomile, luscious notes.

"They threw me in the jail cell with all the putas," she said, doing the sign of the cross. "Ave María y los santos."

"¿Las prostitutas?" he said. He tried to imagine a little old lady in a cement cell with all the streetwalkers who weren't discreet enough to get by.

"¡Ay!" she gasped. "Que sí."

As the tea was steeping, he handed her the mug and brought her a roll of Goya Maria Cookies for dunking. He asked if she wanted milk and she said of course she wanted milk, had he ever seen her drink tea without milk before.

"If you only saw what I saw," she said. "They speak such vulgar words. I tell them that if they don't stop, I will take soap and wash out their mouths, and then their chochos!"

* * *

"Tell me about her," Tyler said one night in bed. He had seen a picture of Hector with his abuela, and another of his abuelo and abuela right after their wedding day. In the foto, they were sitting in chairs somewhere in the campo of San Germán. They faced the camera, unsmiling. "Must have been a crazy wedding party," Tyler had said and Hector laughed.

"What do you wanna know?" Hector said. He didn't know how to answer. No one had asked him before. He didn't think anyone around his own age was interested. "Why do you wanna know?"

Tyler ran his fingers up and down Hector's spine. "Do I need a reason to learn more about you?" Tyler said.

"No," he said. "I guess not. But you never told me about your family in Dallas."

"We don't speak," Tyler said. "They think it's a phase. Like Tyler goes to New York and goes through one of his phases. Fuck them."

Hector leaned in closer to nibble on Tyler's lip. "Can we go back to sleep?" Hector said. "I'm not ready to face the day."

* * *

In the middle of the night, he startled awake. He readjusted the blanket over the both of them and rubbed his foot against Tyler's foot. Tyler nuzzled his nose against Hector's cheek, and they both fell back asleep like this, wrapped around each other.

* * *

The next Saturday Mass at the Garage, the grooves were coming out at a hot pace. Some bitch couldn't take the heat and passed the fuck out. Had to be dragged out, but that only stopped a few people from dancing for about a minute. "Give her some air," his lover screamed. Hector and Tyler went to refill their punch cups.

When the MC introduced a black queen as the mother of such-and-such house, and would everyone give up a round of applause for her legendary children in the audience, Hector clapped. The legends slayed their moves. "Amaze," a bald queen screamed. He did a cobra snap, then walked away in the other direction.

Later, Tyler had to give Hector the 411. "So the white queens have their balls out on Long Island," Tyler said. "And the black queens have theirs up in Harlem."

"What about the Puerto Ricans?" Hector said. They were walking up Varick, looking to get a slice of pizza. He lit a cigarette.

"The mira-miras?" Tyler said. He took a cig from Hector's pack. "What about them?"

"Where their balls at?" Hector said. "Don't say mira-miras."

"Oh," Tyler said, as if he hadn't thought about it. "I guess they just have to join either side."

Hector sucked his teeth.

"Yeah," Tyler said. "Looks like you're gonna have to start your own house then, Mister Boricua." Tyler couldn't pronounce Spanish syllables to save his life.

"Don't tempt me," Hector said, neck back to exhale his smoke. He watched Tyler do the same, and how erotic it was to watch a man breathe out cigarette smoke.

"I can just see the marquee lights now," Tyler said. "Hector Valle: House Father."

* * *

On a scale of One to Betty Ford Blackout, his level of drunk was, say, Half-Finished Martini Glass at Liza Minelli's. He thought it would be a good idea if he and Tyler went to the tattoo parlor. He wanted to get a / , and Tyler would get a \ . Together, their / \ would equal an X. If overlapped. Apart, the slashes would symbolize a separation of two halves. As he explained this aloud, he wondered if it made sense. How many rum and Cokes had he had? He felt like he was rambling, but what he was trying to say, Tyler, is that there was a meaning. He thought that tattoos should have that: meanings.

"I'm going to get mine on my side," Hector said.

Tyler said he was going to get his on his right calf.

"All it takes is a T-shirt," he said, "to hide it from my abuela."

"Yeah?" Tyler said. "Are you hiding me from her too?"

It wasn't even a fair question. He pretended to ignore it as the tattoo artist pricked his skin. It burned him more than he thought it would.

The next morning, when they woke up, Hector looked at his new ink, right below his left rib cage. "Well," he said. "I don't regret it."

He needed water and an ibuprofen or two.

"Good," Tyler said, smiling. "I don't regret it either."

* * *

"What can I tell you about her? Soon after they got hitched and that foto was taken, he went out for work but didn't come back home for dinner. She waited up for him. No phone call, nothing. Can't even imagine what that had to be like. All the worrying. She lit an extra candle for Jesus. When he got home, it was mad dark and he smelled like a bottle of rum. She said, Where'd you go tonight? He said, Don't you ask me questions like that. And he hit her. Well she wasn't gonna take none of that shit. She said, If you know what's good for you, you're not gonna go to sleep in our bed tonight, hijo de puta. But he was tired and drunk, so of course he fell asleep on their bed that night. She took out her chancletas and she popped him real good in both eye sockets. Gave him two black eyes. He never touched her like that again in all his life. It was like she showed him who ran shit. She was not to be fucked with."

* * *

He lost them both that year.

First, his abuela. Died on the toilet seat like Elvis Presley. Massive heart attack, Hector would later learn, but when he first saw her, he didn't know what the hell had happened. Her face made the pain of death look complicated. And that scared him, to think that pain wasn't simple. He called Tyler and said, What do I do now? Tyler came over and took care of things: called the ambulance, the funeral home, ordered a bouquet of yellow flowers so that Hector could have some kind of life in the house.

Then, Tyler. Only two days after he had left to visit family in Dallas, the call came. Hector had been napping. The woman said her name was Karen. She was Tyler's sister. He had been in a fight. Was Hector sitting? No, but he could sit if that's what she was instructing. Two men had slashed Tyler's face, then beat him with a crowbar in the alley behind the bar. Karen was whispering. They were having the burial in two days. Yes, he had heard her correctly. She was sorry. Thought that Hector would want to know. "But please don't call back at this number," she said. "My father doesn't know I'm calling you."

* * *

For days, he wandered the streets thinking, *A crowbar? How many slashes? Did they destroy his beautiful face? How can I call back if you don't give me the number?*

* * *

A graduate student at Teachers College gave him counseling for free, as part of her degree studies. She looked almost thirty, with a severe jet-black bob. Her trousers were wide-legged and pleated. She spoke very slowly with him, and he wondered if this was her counseling voice or her everyday voice. Did she order bagels with cream cheese in this same lullaby voice? It soothed him to the point where he craved a nap after each session.

The first day, he cried the entire hour and said nothing of substance. She asked him to keep a journal. To write letters. To make a list of accomplishments throughout his day, like when he cooked a meal, showered, got out of bed on time. He did these things.

Week three, he told her a memory. When he was six, Abuelo took them out for a drive around the city in his new Chevy. They drove around, Abuelo and Abuela in the front seats, Hector in the back. Nose only an inch from the glass window, he watched the painted buildings in Viejo San Juan pass by. Pinks and yellows and blues. The tiny balconies with clothes hanging to dry. When they stopped for gas at the Esso station outside the city limits, he saw a homeless man and woman sleeping under an overpass. "Who're they?" he asked Abuela.

"People," she said. "No mires así. It's rude to stare."

But for whatever reason, he was convinced that those people were his mother and father. Even though he had no memory of his mother and father, the feeling was real. "You can't ever tell a boy that that's not his mother if that's what he's stuck on believing," Hector told the counselor.

"But she wasn't your mother," she said, writing notes. "The man wasn't your father either."

"They weren't," he said. "But I swear to god, in that moment, you couldn't tell me otherwise."

She asked him how he felt about that. He didn't know how he felt about that though. He brought it up because something similar happened to him the other day. He was doing some compra in the Gristedes when he saw a guy that was Tyler. He didn't just look like Tyler. He *was* Tyler.

"A doppelgänger?" she asked.

"A huh-what?" he said.

"Never mind," she said. "Go on."

"He was holding a bag of almonds and I went up to him and said, 'But you're allergic to almonds,'" he said. "And he looked at me and said, 'No, I'm not.'"

She wrote this down and told him to go on, but there was nothing else to the story. He asked her if this was how it was going to be from now on. Was he going to see Tyler everywhere?

"Perhaps," she said, looking up from her notepad. "Until you meet someone new."

SISTERHOOD

(1984)

VENUS

She smoked her pre-bed cigarette behind the Dumpster where the
nuns and the girls couldn't shoot their words. She closed her eyes,
thought about how to furnish her dream house. It would be out in
the suburbs: Catskills, Hamptons, the country. It would all be white,
even the fence. The kitchen counters would be clean, and her man
would wear a suit. Dior, naturally. He would come home every day
at five o'clock. They would have sex before dinner, and she would
serve him salmon and he would say, Baby, I love you.

Now she was nineteen and home was nothing more than the Serenity House shelter because she was tired of sleeping on benches
around Central Park. She figured she could sneak behind the Dumpster on the side of the building to smoke her cigs without having to
deal with any of the nuns.

The shelter was in Brooklyn near Prospect Park, but not where
all those fancy houses were at. It was far enough from Jersey City
where she felt she had finally left her mother behind, but close
enough to Manhattan where she could feel close to her people, her
sisters.

The nuns were no joke, and it was hard to find one any younger
than sixty. They gave her a scratchy wool blanket, three bland meals

a day, and a roof. No air conditioning, but a girl ain't gonna complain about that. It's not like her mother had AC in Jersey.

She felt a hand on her shoulder. "You got a light?" the guy said.

He was a total butch queen decked out with a tank and chest hair that was curling over the top of it. His pecs were bulging and, as Venus offered her light, she stared at his moustache. He said his name was Jonny, but people called him Sugar Cookie, and would she like some nose candy.

"Nah," she said. "I'm not into that."

"Really?" he said. "You look like the type of girl who likes blow." He sniffed and wiped his nose with the side of his wrist and exhaled a cloud of smoke. "You sure you don't want a little bump?"

"For real though," she said. "Coke ain't my thing."

She watched him dip a key into the little plastic baggie. "I heard of your name before," Venus said. "You're Loca's boyfriend, right?"

La Loca was Venus's roommate. Emphasis on the was. La Loca had given herself that name because, as she said, some bitch from history was named Juana la Loca and she liked the sound of it. She proudly told every girl that she would go loca-crazy on their ass if they tried to pull any shit. Even some of the nuns were intimidated.

On Venus's third night in the place, Sister Milagros, the short Dominican nun who was full of Ay Dios míos and Ay benditos, told Venus to move to a room in the East Quarters. So Venus carried what few things she had with her—a blow-dryer, pink plastic curlers, some clothes—to the new room when La Loca walked in.

"Oh no," she said to Venus, having the audacity to wave a finger all up in Venus's face like she ran shit. "No, no, hell to the no. Get out."

"What's bugging you?" Venus dropped her favorite sequin camisole on the bed.

"You ain't Sugar Cookie," La Loca said. Her neck rolled and she clapped between each word to emphasize her anger. "I told that bitch Milagros that I need to be with Sugar Cookie. And you are not Sugar Cookie."

"You mean Sister Milagros?"

"That's what I *said*."

"You gonna call the nun a bitch like that?"

"Did I stutter, bitch?"

Venus stared at La Loca and tried to contain every ounce of impulse that made her want to slap the fake lashes off her eyelids. "Well," Venus said, "I don't know what to tell you. She told me this was my new room."

"You don't gotta tell me shit, that's what. You just gotta go find another room."

"I just got here," Venus said. "Why do I gotta move my stuff when you're the one with the problem?"

"Don't give me that kind of tone."

"I ain't giving you no tone," she said, channeling all the living patience in the world. "I'm just saying——"

"Do I look like I care what you're saying?" La Loca said. "No, *look* at my face and tell me if I care? I need to see you packing it on out of here."

Venus didn't need an enemy, so she packed it on out and found another room. Her new roommate was an old black woman with swollen ankles who cried all the time and liked to feed pigeons.

Now she was sharing a smoke break with that loca bitch's man out by the Dumpster. "Your girlfriend," Venus said, "got mad issues."

"Yeah," he dragged on the cigarette and handed Venus back the lighter. "Girlfriend—eh. I don't like to use formal terms and shit like that."

Venus flicked her own cigarette butt to the curb. "All I know is that I had to switch rooms so that you two could be in the same room together. She really rose hell and back."

He nodded. "Word," he said. "Don't fuck with her, that's all I'm saying." He held out the baggie of coke and gestured at it with a point of his chin. "You sure you don't want none?"

"Nah," she said.

"You're wack," he said. "Never seen nobody turn down free blow."

He took out a camera from his back pocket and told her to smile. But it all happened too quick. She didn't have time to fluff up her hair or make sure her smile was right. He had taken the shot before giving her the chance.

* * *

She loved to be photographed. She loved to look at the camera lens and think that it was a tiny eye, except this eye reserved judgment. This eye couldn't hurt with its gaze, couldn't throw shade. Only captured her as she was, especially if she was standing in the right light. She knew, of course, that a camera had its own kind of cruelty. It could show a person back to themselves, no compassion. So that's why the hair, the glamour, the costumes had to be just right. Some days, she'd spend an hour in front of the mirror with her blow-dryer. All for the camera, baby.

When she was young, sometimes Nonna took her into Manhattan and told her to look at all the limousines. "You never know who's in there," Nonna had said. "Maybe it's a Hollywood director looking for a new star." Nonna said that was why they had to always look their freshest, bestest. That was Nonna's logic—always smile and always look good because no one ever knew who they'd run into.

So when Venus walked down the street, she liked to think of herself as a ray of light, and the camera was just a tool that a person could use to take that light and transfer it to paper, where it could stay forever.

Her favorite shot: Sitting on the edge of a stage, rocking a summer dress and white gloves. Hair permed out, wearing a costume couture necklace of chunky square beads, holding her snakeskin pump up in the air like she's hailing a cab with it. She's in front of a table full of trophies, sprawled before the judges. The emcee is shouting BODY over and over: BODY, BOD-Y, BOD-AY, GIVE IT TO MAY. So she gives him body. She gives the judges banjee.

The audience whistles and kikis. She gives them what they want, and she always knows what they want.

They want body, they want light.

* * *

"Is that the Bible?" Venus asked Sugar Cookie, who was sniffing like if he didn't hoard what was left of the air, there'd be none left for him to breathe.

"Yeah," he said, "only book in this place." He placed a dollar bill flat on the black hardcover and smoothed it down with a charge card.

It must have been a little after midnight, and Venus had only stumbled upon him because she noticed the common room light was on while she was on her way to the bathroom. "Damn," she said. "Don't you think that's kind of fucked-up? On a Bible?"

He used the card to chop up the rest of the powder like he was dicing vegetables, and then he split it into thick, even lines. "Why? You religious, little VV?"

"Maybe I am," she said for the sake of saying it. Back at Our Lady of the Flowers, the bad boys used to wear their atheism as a badge of honor. Even though Venus had her doubts—the doubts had begun when she learned that Mary apparently got knocked up by god after a conversation with an angel, which made no sense to her—she didn't like to wield her nonbelief as if it were a blade. The way she reasoned it was simple: she didn't believe in paying no attention to people who didn't give a shit about her. Didn't matter if that person was a *person* or god herself.

"Psht," he said. He used his pointer fingers and thumbs to roll the bill into a tight tube. "What kind of sick sonuvabitch wanted to create a world this fucked-up?"

"Excuse you," she said, "but maybe god is a woman. You ever think about that?"

"A woman?" he said. He snorted the line and made a crunching noise with his throat. He wiped his nose with the back of his hand, closed his eyes, and relaxed his head back so that he was looking at the ceiling. "Sure, leave it to some sick bitch to make all this mess. You got a good point, maybe he *is* a woman."

"Or maybe a drag queen," Venus said. "Then she'd have the best of both worlds. I imagine Drag Queen God perched on a cloud, singing 'The Way We Were' as she floods the world for Noah's Ark."

Sugar Cookie laughed.

"But damn, Sugar," Venus said. "What if the nuns see you out here? Snorting coke under a crucifix like that?"

The crucifix in the common room hung in the same place as it did in all the rooms—just above the door frame. Jesus's body was small, with little grooves for ribs and a painted-on frowny face and crown of thorns. "Nah," he said. "What of it? They like me. Not like they're gonna throw me out of a shelter. They'd have too much of that Jesus guilt to do something like that. Right, Jesus?" he said to the crucifix. "Can you hear me? Doing lines with god's kid watching down." He held his right hand up to his ear, as if waiting for a response. "See? Stone-cold silence."

"Yeah, but still," Venus said. "And where's La Loca?"

"She's out cold," he said. "And that bitch can snore."

Venus had to fake a cough to cover her laugh. Sugar Cookie offered her a rail. "Why you being all nice to me?" Venus said, giving him a skeptical look. "Your girl fucking hates my guts for no reason, so why are you being nice to me?"

"She's just jealous of you."

Venus laughed. "Oh, puh-lease."

"It's true," he said. "You can pass for a woman more than she does."

She waved a hand like oh stop it.

"And god knows she sure as hell tries real hard to pass as a woman," he said. "She probably figures that I wanna fuck your brains out."

"Oh, that's never gonna happen," Venus said. "Not in this lifetime or the next."

He put the dollar up to his nose, bent over, and inhaled the next rail, guiding the dollar bill from one end to the other. Venus watched the blue vein bulge out of his arm as he rubbed his finger across the Bible, then wipe that residue against his teeth.

"And how 'bout the next one after that?" he asked. He glided his tongue over the front of his teeth and she imagined what it would be like to fuck him. She imagined he would be the kind of hulking, selfish top who would fuck until he came, not giving a shit about his partner's orgasm.

"It's never gonna happen," Venus said. "Never."

* * *

The next morning, Venus went into the common room and found La Loca sitting on the couch, flipping cards onto the coffee table. It looked like a game of solitaire. The Bible was gone. Cookie was gone. Venus sat down next to La Loca as she continued slamming the cards down, face smeared with pout. Even a game of solitaire was a chance for La Loca to practice her rage.

"I got words for you," Venus said.

La Loca paused with the cards. She turned her head to give Venus a look-over. "What the hell do you want?"

"Why're you throwing so much shade at me since I got here? I didn't do nothing to you. I even left that room for you to be happy and shit," Venus said. "There can be two of us in this shelter, you know."

"Mmm-hmm."

"You think I want to steal Sugar Cookie from you," she said. "Is that it, huh?"

"Pssssht." La Loca rolled her eyes and flipped another card.

The game was strong on the diamonds and spades, but the hearts weren't giving. Homegirl couldn't get an ace of hearts if the world depended on it, and she needed it to free up the twos and threes in the hand. She flipped over a queen of clubs—couldn't use it. Flipped again—two of diamonds.

"Go roll those eyes and your face'll be stuck like that," Venus said. "And no disrespect, but I don't want Sugar Cookie. He's ugly like it's nobody's business. No tea, no shade."

"Girl," La Loca said, stopping midflip to give Venus a hair flip. "What you saying about my man?"

Venus looked at the deck in La Loca's right hand, ready to move to the side if that left arm came out to swing for Venus's face. "What I'm saying is that I don't want his ugly ass," Venus said, "and I never will, so we can be civil to each other and not have to worry all up in here."

La Loca's left eyebrow twitched up and hung out there. Then she flipped the cards again. Nine of spades, no use. Next.

"You and I," Venus said, "are very similar. Look—we both ran away from shit. And we're here. We got enough in common to be friends, not enemies."

"Don't act like you know me."

"You're right," Venus said. "I don't know much about you. But I do know you ran away from somewhere or someone. And you know that I ran away too. I know we're at this fucking shelter with the nuns. I know that my room buddy is obsessed with pigeons. So," Venus said, running out of things to list, "there's all of that."

There was the ace she needed. La Loca placed the two on top of the ace and flipped over the hidden card. A king of hearts, sword right in the head. La Loca turned to her and smiled. She held up the card. "I hate the king of hearts," she said. "What kind of king be all stabbing himself in the head when he's the king of a fucking kingdom?"

Venus laughed.

"Like, would you do that?" La Loca asked.

"I don't really know," Venus said. "It makes no sense. What about you?"

"Girl, I don't want to be no king," La Loca said. "Spent too much time as a man already, almost got enough money for my hormones. I'll be damned if I become some shit other than a queen."

"I hear that."

"K-W-E-E-N," La Loca said. "Queen. And plus, he's the only king in the deck without a moustache. What the fuck is that all about? Everybody knows that moustaches are sexy as hell."

* * *

On the Brooklyn Promenade walkway, Venus rushed to finish her ice-cream cone before it melted into a pool of milk. She licked the sides and caught the trails of sprinkles that rolled like tiny boulders down an ice-cream mountain. "See?" La Loca said. "What'd I say? I'm all about the cup business. Shoulda gotten a cup, not a cone."

"But the cone is the best part."

"Yeah, sure, when your shit ain't melting all over the place. You look like a princess trying to finish a BJ before the clock rings midnight and you turn back into a ho."

"Daaamn," Venus said. "That burned."

"And we all know that the art of fellating takes *time*."

"You're too much," Venus said, and laughed. She rubbed some vanilla onto her lips and licked it slowly, erotically. "You like that?" she asked the ice cream in her best sex hotline voice. "I bet you like that." She stuck out her tongue and licked the ice cream so slow, just scooping it up at the tip. They grabbed each other's arms for support, threw their heads back, and laughed at how silly they could be.

It was all Venus's idea to get the ice cream. Back when she was younger, she went out for ice cream whenever her mother was upset. Which meant, whenever she was upset with Antonio. She would take Venus out for a shopping-and-ice-cream run, all with Antonio's checkbook. One time, her mother wanted to get a pair of jeans. "Thomas," she asked Venus, "what do you think?" Her mother opened the dressing-room door, still wearing the sunglasses that she hadn't taken off all afternoon. Venus had smiled, giving her a thumbs-up. The jeans looked good, but Venus knew that her mother wasn't hiding anything with those sunglasses. The black eye was still there from when Antonio whacked her in the face. Nonna had been at the Elks Lodge that night for Bingo Wednesday. Antonio had found out about the fudged numbers, but didn't know about Henry. Antonio had worked himself into a rage. He was convinced that Nonna was stealing from him and busting the money on bingo and those lotto scratch tickets she kept inside the refrigerator for extra good luck. And there was her mother, looking at her ass in the mirror to see if the jeans looked good, thinking that shaded lenses could hold back the truth from the world.

Venus believed in the power of ice cream to bring people together. Her mother used to get a vanilla cone with chocolate fudge on top, hardened into a shell that she cracked with her lips. And Venus would get strawberry with rainbow sprinkles because she was convinced that strawberry flavoring tasted more like the color pink than the actual fruit, and she liked that.

Now she walked down the Promenade with La Loca, finishing up their ice creams and pointing at the Twin Towers across the river. The Brooklyn Bridge stretched out, connecting the two boroughs. They sat down on a bench and Venus reached into the plastic bag that she carried all her stuff in. She liked to call it her plastic Fendi because she had drawn F logos on it with a black marker from the arts and crafts closet at Serenity.

"Close your eyes," she told La Loca.

"What? Why?"

"Just do it," she said. "I got a surprise."

When La Loca closed her eyes, Venus told her to reach out and open her hands. She pulled out the rock from her plastic Fendi and placed it on La Loca's left palm. "Open," she said and La Loca opened. "It's shaped like a little heart—"

La Loca eyed it hard. "But it's just a rock—"

"Yeah. I know," Venus said. "But it's not *just* a rock. I don't wanna sound cheesy and shit, but I found it in Central Park when I first ran away. And I don't know—I just thought it was cute and shit. Like, it was a really rough time for me, and then I thought it was a sign from the world that everything was going to be okay—

because why else would it be shaped like a heart when I felt like all I needed was some little signal of love? It was like the world was sending that love message to me in the form of that rock."

La Loca ran her fingers over the smooth surface. She moved her index finger into the groove that dipped down, the groove that had convinced Venus in the first place that it was shaped like a heart.

"I want you to have it," Venus said.

La Loca curled her hand around it and put it in her pocket. She gave Venus an air-kiss on each cheek and said thank you.

"What is this now?" A young guy walked up to them. He only looked tall because they were sitting. "What do yous think this is? Tranny Central? Shouldn't you twos be at Meatpacking?"

He looked like he was in his thirties and he was drinking from a bottle that was tucked into a brown paper bag. "Fuck you," La Loca said. She stood up and hawked a wad of spit at his face. It missed, but still landed on his neck.

Venus didn't stand up for him. She wanted to reach out her hand to stop Loca's gold hoops from vibrating in her earlobes. Loca was trembling like whenever they were on the express train and the subway's vibrations traveled up through their bodies.

"What the fuck?" he said, wiping the ball of phlegm off his neck. All it did was smear onto the neckline of his shirt. "This is a family area. You hos shouldn't be strutting your shit around here." He took another swig from the bottle.

"We're not hos," Venus said. "We're just walking down the block, doing our thing in peace."

"Hey, Lady Boy," the guy said. "Shut the fuck up. Nobody likes it when a piece of ass starts mouthing off."

La Loca crossed her arms. She towered over him—she was already six foot, but now with her heels and that big-ass disco hair, Loca probably had half a foot on the guy. "Did you just call my friend a ladyboy?" she said.

"Just speakin' truth to power," the guy said.

"Bitch," La Loca said, "the fuck does your pathetic ass know about truth *or* power? All you know how to do is speak bullshit when your mouth should be zipped."

La Loca knocked the bottle out of his hand. Venus watched as a straight couple stopped and gawked. La Loca grabbed the guy's earlobe and yanked his head so that it was facing Venus. "Her name is Venus," La Loca said, "not Lady Boy. So I want you to apologize to Venus. You want me to spell it out for you?"

The guy winced but stayed silent. La Loca tugged on his earlobe even harder and he moaned. He looked at Venus—his eyes were watering and his breath stank. He said sorry twice and then asked how much they were charging.

"We aren't charging, you ass," La Loca said as she let go of his ear and pushed the side of his head.

He picked himself up off the ground and ran away. The straight couple kept gawking. Venus imagined that anyone who had seen would stop what they were doing and clap, like when subway riders yelled at obnoxious people and the rest of the train clapped for the person who stood up and smacked down. But the people just stared, they didn't clap, and Venus thought that maybe the guy was right. Maybe no one wanted to see them strut it down the Promenade. Maybe they weren't welcome there after all.

* * *

Some days Venus woke up at eleven or noon with the mixed feeling that she had both slept too much and not enough. The room was small and neat and her roommate was always gone to feed the birds. On the bureau, there were plastic bags filled with slices of white bread that her roommate collected and chopped up into pieces that were tiny enough for the pigeons to peck at. During the summer, Venus woke up with sweat all up on her face. The sheets felt damp, and she had to get up to turn on the electric fan. All she wanted was for the breeze to blow a little air her way. She wanted to cool down.

It was the summer months, with their heat and humidity, that made her think of Brazil. She lay in bed thinking about the pictures she had seen of Rio and São Paulo. The beaches, the thongs, the giant Jesus at the top of the mountain with his arms open wide to feel the power of the wind. If she had all the money in the world, that's where she'd go. And she'd drink caipirinhas and chain-smoke in the bars; flirt with all the muscular, tan men; and wear neon-colored thongs at the beach every day.

"I hear that in Brazil," she told La Loca one day in August, "all the men go crazy for the boys in drag. They call them travestis, I think. Now doesn't that sound nice?"

"That don't sound like the world I know," La Loca said. "I think you're lying."

"Am not," Venus said.

"Well then that sounds like it'd be damn fabulous."

"We could wear thongs everyday," Venus said.

"Oh, hell to the no," La Loca said. "Well, first I need to get my surgery. But I don't even like to floss my teeth, what makes you think I want floss up in my cheeks?"

Venus laughed and slapped the side of La Loca's arm. "I'm just daydreaming, you don't have to crush it for me, damn. All I'm talking about is a little bit of whimsy over here."

Venus knew it was just a dream and nothing more. She couldn't even earn enough money to pay for rent, how was she going to hop on a plane and think she could afford rent in another country? She also knew that La Loca was dealing coke with Sugar Cookie to help save money for her hormones and blockers and surgery. La Loca had told that secret one night while they were drinking vodka out of a plastic handle. They mixed it with the orange juice that the nuns kept in the fridge with the other juices.

"I'm scared that Sugar's gonna leave me if I actually get the operation," La Loca told Venus later that day as Venus lay on her bed flipping through a travel magazine with a whole photo essay on Brazil. Ipanema: women lounging on towels, wearing bikinis, throwing peace signs into the air, applying baby oil to their skin, drinking from coconuts.

"Well, don't he love you?" Venus said, looking up from the photos.

"Yeah, but I'm just scared that if I get the surgery down there and become a real woman, he's not gonna be turned on anymore."

"That just sounds confusing," Venus said. She was amazed at how sometimes a girl could know what a man wanted, but other times, it felt like a mystery.

Late nights became a time when they shared secrets with each other. It was perfect because they didn't have to scurry away from Sugar Cookie, who was either out dealing the coke or blowing rails of it on whatever surface was in front of him. Didn't matter if he was in the common room or in the bathroom, if it was one o'clock, he had to cut a line on the flattest surface available to him. "Or I'll die," he was in the habit of saying. Venus thought it was some addict-level shit.

The next night, La Loca told Venus to meet in Loca's room at midnight. Sugar Cookie would be out on a coke run and they could close the door to have silence. They all knew the doors in the entire place didn't lock, but no one had ever busted down a door if it was closed, especially if it was closed after ten at night.

By the time Venus arrived, it was just past midnight and she could tell that La Loca had been crying. The room already smelled like that bad handle of vodka—the smell was borderline rubbing alcohol. The taste too. But it was on the cheap, and even though they didn't like cheap, it was all they could afford to buy at the only bodega in the area that was willing to take La Loca's stamps in exchange for booze.

"I can't take it anymore," La Loca said. She stood up from the bed too quick and almost fell over. That was how drunk she was already. Venus told her to hush and sit back down. That it would all be okay.

"I gotta tell somebody," La Loca said. "I just feel like nobody knows who I was. Like my past is all dead and that I'm just a zombie."

"Honey," Venus said, "I got no clue what that means."

La Loca told Venus that her name used to be Ramón.

"Funny," Venus said. "I never would've pegged you for a Ramón."

"Don't be brutal with me," La Loca said, "and don't you dare ask to see my baby pictures."

"You know I wouldn't."

She told Venus that when she was seven, her mother's boyfriend was watching her while her mother was at work. He said he was going to watch baseball on the couch and maybe he'd teach Ramón how to play catch one day.

"Shit turned real quick," La Loca said. "He was all like, You'd be a cute little girl, because my skin was real smooth, and he said he'd give me a dime if I licked his finger." She downed the rest of the vodka that was in the paper cup.

Venus took a sip of her drink too, not because she was thirsty, but because she wanted to show La Loca that she was in tune with her. That Venus could drink when La Loca drank and listen when La Loca spoke. She watched as La Loca picked up the pack of cards and began fingering through them like she was about to start shuffling.

"So I licked it," La Loca said, "because—shit—I wanted a dime. Get me some gummy candies at the shop, you know? And when I licked it, he grabbed the back of my head and told me to suck the finger and roll it around with my tongue, and then he took his other hand and slid it down my pants and he was watching the tele while my mother was out and he slided down my pants and put his fingers on my nalgas and in my culo, and when my mother came back home later that night, he was sleeping on the couch and I told her what happened.

"Like, I was all excited and shit, because I didn't know he wasn't supposed to do that. I thought it was like a grown-up game, like, that all the kids had people feeling up on them like that. Like it was something special. You know?"

Venus didn't know. Antonio was a real sonuvabitch, but he had never done any of that to Venus when she was young. She looked at

La Loca and shook her head. "I'm sorry," Venus said. She said she didn't know, but maybe she could try to understand.

"And you know what that cunt said to me?" La Loca said, looking at the corner of the bed now. "She told me to shut the fuck up with my lying mouth. That she'd wash my tongue out with suds. She threw a mop at me and some Lysol and said that if I wanted to be a woman, I should learn to clean up my mess."

Venus held La Loca as she cried. "Damn," Venus said. "That's so fucked-up."

"Pour me another drink?" La Loca said.

"Now that I think about it," Venus said, reaching out for the handle. "You should've chopped his dick off. Chopped it right off, then he wouldn't fuck around with you no more."

La Loca took the cup and downed the vodka shot. "I don't want to think about it anymore," she said. "I just had to fuckin' tell somebody about it. I couldn't keep it inside me anymore, because if no one else knew, it'd eat me up, you know?"

"Sort of," Venus said.

"I can't tell Sugar this kind of shit," she said.

Venus didn't ask why. She watched as La Loca reached over and picked up the rock that Venus had given her. She used the rock to hold down papers—all the job applications that she applied for and never heard a word from and all the paperwork from the welfare office.

La Loca got up and poured them both more screwdrivers, using up the rest of the OJ. "Oh shit," she said. "The nuns are gonna be pissed. We drank all the juice."

"Yeah," Venus said. "But it was in the common room. I think if anyone knows how to share, the nuns do. No?"

"You got a point."

Venus heard steps walking down the hall. La Loca must have heard too because she froze midpour. She rushed to put the handle of vodka under the bed and then sat down next to Venus. If they got caught, they might get kicked out, but Venus wasn't totally sure what the punishment would be. They both stared at each other and didn't move.

Whoever it was, they were outside the door. Venus held her breath, and then the steps kept moving down the hall until she couldn't hear them no more and she could breathe again.

La Loca looked at Venus and they laughed. Venus took a sip of her screwdriver, raised her eyebrows, and said, "Damn, this is strong tonight."

"Why drink," La Loca said, "if that shit ain't gonna be strong?"

Venus chuckled. "I don't even know what you mean."

"Mmm—like hell you don't," La Loca said.

It didn't take Venus long to feel the drink. She was two, three down by now. She watched La Loca as she painted her nails glitter-silver, a color she liked to call Glam. Just Glam, nothing else.

"So," La Loca said, fingers splayed out so they could dry. "You gonna share your life story or what?"

Venus stared at the last drops at the bottom of her cup. Wouldn't it have been nice, she thought, if they had never had to front in the first place? Like it was a real shit that La Loca had to posture when they first met. Being all mean like she was Kween Bitch of the place just because she was insecure about people attacking her. And yet there La Loca was, telling her story to Venus when Venus didn't know if she could do the same. Talk about insecurities.

Venus didn't know what it felt like to be protective over a man like La Loca was with Sugar Cookie, but Venus had seen what it did to people. She saw her mother live in a fantasyland where Antonio would be the type of man who never hit her and would leave his wife, bring her to Hawaii, and actually show some kind of interest in getting to know Thomas. What a weird place that fantasyland was in some people's minds. The rent was so high in what it demanded from people—pride, security, money, blood, secrets—but people still wanted to live there. They didn't want to vacation there, they wanted a house with a basement and a fence.

It must have been hard for La Loca to tell that kind of story, about that piece of shit who should have his dick chopped off and set to rot in a vat of bleach. Now that would teach him. Venus took another shot of vodka. She decided to tell a different story. "My name was Thomas," she said. "You ever heard of Saint Elizabeth Ann Seton?"

La Loca shook her head no.

Venus told her that the nuns at Our Lady of the Flowers loved Saint Elizabeth Ann Seton. And they couldn't just say Saint Elizabeth or Saint Seton, it was Saint Elizabeth Ann Seton, like it was one long word. "I must have been a little bit dyslexic, right?" Venus said. "So when they picked *me* to read the story of her life in front of the gym assembly, I was thinking, *Me?—of all people?*"

It had happened on the first day back from Christmas break and everyone was excited to see each other. Vanessa waved at Thomas; Venus waved back at Vanessa. Venus was so nervous to give the speech in front of everyone, and it didn't matter if the words were right there in front of her at the podium. "You'll be fine, Thomas," the sisters told her.

"But instead of saying Seton, like I was supposed to, like it was written there on the paper," Venus said, "I kept saying Satan, but it was just because I was so nervous, not like I did it on purpose. Oh god, it was horrendous."

La Loca gasped. Whenever she was drunk, her eyes were just as expressive as her sassy mouth was while sober. "No you didn't," La Loca play-screamed. "And the nuns completely lost their shit?"

"Uh, yeah," Venus said. "Sister Agnes—I'll never forget her name or that face—she stood next to me at the podium with a meter stick. And every time I fucked up, she beat my ass with that stick until I said Seton all properly."

"Oh shit, I'm sorry," La Loca said. "I shouldn't be laughing."

"No, no," Venus said. "It's fine. It's funny *now*. I was all Satan— no, Seton—yes, See-ton."

Venus hadn't fucked up on purpose. She really was so nervous that the words got flipped and the more times Sister Agnes beat the shit out of her, the more nervous she got. The other students had laughed at first, but then the nuns gave them that stare that said they would raise hell and back if there was even so much as another chuckle. For the rest of the speech, no one laughed. Venus kept her eyes peeled to the words on the pages because she couldn't bear to look up and see Vanessa or Sal or anyone else.

"I feel bad for nuns," La Loca said. "I wouldn't be able to live without dick."

"I know you can't," Venus said, "you chickenhead."

"Hey!"

"I'm saying it with *love*," Venus said. "Every species is valued in the ecosystem of the gay world. Without the chickenheads, the rest of the ecosystem would crash out and die."

"What the fuck are you talking all this science shit to me for?" La Loca said.

"It's a joke, girl," Venus said, putting her arm around her friend. "Calm your damn titties."

* * *

Not all stories needed to be told. She felt that sometimes it was the stories that people didn't tell that spoke more loudly about who they were or where they came from. Venus didn't tell La Loca about Antonio and the dog, and she didn't know why. She could have, and maybe she even felt a little guilty about not sharing with Loca, even after Loca had shared her own secrets. But then Venus began to wonder what other stories lurked beneath Loca's surface, the ones that only La Loca knew. The ones that were held so close to the fibers of her soul, the very act of speaking them aloud would destroy the framework of her being.

If Venus *had* told La Loca that story, this is how it would've gone down:

Thomas was ten years old. His mother and Nonna had to run to a funeral for an old woman in their building named Rose. Rose was a widow who had a son, but then, one day, she didn't have a son no more. All Nonna kept saying was, "By his own hand. His own hand."

Thomas didn't know Rose's son. He had moved to California in search of a dream. That was another thing that Nonna said. She didn't understand why someone had to go so far from his own mother to find a dream when there were plenty of dreams to be found in New York.

Rose died a week after her son did and all the people in the building said they didn't care if the autopsy showed natural causes. The fact that her heart had stopped was proof enough that it was broken. When Thomas heard this, he imagined that his own heart was made of glass, and that there was a little fairy inside of him who had a chisel. Every time something horrible happened—something he saw, something he heard—the fairy would make a small dent. It wouldn't take one small dent to kill a person, but he could see how in the case of Rose, who had lived for long enough to remember different drinking fountains, the dents added up and shattered the heart. And everyone—even people who had never seen *The Wizard of Oz!*—knew that a person needed a heart in order to live.

Thomas asked if he could go to the funeral, but Nonna said no. He was too young. She said it was open casket and she didn't want him to learn *that* about the world yet.

So he stayed with Antonio for the evening. Antonio's wife was visiting family in the Catskills that weekend. Antonio had a dog and Thomas's mother thought that he would have fun playing with the puppy for a couple of hours. Thomas thought that he would like that too, but then he met Antonio's dog. Her name was Eva. She was a seventeen-year-old basset hound with glaucoma. She was also deaf. When Antonio went up to his bedroom and shut the door, Thomas lay on the floor and threw a bouncy ball, but Eva only stood there and stared at him while wheezing. Her eyes looked like clear aggie marbles.

The rowhouse was dark and sad, even though it didn't need to be. Thomas thought that Antonio could open up the curtains, or change the dark wood paneling, or buy a few more lights. Anything, really, could be done to lighten the place up. It smelled like Eva, which is to say that it smelled like wet fur and sagging dog skin. Eva limped around the first floor, her nails clacking away against the shiny wooden finish.

Thomas walked up the stairs and knocked on Antonio's door. He waited and stared at the doorknob, as if the longer he stared, it would magically untwist and open. He heard sounds coming from inside the room, so he knew Antonio was in the room. He knocked again.

A thump, then footsteps. Antonio opened the door with a towel wrapped around his waist. He wasn't wet, and Thomas stared at his chest hair. "What you want, kid?" Antonio said.

"You're not really married, are you?" Thomas said. He wasn't totally sure about his accusation, but it was a hunch. Behind Antonio's arm, Thomas could see two nudie ladies on the TV. They were running their French manicures against their pink nipples. "You're just telling my mom that you're married so that you don't have to marry her."

"I don't have time for this bullshit," Antonio said. Thomas knew he had hit a nerve. He must be right, then. Antonio wasn't denying it. Thomas wanted to say, Of course no woman in their right mind would live in this tacky, wood-paneled hellhole. But of course he didn't say that.

"She's not in the Catskills because she doesn't exist," Thomas said. "And that makes you a liar."

Antonio reached for the remote on the bed and turned the TV off. "Who the fuck do you even think you are, you little son-of-a-bitch brat?"

That was all Thomas wanted to see—Antonio struggling to compose himself. He watched as Antonio bent down to pick up his undies, then as he squirmed to put them on under his towel. "What you want from me, kid?" Antonio said. "Not like you know anything about the world yet."

"I'm hungry," Thomas said. "Can we have dinner soon?"

Once they were in the kitchen, Antonio pushed him to the floor, pulled a big knife out of the drawer, and said, "Here. Make yourself something." He walked out of the kitchen and closed the door.

And what was Thomas supposed to do with that? He stared at the knife. When he opened the refrigerator, it was empty except for a head of lettuce and a rotten bowl of strawberries covered in gray fuzzies. When he moved to open the door and leave the room, he realized he was locked in. He banged and banged on the door, but he knew it was no use. He knew that he had picked the fight and now he was feeling Antonio's fucked-up revenge, and he wanted to scream.

But he was silent as he grabbed the knife and held the lettuce in place. He cut off some bits and ate them. They tasted like—well, they tasted like lettuce. And what the hell was the taste of lettuce other than crunchy water? He was so hungry, he could've cried.

The next day, when he told Nonna what he had done, she flipped her shit. "No grandson of mine eats dog food," she screamed.

She screamed and screamed, but Thomas thought that she just wasn't understanding what his options were in the moment. All he had had was the dog food. He was hungry. He had gotten down on all fours and eaten Eva's bowl of food. It was the slimiest meat sludge he had ever tasted, and he gagged the entire time. He had to stop breathing through his nose because if he didn't, he was sure he'd throw it all up.

"Do you hear this, Isabella?" Nonna screamed from the kitchen to his mother who was absent in the other room. "That dog didn't feed Thomas proper."

"What do you want from me?" his mother pleaded. "I didn't know neither."

"*Porco dio,*" Nonna said. "That man."

"I've almost got him," his mother said. "He's so close to leaving her."

"Ah, *cagacazzo,* and you still want him after this. Just take a nail and crucify your mother to the cross right now."

"No, mom," Thomas said. "He's not married. It's all a giant lie."

Both of them stared at him. Nonna threw her hands up. It was her usual motion, a silent way of saying: You See, This Proves I'm Always Right.

"You lying bitch," his mother said. Thomas was expecting a slap across his face, but nothing came. She couldn't even touch him in that moment, she was total stone. "You think you know my man? Tell me how can that be, Thomas, when you're not much of a man yourself?"

* * *

His mother almost had him, is that what she had said? As if a person were a thing that could be had. Thomas wondered why his mother didn't feel the same way about him. If a man were something that could be had, couldn't a son also be something to be treasured? But he knew the answer to that question. He was young, but he wasn't stupid. He wanted to scream at her, But I came out of your body! I was a part of you! But he knew. He had figured it out years earlier, when Sal and the bad boys had asked him where his father was. He told them he didn't know and Thomas could still see the way Sal's mouth had moved with disgust. *That's because you were a mistake.*

Thomas couldn't deny it. He *was* a mistake. His mother had been so young and Nonna, when asked, told him that his father was a married man from Puerto Rico who was just on vacation and his mother had made a mistake, but that didn't mean Thomas was a mistake, she said, because she loved him and did he know that?

But Nonna's explanation didn't sit well with him. The more he thought about it, the more it became obvious to him: a person like Thomas could be a mistake, and a person like Antonio could be had.

Years later, Venus would come to realize that her mother was just so *young*. She began to understand, though Venus was young herself, what that could mean—to just be *so* young, *too* young. What was it with their fixation with married men? As if the universe was telling them, You cannot have this, and so they wanted it even more.

Venus would later think that her mother was just the type of person who fell hard, who took her desire and translated it into a sense of conquest. Like love's force of gravity just hit that heart one notch too strong. And her mother loved even harder when she knew that the kind of love she wanted was the kind she could never have. Antonio never left his wife. Of course he didn't. If he even had one! And Venus would guess that his mother knew that was the case all along, but refused, for whatever reason, to face the music. *What was a challenge*, Venus thought, *if it wasn't impossible?*

And years later, Venus would look at herself in the mirror and think, *Oh god, I am becoming her. I am becoming* my mother. It was a thought that sent a cold pulse down to her toes. Venus would never fall for a man like Antonio, and she would never tolerate a man popping black eyes anywhere on her face. She would realize that, like her mother, she was the type of person who was so lonely, she would cling to men who didn't deserve to be clung to, just because she was afraid that they would walk out on her. She was afraid that if those men walked out on her, the deepest secret of the universe would be revealed—not the precise number of rings around Saturn, or which order that huge mass of planets was set up in, but rather, that if they left her, it would confirm her biggest fear: that she was meant to be alone because no one loved her, and no one ever would.

ANGEL

Girlfriend didn't want no trouble. She just wanted to get down, dance, dish that shade. She wanted to enter every room like the world was an episode of *Dynasty* and she was Joan Collins playing Alexis: she'd sling mud at any beauty-salon-motherfucka who tried to front. And that's just how it was, take it or leave it.

Years ago, she had to sneak out of her mother's house—her other clothes in a Pathmark shopping bag that was so crumpled, the plastic looked soft. She took the 6 from Hunts Point down into the city, slipping a fresh skirt up over her jeans, dabbing on eyeliner and lip liner whenever the train stopped moving.

"What are you?" a young moreno once asked her. "Some kinda maricón?"

"What's it matter to you?" she snapped at him. "I got nails that'll rip the face off your head, so you better step it on back."

Now she carried around a can of PAM cooking spray for that exact reason—if she had to take someone on, she could do it with the speed it'd take to press her finger down on the nozzle. She knew the subway was a mean place, and an even meaner one for a twenty-year-old with her cojones tucked down to her taint. It took too much work to shave her pelitos down there to get it all looking passable, so she would be damned if someone tried to fuck with her.

Her stomping grounds were the piers at the end of Christopher Street. A real pain in the ass to get to, because she had to transfer at Union Square, take the L, and then *walk*. But she did it. The piers were all fucked-up, covered in graffiti and the chain-link fences were all rusty. This was their special place though. There was a charm to all the metal beams and abandoned overground railway tracks.

Through the holes in the pier planks, she could see the brown water of the Hudson. Sometimes when there was a nice breeze, she would close her eyes and imagine she was on a beach, like in those white-people magazines. One time, she had seen a floating body in the river, all tranquilo and still. It was a man, but she couldn't tell how old he was because he was missing his head. A perfectly good suit gone to waste, and of course, she was eighteen years old at the time and thought nothing of it, other than the fact that she was glad it wasn't her.

She stood on that pier now just like she did every Thursday, waiting to turn a trick and make some cash so that she could buy some new clothes and makeup.

It was Dorian, the old queen that she was, who had taught her how to suck a dick.

"Anyone can put a cock in their mouth," Dorian told her, "but if you want to give professional-level head and make them come back for more, you gotta be ferocious. It's like the difference between hosing down a car and powerwashing it. The suction is key."

They'd been sitting in the back dressing room of Collage, the hellish drag club where Dorian performed. Dorian sat at the old Hollywood vanity that was studded with lightbulbs. She whipped out a black dildo and plopped it on a side table by its suction cup. It swayed like a fresh Jell-O mold. "They don't call it a *job* for nothing, honey. You gotta multitask that shit. Use some tongue, twirl it around, but don't forget your lips. Suction seduction, baby, that's what I always say in the back of my mind when I need inspiration: *suction seduction*."

Now she stood on her pier and gave mad eyes to the other putas who were running up on her zone. She watched as man after man cruised up and down, convinced that her nerves would cave and she'd get a case of the churras. Hector was supposed to call her earlier in the day, which was always an ordeal because Angel's mother was a real pain—always around the apartment. They had to be dodgy about their calls, but it had been not one, but two whole weeks without a word from him. Angel wanted to kiss him up and down *and* kick his ass, all at the same time.

A white businessman walked up to her. He was taller than her, probably a solid six feet high, and he stared at her face. He took her hand and placed it over the boner that was forming inside his pants. The man wasn't fully hard, but Angel could already tell that homeboy was thick. He asked how much for a blow job, and would she swallow. She stared at his suit, the crisp silk tie loosened, top button casually open, and she thought about the money.

When she told him twenty, he said five, as if the concept of twenty was completely wack.

"Five?" she said. "The fuck is a girl gonna do with five?"

"Ten?"

"Twelve," she said. "And don't push your luck."

He nodded and placed his hand on the top of her head to guide her down. She wondered, as she went down—as she always wondered when she went down—if *this* was the guy who would finally do her in: grab her throat and strangle her silly until her body was like an unfilled balloon. The head of his polla hit the back of her throat and she closed her eyes as she felt his cum drip down.

When he was done, he thanked her and walked away. She folded the money and put it in her clutch. *Fucking Hector,* she thought. Where was he? Why was he fronting?

The neon Maxwell House coffee ad across the way flashed once, then twice, as it tipped itself over to spill light-drops of coffee into a cup. She looked across the river, among the trees and the fancy new apartment buildings of Jersey. She'd have to call Dorian now to see if she knew what was up with Hector. What a pain. What a damn shame too.

* * *

That bulge! Ay, Dios mío. She had dreams about the fucking bulge in his pants. Because Hector always wore the same basic getup— tight crop top with high-waisted pants that made that package look like a meal. *Yes, girl,* Angel thought, *please.*

But now he was missing and he wasn't at the pier and Dorian hadn't called back to give a heads-up as to his whereabouts. In all seriousness, it wasn't just about his dick. It was about his heart too. Angel could sense that there was something special about him. That smile of his could melt her like the manteca on a roasted potato— todavía because that smile never got old.

Maybe if they didn't have to hide things from her mother, he wouldn't have disappeared like he did. Two whole weeks, almost three. Angel checked the papers to make sure none of the bathhouses had burned down—not that Hector ever went to those, but just in case he had. She was pulling at straws. She knew that much.

"I feel like his soul is a conga and a clave," she once explained to Dorian, "and my soul is playing the bongos with a güiro. Then, when we come together, the ritmo harmonizes just right, like it can't with nobody else."

She was at wit's end, about to stomp all the way to his apartment in Alphabet City and keep her finger on the buzzer. Where would they even be if it weren't for that apartment? Fifty-five dollars a month in Alphabet City. Hot damn. Hector always said, "Thank god for this apartment, otherwise we'd be out on the street just like the others."

She walked up to a payphone now to dial Dorian. She'd tell Dorian that homeboy wasn't calling her back, wasn't answering his door, hadn't said a single word.

As the phone rang, she thought about how beautiful Hector was. How he drank his Café Bustelo black, how he was as flexible as any dancer in Lincoln Center, which was his dream. She loved that he wanted to be a dancer. He wanted to express all his love and pain with that body of his.

The phone kept ringing. The love she felt for him was the kind that made every word sound like a smooth jazz album. Her heart was turning like a freestyle beat. Best believe that Hector was that fine specimen of a man called a papi chulo. A man so fine, it made a queen wanna get on her knees and weep to the lord Jesus.

Dorian didn't pick up, so Angel hung up. Even if she didn't believe in god, a man as fine as Hector could make a girl believe.

* * *

When Dorian called three days later, he said that Hector was working a new job at Yogurt Delite on Eighth Avenue in Chelsea. So, when Angel stomped up into the Yogurt Delite on Eighth Avenue, she saw him wiping down a counter with a white rag, looking as suave as a member of Menudo. When the door closed behind her, a little bell jangled as it hit the glass. Hector looked up and saw it was her. He smiled and chuckled to himself, just like he always did when he knew she was about to unleash on him.

"Uh-oh," he said. "I'm in trouble, right?" He laughed as he

wiped up some stray sprinkles on the countertop that he had forgotten to clean up. "I swear I wasn't dipping out forever," he said. "It's been a rough few weeks and we gotta talk about some shit. How'd you find me, mama? Dorian?"

"Hell yes, Dorian did," she said. And it wasn't easy. She had called Dorian not once, not twice, but three damn times, almost in tears by the time Dorian had *finally* called back.

"That man can't keep a secret, can he?" Hector said, and she thought, *You have no idea*. Angel had had to promise Dorian a new blouse from Saks, which she still had no idea how she was going to mop.

"Three weeks, Hector," she said. "Where you been? Are you dropping me and I'm not taking the hint?"

"No, nena. It's not that. You know I love you."

"What is that supposed to even mean?" Angel said. "Can you make me a cup of vanilla?"

Hector stared at her and made eyebrows at her. "Is that what you want?" he said. "You came here for yogurt?"

"Of course I didn't come here for yogurt," she said. "But it just happens to be here, so it's the least you can do."

He asked her small or medium.

"Large," she said. "Damn, give me as much as you can."

As he turned his back on her, she watched his skinny body move slowly. He had the grace of a swan, whether he was working behind a counter or working to dish a vogue. A white girl was in the corner with her mother. She licked at the chocolate cone with the craze of a crackhead hitting a new pipe. The mother told her to be more gentle or the yogurt would go everywhere. "Lick the sides, sweetie," the mother said, "so it doesn't go drippy-droppy everywhere."

Hector handed her the cup and rang up the order on the register. When the lid opened, he popped it back closed without putting any money in. They stared at each other wordlessly as she guided the spoon from vanilla to mouth.

"I'm sorry," he whispered.

"¿Por qué?" She rolled her neck to emphasize that she knew exactly what for, but wanted him to say more.

"For keeping you out of the loop," he said.

"Why haven't you called me back?" she asked. "I know my mother's wack and I know that you know that, but she's not home all the time. We can talk then."

"It's not that," he said. He cracked his knuckles and winced at the pain it probably brought him. "Mira," he said, "we close in fifteen minutes. Just wait 'til they leave." He motioned his eyes to the little girl, who had reached the cone. Her face was covered with chocolate and the mother looked pissed.

Angel waited and watched Hector as he powered down the yogurt machines. She tried to imagine what it was like inside one of those metal machines, how much energy it took to turn all that into something edible. She watched as he Windexed the counters and mopped the floors. His body moved with grace, like he wasn't trapped behind a counter. He had always been flaco, but now he looked too flaquito. He looked like he needed a good cheeseburger. She checked her clutch to see if she had enough money to take him out to the diner on Tenth Avenue. Get something fatty and delicious-nutritious. It was a running joke between them—to evaluate all the food they cooked together on a scale of no-way-no-how (unhealthy) to delicious-nutritious (super healthy), except when they said the words, they had to do their best impressions of what they imagined a fancy French waiter would sound like. Hector's impressions were always more banging than hers, and it made her giggle. She fingered the loose bills in her clutch and counted—she had three crumpled tens.

When he finally locked the door, he motioned her to the back of the store. She asked him where they were going. He said they were going to the bathroom.

"Ay, Dios mío," she said. "*Here?* Are you bugging? Do I look like the type of woman who fucks in a bathroom?"

"Angel." His face was stern. "We're not going for hanky time.

This is important. Besides, you got no problem sucking people off on the fucking streets."

"Fuck you, Hector. Don't act like you've never done none of that and that you're somehow better than me because you work in *yogurt* now."

He apologized and she immediately regretted what she said. That look on his face could break the hands off a clock, turning time into something weightless and slow. Something was wrong, she could tell. She wanted to put her arms around him and take that pain away from him. She walked over to him and kissed him on the cheek.

The fluorescent light in the bathroom buzzed and she could see the black flecks of dead bugs that had flown too close to the light. He took off his shirt.

"Seriously, Hector," she said, trying to be more gentle this time. "You just said we wasn't—"

"I need you to look at me," he said. He pointed to his right nipple. His skin looked like it was squeezing at his ribs.

"So you have a mosquito bite?"

"It's not itchy," he said. "It don't feel like nothing."

"So why worry if you can't feel it?" she said. She looked closer, knowing that even things that had no feeling were worth attention. There was a deep red mark, bordering on purple, right next to the ring of pelitos that circled his nipple.

"You think this is it?" he asked. "Am I gonna die now? I'm gonna die now, right?"

"Stop being wack," she said. He leaned against the sink and she leaned with him. "You're not gonna die from a bug bite."

"Oh, come on, Angel," he said. He squeezed his T-shirt tighter as he held it up above his head. "We can cut the shit. I know you know what this is. Everyone knows what this is."

She did know what it was. Or at least what it might've been. It was the bruise, the mark that everyone talked about and dreaded. What else could it be? She asked him if he had been to a clinic.

"What for?" he said.

"What do you mean, what for?" she said. "To find out. Don't they have some pill you can take?"

"Where have you been?" he said to her. "What magic pill are you talking about? There's nothing, not a thing. The results come back in another week."

"Okay, so we have another week—"

"What do you mean *we*? You've got all the time in the world," he said. "*I* got a week."

"—and then we can talk to Dorian," she said. "I bet he knows how to handle this and where we can get you the minerals and stuff. Protein powders, vitamins, whatever."

"And with what money?" he said. "I don't even got a pot to piss in, you know that."

"I'll give you some money."

He closed his eyes and leaned his head back and opened his mouth as if to scream. She imagined that this was what deafness would feel like—watching someone in open-mouthed agony, hearing nothing. The pipes made a loud churning and Hector opened his eyes to look back at her.

"It's not going to be enough," he said. "We don't have enough money for that. For this."

*　*　*

Two days later, on Thanksgiving morning, Angel climbed out of Hector's bed and up the fire escape to the top of the roof in order to watch the sun rise. The streets below were empty, except for a couple who were bickering over something. Angel was too far away to hear what they were arguing about. The woman was waving with her hands and the man was pointing at himself. Angel exhaled a strong cloud of smoke and looked at the fading advertisement for a soup company that was on the side of an eight-story building on the corner of the block.

She wasn't wearing a jacket because she didn't think it was going to be as chilly as it was. As soon as she was up there, she regreted that decision. She tried to rush through her cigarette so that the air wouldn't wear her body down. The last thing she needed right now was to get sick.

She was worried about Hector's test result. The anxiety flashed in her mind at least once an hour, but she wanted to get out on the roof to smoke and not have to sit with all that worry. November was her favorite month. It was the month that the trees dropped their leaves, and sweaters came out, and the sales associates at Saks and Bergdorf did up their Christmas windows real good. The tree in Rockefeller Center would soon be lit up bright and the streets of New York would be packed tight with people buying gifts. November in Manhattan felt like the entire city was huddled together under a soft cotton blanket that was fresh out the secadora.

Every November, she fantasized about coming out of the Plaza Hotel dressed in silk, stepping onto a carriage led by a horse into the orange-and-yellow swirl of leaves. She liked to imagine that the trees were reaching up to grab a piece of the sky, then they would curl themselves into a ball and sleep through the winter on a bed of four-hundred-thread-count Egyptian cotton, until spring, when they would doll up for the season's next ball.

Snow had been forecasted that morning, but as she finished up her cig on the roof, no flakes were falling yet. She climbed down the fire escape and back into Hector's apartment. He was still in his pj's and brought her a cup of coffee just as she liked it: lots of half-and-half and sugar. He liked to joke with her that she put so much half-and-half, she should just call it full-and-full. She thought that was mad corny, but she always laughed at it.

Later that morning, Angel watched the Macy's parade on the TV with Hector. She had to focus on the dancers, the singers, the marching bands in order to not think about the test results. Santa and Mrs. Claus paraded down the street in their sled, and Angel said, "How many more days until the test results come back?"

"I told you already," Hector said. "A couple more days."

"Right, right," Angel said. "I knew that."

"If you keep bringing it up, you're gonna make me go stir-crazy también," Hector said. "Please. Everything's gonna work out fine."

Now that Hector was singing a different tune and pretending to be calm about it, she felt guilty. It was like they had done a role reversal. She felt like her questions were pestering him and stressing him out. She was worried that Hector was pretending to be the calm one because they couldn't afford to have two people melting down in their apartment at the same time.

The TV cut close to a shot of Mrs. Claus waving to the little white kids in the audience. The Christmas season had officially arrived, the announcer said.

"You think they get a different Santa every year?" Angel said. "Or do you think they stick with the same guy?"

* * *

By the time they stood outside Mami's building in the Bronx, the sky had a twinkle of orange in the gray clouds. Angel hoped that the earlier promise of snow would come for real. Before they walked into the building to face Mami, Hector squeezed her hand and told her not to worry.

"I ain't worried," she said, but it was a lie.

When she led him into the apartment, she could hear Miguel belting out tunes from the shower. She kissed her mother on the cheek and took over the tasks—checked on the pernil in the oven, sprinkled garlic powder and salt over the tostones, piled the lumps of maduros onto a plate with sliced tomatoes. It took Hector negative-two-minutes to chat it up with Mami. *That man*, Angel thought, *could charm the pants off a tree*. Angel peeked out from behind the cocina wall—Mami was only drinking a coconut soda. *For the better*, Angel thought.

During dinner, Hector dominated the conversation as Angel took care of the food situation and brought the dirty plates to the sink. As Angel sprinkled the cinnamon over the tembleque and served it with dessert spoons, Hector was in the middle of his El

Yunque story. The rain forest was wet with magic, he said, when he and his abuelo had walked a random path until they came to a water hole.

"Ay, Dios," Mami screamed like a church lady, "I love a good watering hole."

"I couldn't believe it myself," Hector said. Angel sat and spooned her tembleque and wondered if she were in a special edition of *The Twilight Zone*. She tried to make eyes with Miguel, but he was also enraptured by Hector's suave-ass storytelling abilities.

"I took off everything 'cept my calzoncillos and swam under the waterfall," Hector continued. "And I was begging my abuelo to come in with me."

"I always say," Mami said, waving her dessert spoon in the air, "whenever the shoe fits—you gotta swim."

"What?" Angel said, but no one responded.

"Did he swim with ya?" Miguel asked.

"Naw," Hector said. "He just watched and gave me one of those gummy smiles because he forgot his denture-teeth at home." Hector curled up his lips over his teeth and did his best jibarito-abuelo impression, eating the last syllables of all the words. His sense of stage presence always amazed Angel. It was as if the man could just turn it on for anyone he wanted to dazzle. Angel watched as Hector told story after story. He spoke with his hands. He placed an arm on Mami's shoulder. He threw his head back to laugh. She watched his charm unfold just the way it had when she first fell for him.

After dessert, Miguel started talking to Hector about his homeys at school, smoking reefer and listening to Pink Floyd.

"You know they say you can watch *The Wizard of Oz* backward and listen to it," Miguel said. "Or maybe it's the other way 'round, like you listen to it backward and watch it forward. I dunno, it's one of those."

"Who's *they*?" Hector said. "*They* say, *they* do. I just wanna know who *they* is, my man."

"Pues, no sé," Miguel said. "Just *people*."

* * *

When dinner was over and Hector had gone downstairs to bring out the trash, Mami was folding the floral tablecloth and the plastic cover that went over it. She asked if Angel and Hector were fucking.

"Madre mía," Angel said. "Por favor, could we not go there. Can we not have that moment right now."

Miguel was blasting music from his bedroom, loud enough that the neighbors would be banging on their door in no time. The smell of reefer flowed up from under his door and it smelled like freshly dead skunk.

"He's gonna give you that virus," Mami said. "I seen it on the *NBC Nightly News*. I thought you were bringing a friend over—not some fucking maricón, Angel."

"Where's this coming from?" Angel said. "I thought you liked him. Just a half hour ago, this apartment was like the fucking Puerto Rican rendition of *Leave It to Beaver*."

Miguel's music was all bass, just a thump-thump verberating the walls and floor.

"Mira, it's hard enough for me to deal with you coming into my house dressed the way you do," Mami said. "But you're gonna get ese virus—that gay cancer shit. Don't do that to me, Angel. Coño, what're the neighbors gonna say?"

"You were laughing at his stories," Angel said.

Mami put the two table-protecting cloths over each other and shoved them into the lowest drawer in the plate cabinet. She told Angel she was going to call the santera lady from the botánica to set up an in-home appointment.

"You're not calling no santera," Angel said. "I don't need no es-píritu bullshit."

"Only a spell to help protect you," Mami said.

"I don't need some fucking hoodoo magic," Angel said. "He doesn't have the virus. Not all maricones got the damn virus. We're not all walking time bombs, for fuck's sake."

Later that night, she lay on the floor of the sala, staring up at the ceiling while smoking a cigarette. The nieve was falling down so light, it looked like white dust floating in the sky. As the smoke swirled up toward the white ceiling, she wondered if maybe Mami was right. Maybe she did need all the protection she could find. But that gave Angel the terrors.

What terrified her were the ways in which the world, with or without magic, was capable of doing anything, and there was no way to see or say what kind of jodienda was going to come next. What terrified her was that even without magic, anything could happen. Anything at all.

HECTOR

Dear Alvin Ailey,

My name is Hector Valle. I live in New York. My counselor said it might help if I keep a journal. Maybe write some letters too. She said I don't need to send the letters if I don't want to. The important part is just getting the feelings out there. So forgive me, Mr. Ailey, because I probably won't ever send this letter to you. It's just that I'm going through a difficult time. I hope you understand.

I wanted to say that I'm a huge fan. I watched a video of Revelations and I was so moved. The dancers glided like they was moving through water. When I was young, my abuela managed to save enough money for me to take one dance class a year. My ballet teacher was an old Cuban woman who trained in Paris. She used to tell us that a proper dancer stands up straight, so we should imagine that our spines are hanging down from the ceiling like a string of pearls. Whenever we fucked up, she slammed down her walking stick and screamed, "Pedestrian!" at us. (The goal, I guess, was not to be pedestrian.) And I thought of that when I watched Revelations. Your dancers was moving like they was dangling from the ceiling off a pearl necklace. They definitely wasn't pedestrian. It made me so happy and so sad, but I mean that in a good way. That's how I feel whenever I see something really beautiful. That's how I know it's beautiful.

In Revelations, I remember there was a group of dancers on the stage that used a giant tree branch to sweep the earth. And there was a white cloth to cleanse the sky. That made me happy-sad too. And the couple getting baptized! With yards and yards of billowing silk stretched across the stage. Was it silk? I always thought, wouldn't it be nice if the sky was made of silk, and whenever we walked and the wind blew, the sky would billow also. I think that would just make me happy. Not happy-sad, just happy.

But it's the last part that really kills me. I watched it and re-watched, the part when the man does the "I Wanna Be Ready" solo. Just him alone on the stage with the one light shining down on him. Everything else black. He's just there, can't even get up off the ground almost. Ever since I saw that, I go up to my roof and lay down a couple of flattened cardboard boxes and do that dance. Every morning. Because I wanna be ready too, Mr. Ailey.

I always wanted to be part of your dance group. What a dream that would have been. But then someone told me that you can't join if you're not black. I thought, Well, gee, I'm not black—but I certainly ain't white. Especially if I'm talking Spanish, all the white people in Manhattan look at me like I might as well be black. But that's okay, I understand why all your dancers are black. And I like that. I like what you do. But most of all, Mr. Ailey, I love your range. You can do ballet and jazz and hip-hop and gospel. It feels like something real special.

I'm trying to teach my girl, Angel, how to dance. She's alright. Sometimes I think she overthinks it. You know how you have to get past that stage of thinking and let your body take over. Like the world is made of water and it only has to flow into you and out of your arms and legs. I'm going to keep teaching

*her though, and then maybe one day, her and I can dance on the
roof without music, letting our bodies tell each other everything
we think and see and feel.*

With love,
H.

VENUS

Fluorescent lights were pure hell and she would never understand
their purpose, but there it was, flickering in the bathroom as she
stared at her reflection in the mirror to do her makeup. Mirror was
a generous word—it was the kind of mirror that used to hang in
the bathrooms at Our Lady of the Flowers, where she would look
at herself and see a lost boy, and the mirrors in the disgusting bathrooms at Port Authority, where she would refuse to look at herself
as she sponge-washed her armpits. She could barely make out her
face, but it would have to do—whatever it could reflect back to her.
She closed her eyes and arched her eyebrows up so that the skin on
her eyelids was flat. She dabbed on the cover-up, which felt damp
against her skin. She smoothed it in, creating a base layer for the
color that would come next—a brand new blue that she had just
mopped from Duane Reade. She heard the door open and close.

She opened her eyes and saw Sugar Cookie standing in front of
the door frame. She apologized and said she'd be out in just a sec.
She was just doing her face right. She only had to finish up her eyes
and put lip liner on, then the bathroom could be all his.

"Nah," he said. "We got something to conversate about."

She heard the light buzz as it flicked on and off quickly. "If it's
about La Loca, don't worry, Sugar. We're close now."

"It's not," he said. He turned the door's metal lock, and Venus
heard it click as she put down her brush.

He started walking toward her and she put down her compact.
"What do you want? Why'd you lock me in?"

He took a step toward her and she backed up against the bathroom's side wall. She could feel the cold pink tiles against her back. She could even feel the groove where an old tile had popped out and crashed to the floor. Now there was nothing left there except a small hole in the wall in the shape of the square that used to fill it. It was cold enough to feel through the sheer fabric of her tank, a fabric she had picked because it showed a little skin without being trampy. She had wanted to suggest, not reveal. He pressed his body against hers so that her face was pushed in his chest. He told her to just make it easy for the both of them—he wanted her to suck his dick.

"And what is this hairspray you are using today?" he said, taking a deep inhale breath.

"Stop, Sugar."

"It smells sweet. All tropical scented."

"Stop it," she said. "Why are you bugging?"

"Why stop," he said, but she could tell that it wasn't a question. "You know you like it. I see you, wearing that sexy tank top. I see you, just getting close to Loca so that you can have me."

She could feel him getting hard as he pressed his legs against her waist. He reached his hands into the side of her tank and grabbed her nipple. His pinch sent a sharp pang through her body. She tried to wiggle her way out, but he had her pinned.

"You don't have to pretend to make it all difficult for me," he said. "But if you're at it, just don't make a fucking sound." His left fingers pinched harder and she held back a scream because she was scared that he would cover her mouth and fuck her up real bad. She scrunched her face because of the pain, and when she heard a click, she saw the switchblade in his hand. "If you're not gonna give in," he said, holding the blade to her neck, "then we're gonna have to do it my way."

He told her to get to her knees. He unzipped his pants and, once she was down there on all fours, he backstepped to the sink counter. With his hands rooted in her hair, he pulled her closer to the sink so that he could lean against the ledge.

His cock was thick and curved and he was unforgiving as she

gagged on it. He was so thick that the hinges of her jaw hurt as she tried to keep her mouth locked open, fearing that her teeth would scratch him and he'd slice her neck open. She couldn't bear to swallow, so the spit leaked out of her mouth as he facefucked her. She thought she was gonna throw up, and she hoped she would so that the acid from her stomach could burn him.

When he was done with her, the back of her throat felt warm and sticky. She used the sink counter to prop herself back up, and she didn't know where to look because she didn't want to see herself in the mirror and she didn't want to see him. She sat back down on the floor and reached for a wad of toilet paper to blow her nose. She wiped the side of her mouth. She could only imagine what her mascara looked like.

Someone knocked on the door and Venus thought, *Thank god*. Sugar Cookie zipped back up and unlocked the door. Venus balled the toilet paper up into her palms and leaned her head back against the wall, neck loose.

"Baby," she heard Sugar Cookie say and she thought, *Don't fucking call me baby*. "You're never gonna believe what this maneater bitch did to me?"

That son of a bitch—Venus was too shocked for words as she looked up and saw La Loca standing at the door with her makeup bag.

"You were right about her all along, babe," he said.

Venus concentrated on her breathing or else she knew she'd pass the fuck out. She turned her head left and right, as if to signal no-no, that's not how it happened at all. "She said that if I didn't let her suck me, she'd take that blade and stab me in the balls."

La Loca stepped into the room and towered over Venus. They all looked at the switchblade that was on the counter. "Stand up," La Loca said.

Venus licked her lips and stood up, shoulders back, breathing hard. "He's lying to you," Venus said. "It was *him*."

"I didn't say I wanted words," La Loca said. "All I said was to stand the fuck up."

Venus leaned her left hand on the sink for balance, wondering if Loca would take her other hand.

"Now look me in the eyes," La Loca said, "you lying bitch."

She looked into La Loca's eyes—so blue, so hard. "I'm not lying," Venus said, staring at the long eyelashes that Loca must've glued on only minutes earlier. La Loca reached into her makeup bag and pulled out the rock that was shaped like a heart. She slammed it on the counter.

"You can have your shitty rock back," La Loca said. She watched La Loca's nostrils flare, and the last thing she felt was the slap: the side of La Loca's calloused palm flat against the side of her face.

"You're just like your mother," Venus said, "staying by your rapist man even when you know better."

La Loca slapped her again so hard, she saw stars as her head hit the wall. Whatever remained of Sugar Cookie's cum spat out of her mouth, along with some blood.

*   *   *

Leaving. It was a funny word. How could a person leave a place that was never theirs to begin with? It seemed to Venus like she had become a master of leaving—leaving Jersey City, leaving hotel rooms, leaving behind everyone she had ever met, whether or not she had given them the impression that she would stay in the first place.

She left for the first time when she was fourteen and Antonio taught her the difference between bail and jail. She had never been thrown in jail, and she hoped she never would be. But if it happened, at least she now knew what bail meant. Bail and jail. Rhyming words, that was a doozy. The difference between *bail* and *jail* is that the first is used to get out of the second, if there's enough. First to get out of the second, she'd repeat to herself. Seton, Satan. Bail, jail. Letters could be such a pain in the ass.

It had happened the day before Halloween. Thomas was unpacking his costume from the plastic bag it came in from the party store.

It was a cowboy outfit even though he wanted to be the pretty princess. The shirt was a polyblend thing, the kind of fabric that could completely go up if he stood too close to a match or candle. There was a boom-knocking at the door while he was putting the shirt on a hanger so there would be no wrinkles the next day. It all happened so quickly. Nonna opened the door, the stream of policemen came in, the words and the tears, Nonna and his mother away in cuffs.

Antonio had to spell it out for him. They were selling numbers and that was a no-no according to Uncle Sam. "It's fucked-up," Antonio said.

"Who is Sam?" Thomas asked, but Antonio said never mind, he was trying to get bail, but Thomas didn't know if Antonio was even telling the truth. If he couldn't get enough money to take his mother to Hawaii, then how the hell would he get this bail? A week went by and there was still nothing, so Thomas packed a bag with his clothes and some Wonder Bread and cold cuts, and he booked it out of there.

Leaving. It wasn't that hard to do. All he needed were feet and eyes that marched forward—anyone could do it. He took the bus to Port Authority at midnight. Swarms of girls so young, men with canes and fedora hats and round bellies, all of them buzzing around like flies at the doors. He walked all the way up to Central Park, must have taken an hour or two to get to the lake at night.

The water was calm and the boats were asleep at the dock. It was too dark to see the buildings rise up above the trees, but he knew they were there, waiting for the morning light to come. He found a rock shaped like a heart and he put it in his pocket, thinking it was a sign from the universe that everything would turn out alright.

A man in a suit blazer, with chubby fingers that sweated a lot, picked him up that night and brought him back to the Plaza. "If anyone asks," the man told him, holding his hand, "just pretend that you're my son."

It was the same hotel from the Eloise books that Nonna had read to him as a kid. When he asked the man if the Eloise story was true all along, he laughed and told Thomas that was only a story. Thomas watched as he unbuttoned his shirt and folded it over the chair. "What's your name?" the man asked.

Thomas looked down at the cover of a magazine on the table. "Venus," she said, looking at the words on the cover: Venus de Milo. In the quickness of her glance, she took in the picture on the cover—the white marble of the statue, the robe, the perky tits, the lack of arms. Yes, she thought, to be naked, armless, and made of marble. To think: a woman from Milo named after a planet!

"That's a beautiful name," the man said. "Like the goddess. I bet you do look like a goddess underneath those clothes."

"No," she said, blushing. "Like the planet."

The man laughed and played with the wedding ring that looked like it was choking his fat finger. "The planet is named after the goddess."

"Oh," she said. "Well, I don't know all about that—"

"Don't worry," he said. "I'll give you three-hundred."

"Okay," she said because she didn't know what to say.

"And when we're done, I'll order room service."

"Okay."

The man shed his clothes and stood in front of Venus. She didn't want to think about how old he was, but maybe in his fifties. She was never quite good at guessing ages and she knew this. The man kept his gold watch on, and he stepped closer to her to rub his hairy chest against her. He started to undress her, first her shirt, then her pants, then the slow slipping off of the white briefs that Venus had made sure were hole-less. "You're a cute kid," he said and she was aware of his gaze as he looked at her smooth body, her skinny legs, her ribs, and she wondered if this man could sense her desire to be a woman. He looked at her face, then, and said, "You *are* hungry, right?"

He downed four tiny whiskey bottles that he pulled from the mini fridge and then he turned off all the lights and fucked her. Wanted her on her stomach so he didn't have to see her face. He wrapped his arms around her so that she couldn't move away while he entered her. She smelled the sour and bitter curling of his breath as he exhaled into the space between her ear and her shoulder. He was kind enough not to cum inside her. "I only cum inside my wife," he said. And when he was done, he fell asleep on top of her.

At first, she had been too nice to want to wake him. But then she felt uncomfortable under his weight, plus the snoring and the occasional body twitches were annoying. She knew it would be impossible to fall asleep buried under him. When she woke him up, he went to the safe and pulled out a wad of bills that were rubber banded together. He pulled out three and handed them to her.

"What about the room service?" she said.

"Oh," he said. "I'm too tired for that."

But I'm hungry, she wanted to say, yet didn't want to push her luck.

That night had been about five years ago. Now, after finding Serenity and all it had to offer her—a momentary pause in the hustle of street life, meals, some form of stability as she got those job applications in and waited to hear back, the occasional cigarette behind the Dumpster—she would have to leave again. She *knew* she had to leave. There was no way in hell she could stay there—not with Sugar Cookie around. Not with the wrath of La Loca that she knew was coming her way. She hadn't just crossed over a bridge, she had burned it all the way to the motherfucking ground.

Now she stood in front of that same lake in Central Park with Serenity behind her for good. She was back on that cruising grind and she thought about that nice man she had met a couple years ago. He had a special place in her heart because he was the first one who had taught her what she was worth, and how she could go about working in the parks, the piers, wherever. He had taught her that nights spent in hotel rooms beat out the nights spent sucking dick under the god-given sky and all the world's harsh elements. At least the hotel rooms provided a little warmth.

* * *

She was alone in the bushes, crouched down like the girls did out-side bars and concert halls when they wanted to take a piss, when she heard the footsteps walking toward her. She didn't have a blade on her though, and she was kicking herself for forgetting one. She hiked up her skirt so nothing would rip and then she rested her head in her palms so that she could sob without making a sound.

"What's a-matter, nena?" the voice said.

Venus looked up and adjusted her tube top and wiped some snot on the outside of her arm. There was a body standing in the shadow of a street lamp, and the light slashed across the person's face like an orange triangle. The voice asked her what her name was and why the fuck she was crying behind a bush.

Venus said her name and thought about lying, but she was inter-rupted before she could get out more words. "Venus?" the voice said. "Hold up the phone for a hot second. Like the planet?"

"Yeah," she said. "You know it?"

"Do I *know* it? Girl, of course I know it. Second planet from the sun."

"Yeah," Venus said. Her knees were shaking from the squat she was still in. She wobbled her ankles so that she could stand. "And it's also the name of a goddess."

"Oh, really? I didn't know that. Shit, which goddess?"

"Well," Venus said. "I'm not sure, exactly. But someone told me that Venus was a goddess."

"Ay, pues mira, goddess! Look at choo," the voice said. "I'm An-gel. *Enchanté.*"

Angel grabbed Venus's hand and kissed her fingers like a prince in some Russian ball movie. Angel was decked out like a Christ-mas tree, all sparkle and glitter. Her golden chandelier drop earrings framed her neck, and they weren't clip-ons or nothing. They were the real deal.

"You Spanish?" Angel asked. "You look Spanish."

"Italian," Venus said, pulling down on her skirt to smooth out the wrinkles. She didn't want anything to pop out and give the street a show.

"Damn, coulda had me fooled with those legs," Angel said. "I'm Puerto Rican and I can spot Rican legs from a block away. And those right there look like some fuckin' *legs*."

Venus laughed and rubbed her freshly shaved thigh like Vanna White displaying a new letter. Angel cackled and whistled. "Work that pierna, chica," Angel said. "You speak Spanish though?"

"A little," Venus said. "Had to pick some up in the shelters to make sure nobody was talking shit about me."

They laughed and then Angel said, "Pues, ¿qué pasó contigo, nenita? Why you all crying in a bush under the moon?"

"Nada."

"What is it?"

"It's *nothing*," Venus said.

"Don't lie," Angel said. "You ain't trying to run up on my zone, are you? Because this is my block. If you gotta work, you can do it all up over there near the Duprees' zone."

"Nah, I'm not working. Don't worry."

"Well then why you crying? Look at us," Angel said. "I can just tell by looking at you that you and I got a lot in common. We gotta stick together."

Venus winced at those words. She had heard them before, hadn't she? The idea of sticking together with another person meant that she'd have to trust, and she didn't know, after all the bullshit she had gone through, if she wanted to do that.

"I don't even know you," Venus said.

"Well not yet you don't," Angel said. "What do you wanna know about?"

"Oh fine," Venus said, "I'll tell you."

"That certainly didn't take much," Angel said. "See, nena. You act all guarded, but I can tell you really just wanna tell people who you are. I can be the same way."

Venus told Angel that she was crying in the bush because *before* that, she was strutting down Hudson Street. Now, girl, she was strutting like she owned that asphalt. Thinking, *Look at me,* rocking this new white-washed denim mini-falda she had mopped from Saks with a loose-fitting T-shirt that she cut off herself to show the world what her belly button looked like.

"God, I love Saks," Angel said. "And, atención, mundo. Look at that naval. Sizzle-sizzle."

"I was smoking my Newport and minding my own," Venus said. "I was exhaling my smoke into the air with my head back so my blow-out could blow in the summer wind."

"You got a gift for storytelling," Angel said. "I feel like I'm there with you."

"And as soon as I finished my cig and flicked the butt to the curb, I felt a hand on my ass."

Angel gasped. "Oh no you did not."

"Oh yes I did too," Venus said.

"Did you know the guy? Angel said. "Because if you didn't, I hope you smacked the shit out of him real good for being nasty."

"Nah," Venus lied. The thing is that she did know him. It was Sugar Cookie, after all those weeks, he had found her. But she thought that would be too complicated to explain to Angel.

Venus had told Sugar to fuck off. She had to pick up her stride so that his scummy hand would find itself off her ass, but he picked up his pace so that they were walking together. "Get your hand off me," she told him.

"What's the matter, baby girl?" Sugar had said. "You ain't happy to see me?"

She had to stop walking to look at his face, that goofy-ass smile. "Hell no, I'm not. And I said get that hand off me!" She hawked a wad of spit at his face.

He scrunched his face and wiped away the spit with his hand. "Now that wasn't very nice."

Now Venus told Angel that she tried to run away, but her kitten heels made it difficult because when she tried to run, her ankle got twisted and she fell. "And he reached out a hand," Venus told Angel, "but I didn't want to touch him."

"And of course not," Angel said, fingers splayed over her heart like every breath was a gasp she had to take.

"You know what I want to do to you?" Sugar Cookie had said. "I want to run my tongue all inside that juicy ass of yours."

Venus had stumbled up to her feet, grabbed her clutch, and looked at the corner of the street. There were two cops drinking coffee, so she yelled at them and when they looked over, she screamed help.

"Fuck," Sugar Cookie said. "I'll just tell them you're soliciting. And who do you think they're gonna believe—a man like myself, or some fem-boy faggot like you wearing a miniskirt at the piers?"

When Angel heard this part of the story, she gasped. "How dare he?" Angel said. "Did he not see that skirt looks so fucking good on you? That asshole. I can't believe it."

The problem was that when Sugar had said that, Venus knew that he was right. She knew that the cops would see her, then see him, and she would be the guilty one. She resented them all for that.

As the cops walked toward them, Sugar Cookie yelled, "Get away from me, faggot. I don't want none of that. Officers!"

"So I told him to go fuck himself," Venus told Angel. "And then I took up my heels and ran barefooted down the street until my lungs couldn't do no more."

"And here you are," Angel said.

"And here I am."

"So let's go." Angel grabbed Venus's wrist.

Venus was confused. "What do you mean let's go?"

"We're going to find that bruto motherfucker and show him what's what."

Venus would've been fine with letting the whole Sugar business pass, but Angel? Homegirl seemed about as reasonable as a blowtorch in a hurricane.

"But, Angel, look at your hair," Venus said as Angel dragged her down the street by the wrist. "You don't wanna start nothing and get it all messy."

Angel kept stomping down Christopher Street. Three men in tight denim jackets and moustaches were smoking cigarettes outside of some dive. One of the men whistled at them, and Angel screamed, "Take a picture, it'll last you *much* longer." Then to Venus, "Pues nena, I'm not worried about my hair. Why do you think god invented hairspray?"

"Yeah, but your dress. What if it gets ripped?"

"And *who* in their right mind is gonna rip it?"

"Shiiit," Venus said. "How do you walk so fast in those things?" Angel's stilettos must've been seven inches high and were pointy enough to be classified as a weapon. They were no match for Venus's kitten keels, which earlier that evening had seemed so right, and now, less so.

Angel shrugged off the question, maybe because she didn't hear because she was so intent on finding the right street to turn on, but Venus couldn't be sure. Venus didn't even know where they were heading.

"Cálmate," Angel said. "What's this Sugar Ass motherfucker look like?"

They stopped in the middle of the street and Venus was able to catch her breath. "Come on," Venus said. "This is wack. What are we even gonna do if we find him? And why do you wanna get revenge for someone that you just met?"

They were stopped near the corner of Christopher and some street that Venus couldn't read the name of. "Revenge for someone that I just met?" Angel repeated. "Nena, I gotta stick up for the people who look and sashay just like I do because if he hurts you, he's also hurting me, don't you see?"

Venus nodded.

"If you let these motherfuckers treat you like that," Angel said, "they're just gonna keep on doing it—to you, to me, to all of us. Not ever gonna learn. So let's take this Sugar Ass to school, teach his bruto ass a little something about r-e-s-p-e-c-t—Aretha style!—and that's what it's gonna be."

"I'm just afraid," Venus whispered. She moved her face closer to those drop earrings that dangled from Angel's ear. "I'm afraid he's gonna kill me."

"Not with me around he ain't."

"No, but for real," Venus said. "I wasn't completely honest with you before."

"Oh?" Angel's eyes grew all big.

"You don't know what he did to me at the shelter. He pulled a knife at me and forced me to give him head. Then when his girl walked in, he blamed it all on me."

Angel moved her neck back and squinted her eyelids a bit, as if to hone in some kind of eagle-eyed focus on Venus's face. "So you just wanna let it sit?" Angel asked.

"Yeah, no," Venus said. "I don't know."

Angel grabbed her hand and they turned around back the way they came from. "Fine," Angel said. "Some motherfucker pulls a blade on you and you just wanna let it sit. Okay. Alright."

Venus reached for her clutch to get her pack of cigs, but when she opened the box, there weren't any left. She asked Angel if there was a bodega nearby and Angel pointed to the corner. She asked Angel if she wanted to share in on a pack of Newports.

Just as Venus walked up to the bodega, with its lit-up posters for the New York state lotto, there he was, sitting with his legs wide open on the stoop of the building across the way. He was chugging from a bottle that was covered in a brown paper bag. She watched his head turn, back and forth, slowly, as if the tip of his nose had a magnet that was attracted to every passing man's ass. The pig.

"That's him," she whispered to Angel. "I can't believe it."

Venus stood where she was and watched Angel glide over to

Sugar Cookie in those seven inchers. Angel's dress glittered like little pieces of floating tinfoil. Her stilettos clacked on the sidewalk like flip-flops at the Coney Island boardwalk on a hot summer day.

"Escuse me," Venus could hear Angel say. "But, in the happenstance, did you manage to call my girl a faggot?" Angel pointed to where Venus was standing. Venus didn't know what to do—if dropping dead in the flip of a second were an option, she'd take it—so she held up her hand and wiggled her fingers and offered a pained, toothless smile. Sugar Cookie looked at Venus, took another chug from his bottle, then looked at Angel as if she were carrying a garbage bag full of rotting fish.

"And what the fuck is it to you?" he said.

"What is it to me?" Angel said, bringing her finely did nails to the side of her face, as if expressing shock *and* a desire to fan herself. "She's my child, that's what."

"Your child?" Sugar Cookie's laugh sounded like a roar. He was laughing so hard, he had to pause to make sure he didn't vomit. After he dry-gagged, he said, "You're not old enough to have a boy that old."

"Apologize to my daughter," Angel said. "And do it right now."

Sugar Cookie burped a loud, wet burp. He scratched his crotch. He wiped his mouth with the part of his T-shirt that covered his shoulder.

"Honey," Angel said. "Don't let this *beautiful* dress fool you or give you any kind of misconceptions. Do what I say and apologize to my daughter right this instant."

"Oh, fuck off."

Angel took off her shoes, one by one. Venus watched as Angel whipped her arm up and back, and then slammed the heel part of the shoe against the side of Sugar Cookie's face. He wailed while she clocked him. Again and again, like the goal was to drill cement. Angel was aiming for temple, for eye socket, for ear. Homegirl had gone Level Stiletto Powertool on his beat ass.

When she was done, there was blood dripping down his face and his body was slumped on the stoop. She slipped on her shoes in two elegant motions and walked back to Venus as if nothing had happened. There was a line of blood on her hand.

"Oh, my god," Venus said. "Did you kill him?"

"No," Angel said. "He's very much alive, but we need to run before he gets up and whoops both our asses."

Before they ran down those dark streets, Venus looked back to get a last glimpse of Sugar. Angel was right: Sugar wasn't dead. He wasn't even passed out. He just looked like he got into a boxing match with the wrong, angry drag queen. The sight of his blood didn't make Venus feel happy, but it certainly did make her feel content.

"I warned you," Angel screamed at Sugar Cookie over her shoulder as they ran. "You shouldn't have let all of *this* fool you."

* * *

Angel guided Venus way west to an area near the Hudson where some boys were laying down cardboard boxes so they could spin on their heads without cutting skin up. When they sat on a bench, they stared at each other and laughed so hard, Venus was convinced she would bust an organ.

"Did you see the look on his face?" Venus said.

"I was took quick with running."

"You made him *bleed*," Venus said. "He didn't see it coming."

"Good," Angel said. "That was the objective. I told him not to fuck around. And I gave him the chance to apologize."

"Day-um."

"Why don't you sleep?" Angel said. Venus could feel Angel's fingers massaging her scalp, then guiding Venus's head into Angel's lap as if it were a pillow.

"Hey," Venus said. "Thank you—you know, for everything."

She watched one of the boys squat down like a frog, with his forehead on the cardboard like his chin wanted to kiss the ground. Then his knees rested on his arms above his bent elbows. Once he was there, he sprang his legs up and used his hands to spin his body, and Venus was worried that the boy's scalp would start to bleed.

"No pasa nada, nena," Angel said. "You know he deserved that shit. I'd like to see him pass me or you on the street one more time and try to play."

"You're a sass machine," Venus said. "I wish I got your sass."

"I'm giving some away," Angel said, "all for free."

They sat and watched the boys break it down to Afrika Bambaataa and Soul Sonic Force. They made Venus envy that kind of arm-leg coordination. She wished she had the kind of strength to balance everything on her hands so her legs could spin in circles. She watched as the main man of the group did a worm, then shot back up to his feet and waved his arms out like he was saluting the moon. Then a rat the size of a small cat scurried out from a nearby bush and they both jumped up and screamed bloody murder at the same time.

"So many damn rats on this island," Venus said.

"Mmm," Angel said. "Not just here, nena. But all over."

"Can't believe we just screamed that loud," Venus said. "My heart is still coming out of my chest."

"That's what I'm saying," Angel said. "Sometimes I get scared of my own shadow."

"Now that," Venus said, "I don't believe." She lay on her side so that her knees curled up to her chest in a fetal position. Angel was playing with the hair near Venus's earlobe—it had taken months for Venus to finally grow it all out to that length.

"You know," Angel said, "I don't even know where you're from?"

"Somewhere over there." Venus pointed across the river, to the patchwork of trees on the Jersey side of things.

"And why'd you bust out?" Angel said. "Please don't tell me it's a sad story."

"My mom and grandma got busted selling numbers for some guy."

"Numbers?"

"Yeah," Venus said. "For some guy my mom was fucking."

"Shit," Angel said. "The things we do for our men, can I get an amen on that? That is so fucked-up."

"You're telling me," Venus said. "What about you? Why'd you leave?"

"I didn't—not quite, at least," Angel said. "I'm living with my man, Hector. His abuela was also selling numbers back when she was alive."

"Oh yeah?" Venus sat up on the bench, suddenly energized by this talk of a man. "Where you two living? Westchester?"

"Girl, I wish. Get me a car and a little house and I'd be the happiest little thing in the world." Angel reached into her clutch and took out her lip liner. "Alphabet City right now, so we'll see what happens, sabes?"

She watched as Angel carefully drew on two thick maroon lines around her lips. She nodded when Angel asked if they were even. Angel blew her an air-kiss.

"Where's your mother?" Angel asked.

"I don't know," she said. "Either with Antonio or in jail. I don't even care."

"Ay, look at you," Angel said. "You don't even know where your mother is?" She giggled and looked up at the edge of the sky that was turning pink. Soon the city would start the slow curl out of bed, the sky would change from pink to orange to purple. People would leave the bars and the late-night diners, and go home. The bagel shops would open and the streets out front would smell like dough and butter. Then the purple in the sky would become a soft blue, and the sun would rise higher.

Angel put her arm around Venus and looked her directly in the eyes and said, "Ay, nena, your mother is right next to you."

ANGEL

They climbed the fire escape to the top of the roof. Two taxis were on the corner of Avenue A, one had hit the other, and the drivers were having words. "Oh," Angel said, "you shoulda seen the nails on her though."

Hector didn't laugh.

"Honey, really, I'm joking," Angel said. "That woman is a scam artist, but you can laugh when I throw the shade," Angel said. She was talking about the santera that Mami had called. "With the money she's charging, she could get those nails done three times a week, and I'm sure she does."

"You're so bad," Hector said. The sun was setting on the other side of the island, near the West Side Highway—avenues of buildings and blocks away, but they could still see the sky's colors giving way. It was cold and the sky was a soft pink. If they couldn't see the sun set, at least they could be around to feel it happening. "We gotta talk about something."

"Can't we talk after the dance?" Angel said. She had popped the lids off some Goya cans and duct-taped them to the bottoms of their shoes. She told Hector that she wanted him to teach her how to tap dance. They had watched *Too Hot to Handle* so many times that they could recite the back-and-forth between Fred Astaire and Ginger Rogers like it was a thirty-second soda jingle.

"Angel, come on," Hector said, but she pouted and he gave in. "This reminds me," he said in his Fred Astaire voice, "of the old days when we used to do shows at the old ball."

"Yeah," Angel said, throwing Rogers realness, "we used to fight about the gate receipts."

She stared at him and thought about what a silly thing it must be for Fred and Ginger to fight over receipts. She knew that Hector had something to tell her. She knew what it was, but she wanted to avoid it. Had the results come back? She just wanted him to teach her how to tap.

"You remember the Valentine I sent you?" he said, puffing out his chest. "The one with the heart and the arrow dripping blood?"

Angel broke character but then got serious again. "I do remember," she said. "I think that's the only Valentine I ever received."

(*And who was Ginger kidding?* Angel thought. *There was no way a fox like her could've only gotten one Valentine.*)

"That's the only one I ever sent," Hector said. He grabbed her and spun her around, their hands connected.

"Those were some happy days then," she said. "You know, I think I was in love with you then." She spun into his chest and looked at his face—the dark circles under his eyes, the stubble. He squeezed her into his chest and she could feel his ribs.

"I know you were," he said.

"Oh, you," she said.

"Oh, me," he said. "And what's more, I was madly in love with you." He tapped around her but the lids on the bottoms of his shoes hardly made a sound. Even though she could tell that he didn't want to do this performance for her, he continued.

She wanted to stop it all, but it was too late, they were already in the middle of it. He brought his arms up and and flailed them back and forth. He rained down jazz hands.

"We were funny, weren't we?" she said, forcing Ginger's line and thinking, *There is nothing at all funny about this now.* "Aren't we?"

Hector stopped. "I can't do this anymore," he said.

"No," she said. She walked up to him and by now the sun had set fully. There was no more pink in the sky. She put her hand up to his mouth and said, "Don't continue."

She undressed him. It was so cold, both their nips were getting hard. She glided her hands over his body, searching for the areas that were so sensitive, he would gasp. They explored each other's skin as if they were mapmakers in new territory.

"We can't," he said, "have sex."

"I figured," she said.

He told her that the test had come back positive. They were lying on the roof now, too many clouds for any stars to be in sight.

"I don't give a shit anymore," he said.

"Don't say that shit, Hector." She didn't know whether she should squeeze his hand, say it would be alright, or if that kind of thing would come across as corny, forced, or cheesy.

"But it's the truth," he said. "Look at you, you have so much hope for the world, for the people in it. I hope the way you see shit never changes, but damn yo, sometimes life just sucks you in and chews you up. Just like this city. This city moves so fast, it don't care who we small people are. It never did and it never will."

"I'm sorry," she said, fearing that she wouldn't know what else to say. "I'm sorry for everything."

"Why're you apologizing?" he asked, but she didn't have an answer.

* * *

The next day, she went to the clinic in Chelsea to get tested. There were only six chairs, so some people were standing. Skinny young boys, no families. The only woman there looked like a butch and she was sitting next to her fem queen friend, holding his hand and rubbing his palm and wiping the sweat off his forehead every couple of minutes.

Angel was alone because Hector was working at the yogurt place. He had told her he would take off, but she said no. The nice nurse was wearing rubber gloves when she took the blood. She told Angel that the results would come back in two weeks, and asked for her phone number and address.

Two weeks later, the test came back negative. She wasn't relieved because it was more than that. Her first thought was that the test was wrong. There was no way in hell she could've been negative. But the nurse assured her that it was the case. She could come back in three months to get tested again, and the nurse even encouraged that.

When she got back to Hector's apartment, she didn't say any-thing. She prepared a picnic of cheddar cheese sandwiches and cheap red wine. The white bread was so soft, it stuck to the top of her mouth. She was scared to drink the wine because she didn't want her teeth to look like they were stained with blood.

After everything was set up on the roof and they were about to start eating, she told him the test came back negative. "That's great news," Hector said. He gulped down the wine in his cup. "So is this, like, your celebration party?"

"What? Why would you even think that?" she said, looking at the bottle of wine and the sandwich spread. It wasn't supposed to be celebrating anything. It was just supposed to be dinner."

"Well, that's great news," he said again, looking down at which sandwich wedge he wanted to take.

"Is it?" she said.

"¿Y qué dices?" he said. "Of course it is."

She watched him pour himself another glass of wine and peer down at the street. He started to cry, but it was so gentle, so silent, that Angel wasn't sure at first if he was. The rooftop was dark and they only had one candle up there. The mosquitoes were out and biting and Angel slapped her leg, thinking she had been bit.

"I don't really know what I'm saying," she said. She didn't know how to tell him that she felt guilty without using the exact words.

The truth felt like a complicated mess, and yet, it was so simple if she had to boil it down. Hector had the virus and she didn't. Hector would die, and even though she knew that everyone would die someday, this meant that Hector would die sooner. Much sooner. And she would go on living. She would have to learn how to live in the world after the man she loved was dead.

His crying was so quiet, she didn't say anything because she thought that he didn't want her to notice. So she remained silent. She didn't want to call out his tears, ask him what was wrong when she so clearly knew what was wrong. She let him have his moment, and she became furious at the most foolish of things. She was angry that the picnic had come across as a celebration dinner. She was angry that space existed. She was angry that she couldn't turn herself into the tiniest speck of dust so that she could enter Hector's body and soothe him. Not just soothe him, but cure him.

"So what do we do now?" she said.

"Oh, now you say something," he said. He still wasn't facing her, looking down at the street. "What do you mean *we*? I'm the one that's gonna die."

"I thought Dorian told me about some people getting on a government trial," she said.

"Fuck," he said, "might as well play the goddamn jackpot lottery."

* * *

Later that night, after they finished their sandwiches and cleaned up the mess that they had made up on the roof, they climbed down the fire escape and used a latex condom to fuck. They needed to use extra KY so the added rubber-friction didn't hurt her. When he first entered her, she held her breath, careful to show him that everything was alright, nothing hurt, and things could continue just as they always had been.

When they finished, Hector pulled the condom off and his cum gathered down at the tip like a wad of spit. The condom looked so sad just dangling there under the weight of gravity. Angel couldn't stand the sight of it. She cried.

"What's wrong?" Hector said after he got up to throw the condom in the basura.

"I don't like it," Angel said. "I don't like the way it feels."

"I guess it does feel," Hector said, "a little different."

"A *little*?" she said. "It hurts me. I can't even feel you anymore."

HECTOR

Dear Martha Graham,

Sometimes I wonder what the world would be like if all of us people never had to use spoken language and we could only communicate with the movement of our bodies. I say that there'd be more love and less misunderstandings. Even when we have to yell, it would be beautiful.

The nurse at the clinic told me that I tested positive for the virus and I got no words to describe it. I don't even think I got the movements neither. My girl tested negative and now it feels like everything's gonna go to shit.

When I found out, I walked from the clinic to the public library. You know the building with the lions outside? That one. I got to watch your video of Lamentation. I watched you wrapped in that tight fabric—it looked like it was a combo between a bedsheet and a turteneck, all over your body—and you was, like, trying to rip yourself out of it. I cried one of those ugly cries when I watched you that I was worried someone was gonna pop their head in and see if I wasn't being murdered right there on the spot.

I took it to be that your lamentation's dance was you trying to escape the self. Maybe I'm wrong, but that's just what I felt. It was like you was trapped in that fabric just like we all trapped in our bodies. Just like this virus is trapped inside me and there's no way it's getting out of me.

As soon as I got home, I went to the roof and practiced my floor works and standing exercises, but I didn't feel like standing no more. I didn't want to do my jumps or my runs or my across-the-floors, so I worked on my falls. Even on that concrete, now that takes some dedication.

The core of the technique during the fall was to use my back. I thought about each little bit of my spine cord, dangling like I was a pearl necklace hanging from a ceiling. What's important is the contraction—makes me look like an electric shock is being pumped in my body. I had to let the weight of my body go against the floor. I couldn't deny the weight of my body to gravity. There's no use in even trying to fight gravity, and I wanted to make my fall look as graceful as I could.

You talk a lot about life force. Especially in the hands. The palm of the hand's gotta be straight out to the audience. I didn't have an audience up there, 'cause I was just doing it alone. But I pretended. I said, I give you (my audience) myself, I give you what I have to give, because that's what it means. I imagine it *like there is light in my core and it moves to my hand and then I contract it out and the audience can see it.*

How many drops of blood have gone into the making of you, you said. And I didn't understand when I first heard it, 'cause I thought, Now Martha girl, we can't possibly count all those damn drops of blood. You said, how much memory is in each drop of blood. And I thought, Now this woman has lost her damn mind thinking that blood can have memories. But you pulled the stunt of the season on me, Ms. Graham. Now I just think each movement I make is just blood coming together to form my body, and each of those blood drops got viruses inside them, growing and multiplying. What I want to know is: If, when the virus advances and I'm still dancing—if I can still move—ain't that just the virus dancing too? Ain't that just the ugly beast of a virus trying to mask itself into something beautiful?

That doesn't seem fair at all. It all doesn't seem fair. Because I'm in love again, Martha, and it's the kind of love that makes you wish you could live forever.

And I think about your words that any moment of choice is a sacrifice. How every single last one of us has life within us and we make a choice about what we will reveal. But I don't got an audience, so what can I reveal if no one is watching me contract and fall?

The thought that this virus might be little pieces of Tyler inside me is killing me. I don't know how I'm gonna muster up the damn words to make sense of it. (I'm not gonna be a father. I'll never see her be a mother.) Even if the world was like I dreamed it could be—no mouth sounds, just dance—I don't even know how I'd find the movements to communicate everything that I'm feeling.

Love,

H.

PART TWO

THE
HOUSE

(1986–1988)

We all live in a house on fire, no fire department to call; no way out, just the upstairs window to look out of while the fire burns the house down with us trapped, locked in it.

—Tennessee Williams, *The Milk Train Doesn't Stop Here Anymore*

ONE

DORIAN

Oh darling, nobody was about to run up a cover of *Vogue* with my face on it, but I suppose you could say that I did have the name recognition in the ball scenes. And I remember when the balls were balls. We would make our outfits ourselves. Gowns and boas and more bugle beads than a bitch knew what to do with. Now it's all about the designers. Anybody can lift a designer out of a store. Where's the art in that? But times change, I know that. Now everyone wants to be looking like Marilyn Monroe or Alexis. Me? I wanted to look like Lena Horne, and let me tell you—when I was young, not nobody wanted to look like Lena Horne.

When I first met Angel, I knew she was different. She had a spark to her and I could see it that first instant. Nearly broke down my door that night at Collage looking like a damsel in a baseball cap. Huffing and puffing like she ran down that hall. I wasn't going nowhere, so I never know why they run. I always say, nothing going to get me to run unless a lion was chasing after me for a dinnertime meal. Then I'd *have* to run and look for a tree to climb. But that hasn't happened yet, so I don't understand why they still running.

And sure, I had some of the kids come to me all the time asking for advice. I liked that. Made me feel special in the way that any kind of attention makes you feel special. But no one really dazzled me. I'd give them some advice and send them along. You absorb it, you take it, and you like it. But Angel was a different story. She was a much different quantity.

She came in there when I was disrobing and chatting with Hector and even though she was dressed in that dreadful outfit like some little boy, I could see the fem realness queen deep within just waiting to burst out. Some people are just born to be fem realness queens, and that's a good thing. They can get out of a ball, onto the subway, and home without blood running down their hair. And whenever I discover one who comes to me, I take them on because I don't need to be teaching them how to hold their own. I need to make sure they can do that for themselves already, because I'm too old to be losing children to those mean, straight street fights.

But when I first started teaching her how to bring out that inner queen, I had to make it real clear that I wasn't going to be no fairy godmother. Life isn't about the Cinderella bullshit and I wasn't there to give her a set of glass heels and send her on her way. Hell no. I taught her the practical things. How to sew, how to select fabrics and make a gown, how to suck a cock so that you'll never starve. I said that when things got hard, make rice and beans and put a fried egg on top because then you got your carbohydrates, your fats, and your proteins. Because look, you gotta work in this city. Work or starve, legal or otherwise. And we aren't fools. We know that there just aren't many opportunities and doors open for a natural-born man to walk into a corporate office like a fem queen. So we do what we can, and if we have to suck a cock, then we have to suck a cock.

Angel was a fast learner and sometimes I think that maybe she didn't need me to teach her shit. Sometimes I think that her inner queen would have come out just as natural even if I wasn't in the picture. I really took to her. There was a certain kind of charm to her sass that reminded me of myself when I was younger. And sometimes, but only sometimes, I would think that maybe being a fairy godmother would be a nice gig. You'd get to see these young queens grow into their own. But then I pop that bubble real quick, because that's some whimsical fairy-tale shit. I would never let my queens ride inside a pumpkin or wear glass shoes. (Think of the corns on those damn feet! Glass does *not* breathe.)

And then there's the time limit. Who the hell wants to be a queen until the clock ticks midnight? That's not nearly enough time. Darling, this is a *craft*. You can't put a stopwatch on it like that. So, if I were a fairy godmother, I'd have no fucking time limit. I say that's got to be the shame of it all—these queens should have the ability to live their lives without looking up at the clock to see when midnight comes. Because before you know it, it's already midnight and the party is over, but just for you, because you see all the other young people still out enjoying their parties. And then what?

That doesn't seem fair at all.

DANIEL

He went down to the piers because that is where he thought boys like him were supposed to go. He had only packed a couple of needed things, the basics: a couple of camisetas made of cotton—a fabric that could breathe and be washed easily, plus some socks and undies and an extra pair of pants. Not to mention two packs of Newport 100s for an extra kick. He was never one for the longer cigs, but now was as good a time as any to start. He had a C-note tucked into the back of his briefs so that he could always feel the bill against his skin. A constant fear that it would slip away, just like all the other things, except this was money, and money he needed. He didn't leave a note for his mother, but she should know why he had left like a bat flying away from a hot fireball sun. He didn't want to think about her.

Now that he was there at the piers with the other maricones, he didn't know what to do with himself. There was a group of guys leaning on the end of the cement pier walls. Freestyle and disco and house were playing on random boom boxes here, there, and everywhere. One dude in particular caught his eye. He had curly brown hair and biceps that could kill. He was smoking a cigarette, looking up like he was bored with all of creation and wanted the sky to surprise him with something new for a change.

Daniel thought about walking up to the guy for a chat. Hopefully, if things worked well, that convo would lead to a bed for the night. Daniel stared as he exhaled his smoke. It made him crave the nicotine too. The guy stared at Daniel and smirked. As the man's eyes sized Daniel up and down, Daniel felt the heat in his face. He didn't know if he could do this song and dance. Just as the man flicked his cig and started walking toward him, Daniel broke eye contact, turned around, and walked away.

This whole cruising thing, he didn't know, he just didn't have the nerve to do it yet. There was a butterfly the size of Mars up in his stomach. Beginner's jitters, he'd call it. Instead, when he was at a safer distance, he could stare and long and pine for. Those tight denim shorts exposing thick, hairy quads. A tight tee that showed a body that made Daniel think there wasn't anything fair in the world.

"You better give me my fucking money back," a voice screamed out behind Daniel, but he couldn't see where. "If you think I'm some wholesale ho giving out sale coupons, you must be one mistaken motherfucker."

Daniel spun around. The girl was near a cement traffic barricade, holding up her maleta in one hand and a can of hairspray en la otra. A body was on the ground at her feet. She kept screaming, My money, my money, piece of shit, as she kicked him in the balls.

"Damn yo," Daniel said to her. "You trying to kill the dude or give him a perm?"

She gave him a look that told him to knock it off or he would be next.

"This cheap motherfucker tried to stab me," she said. "He's having a lucky day that I'm feeling generous and not pushing that blade down through his shoulder blades, do—you—hear—me—you—cheap-ass?"

"Whoa now," Daniel said, "no need to scream."

"Excuse me, Mr. Diplomatic," she said. "But did I ask you?"

"No, I guess you didn't," he said. He didn't believe her about the knife, but what could he say. Stabbing was a drastic thing to accuse someone of, but he didn't know either of them from a hole in the wall.

The guy made for her ankles with one hand. With the other, he whipped a blade out of his back pocket. The motherfucker was about to play, but Daniel wanted none of it. Daniel kicked the guy's back so hard, a splat of blood came out of his mouth. He was out cold on the sidewalk.

"Damn—look at you, Mr. Hercules," she said. "That was some kick."

A drag queen walked by in a silver jumpsuit and big neon-green hair and said, "Yes, honey, you tell that man how it is."

"Fuck yo," Daniel said. "Tell me the motherfucker's still breathing."

"I could give two shits right now if he's still breathing," she said. She crouched down and screamed in the guy's unconscious face, "Two shits, you hear me, pendejo piece of shit!"

When she stood back up, she asked Daniel for his name. When he told her, she said, "Daniel what?"

"Just Daniel."

"Honey, what do you mean just Daniel?" she said. "Like you're Prince and about to get down with some funk right about now."

"I'm sorry?" he said. "My last name is Sanchez, but I'm not sure why—"

"No, no," she said. "Like what house? Like from whence you came, you understand me when I speak all formally?"

"My mom didn't own a house," he said. "We had an apartment in the Bronx, but—"

"Oh," she said. "Oh-oh. I'm having an aha moment."

"Are you always this confusing?"

"No, darling," she said. "My name is Venus Xtravaganza and I'm from the House of Xtravaganza. My aha moment is that your pretty-boy face don't belong to a house yet."

She thanked him for helping her and opened her clutch to take out a crumpled up five-dollar bill. "Don't spend it all in one place," she said, then she laughed at herself. When he didn't take the money from her hand, she looked at him like what was wrong with him. "Well, I ain't gonna blow you too. This kitchen is closed for the night."

"No," Daniel said. "I'm not looking for none of that. Why are you so defensive and shit?"

Venus put the money back into her clutch and snapped it shut right in front of his face. "You should never ask a real woman what she's up to."

He couldn't tell if she was being dismissive, flirty, or just dishing out sass for the sake of dishing out sass. "A real woman?" he said and he could feel his forehead was all eyebrows.

"Oh, you're being shady now," she said. "Don't even start with me because I'll spray your ass too."

He couldn't help but laugh at her. She was so short and flaca that her energy was like an excitable small dog that loved to yap-yap-yap just to hear themselves. But then he saw her eyes became angry and he realized that she wasn't joking and that he shouldn't have laughed.

"Sorry," he began, "I was just—"

"Earth to the maricón in denial," she said, "go back to your wife and leave me a set of peace on your way out."

The words just came out of him: "I don't have anywhere to go." He wished he could take them back. Who was he to think that this stranger, with her can of hairspray and sass, could be capable of caring for the fact that he needed to find an easy guy to fuck so that he could rest his head on a pillow that night, the next night, for a week or month or however long, until he could find a job and make his way in the world.

She let out an *ahh*. Her stare looked right into him, and he felt like she was really seeing who he was, had been, and always wanted to be. She lowered her voice to a whisper, "Don't you tell me that you just busted out and ran away?"

"Or else what?" he said. "You don't know me."

"I knew it," Venus said. "All the same, I tell you. You really do need to find a house, you pretty thing."

Daniel didn't say a peep.

"Well, I been there, girl," Venus said.

"Girl?"

"Hush, it's just a phrasing," she said. "I call everyone a girl, even the muscle boys like you. Unless they're being bad! Then I don't call them nothing!"

She stepped over the body between them, careful not to let her heel get caught on the guy's shirt. She grabbed Daniel's hand and said, "Come here, baby boy. Maybe Angel and I could help you out."

"Who's Angel?" he asked.

"I'm going to pretend you didn't say that," Venus said. She smiled at him and kept walking over to an area of grass near a bench. "Good," she sighed. "It's still here." She picked up a fur coat and draped it on Daniel's back. She told him it was a mink, from Paris.

"Bull to the shit," he said. Even he knew that there was no way this pre-op transsexual with the cheap stilettos could afford a Parisian mink coat.

Venus laughed and said, "Oh good, for a second I thought you were gonna be the worst baby gay. You're absolutely right, darling, but Hector always liked to say this was a mink from Paris but—" now she was down to a whisper, like it was a secret they both needed to keep from the world, "—you know, Angel said she got it for him at a sale in Queens. I didn't tell you that. That information is just between you and I, darling. I assume you can keep a little secret."

* * *

Six. When he was six years old, what he wanted more than anything was a Hot Wheels track. It didn't matter if it was the mongoose track or the drag 'chute stunt track, he just wanted a track with a loop-the-loop where he could put the cars on and send them flying.

"Okay, Daniel," his mother sighed at the kitchen table. "We'll see what Santa Claus can do this year, but it's been a hard year in the North Pole."

He didn't think he had anything to worry about. He had been a good boy. He had done okay in his classes. He didn't push anyone on the monkey bars. Okay, he pushed Jimmy—but it was only once, and Jimmy had deserved it because he was mouthing off at Kyle. But that didn't count, or if it *did* count, Daniel was sure that when Santa looked at the grand scheme of things, he would be forgiven.

* * *

They ate a lot of peanut butter sandwiches for dinner that month, but Daniel wasn't going to complain because he wanted to be on Santa's good list. When Christmas came around, there were those Hot Wheels. There was the drag 'chute stunt track. And when he gave his mother these big-ass, hoochie-mama, gold-embossed bamboo hoop earrings, she laughed and said, "Oh god, Daniel, these are something else."

He squealed and told her to put them on.

She did. And she wore them all day long. Until night, when she made a hurt face and took them off. "Mommy's gonna have to make these her indoor earrings," she told him. "They're kind of heavy and Mommy needs to rest her earlobes. And, oh look—they made my piercing hole turn green, well that's not good."

* * *

Eight. He could tell that his mother was always in a good mood when a nice man took her out to dinner and movies. She used to say to her friend Nilda on the phone, Yes, he was such a nice man, or, No, girl, that man is nasty or cold or just downright mean and I wouldn't fuck him with my enemy's vagina.

Then she met Rob and she talked on the phone with Nilda for longer in the evenings. "I'm just over the moon, Nild," Mama said, and Daniel watched her twirling the cord with her index finger as she rested the phone between her ear and her shoulder. She was painting her toenails, and her foot was plopped straight up on the kitchen table as Daniel watched his cartoons. "He's got me believing in all kinds of magic," Mama said. "Let—me—tell—you, shoo."

So for the next week, whenever his mother was out of the apartment and he was doing his chores at home, he developed some rituals to help her out. The goal was for Rob to be nice to his mother, to take her out to all the dinners she could handle without getting fat, and then he would marry her and be Daniel's father. He dug into the bathroom cabinet and pulled out some tealight candles and set them up on the dining room table next to a faded painting of La Virgen María that Nilda had bought Mama from the dollar store on Tremont. He did the sign of the cross and said, "Dear María, let all these things happen," and then he listed his wishes.

Monday and Tuesday came and went. His mother went on two dates with Rob. But still no wedding. He was gonna have to go in with the big guns. On Wednesday, he faked sick so that he could dedicate the whole afternoon to the ritual. While his mother was working at the Duane Reade, he turned on *All My Children* and watched that Susan Lucci woman slap the hell out of her former best friend. He held one of the tea candles in his hand and walked around the room in circles. He chanted Jesus's name because he was starting to worry that maybe María wasn't enough heavenly power to assist on this mission.

When the show went to commercial and kids were singing for more Ovaltine, there was a pounding at the door. "Yo, Carmen," a man's voice boomed. Daniel froze and blew out the candle. The guy at the door banged again. "Carmen, I know you're in there," he shouted. "Let a brother in, woman."

Daniel glided over to the door and pressed his ear to it. "Um," he said, "she's not here."

"Daniel?" the man said. "Is that you?"

Daniel was stunned that this man knew his name. He didn't recognize the voice at all. Now he was curious. He knew that he shouldn't open the door, but maybe if it was just for a second, everything would be okay. "Maybe," Daniel said. "How do you know my name?"

"It's Ricky," the man said. "Your moms ever tell you about Ricky? I need to talk to your moms. You sure she ain't here?"

Ricky did kind of ring a bell. He had heard the name once or twice before when his mother was on the phone.

"I'm sure," Daniel said.

"Damn yo," Ricky said. "I'm flipping shit out here. Can you help a brother out and let me in? I used to be your mom's boyfriend, can't believe she didn't say nothing about me."

"I don't think I can."

But he did let Ricky in. Nothing happened. Ricky just sat on the sofa with flowers in his hand. Daniel offered him a glass of water and felt like an adult when he did, but Ricky said no, he didn't want water.

When his mother got home, she raised hell up one level closer to Earth with her screaming.

"Bitch," Ricky said. "All I wanted was to give you some flowers."

"I don't need your flowers," his mother said. "You come here and make my son let you in this house. I should beat your ass, Ricky, so just go away."

"Ingrateful," Ricky said. "I should beat your ass for being a goddamned whore with that Robert."

"Don't talk about Robert."

"You tell your son what you did to me?" Ricky said.

His mother sighed loudly. "I didn't *do* anything to you, you fucking narcissist."

"How long after me did you wait to fuck him?" Ricky said. "You gonna make a grown man cry in front of a child?" Ricky looked at Daniel, who was watching from the sofa like he was watching a soap opera fight.

"No one asked you to come here," his mother said. "This isn't about you."

"You're a cold bitch," Ricky said.

When he left and she slammed the door behind him, she sat down on the couch next to Daniel and cried.

"Why'd he call you a cold bitch?" Daniel said.

"Don't say that," she said, and Daniel wondered if maybe his rituals had backfired and gone all wrong. Maybe he had set all of this in motion with his prayers and candles. He vowed to never light another candle and just let things happen like they were supposed to.

Cold bitch, cold bitch, he mouthed the words to himself later after he got out of the shower and had to wipe the steam off the mirror. Cold bitch, cold bitch, that man Ricky was surely gonna get a large sack of coal.

*　*　*

Ten. Rob left and he took her happiness with him. Daniel didn't know what to do. He would've brought out all his Hot Wheels cars and sold them to the pawnshop dudes. Heck, he was double digits now and that meant he wasn't some little kid. He needed to be a man about it now. He needed to help the woman of the house.

He decided he would start by making his mother eggs and toast for breakfast. When he brought them to her, she looked at the plate and blinked all slow. "They're running," she said. "The eggs are too watery, they're running."

Silly, silly, he thought. *Eggs don't have legs for running.* "I tried my best," he said.

She took a chunk of the scrambled eggs with the fork and laid it on top of the toast and took a bite. "Oh fuck," she said, sticking out her tongue so that the half-chewed mess in her mouth just fell out. "What did you put in these?"

He watched as her head leaned back into the pillow and she moaned as if she were in pain. "It's too bright in here," she said. "When did it get so bright?"

"I put oregano and"—he had to think about what else he had put—"and there was butter on the pan. Oh, and I sprinkled Adobo on too."

She swiped her arm across the bed so the plate could fall onto the ground. It made a crash sound but no glass broke. The eggs slid onto the floor. "Who the fuck puts Adobo on eggs?" she shouted. "What've you done?"

"I didn't do nothing," he said, on his knees, scooping eggs into his palms.

"Why don't they ever love me?" she asked. Her voice was so still, it gave Daniel goosebumps on his arms.

"*I* love you though," he said. He put the fallen eggs onto the plate and put the fork on top so that he could bring it back to the kitchen. "Here," he said and kissed his mother on the forehead.

He asked her why she was crying.

"You're not my little boy anymore," she said. "You weren't supposed to get this old so quick, and then you're just gonna grow up and leave me all alone and then who's gonna be with me. They always go away from me, Daniel, why do they always go?"

He didn't know what kind of answer to give to a question like that. *Maybe some questions just didn't have answers,* he thought, so he leaned in and gave her another kiss.

"Stop," she screamed and pushed him away. She was crying now for him to close the blinds, to make the sun go away.

And he did. He cleaned the plates and threw away the food. He closed the door and let her sleep all day, and the next. He couldn't make the light disappear back into the sky, but he could close what needed to be closed.

* * *

Eleven. The thing about desire, he thought, was that it was unpredictable. Desire is what led him to watch his first porno. It was fairly vanilla—an overdone production where the white woman lit candles and the bed was very cushiony. The white man was tall and tan. He had gym muscles and a huge cock. Daniel looked at the woman's titties, but he was more interested in the guy. He watched him eat her out, then fuck her, and he realized that he wasn't interested in the woman. He wanted the man. Actually, he wanted to be the guy *and* fuck him. That would make him gay, but whatever. He didn't feel any shame about it. He knew what he wanted and he didn't give a shit if other people were gonna give him shit about it. It wasn't like he was gonna get fucked. He wanted to do the fucking. He watched the guy's ass squeeze as he fell into the woman, up and down, and Daniel jerked himself until he shot all over his torso.

* * *

Twelve. He could no longer recognize her. She became so thin, it looked like her body was a shrink-wrap machine and it was sucking her in. She grew pillows under her eyes, and then those pillows turned a purple-blue that made Daniel wince whenever he saw her. She lost her job. She made him go to Pathmark by himself to make the food stamps stretch, and every time, the cashiers looked at him like he was too young, but he acted like he didn't see those stares.

He knew she was using, but he also knew that she didn't know that he knew. He had found a needle in the bathroom, and for fuck's sake, she wasn't no diabetic.

"I really fucked up," she said to him one day when he came back from school. It was May and the city days were starting to get warmer.

"Oh no," he said. "What'd you do?"

He was expecting her to come forward with it. He imagined it would go something like this: she would sit him down at the kitchen table, present her needles and tinfoil and lighter and plastic baggie of powder stuff. The more he tried to imagine the scene, the more it slipped away from him, just like when he woke up in the middle of a bad dream.

"The bitch at the help office," she said, "is stopping our checks until I go to court."

She was crying now, saying she didn't know what she was going to do, how they needed to eat and pay that rent check. But he didn't want to hear any of that. He could find a way to figure things out. "You sure there isn't nothing else you wanna say to me," he said.

She wiped her nose and sighed. "I'm craving," she said, "a god-damn cigarette."

He looked at her thick, messy hair that was so uncombed, it was surely full of knots by now. He looked at her chicken-bone arms, thin enough for the wind to snap in two. He looked at the dotted marks in the middle of her arm, where the needles searched for veins. "You really fucked up," he said.

"I know," she said, "I know." She was crying hard now, so hard that he wondered if she would hiccup when she had to gasp for air again.

What can I do to help? he should have said. But: "You're a cold bitch, mama," is what he actually said. "I can't believe you did this."

* * *

Thirteen. He gave her an ultimatum: get off the smack or that's it and I'm walking out the door. He said please do it for me and she said she would and he believed her. He thought that when he got older, he would take her away from this place to a new city, a new building, a new life, where she could get clean and stay clean and that was it, she just needed to start now because he couldn't take it no more.

Clean, he thought, *what a strange concept.* Like a person was fresh out the shower and nothing had dirtied them. Turn over a new leaf, stay clean, yada yada, they were just bullshit phrases. His mother was a junkie, but she wasn't dirty. And it wasn't like being clean made a person any more or less worthy of love.

Please, he thought, *please let it be true this time. She gave her word. Let her get off that junk. Please.*

* * *

"How old are you, anyway?" Venus asked him. They were sitting at the dining room table with another kid who was introduced to him as Juanito.

"Fourteen," Daniel said. He was still wearing Venus's fur coat, even though there was no air conditioner and it was stifling inside.

"Oh, look at you," Venus said, "just like Juanito."

"Yes, say it loud and proud," Juanito said, taking a pause from the sewing machine that was gobbling up a web of fabric from the tips of his fingers like he was some kind of diva spider. He moved his fingers over to Daniel to pet the fur jacket. "Venus isn't supposed to be bringing just *anyone* back here." He winked at Daniel.

"Ay, cállate, Juanito," Venus said. "Dani's just a new friend of mine. Ain't that right, Daniel?"

Daniel nodded yes as Juanito's eyebrows stayed risen over his eyes.

"He's gonna live with us now," Venus said.

"Oh, is he now?" Juanito said. "Girl, you know you gotta pass this through Angel first before you start making decisions around here." Then Juanito turned to Daniel but didn't take his eyes off the gobble-gobble of the sewing machine. "You ever walk in a ball? 'Cause I'm preparing for my big debut now and I wanna know if you're gonna debut too?"

Daniel looked at Venus and tried to communicate with a squeeze of the face that he didn't know how to answer Juanito's question.

Venus must've taken the hint because she put a hand on Daniel's arm. "No," Venus said. "He's not a ball queen like you, Reina Juana, with that ugly-ass silver shit you got going on over there. What the hell *is* that?"

They both cackled like it was the funniest joke in the world, but Daniel had no idea where the punchline was hidden. He was pretty sure it was a straight-up insult, but why the laughter?

"You are a shady one," Juanito said. "Pero excuse me, this is a silver lamé bodice. And it's going to win me the Banjee Girl Realness trophy, so you better back that truck up. And since we're reading, tell me, what the fuck happened to your face? Did you run into a police officer on the street?"

Venus touched the bruise on her cheek and now it was Daniel's turn to chime in. "Some motherfucker tried to get real with her," Daniel said.

"Yes," Venus said, "And Daniel helped me out, otherwise I was going to beat the shit out of that sorry excuse for a man."

"Didn't he try to stab you?" Daniel asked, adjusting the fur so it wasn't sticking to the beads of sweat forming on his neck.

"Yes, he sure did." Venus threw her hands in the air, like can-you-believe-that-shit, what-is-a-girl-to-do.

"Ay, Dios mío," Juanito said, shifting the fabric to a new direction. "No no no no no me lo puedo. I simply *cannot*."

* * *

When Daniel knocked on Angel's door and peeked in, Angel was placing various gold earrings up to her right ear and evaluating them in the mirror. Angel singsonged for Daniel to come in, and he sat down on the edge of her bed as Angel still considered her earrings in the mirror.

"Venus tells me you wanna live here, verdad?" Angel said, still looking at the mirror.

Daniel hesitated. The answer was yes, he did want to live there with them, but having Angel speak to him without looking at him at the same time was throwing him for a loop.

"Yeah," Daniel said.

"She also tells me that you saved her life," Angel said.

"Yes, ma'am," he said, even though he believed that Venus would've been fine if their paths hadn't crossed at the piers. Venus was probably more than capable of kicking that guy's ass. If anything, he had stopped Venus from killing the guy.

"Don't," Angel said, laying one of the gold earrings into a wooden jewelry box like she was laying down a sleeping baby. "Don't ma'am me. I'm not some irrelevant vieja," she said. "I'm not even a full woman yet." She laughed at this.

Daniel apologized and Angel picked up another earring and put it up to her ear. She leaned in and squinted her eyes, as if that might hold the answers to the mysteries of selection.

"Which is better?" Angel said, holding up a gold hoop to her left ear, and an even larger gold hoop to her right ear. They were so large, they looked like towel rings for a bathroom. Daniel pointed to the one on the right because the gold looked textured.

"Good choice," Angel said and finally turned to face Daniel. He saw her give him a one-up and her face soured. "Where'd you get that coat?"

"Oh, um," Daniel said, "Venus gave it to me after—"

"She *gave* it to you?" Angel said. Her tone was acid rain, and Daniel realized that this may have been the wrong answer. Before he could backtrack, Angel was screaming Venus's name.

It took all of five heartbeats for Venus to pop up in the door frame.

"Daniel tells me that you *gave* him Hector's fur coat," Angel said.

"Ay," Venus said, "what he meant is that I *gave* it to him for the day, as a token for helping me out."

Angel's eyes were stone as she stared at Venus, then back at Daniel, then at the heart of the fur coat.

"Right," Daniel said. "I didn't know it was Hector's coat. I can give it back to him when I meet him—"

"That won't be happening," Angel said, turning her face back to the mirror so she could put on the earrings with textures. The set that Daniel had selected. "Hector is dead," she said.

"Oh fuck," Daniel said. "I'm really sorry. I didn't mean to—"

"It's fine," Angel said. She turned to Daniel to give him a quick, forced smile. "I'm not here to be your friend. I'm here to be your mother, and I must say," she said, "the coat does fit you well."

* * *

Regret. He couldn't help but think he had jumped the gun. Maybe he had left too fast. Maybe he should have done more for her, help her get through rehab programs. Maybe a court could've ordered her to Jacobi for that acupuncture thing they had. Maybe it did work for strangers to poke needles into the ear to alleviate withdrawals. Maybe he just wasn't patient enough. Maybe he didn't imagine what she had gone through. Maybe he could have done more.

As he lay tossing and turning in this new bed down the hall from the other Xtravaganzas, he realized that he had become just like all the other men in his dear mother's life, just like all the other fuckers who left her behind, whatever their reason. He thought about praying, but then he figured, fuck it. He didn't want to talk to a god that had allowed smack to walk this wide world. To a god who designed humans to have blood, blood that pumped through veins, veins that circulated bodies, bodies that could thirst for smack. *What kind of sick world is this,* he thought, tossing again under the shadows of the moon's light splatted against the ceiling.

The next morning, he woke up and thought, *I will go back to her.* He wasn't going to abandon his new friends, but he was going to go see her and promise her that he would help her get through this. That they could get through this together.

When he got there, she must've just left a few hours before. All the furniture was still there, but some of her clothes were gone. Her luggage, gone. He waited all day, chain-smoking out her bedroom window, crying here and there. *What have I done,* he thought. He slept there overnight, and when she didn't come back by noon the next day, he knew that she was gone and he had no idea where to go to find her.

ANGEL

This is the house. It is an apartment, but it is still a house. A walk-up, but still a house. This is our home, which is like a house, but with more oomph, more feeling.

This is how a house becomes a home. This is how a house becomes a family. It had been Hector's idea from the start to form a community of runaway Boricua queens. It's not like she could steal credit from her man, oh no. Her fear was that they would become like some Peter Pan Never-Never Land reenactment. If her body couldn't bear children, at least the thought of becoming a house mother could make her happy. And Hector would be the father. The dream was for them to have a group of chickadee children banding together in their home. Alphabet City would be their stomping grounds.

Hector was wedded to the idea of Alvin Ailey and the dancers. Hector wanted to be just like them and Angel would nod her head yes-yes, but think no-no. She didn't need to read a paper to know what was happening. People were dying. Not just any people. *Their* people. Even Ailey was gonna go—she wanted to tell him this, but she didn't have the heart. There was no point in speaking it aloud.

And then it happened. Hector died. Died, died, died, she said the word so many times that it no longer felt or sounded like a word that made any sense. It was beyond sense. Senseless. She refused to say that he passed on, because there she went with those damn phrases again. That would mean that he was passing from one form to another, and she didn't know how to rationalize that. It's not like *that* made her feel any better. The bottom line was that he wasn't here, on this Earth, with her.

Juanito wasn't around then, but Venus was, and she cooked Angel breakfast-lunch-dinner for how many days? Angel couldn't count a total, but she knew it was a lot.

"We can't stay here anymore," Angel told Venus one night while they smoked cigarettes on the fire escape.

"What," Venus said, "do you mean? Where the fuck are we gonna go?"

"No sé," Angel said, "Sure, I got my dudas, but I know we can't stay here anymore."

What she wanted to tell Venus, but couldn't, was that whenever she walked around the empty Alphabet City apartment, she could feel Hector's absence like a pain between her temples. His memory was a ghost that would keep haunting her ass. She knew they had to move.

A friend of Dorian's had a rent-controlled place in the Bronx and a yearning to be closer to the Garage in Manhattan, so they fudged the paperwork, switched off apartments, and dared the city's offices to make heads of tails.

Now there she was, two years later, sitting at the dining room table next to Juanito's sewing machine, wondering about this new boy, Daniel. He seemed like a good kid. More macho than she would've expected, but hey, a new banjee boy could be an asset. She wanted to sit down and ask him how it was, exactly, that a year could pass so quickly. It only seemed that as she got older, time decided to dial it up a notch and move faster. She wanted to know what this Daniel's thoughts were on the process.

She twirled her fingers around a piece of red string and the spool started to spin slowly. Well, if Daniel were going to have the absolute cojones to wear Hector's fur—the fur that *she* had bought him with her own hard-earned money—she should be able to say whatever she wanted. Like damn, if she wanted to mope, then mope she'd do.

She walked over to the nevera and pulled out the cold bottle of white wine. Only one more glass left. She poured it into a coffee mug and leaned against the kitchen counter as the alcohol burned the back of her throat. This was her house now—a single sofa, three twin beds, nevera, parquet floors that were *made* for tacones to clack against, some walls, a roof.

Before she turned the lights off to go to sleep, she unwrapped the frame that she had just bought at the Salvation Army. It was an old painting of flowers in a vase. She bought it for two dollars. It wasn't nothing lavish. Actually, the more she stared at it, the more it seemed like somebody's old paint-by-numbers thing. But what could she say? It caught her eye.

She put the mug down and picked up the hammer. She nailed the frame in the sala, right above the sofa. When she finished, she looked up to marvel at the creation. Now the walls didn't look so bare. Sure, the frame itself was kind of shitty: a wooden frame that was barely holding the thing up for dear life. But she looked at it and smiled, thinking about all the future breakfasts she would eat under it, trying to focus on the little glimpse of still life it offered, hoping more than anything that the wooden frame holding it together wouldn't give up just yet.

* * *

Angel hated when Miguel got to pick the restaurant because he always picked the expensive ones that she couldn't afford to pay for. He always insisted on paying, but she didn't want none of his drug money. So this time, she absolutely wouldn't take no for an answer when she suggested they go to the cheap Rican place on Eighth Avenue in Chelsea.

"Well look at you," Miguel said. He had started growing a goatee since she last saw him a week ago. She didn't know anyone else who could grow facial hair so damn quickly, but then again, she realized that it wasn't like she knew that many people who had beards. "My beautiful big sister over there."

He said this to her every week when they went out for lunch. At first, she ate it up, thinking it was his way of showering her ego, rewarding her for dolling up. But then she realized it was just his charming nature, and that it didn't matter if she came wrapped in a black garbage bag—he would *still* say those same words in greeting.

"Don't you start buttering me up with compliments," she said, laughing.

"I ain't smooth talking," he said. "Red is so dashing on you. So daring. I admire your bravery."

"You're so sarcastic," she said. Like hell he wasn't smooth talking. He could smooth talk his way to the moon and back.

"I got the bill this time," he said. "Order whatever you're feeling for."

They sat down and Angel said no, what did he mean this time? She had picked this place and therefore she would pay for it, and she didn't want to hear anything more. She unwrapped her utensils and took the cheap, white napkin and opened it on her lap. When he opened his mouth to say something, she hushed him. She didn't feel like talking about this again.

"So, I've been talking with Mami," Miguel said.

Angel put her hand up. "Nope," she said, marveling at how quick Miguel could be to get straight to the point on all the harsh topics. She'd make sure that this conversation went nowhere, fast. "I don't wanna hear talk of that woman."

"Angel, come on. It's been enough already."

"Nope."

Angel had no patience for it, that's all. She knew that Miguel still lived under the same roof as their mother. Angel still didn't talk to that woman, and wanted nothing to do with her. Na-da.

"She wants to see you," Miguel said.

"Well then that's a sorry case of the benditos," Angel said, playing with the corner edge of the napkin in her lap. She avoided her brother's eyes. "Porque I don't wanna see or hear from her."

Before Miguel could chime in again, Angel got riled up in her seat, sat straight up, and said, "And why you always thinking about what Mami wants and not what Angel wants, huh? Why you always gotta take her side? You know what she used to do to me, what she used to say, you were there for it all—"

"Damn, Angel," Miguel said, "could you take it down a notch? People are staring."

"Let them stare," Angel said in the harshest whisper she could muster.

"You're stubborn sometimes," he said.

"You know I got reasons to be," she said. "Let's leave it at that."

The waitress came over with eyes so reluctant, it looked like someone had sent her to their table and she was afraid of being chewed out alive. Miguel ordered the bistec encebollado and Angel got the mofongo with a flan that she told Miguel they would split for dessert. It wasn't up for discussion, they were gonna split the flan. And yes, let them leave it at that. Angel didn't want to talk about the beatings, the santería hoodoo magic that Mami had inflicted on her just because she was growing up into the fine woman that she wanted to be. Those memories angered her even more because she never had the cojones to call out those rituals for what they were: porquería-bullshit, that's what. It made Angel think she was seeing a version of herself that she didn't want to face—a version of herself that made her out to be less strong than she thought she was.

"She asked me, the other day," Miguel said, "where you're working. If you're working, I should say."

"Like she gives a fuck," Angel said.

"Come on, Angel," he said. "Don't be so brutal. That's the thing. She *does* give a fuck."

"Well what'd you tell her?"

"I didn't know what to say," he said. "If I tell her, you know she's gonna show up to that Pathmark. You just know she's that persistent."

Persistent. That was a generous word for what Miguel was describing. Angel didn't think it was wrong though.

"Don't tell her," Angel said.

Miguel sighed and threw his head back so he could stare up at the ceiling. "Why're you two putting me in this situation?" he said.

"Is she asking you where you're working, huh?" Angel said.

"Oh, we're going to go there again? You wanna talk about the weed?"

Yes, Angel thought, maybe. Was it not proof that he was being a hypocrite? No, maybe she was being harsh. Their conversations about weed never went far, she knew the routine. She would beg him to stop dealing, she would tell him to think about what would happen if he got caught, but then he would call her a hypocrite for selling ass to make ends meet and wasn't that worse? It was completely different, she always said. But he couldn't see it.

"Fine," Miguel said, "let's not talk about our poor mother who wants to see you."

The waitress came with their plates and asked if there was anything else she could get them. Miguel said they needed a bottle of ketchup, and when she brought them the red plastic tube of ketchup, he handed it to Angel so she could put some on her mofongo, just like she always used to do when she was a kid.

"So I'm seeing a new girl," Miguel said and Angel was relieved that there was a new topic for them to discuss. Something easier. Something tame, unloaded.

"Wondrous," Angel said, careful to make her tone sound excited, but not *too* excited for fear of sounding fake-genuine. "What does she look like? She's not tacky, right? Let me see a foto already."

Miguel leaned in his seat to take out his wallet from his back pocket. As he unfolded the black leather tri-fold, some folded-up hundreds slid onto the table along with some random fotos. As he rushed to gather them back together, Angel caught a glimpse of a picture of the two of them from years ago. It was under some other fotos of people she didn't recognize—must've been friends from school. Angel used her pinky finger to dig through the pile of fallen fotos until she could find the one she was looking for.

"Espera," Angel said. "Let me see that one."

Miguel handed it over and Angel put her spoon down to give the foto her full attention. "I didn't know you had this foto. Look at Papi—you're a spitting image, holy shit. I never realized until I see you both side by side," she said. "We look so young."

Angel held up the foto to the side of Miguel's face. "We're still young," Miguel said and shot a sad smile. "You're not even twenty-two yet."

"How old are we here?" she said. "Like seven?"

In the foto, they're standing in front of a fire hydrant with their father. One man, two boys, all smiling. Angel looked so happy then, so carefree. She wanted to cry, but she didn't want to be that girl— the one who cries in a Chelsea diner during lunch hour. "I look so pretty there," she said instead. "What happened?"

"Oh, come on, Angel," Miguel said. "You're still pretty."

She smiled but she didn't know if he meant it or if he was just trying to be kind. She wanted to tell him that she didn't need for him to comfort her with lies.

"This is Yvette," he said, handing over a tiny foto. It must've been Yvette's high school shot. She looked like a pale girl who was obsessed with eyeliner. Probably Rican, but maybe Cubana. Angel stared at the foto, trying to think of what to say to her brother. Yvette certainly had the bold eyeliner thing going on, but she couldn't say that to Miguel.

"She's cute," Angel said. "Is she goth? No tea, no shade. Just curiosity."

"Curiosity killed the cat, Angel," he said.

"Ho, do I look like a cat to you?" she said. "I am a full-grown human woman."

"Alright, alright," he said. "She's not goth. She's just going through an eyeliner phase. I kinda dig it though. She gives me eyes from across the room and I get mad chills."

It was no matter to Angel that Miguel's new love was tackier than a chandelier in a cheap Russian tearoom. And damn—she knew she had to be less judgmental, but sometimes she couldn't help it. Sometimes the sass just popped into her mind and there was nothing she could do to hold it back. "She's definitely cute," Angel said.

"Cute?" Miguel said. He snatched the foto back out of Angel's hand. "You don't ever call anybody just cute."

Damn, he knew her well enough. "She's," Angel had to think about how to answer, "looking like she is growing into the fine, beautiful mujer that god meant her to become."

"Oh, bullshit," Miguel said, "you are such a sarcastic ass."

"Okay fine, Jesus!" Angel said. "You are a pill, sometimes. I can't even tell you a white lie without it getting past you."

Miguel nodded yeah.

"She's kinda tacky, Miguel," she said. "I'm sorry it sounds so brutal. Pero mira, I can deal as long as I know you like her. Maybe I can just—show her how to put on eyeliner so that it brings out her eyes instead of holding them back."

Miguel sighed and rolled his eyes. "Don't even." He chuckled. "Sometimes you're so predictable."

"What's that even supposed to mean?"

"I believe you gays would probably call you a queen, right?"

"Oh yes, absolutely, and don't you forget it." She snapped her fingers left, right, and center.

"What about you?" he said "You got somebody new yet?"

The words hit her cold. She looked down at her plate and shifted around a small mound of mofongo onto the other side of the plate.

"I'm not ready," she said.

He apologized and swirled the ice in his soda with the twisty straw.

"I'm sorry," he said. "I didn't mean it like that."

"It's whatever."

"One day you'll be ready," he said, but even the way the last words trailed off made it sound like a question. *No*, she thought, she never ever would be ready.

"Here you go," the waitress sang, setting the plate of flan on the table between them. "Enjoy it!" Angel stared at the flan, which was already cut, straight down the middle.

*　*　*

Pathmark was the only place where she dressed like a boy. That's why she decided to work at the location on East 125th and not one closer to home in the Bronx—she didn't want anyone she knew to see her outside of women's clothes. She wouldn't be able to bear the humiliation.

The job was easy enough. Stocking shelves, telling people where to find the beans, the spices, the pasta. Sometimes the manager put her on cash register and she got to see what people were feeding themselves these days. She even got a little discount on her own groceries, which was a real benefit.

But don't even get her started on the uniform they all had to wear over their outfits. She didn't even know how to describe it, if she had to. Coverall? Apron? Whatever it was, it made her look like a butcher. She liked to hold meat in her hand, but that didn't mean she needed to go around passing like some butcher. She had never before worn anything that felt like a sack, and *this* felt like a sack. It was bad enough that she had to keep her hair tied back in a ponytail and take out her earrings. She felt naked without her jewelry, for fuck's sake.

When she walked in a ball, MODEL EFFECT was her category. She always looked elegant when they saw her: sometimes in a tapered silk dress, carrying a Sevillana fan as an accessory. She wasn't about the costume posturing, nor did she want to strut her stuff looking like a hoochie. Her goal was to look like a wealthy woman with purpose. At Pathmark, on the other hand, she wore her frumpy outfit and looked like a male. She'd be damned if someone from the ball scene came in and saw her like that. The only thing worse would be if her mother came in. Oh, she wouldn't know what to do. Surely she'd get fired if she smacked a customer in the face.

Before going into work that day, she stood in front of the mirror and flared out her nostrils to see if there were any straggler pelos that needed to be cut. She doused a cottonball in polish remover so that she could wipe the gold off her uñas. She wiped her lipstick off with a baby wipe and tried to relax all her face muscles so that she could look more masculine. Boys don't show emotion, she repeated to herself as she deadened her muscles. No emotion, no emotion.

She had taken the job because, por lo menos, it was easy money, something she could do as a side hustle when she wasn't at the piers. And it was stable. Porque she'd be damned! Damned if she ever had to stand in line at the welfare building! Not no way in hell was she going to beg. For what? So she could stand in line? She undid a string of floss and smiled at herself in the mirror to make sure nothing was stuck between her teeth. She stuck out her tongue. Her motto was this: If it can't be done in heels, she didn't want to do it. And could she wait in line in heels? No. Could she break out the heels for a day shift at Pathmark? Unfortunately not, though a girl could daydream about it.

When she got to work, she wasn't put on register. They had her ass mopping up the milk aisle. *Ha!* she thought. If only someone could put *that* on a badge: ANGEL XTRAVAGANZA—SHE'LL MOP UP ALL YOUR MILK. Oh, she was being nasty.

She kept an eye on the entrance door, as if that could do anything to prevent her damn mother from stepping foot into that store. No, she was being irrational. Miguel hadn't said anything to Mami. Or maybe he had, and lied about it. An old black man walked in, holding a giant book up, marching toward the chips aisle.

"Hallelujah," the man shouted. "Jesus, I love you. Hallelujah."

This man came in from time to time, enough times for her coworkers to refer to him as Hallelujah Man. He was bone thin, had tight white curls, and wore suits that had way too much fabric for his body. Angel didn't know why he was celebrating all of creation in an overly lit aisle filled with Fritos and Funyuns and Cheetos, but there he was.

There was nothing to mop up, so Angel just worked the motions, pretending to clean up spills that didn't exist. It was easier than putting things on shelves for hours on end. If her mother showed up, she'd cry. No, she wouldn't cry. She would stand tall and say, Ma, you shouldn't have come, I don't want to see you.

Pero she knew that wouldn't work. Mami was persistent like it was nobody's business. What was she so afraid of? Angel was a grown-ass human being. It's not like Mami would throw down and whoop her ass in the middle of the cereal aisle. She was a mess, but she wasn't *that* much of a nightmare.

Then it hit her. She didn't want to face her mother because she was afraid she'd have to lie. Mami would want to know how Hector was doing and Angel would either have to tell the truth and own up that Mami was right all along (she'd rather eat a salad washed in Port Authority toilet water), or she'd have to lie. She could just see it now: she's holding onto the mop and looking straight at her mother as she tells her that Hector is fine, doing fabulous actually, and that they are going to move to Long Island, to a real house, once they saved up enough money. They'd become the type of couple who'd say "burbs" instead of "suburbs." Then what?

The man was in front of her now and he threw the Bible on the floor, in front of Angel's mop. "I love you," the man sang to the sky and Angel was crying in front of the applesauce shelf. "Hallelujah."

* * *

When she got home that night, the house was empty. Juanito had probably taken Daniel out. Venus was—wherever that girl felt like going that day, hopefully keeping herself out of trouble. A mother could only worry so much. Angel went to the back of her closet and pulled out the box where she kept the envelopes.

There were two envelopes that kept everything in her life in some kind of order. She had taken a black Sharpie and labeled them, months ago, when she knew that Hector was gone and that the entire weight of the house was gonna be on her arms. *Needs:* envelope one. *Dreams:* envelope two.

She took out the stack of bills in each envelope and counted them. All the ones and fives and tens, sometimes a twenty here and there, pero never a fifty or hundred. All those white men on the bills, but it was whatever. At least Mr. Hamilton had nice bone structure. Now *that* was a face she could carry in her pocket and think, *Damn, papi*.

She licked the tips of her fingers as she counted each bill and added it up in her head. Always the small change, but small change was small change until it could be added up to big change. There was no forgetting that.

Needs meant food—huevos for breakfast and boxes of Cheerios, milk by the gallon, bread for toasting and grilling cheese, and lots of deli meats sliced real thin. Then dinner meant cans of Goya beans and white rice by the pound, sometimes chicken breasts if they were on sale.

Then there were the *dreams*. This was where she saved up money to buy that darling Chanel suit at Saks that she was lusting over. And the newspaper cutout for the Model Search at Bloomingdale's, where she would go in a few months to show the panel of judges—and Wilhelmina her damn self—that she, Angel Xtravaganza, mother of the House of Xtravaganza, known on the streets as La Nena del Bronx, could be a supermodel.

Angel slipped out the two pictures of Hector that she kept in that very envelope. She kept him there because she couldn't bear to put him in a frame and stare at him every day. She couldn't see his face as a constant reminder of what she had once upon a time, and at least when he was stored away in the envelope, she could go searching for him whenever she could handle it.

While she waited for her children to come back home to her, she lingered a little longer than usual on Hector's fotos. One was just him, wearing a chunky sweater and tight jeans, hand on his hip and a sonrisa so big, the camera flash bounced off his pearly whites. The other foto was of the both of them: a day at Coney Island ending in a foto-booth session of four fotos in quick succession: a side hug; a goofy one, where they leaned in and stuck their tongues out; and the last two, where they took turns pecking kisses on the other's cheek. The film was proof that what they had was real. They had made the mistake of sitting too close to the camera, so their faces were up close and personal, and some of their hair got chopped off by the top margin of the foto. Angel stuck out her index finger, where the golden nail polish had split in half before she had completely removed it before work. She rubbed Hector's face.

"Ay, Hector," she whispered to the strip of paper. "We've got ourselves a new Xtravaganza."

JUANITO

It wasn't any kind of sorpresa that Angel had given Daniel the green light, but Juanito was a little taken by the fact that Venus was the one who picked Daniel up in the first place at the piers. Juanito had trouble imagining how that even went down. Did Venus think he was a potential client, por fa-vor, could anyone *imagine*! Especially since Venus could be so cold sometimes—so closed off to the world. Always hard to tell with Vee's moods, because one minute she'd be an ice queen, then homegirl would bounce back, as warm and abierta as a flamenco dancer in a hachi-mama red dress, ready to stomp all up on a plank of wood.

As soon as Angel said yes, that Daniel could become an Xtravaganza, Juanito put a pause on his sewing machine, set the red silk fabric down with a gentle glide of his fingers, and said, "I'll take him down to the piers." He tried not to sound as excitable as the locas on *The Price Is Right*—the ones who launch up out of their seats when their name is called like their ass is gonna zoom all the way to Mars, screaming like Jesus was making a second coming back to Earth. Juanito tried to sound like it was no bother, like if he *had* to give a tour, he would. But on the inside, his heart was singing a tune—something fast and wild.

When Daniel woke up on his third day in the house, Juanito made two extra eggs in the frying pan. "You like eggs with butter?" he asked Daniel, who walked into the cocina in Venus's sweatpants, which were too tight and short on him. Daniel must've had half a foot on Venus's height, and Daniel's muscular quads and ass were wrapped tight in the gray cotton.

Daniel said yes and rubbed his eyes with closed fists. "Like, how much butter are we talking though?"

"Like, just enough to make it not stick to the pan," Juanito said.

"Then yeah. You gonna share some with me?"

"If you want," Juanito said, trying not to rush his manos to the cabinet door to get a plate for the eggs. Once the plate was on the counter, he took the wooden spoon and cut the omelet in half.

"You can take the bigger half," Juanito said and handed Daniel his plate.

"You sure? You made it."

Juanito nodded and moved his sewing machine from the dining room table to the sofa so that they had enough room to eat. They ate in silence because Juanito was too nervous to say a thing. He thought about things he could bring up for chitchat, but just when he was going to say a word, a garbage truck passed on the street below. Four stories down and the sound was still thunderous enough to make words impossible to hear.

Juanito wondered if Daniel were the type of gay who would want to talk about fabric with him, or sewing machines. How the needle could gobble up the swatches, connect whatever was fed into it with the quick needle motions, up and down and up and down. So he picked something easier. "When'd you get your ear pierced?" Juanito finally asked. He resisted the urge to take the gold hoop into his fingers, and by default, play with Daniel's earlobe.

Daniel smirked and finished chewing his eggs. "Uh," he said. "Like a year ago? Two?" He shrugged.

"Well, I only ask," Juanito said, forking his next bite, "because I think it looks nice."

Juanito knew that his eyes could hold no secrets, so he looked back down at his eggs. He didn't want Daniel to read his eyes like a palm reader reads a palm. Juanito was convinced that if his eyes had lines that people could read, the heart line would be the strongest.

"Gracias, guapo," Daniel said, and Juanito had to hold himself from melting like a tub of butter over a nice blue flame. "You're too sweet."

Juanito smiled and play-punched Daniel on the shoulder. "You don't even know the half of it."

* * *

They waited two days to go down to the piers because two days meant Friday, and Friday was always a good day for cash. Juanito's job was supposed to be easy. He would teach Daniel how to hustle for some cash—how to spot the white men who cruised the piers for their little Latin lovers, how to exaggerate the vowels of their Nuyorican accent to give the johns the exotic flavor that they wanted, how to go behind a bush or deep into a dark alley, how to kneel down on cement so that his knees wouldn't get cut up, how to always negotiate higher because the price they give is always gonna be so, so low. And, most important, how to get into a car, if they *had* a car, but cars were complicated because cars meant rules. Cars meant that at any moment, the client had the power to lock the doors and drive away without letting anyone out for fresh air.

"But if you find a dude with a car," Juanito told him, "then you gotta take this."

This was one of those Swiss Army knives, hooked up with a corkscrew that he could use between his fingers to land a fierce punch. Or if he had a bottle of wine and some free time, he could always take a break to sip on some vino. Then there were little scissors and a tiny, but sharp, blade.

"This blade is all you gotta flash," Juanito said. When Daniel's eyes looked wide like deer, Juanito said, "No, don't worry. No tengas miedo—you probably won't have to use it. Like ever. It's mostly just to feel safe. And maybe you gotta flash it once or twice to let them know that you are not to be fucked with, sabes?"

Daniel was quiet. His hands were in his jeans pockets, shoulders so tense that they were jutting to near his ears. He was kicking the curb with the toes of his shoes.

"¿Qué pasa? You cold, papi?" Juanito said. "The March air got you needing a fleece blanket still?"

"Nah," Daniel said. "I'm just surprised that you're the one telling me to take a blade and knife a john, you know?"

"¿Y qué? Why does that surprise you?"

"Porque you're so little, Juanito. So innocent looking," Daniel said. "With your sewing machine and your fabrics and shit. Now, here you're telling me to keep a knife just in case I gotta flash it."

"Mira, some of these guys are gonna fuck with you," Juanito said. "And you gotta be ready."

"I mean, I figured that. I just wasn't expecting you to be the one to be giving me a blade. I ain't never cut anyone before."

"And you think I have?"

"No, well I don't know, I didn't say that. I'm just surprised, that's all," Daniel said. "I didn't think you was capable of cutting anything other than a piece of silk."

Daniel put his arm on Juanito's shoulder and looked both ways to see if there was anyone around them.

"If it makes you feel better," Juanito said, "I never had to cut anyone before, and I hope I don't ever have to. Pero hold up un momento—you like my fabrics?"

"Yeah," Daniel said. He kicked against the curb again, gently. "No sé—I think it's pretty adorable."

It was too dark to see if Daniel was blushing, but Juanito was pretty sure that his own face was going red. "Well maybe I'll make you a pair of pants some time. Or a shirt! Yes, I think a shirt, maybe."

Daniel smiled and held out his hand. "You gonna give me that knife or what?" His arm was reaching like he wanted to take it and hold it.

"No," Juanito said. He held the army knife, then put it into his pocket. "Not yet. I don't think we're gonna hustle tonight. I think we should do something else."

* * *

They bought two bottles of orange soda instead, then found a little patch of grass to claim their own. Only a block from the water, the Friday night pier crowd was making all kinds of noise—stereos with freestyle on blast; laughter and kikis; hands clapping and shoes clacking; the occasional, Girrrl, no you did *not*. Daniel and Juanito sat on the grass, opened their soda bottles, and leaned against each other for support. A young black queen walked past them with her right arm raised to balance a boom box on her shoulder. It wasn't playing any music yet. Homegirl's nails were vampire-red and thick gold nameplate hoops hung from her earlobes. Juanito's eyes weren't sharp enough to read her name.

Juanito turned to Daniel and whispered, "What do you think her name is?"

"Umm," Daniel said. "I'm thinking she is giving vibes that she is—Mildred? No, now I'm seeing Leonora? No—"

"Ay, Dios mío." Juanito laughed. "You're the silliest. She is definitely not a Mildred or a Leo-whatever and you know that."

"Yeah, I'm just playing with you."

They watched the queen sashay her way to the pier. "Shawna," she shouted out toward the river with her free hand up to her mouth like her fingers were some kind of megaphone. "Don't choo even *think* about that bitch from the DMV—"

"Sounds like Shawna's having trouble getting her car papers done," Daniel whispered to Juanito as the queen glided away too far to hear the rest. "I hope she takes her friend's advice and doesn't think about it for a single-little-hot-second."

Juanito giggled and smacked the side of Daniel's arm. "You're too much," he said, and dipped the straw into his bottle. Daniel leaned his head back and took a big gulp out of his own drink.

"You know what I love about orange soda?" Juanito asked.

Daniel raised his eyebrows and shrugged. A smile lingered on his lips.

"It's so much sweeter than all the other sodas," he said. "So much sweeter that it's like tangy-tangy and it makes it feel like the top layer of your tongue is pinching together."

"Like a soda-sugar tongue burn?"

"Sí sí," he said. "Azúúúúcar."

Juanito lay back on the grass so that he was looking up at the night sky. He could see Daniel out the side of his eye, could see the barba-stubble growing on the side of his face and the tip of his chin. He could see how that one thick vein bulged out of his left arm—the arm that he leaned on as he held the soda with his right hand. He wanted to kiss Daniel, but he didn't want to go in for it. It was like he just wanted it to happen, like *bam!* He wiggled a little closer to Daniel and traced the vein on Daniel's arm with his forefinger.

Daniel sighed and tilted his head back. "That feels good," he said. "My arms are sensitive like you got no idea."

And Juanito, in that moment more than others, wished that he could sing. He wished that he could sing a slow jam about kisses and night skies and sensitive brazos. He wished that he could open his mouth and something beautiful would come out of it, so that Daniel would turn his head to face him and say, That song, those words, are so, so beautiful—please don't stop singing to me.

But he knew he couldn't carry no tune. Not even a note. And it seemed like just when Daniel turned to look at Juanito, some queens started wailing.

Juanito and Daniel both sat up straight and turned around to face the epicenter of the throwdown. It looked like, as best as Juanito could tell, two Latina queens were going at it. He could tell that it wasn't going to end well. They both had studded clutch purses, which meant that someone was probably going to end up bleeding by the time that fight fizzled.

The queen on the left was wearing a tight leopard-print mini-falda that barely covered her panties. The other queen was wearing a little black dress and had thick lip liner that made her mouth look clown-level fochi.

"Oh shit," Daniel wrapped his arm around Juanito's shoulder and held him closer. "What you think they're fighting about?"

"No sé," he said. "I gotta listen."

Pero, damn, listening was difficult in that hot moment. Daniel's arms were around him and Juanito had to pay attention to the fact that he was breathing still out of a fear that he would forget to inhale.

Lip Liner was scream-yelling at Leopard Print, calling her a puta. Over and over again, puta, puta. "Uh-oh," Juanito said. "I bet you they're fighting over a man."

"Scandalous," Daniel said. "Alert the *New York Post*."

"They'd eat that up for breakfast."

"*And* lunch, who you kidding?"

"Snacking on that bochinche," Juanito said.

Leopard Print's heels were too high and her ankle wobbled and gave way. She went down hard. Lip Liner raised both hands high up in the air and whipped her clutch bag down like a whip. Leopard Print cried out, "I didn't fuck him, you delusional crab-infested bitch."

"You lying puta," Lip Liner screamed. "How dare you bring up the crabs." She whacked her bag down again. "That was a horrible two weeks in my life. Your ass is lucky I don't have a blade on me."

"Oh please, bitch," Leopard Print said. "I wouldn't even fuck your man if his cum was the fountain of fuckin' youth."

"Is that how you talk to your mother?" Lip Liner said. "I didn't bring you in off the streets and into our house so that you could be a shady bitch on wheels."

"Oh shit," Daniel said. "She is getting her ass served back to her. Do you think we should go break up the fight?"

"No," Juanito said. "Not unless you want to give them a reason to tag team on you and make you bleed. Never break up a fight between house sistas."

"Okay, then I'll pass on that," Daniel said. He stood up and Juanito lay in his shadow. Daniel had his hand out like he was waiting for a low-five. "Hey, Juanito, you gonna give it to me?"

"¿Qué?" Juanito said. "What do you want?"

"The soda bottle," Daniel said, "I'm gonna go throw it in the bin. Let's head over there together."

*　*　*

Juanito knew that Angel wouldn't be a happy camper if, at the end of the semana, they came home empty-handed. Every Sunday evening, Angel sat at the dining room table while Juanito worked on his sewing projects. Half the table covered in fabric, the other half covered with crumpled bills that Angel stuffed into an envelope for food, rent, heat. Mama had that shit on lock down, and for that, everyone was grateful. "But I'm not some pimp," Angel had said, a year earlier to Juanito when he had first arrived off the streets. He was only thirteen then, with a backpack full of old clothes and a couple of hundred dollar bills. "I'm not pimping out nobody."

"I know that," Juanito said back to her. "You're just keeping the house afloat."

"Pero sometimes," Angel said, "sometimes I feel like a pimp and I don't like that feeling, you know?"

A week later, Angel bought Juanito that sewing machine, saying, "I know it's not nothing magical, but when you plug it in, it sews. So work those fingers between the needles and make your crazy-colorful outfits, Juanito baby."

And Juanito had said, "Gracias, mamita. You didn't have to do that."

"I know I didn't," Angel said. "But now we're family, and I know you like to sew. You should have the chance to develop that, verdad? Maybe you'll walk in a ball one day with an outfit all your own."

Now, Juanito didn't want to think about letting Angel down. He couldn't show up with Daniel on Sunday—Daniel's first Sunday in the house—with no cash to hand over. But he also couldn't stomach the thought of Daniel fucking with other guys on the piers, in those cars, down those dark streets in the Meatpacking. And he couldn't even wrap his mind around the thought of Daniel taking the army knife for protection—he seemed too sweet for that and Juanito didn't want to be the one who, even if it was indirect, pushed Daniel into the kind of danger that would require a blade.

So Juanito taught him how to steal. Not nothing violent—Juanito was clear with that: no violence, ever—just a simple picking of the pockets. They spent Sunday morning on crowded trains, looking to spot tourists. They walked by outdoor cafes to look for purses that could easily be snatched.

"The key to purses is," he told Daniel, "you gotta find the ones on the ground that you can grab and walk away with, never making eye contact. Don't run, because then they'll see you and scream."

"You sure about this?" Daniel said. They sat down on a bench in Central Park near the open meadow. Groups of people were tossing around inflatable beach balls, the kinds that seemed to float in the air for a second or two before giving in to gravity and dropping back down, waiting for the next fist to punch it back up again.

"Yeah," Juanito said. "So the trick here is to sit close enough to the bag, and then put your jacket down next to it."

Daniel nodded and then darted his eyes around.

"And then you can reach your arm under your jacket and slip it into the bag," Juanito continued, "until you can feel a wallet. Then you slide it out of the bag, under the jacket and simply get up to walk away. If you're smooth enough, no one will spot you."

"Smooth enough," Daniel said. "Ay, Juanito. I don't know about this. At least at the piers, we can do something and get money for it. Pero this is like stealing from people and we didn't earn it or nada."

"You'd rather fuck around with someone and get the cash that way?" Juanito tried to keep his tone even. He didn't want to show Daniel that the idea of it would somehow hurt his feelings.

"Pues, I mean," Daniel said, "isn't that what you do?"

The words stung, not because they were mean, but because they were true. Juanito never thought of himself as a whore, pero as someone who supported his sewing and creating hobby by hustling on the side. It was just something to get by.

"I do it because it's not like there ain't nothing else I can do," Juanito said. "You don't think I haven't tried to get some kind of other job?"

"I didn't say that," Daniel said. "Damn, why are you yelling at me?"

"I dropped out of high school to get away from my old life," Juanito said. "You don't think I'd rather be one of those fancy lawyers or doctors or whatever?"

"Chill out, Juanito. I'm just trying to understand what I've got to do here. I'm not throwing shade at you."

He regretted overreacting and had never meant to scream. The words had come out like water out of a hydrant—he hadn't meant to put his emotions out there on full blast. But he still couldn't bear the thought of Daniel fucking someone else at the pier, which he knew seemed ridiculous now that he thought about it. He had just met Daniel, they weren't dating, Daniel didn't even *know* how Juanito felt about him.

"Alright, we can go to the piers next week," Juanito said. He looked at the beach balls floating in the air, and then at the sun that was so bright, if he looked at it long enough, it would cause all the other colors around him to fade. "If that's what you want to do, we can do that. But now, we gotta take one wallet to bring back some money to Angel tonight—for food and stuff."

Daniel took off his jacket and placed it on the grass near the closest purse. The straight couple nearest Daniel was sprawled out on a blanket, taking bites of sandwiches and apple slices. They had a wooden picnic basket, which made Juanito think of Dorothy and Toto. The girl whispered something into the guy's ear and he laughed and looked into her eyes so gently that it made Juanito want to cry. He had never had someone look into his eyes like that. He didn't like to see reminders in the world that looks like that even happened to other people. If he didn't have to see it, he wouldn't have to think about it. He watched Daniel's arm slowly stretch under the jacket, and he leaned back to look again at the blinding sun.

* * *

After a long day at the piers, after a long afternoon walking around the city in search of whatever they were in search of that particular day, after Angel had sorted through the money at the dining room table and went off to work herself, Juanito liked to lay on the roof as Venus smoked a joint. Now that Daniel was part of the picture, Venus insisted that all three of them go up the stairs to lay out and smoke.

But Juanito wasn't that big of a fan of weed. After a long day or a long week, not nobody was looking for some rah-rah cheerleader cool down—porque that was the phrase that Venus used: *cool down*. As in, she just wanted to *cool down* and smoke a jay. Pero weed gave

Juanito panic attacks most of the time. What could he say, he just couldn't help but feel the feels—a dull ache in his shoulders whenever he'd tense up without realizing it. He could go twenty minutes without realizing that his shoulders were scrunched up and tense in a position that, to anyone looking at him, would look completely stiff. Whenever that happened, Juanito would search within and take a moment. Breathe, he'd say to himself, cálmate.

"But why do they call that shit a *toke*?" Juanito asked. Venus had already lit the joint and Daniel was holding in his puff. They sat cross-legged on the roof and Juanito could feel the cement against his ass-bone.

"No sé," Venus said, primping her hair like the joint was gonna look her up and down before she took it in her fingers. "Why do we call shit anything anyways?"

Juanito could see Daniel's exhaled nube glow orange under the building's only rooftop light. Daniel put his arm around Juanito and pressed his fingers into Juanito's neck muscle like he was dialing a telephone. "Relax," Daniel whispered to him. "Your shoulders are rock hard."

"Okay, party people," Venus sang, whipping out a comb and using it as a fake microphone. She got up to her heels. "Deejay Vee-Vee, lyrical master, giving it to you faster, on the blaster, flashing like the grandmaster—"

"Drunker than plaster—" Daniel sang.

"Uh—" Juanito said. "Walking up that StairMaster?"

They laughed and now it was Juanito's turn to take the joint. Venus kicked out a leg and said, "Mira, muñequitas, pero with these kinds of legs, you know your girl Venus don't got no need for a Stair-Master. I'll just walk up and down that crazy island Manhattan—and don't make me do my Rita Moreno show tunes for you now, darling."

"I wasn't doubting," Juanito said. "It's not like I got those rhyming skills like you. How many damn words rhyme with faster, and you got me going at the end of the game—like shit, girl."

Juanito trembled as he put the joint to his lips. It was already half burned down. Venus eyed him hard. "You don't gotta smoke it, Juanito," she said. "It's just supposed to cool us down, not give you a mad case of ansiedad. Pass it over if you don't want it, no pasa nada."

The last time he had smoked on the roof with Venus, it had been way too much for him to handle. He had trembled even though it was nowhere near cold, and he was convinced that he could feel his heart pounding in his chest. Venus had had to bring his nervous ass back down to the apartment, where he wrapped himself in one layer of taffeta, a fuzzy winter blanket, and crowned it off with a thin layer of tulle. He had called it his little cocoon of love.

But that had been months ago—last summer—before Daniel had shown up. And now there they were, looking at the clouds take shape. Daniel was wearing a tank top and had his arm around Juanito's shoulder. Juanito took a little sip of the joint, pinky up, and rested his head on Daniel's shoulder. Maybe this would be his new cocoon of something.

Night was something magical in New York and Juanito loved the sparkle view of the buildings downtown in Manhattan. Over that river, past that bridge, past the ripples of buildings of Harlem, there were the big glass boxes with yellow dotted lights. He thought of this view like he thought of snowflakes—just like each flake was a different shape and no two were the same, no two views of that city were the same no matter which night he saw it.

He was high, pero only un poco. He could feel Daniel's fingers gliding up and down his neck and he liked that. When "I Feel for You" came on the radio, Venus shouted out, "This shit is my jam—well now this is the perfect night."

"You and your Chaka Khan," Daniel said. "I feel like I just met you but I know you love that woman."

"Well there's clearly a lot to love," Venus said. "Ch-ch-aka Khan is a star."

Venus and Daniel took turns using Venus's comb as a mic. "Mic check one, two, one, two," Daniel said, tapping his finger on the tip of the comb as the radio went to commercial break. "Can you hear me? Am I coming through to you?"

"We can hear you," Juanito said, sitting upright and clapping. "Sing that song. Belt that tune, sister."

One minute into "Burning Up," Madonna went silent midword. The music stopped and Venus whined, "No me digas que los batteries freakin' died out on us!"

But what could Juanito say? The batteries had freakin' died out on them. Daniel held out his hand, like he was gonna push the air out in front of him. He did a slow-jam breakdown of "Burning Up," and soon they were all on their feet, singing and dancing and filling the silence with their breathing.

The three of them smoked through another joint and lay down on the cement roof. Juanito was so high that he could feel precisely where the cement was uneven. He rested his head on Daniel's stomach and laughed hard. "My body feels so heavy," Juanito said. "Like one of those sumo wrestlers. I can't get up."

"Help us," Daniel joke-screamed. "We can't get up, we can't up. We're too stoned to function."

Daniel snuggled closer to Juanito and squeezed their bodies together. Juanito could feel Daniel's heart a-thumping through his light wool sweater. He stuck his finger in one of the holes on the side of the sweater and scratched Daniel's nipple.

Venus cleared her throat loudly and Juanito turned to her to flash a smile. Venus raised her eyebrows like she always did when she wanted Juanito to know that she was watching him. Juanito giggled and bit his lip.

"I know, I know," Venus said. "When I smoke, I feel lovey-dovey too. I just wanna go up behind Angel and give her a diva-hug and tell her that I love her."

"Y yo también," Juanito said. "Like she always got food on the table for us. That's some real-level love. Making sure we always got a bed to sleep in. Making that bomb-ass chicken soup."

"Pero she'd kill us if she saw us smoking," Venus said. "Y ya tú sabes, Juanito."

"Mmm, why you think she'd kill you for smoking a little joint?" Daniel asked.

"Because, papo," Juanito started, and Venus finished, "She don't like any kind of drug other than liquor. Says that white people already got conceptions of what they wanna see when they see us, don't need to fit into any kind of premade stereotype."

"Like it'll piss her off," Juanito said, "if we do anything that confirms their racist bullshit. Or something like that."

Juanito could feel Daniel's fingers massaging his scalp, and his eyelids fluttered. "I could see that," Daniel said. Juanito could feel Daniel nodding.

"Pero I don't like to think like that," Venus said. "I'd rather lay up on this roof, smoke my jay after a long-ass day at the piers, and dream."

"You got any rhymes about dreams, Vee?" Daniel asked.

"Nah," she said. "Rhymes are fun and shit, but dreams are the serious-level shit."

Juanito bolted upright and Daniel's hand fell back onto his pecho. "Dime, reinas," Juanito said, "if we lived in a world where you could be, do, or want anything, what would it be?"

"Oh, I got an answer, sin duda," Venus said. "No question about it. I want a house in Westchester. Wouldn't that be nice?"

"Yes," Juanito said. "All kinds of yes, por favor."

"Sí," Daniel said, "But then you'd have to mow the lawn every week. And shovel snow."

"Well," Venus said, waving her left hand like she couldn't be bothered. "That's why my man would do it for me."

"I would have a custom-made Fiorucci one-piece," Juanito said, "with a drop back, and elastic near the calves so it don't go down all the way. And—a gold wristlet to accessorize with it. I could wear it to my first ball. Just think of the debut I'd make."

Venus opened her mouth but then must have decided that there were just no words. She clapped slow and hard, shaking her head and closing her eyes like yes-yes-*yes*.

"I think I'd go the route of simplicity," Daniel said. "But still practical, sabes? I'd get us a washer-dryer set. Can you picture it without buggin' out?"

Venus bit her lip. "Yes, queen." Her eyes were closed and she looked up. "I *can* picture it."

"Clean clothes all the time," Juanito said. "And no trekking to that stank-ass laundromat."

"And no more quarters," Daniel said.

"So practical," Venus said. "You're the new man of the house. I can just see it now." She put her hand in the sky like she was blocking a blinding sun out of her eyes.

Venus recounted the time she had let a gentleman take her home after dinner. She said that she had excused herself to powder up in his bathroom, and as she walked down the hallway, she saw the washer-dryer combo and was so turned on by that display of dinero, she insisted that he fuck her on top of it while it was on a vicious spin cycle.

"Damn," Juanito said. "You know Angel would kick your ass if she heard you went to his house."

"Yeah," Venus said. "Ya sé, no going back to their places. Pero he was a classy mothafucka. I knew nothing was gonna happen."

"You always get the classy mothafuckas," Juanito said.

"I know, right?" Venus said. "He even took me to Bloomies to buy me a new dress. What can I say? He just wants me to look good for him."

"Shit, girl," Daniel said. "You working it down there."

"Maybe he'll pay for your tits," Juanito said. "And take care of that other problem you've got going on down there."

"Nena, please," Venus said. "Don't be playing with me like that, getting my hopes up and shit."

Juanito sighed and said, "I'm really happy right now." Daniel pulled him in closer.

"Ha—I know that just being in my presence has a sunshine effect, now don't it," Venus said and laughed. "Even at night, I give off them UV rays."

Juanito play-slapped her leg. "Don't be a goofball. I meant that I'm just happy that I didn't get no anxiety from the weed. You know me, Vee, always unpredictable."

Venus leaned in and planted a tiny beso on Juanito's cheek. "Oops," she said. "I smudged a little pink Revlon on you, nena. Don't mind me."

Daniel turned to Juanito and rubbed the lipstick off with his thumb. He leaned in and whispered to Juanito, "You've got the prettiest eyelashes, guapo."

Alert the *New York Times*—Juanito's heart thumped twice in a second and then took another second to take a breather before pumping again. He leaned his head back and ate up the purple-blue sky with his eyes. "Look up," he told the others. "Don't the sky look like a sprawled-out spool of purple taffeta?"

Venus and Daniel looked up. Juanito glanced over and saw Daniel's Adam's apple bulging out of his throat. He wanted to shoot an air-kiss and imagine it landing square on the tip of it.

"Ay, taffeta," Venus said. "What an unforgiving fabric."

* * *

While Venus went down to the apartment to see if Angel had got back home, Juanito curled into Daniel's body. Little spoon, he liked to say. Little enough to pour the sugar in a cup, but big enough to cuddle forever.

The rooftop door opened and the door slammed against the wall. "Ay, sometimes I don't even know how to measure my own strength," Venus said. "I'm like the freakin' Wonder Woman up in here."

Juanito snuggled his cheek against Daniel's wool sweater. His ear was against Daniel's body, and when Daniel said hi to Venus, Juanito could feel, through his ear, the vibrations of Daniel's voice.

"Ay, look at you two," Venus said, her tacones clacking against the cement as she shimmied over to them. "Lucky for you that I got a little something-something from downstairs."

She was carrying the mixed-fabric quilt that Juanito had finished sewing a couple of months earlier. He had hunched over that sewing machine, cada día, connecting the various swatches of leftover fabrics that he had found around the Garment District.

He watched as Venus's scrawny arms extended out as she threw the blanket on top of them. Juanito couldn't help but flinch and turn his head back into the side of Daniel's torso. "There you go, nenas," Venus said, hurrying away. "I don't need you two getting a cold, saben?"

Her tacones clacked until the door slammed shut and the gentle tapping of heels against stairs got softer and softer.

Daniel sat up and pulled the quilt over both of their bodies. They sat facing each other, cross-legged, and Juanito imagined that this was what the rich kids used to do at summer camp—stay up all night in tents and under blankets. Daniel put his hand on Juanito's neck, then down to his chest, torso, hip, thigh. "Is this okay?" he asked Juanito.

Juanito nodded.

"Tell me, yes," Daniel said. "I want to hear your voice."

"Yes," Juanito said, now putting his hand over Daniel's hand and guiding it over to his lower back. "This is where I'm most sensitive," he said. "But don't tickle me. I don't like to be tickled."

Daniel smiled and Juanito could feel the goosebumps forming just above the waist band of his sweatpants. When Daniel moved forward to kiss him, Juanito closed his eyes. He was shocked by how soft Daniel's lips felt against his own. Shocked by how tender Daniel was being.

"Juanito," Daniel said. "You've gotta relax. You're so tense, you're wincing. Is everything okay?"

"Yes," he said, this time leaning in to nibble on Daniel's lower lip. "I think everything is getting better now."

VENUS

The first rule, or as she liked to call it, The Golden Rule, that she needed to make sure Daniel understood was that the client had to pay first. "So if they try any porquería bullshit with you and you don't feel safe," she told him, "just bite it."

They were standing in the Meatpacking District near the Hudson, a little farther down than the piers off Christopher Street. If she was going to show him how to work the cars, then they needed to be near where the cars were at.

"Yeah," Juanito said, fidgeting with the zipper of his coat. He was pulling it up, down. "Blow 'em for ten bucks, fifteen if they're willing to go that high, but don't take too long."

Venus slapped Juanito's nervous hands away from the zipper. "But if you feel like shit is going down and he's gonna hurt you," Venus repeated, "just chomp on it. That'll buy you time to open the door and get the fuck out."

"You mean—bite his dick?" Daniel asked.

"Yes," she said. "Chomp down as hard as fuck."

"Ave María," Daniel said.

"God gave you teeth for a reason," Venus said. "Use them."

"Yeah, for eating," Daniel said.

"It's only," she said, "if you gotta save yourself from getting hurt."

Venus saw Daniel look down at the ground and then at Juanito. Something was up with those two! Juanito forced a closed-mouth smile. His hands were back on the zipper, up-down, up-down, up— she slapped his hands again. "You're gonna break that damn jacket if you keep fussing," she said.

It only took a few minutes for a car to roll by. Venus ran up to the car window as best she could in her tacones, which were these five-inch ordeals in emerald green that she had picked up in the East Village a month before. They didn't match anything she owned, but that didn't stop her from buying them. She would find a way to make them match. Además, she felt like she was living on the edge because she was only one wrong step away from twisting her damn ankle. She always believed the old mantra, which she whispered to herself when she was trying to get her footing right: fashion over pain, fashion over pain, if it don't hurt, then there ain't no gain.

She stood at the car door next to Daniel. "You know the drill, verdad?" she said. He nodded back and got in the car. She crossed her arms and sighed a happy sigh. She felt excited when a new child was learning the strings. There was Daniel, their newest house banjee, getting into his first car. It made her heart tingle just to think about it.

When she walked back to the corner to stand with Juanito darling, Venus practiced a slow catwalk to the basura can on the tip of the intersection, then walked back to Juanito with her hands on her hips, posture so stiff like she was balancing a wooden bowl on top of her head.

"These tacones are doing *wonders*," she said to Juanito, who was still looking at the car like it was full of kittens and the thing was about to blow up. Venus snapped her fingers in front of Juanito's line of sight. "I said, these tacones are doing the seven wonders of the world over here on my toes."

Juanito looked at her shoes, then back up to her eyes. "You're about to break your neck with one wrong step," he said. "These cobblestoned streets be like landmines under stiletto heels, nena."

"Pues, that's why I'm *practicing* my catwalking, girl," she said. "You gotta trust me with these things."

Juanito sighed. "You think he's okay in there?"

Venus turned back to look at the car. They were too far away to see exactly what was going down, but she could see the outlines of their bodies through the dash. "I'm sure he's fine," she said. "It's like riding a bike. Once he got his balance, he'll get it down pat."

Juanito didn't laugh at her little broma.

"¿Qué pasó, Juanito?" she said. "I see you falling hard for him."

"Por favor, Vee." Juanito waved a hand at her like she was a pesky tsetse fly about to enter one of his nostrils.

Venus let out a cackle. "You thinking I don't got eyes in this head, nena."

"I know you got eyes in the front *and* the back of that head," he said. "Nothing gets past you. But what do you know about love?"

"I love real hard, Juanito, and you know that. So don't get sassafrassy on me right now," she said. "I think he's got the hots for you too, so don't you worry. He'll be just fine in that car. We all gotta pull some weight in this house, legal or otherwise. You know that."

Venus watched Juanito stare at the car door, and then she looked over también. "That's a shiny thing, that car over there," was all she could think to say. She put her arm around Juanito.

"I'm gonna apply to clean apartments tomorrow," Juanito said.

"Where at?"

"No sé, but I know I got to."

Venus stood there feeling taller than Wonder Woman in those heels, arm wrapped around Juanito like they were posing for some badass album cover. Her hair was extra high that night, thanks to a fresh perm and a shit ton of aerosol.

"Mira," Juanito gasped. "The door. Something's up."

Venus watched. The door opened un poco, then slammed shut again. Then it opened again, but shut real quick right after.

"Ay, fuck," Venus said. "Alright. I got this."

She took off her tacones so that she could run faster. She carried the things with her right pinky, by the straps, hand up in the air like she was waving for a taxi. When she got to the car, she opened the door from the outside and Daniel nearly fell on her ankles as he spilled out of the passenger seat.

"Give me my fuckin' money back," the man screamed.

"I'll get you napkins," Daniel said as he pushed himself up off the street.

Venus looked inside at the john. "Wooooof," Venus said. Homeboy's crotch was covered in a little bit of vomit. Oh, Daniel baby. Who knew he had such a gag reflex?

"Your boy fuckin' upchucked all on me," the man screamed at Venus.

"I said I was sorry," Daniel said, but Venus held her hand up high in a shush motion.

"Look, honey," Venus said, leaning over with her hand on the door, ready to shut it closed. "Back the fuck off and stop messing with my friend."

"Give me my fuckin' money back," he screamed.

"Yeah, I heard you the first time," Venus said. "But you're just gonna have to deal with it 'cause do I look like some kind of customer service representative?" She slammed the door and screamed, more at the window than at the dude himself, "Fuck you and the horse you rode in on."

*   *   *

She never had a temper when she was around her newest man, Charles. Even the mention of his name made Venus want to slow down gravity like a Michael Jackson video. On the surface, Charles was nothing to write home about. He was in his forties, white, a little bit stocky, but that didn't bother her. She always thought, *Hey, a little more to hold on to when I need to do some holding on to.*

Venus had met him a couple of blocks away from where Daniel had gotten into his first car. She met him a month ago, give or take a week. On their first night together, once Venus was done doing what Charles had paid her to do—she didn't believe in spelling out particulars because that was déclassé—Venus sat in the passenger seat of the BMW and pushed her dress back down so that it wasn't inching up on her privates no more. Charles told her to buckle up as he pressed on the radio.

"You like jazz?" he asked.

"I'm not sure," she said. "Don't think I ever heard any before?"

He told her that the tape he was playing was a woman named

Ella Fitzgerald. He said that she used to live up in Harlem back in the day. Venus watched as Charles leaned his head back against the leather headrest as the car idled. He closed his eyes like he had only a few minutes earlier, when her lips were wrapped around him and he told her to glide her tongue around back and forth. When she was down there, she had looked up to watch his face—a face she could fall for, she knew. All she could see from down there was the tip of his chin inching toward the roof of the car.

"That voice," he said, "is like a cold glass of water on a summer afternoon."

Venus didn't want to think of this woman's voice like a glass of water. Water had no taste—okay, yes. Water was necessary and sometimes refreshing and fresca, but nothing could be more *boring* than a glass of damn water.

Pero as she listened, the woman's voice broke Venus's heart. It was beautiful, crisp like fresh linen, but there was also something painful in it too. She wanted to know who this woman was, where she could go to find her.

"Who is she?" she asked.

"Buckle up," he told her.

"I can't," she said. She leaned forward and put her hand on the door clasp. "Where're we going?"

"Come back to my house," he said. She watched as his eyes scanned her: her eyes to her chin to her chest to her hand on that door clasp.

She hesitated and looked out the window. There was no one on the street. The car clock's green light said 3:00 A.M., but she wasn't sure if it was accurate. Maybe he hadn't fallen back for daylight savings.

She knew that he hadn't locked the door—she hadn't heard any click. And she knew she couldn't go back to his place. It was one of Angel's rules, and for good reason. A street girl never knew what could happen back in the confines of a client's house. Not to say that she hadn't done it before, but still. At least the streets were out in the open and safe in their own way. Our house, Angel used to say, is the only safe house.

"You know I want to, baby," Venus said. "But I just can't. I only do cars."

"Then at least stay and listen to one more song with me." He glided his hand to her earlobe. "You have such beautiful hair," he said. "You should grow it out for me."

She sighed. She felt that he had seen her and her needs—her desire to be beautiful in someone else's eyes. She could maybe count on her fingers and toes the number of johns who had ever complimented her *after* they had already cum. And that wasn't saying much.

She knew she was going to fall for him, and in the mean beating depths of her corazón, she wanted to. But her head was saying no. Her head was being practical. Or trying to, por lo menos.

She opened the door. "I can't go back tonight," she said as her heels touched the cement. "But I'll be here tomorrow night, same time, and we can go from there."

* * *

The next night, she was there in a silver lamé jumpsuit looking like a disco ball with legs. And the night after, she was decked out in a leopard-print wrap dress. It was a fake Diane von Furstenberg that she had picked up in the back room of a Chinatown dig that sold fake Gucci bags behind a trapdoor. And the night after, she went all out in a white dress à la Marilyn Monroe, with a rabbit-fur jacket because the wind was a little nippy. It was just like her, too, to associate memories with the outfits that she paired them with, as if she could check back into her mind like it was a library card-catalog, and she could say, Oh yes, Thursday the 24th, I was wearing this and that, and he was being such a *doll*.

Charles always wore the same thing, which wasn't to say that he was schlepping it up. He always wore tailored suits and a white button-down shirt. The only thing that changed were the patterns of his silk ties, and whether his blazers were navy or black. Pero in the dark streets where they parked the car, it was hard for Venus to tell the difference between navy and black. After a couple of weeks, it didn't matter what he was wearing neither.

On their third week, her hair had grown out long enough that she didn't have to wear wigs. He played with her hair, twirled it in his fingers while they listened to an entire Ella album. She was discovering something new about herself: she loved when people played with her hair. No one had done it before. Sure, men had grabbed, yanked, pulled her hair like it was a rope signal for her to go down further, to deep throat, or whatever. But Charles was being gentle with her.

When Ella was done and the tape went mute, Charles popped in a new cassette. This man, he said, was named Something Armstrong. She hadn't heard the first name and she didn't feel like asking again.

"Are his arms as strong as yours?" she said while pinching at his biceps muscles, which weren't even that strong. She knew it was a corny thing to say, pero she wanted to make him feel manly and guapo. She always told him how much she loved his body, which wasn't a lie.

"I love the way the trumpet sounds," he said.

"Sounds like a mighty strong trumpet," she said.

They moved to the back seat where they could at least cuddle a little. He took off his blazer and unbuttoned his shirt so that she could see the squiggly chest hairs that popped out of his white undershirt. She played with those pelitos with the tips of her fingers, then she scratched him lightly around his chest and neck area and he sighed.

"I got you something," he said. He leaned over to the front of the car so that he could open the glove compartment.

"Don't tell me you're trying to butter me up so that you can get me to your house."

When she saw the bag, she already had some kind of idea of what it was. She had been expecting it to be a kind of gag gift, like all the times when machos would say that they had a gift for her, then whipped out their dick for her to suck on, like *that* was supposed to be the special regalo of the season that they got at the Sucia section of Macy's. That had happened to her at least four times before, and each time, she had to pretend a surprised face to keep her eyes from rolling around their sockets.

Charles held out the small bag. His fingers pinched the top of the white strings on the handle. Even in the dark, she could see that the bag was robins-egg blue. She took out the box inside and untied the white ribbon knots. It was from Tiffany & Co. A sterling silver bracelet.

"Oh, wow," she said as he put it on her wrist. "For me?"

"For you?" he said. "For who else would it be?"

"I don't know," she said.

"And something else," he said. "But it's a surprise. I got tickets for a show, but I'm not telling you which one yet. Just meet me here tomorrow at six o'clock."

Six o'clock! So early. At six o'clock, she would be in the bathroom singing her Gloria Gaynor and shaving her piernas, trying not to slip on the tile floor so she wouldn't get a disco concussion.

"It's too early," she said.

"It's never too early," he said. "You won't regret it, I promise you."

She stared at the chain-linked bracelet on her wrist, then jiggled her hand around so that she could see the silver glimmer in whatever light was spilling into the car. "Oh, alright," she said. "But only because you promised."

* * *

Angel was always accusing her of confusing the heart and the head, to which Venus snapped back, "I'm not confused if I feel them both at the same time." Every time Angel hurled her accusation, Venus would flash out her fingers and run them through her hair and say, "When you got good hair, you don't got to care . . ."

"What am I gonna do with you, nena?" Angel always said back, like a film reel on repeat. It was so predictable of her.

And because of that, Venus wasn't gonna tell Angel about Charles. What she didn't know wasn't gonna kill her. Plus, Venus was in a good mood. Like so damn good. Her emerald cha-cha shoes were on point, her hair was looking especially fly, and Daniel baby was getting into cars like he was a big ol' gay mechanic. And no one had tried to stab him yet! Pues, never mind that Daniel had thrown up on that first guy. That was no matter. Time would soften that blow. Eventually they would be able to laugh about it. If Venus had a nickel for every time someone made her gag, well, she'd have enough coins to do a load of laundry, and ain't that the truth.

It was almost time to meet Charles at the corner, but she didn't see his car yet and she needed a light for her smoke. She walked down the sidewalk and opened her clutch to make sure she had her ciggies. She popped out a Newport and asked the next guy who passed her for a light. When he ignored her and kept on walking, she huffed. "I just wanted to be lit up," she screamed. "I wasn't so- liciting your sorry ass."

She held the cigarette between her fingers and popped out her right hip. Across the street, she thought she saw one of the LaBeija children, but she couldn't tell which one. She scurried over to her, careful not to twist her ankle on any of the small holes in the cement.

"Girl, I been jonesing for one of these bad boys," Venus said, holding up her cig as proof. "Please tell me you got a lighter handy."

"You're in luck," the black queen told her. "Because lord knows I been jonesing for one of *those* bad boys over there," she pouted her lips and chin-nodded across the street to a group of three, fine as hell morenos smoking cigarettes around a botellón of Colt. "And they ain't payin' me any light of day."

She lit Venus's cig and then whipped out one of her own so they could smoke together. "Well, they must be acting a fool," Venus said, "not realizing what they are missing out on because you are a radiant queen in that hot pink dress."

"Thank you, darling."

"Hold on, stand in closer to the curb so I can see it in the light." Venus took a drag on her cigarette. "Oh yes, confirming what I already felt to be true. Lurex is one hell of a fabric. Look at you shimmering in that light."

The queen did a slo-mo 360 with her cigarette hand in the air, looking like a princess on a rotating pedestal. "Well I'm certainly glad to meet you, honey," she said to Venus, "because I just been standing here, so sad and angry that I could shit a diamond."

"Mmm," Venus hummed. "If only it were that easy."

The queen nodded and dragged on her cig.

"I'd have so many carats, my eyesight would be laser sharp." Venus blew a puff of smoke. "Just blinding, I tell you."

* * *

The surprise tickets that Charles had were for the Winter Garden, to see *Cats*. The whole time she sat there thinking, *Whaaaat the fuck is this?* Pero at least the dancers could glide. She couldn't even imagine how hot they were in those furry getups, under all those lights. She cried when that Grizabella kitty sang her memory song. Who knew that an old cat's sadness would cause waterworks?

That night, he didn't ask her if she wanted to go back to his house. He said that he was taking her to a hotel in Times Square. *Hotels,* she thought, *aren't as dangerous as houses because at least in a hotel room, a girl can scream and someone might hear.* When she walked into the room, he asked her what she thought.

"About what?" she said. "What I think about what?"

The question could have meant anything. What did she think of him, of cats singing jellicle meow-meows on a Broadway stage, of Nancy Reagan's closet, or what?

"The room," he said. He held his hands out like they were standing at the Waldorf.

"Well it ain't the Plaza," she said, regretting how harsh it sounded. "But it's nice. It has a bed. It has"—she peeked into the bathroom to confirm—"towels."

The room smelled like stale cigarettes and the wooden furniture looked like it was a couple decades old. Charles pulled the window treatments closed and he fucked her on the sheets that were white and smelled like cheap detergent. *At least they're clean,* she thought. *At least it's more cómodo than a car.*

He used his spit as lube and he came inside her and touched her hair. He cuddled her afterward and, the next morning, he gave her an extra hundred dollars. He smiled as he gave it to her and she looked down at the bill. "Thank you," she said, not meeting his eyes. She didn't want him to see her disappointment. She thought the show had been a gift, not a payment. If he hadn't given her that extra money, she would've forgotten that the night was nothing more than a business transaction.

When they stood in the elevator and he looked up at the floor numbers descending, she said, "Next time, take me to your house."

"Are you sure?" he said.

"Yes," she said, even though she wasn't sure at all. She wanted his tenderness. She wanted white cotton sheets, cuddles, the feel of his five-o'clock shadow rubbing against the side of her neck and the insides of her thighs. If going to his house was the way to get that tenderness, then take her to that house, open that door, and welcome her in, damn it.

* * *

Two evenings later, it was the kind of night for the roof to be down. She was in the passenger seat with her right arm up to feel the air whoosh past her. Her left hand was on Charles's leg as he drove them from the piers to the Brooklyn-Queens Expressway. She could see the blue twinkles of the Verrazano Bridge on the horizon.

Venus didn't like Staten Island. She had always felt like it was more a part of New Jersey than the city. She didn't like that the ferry was the only option to get there if you didn't have a car. And she didn't have a car.

The last time she had taken the ferry to Staten Island to visit a client, the man had handcuffed her to his bed and invited two other men to come over. The man had blindfolded her so she couldn't make out any faces, only their voices, as one of them told the others that they should use condoms because who knew what the bitch had festering down there. She would've smacked them all with the heel side of her shoes if she hadn't been tied down. The latex was dry and hurt her and she screamed so that, at the very least, the sons of bitches could hear the pain they were putting her through.

That had been two years ago and the only reason that she didn't stop Charles from heading over the Verrazano this time was that Venus knew he was more gentle than that. And okay, Staten Island wasn't Westchester or the Hamptons, but at least it was a suburb with houses and lawns and driveways. As they headed over the bridge, she looked to her right to see the lit up skyline of Manhattan. The Twin Towers, the Empire State, and all the other scrapers that sprouted up out of the cement.

And there was Charles, next to her, humming his jazz beats and getting a hard-on. She moved her hand around his upper thigh to excite him even more. She thought of Juanito and Daniel, probably up on one of those distant building roofs, falling hard for each other. She hoped that Daniel wouldn't hurt Juanito. She thought of Angel, sitting at the kitchen table staring at the two fotos of Hector that she thought Venus didn't know about. She thought of Charles and if maybe she had found the man who would finally support her just like the white girls got treated by their rich husbands. Charles took the first exit off the highway and down streets that had trees and row houses. When they hit Howard Avenue, there were houses that looked like villas with long driveways. The Verrazano Bridge twinkled baby blue. The wind blew through her hair and she let out a laugh. "Who knew the wind was so fierce," she said, "when the roof is let down."

It wasn't a question, even though it sounded like one. She felt like the universe had just let her in on a secret that only people with convertibles knew about—and she loved to hold on to little secrets like that.

TWO

DORIAN

Skinny bitches think they are hot shit. The poor damsels. If only they could get some sense knocked into them and realize—well, they need to realize many things. First of which, they aren't gonna stay skinny for long. Metabolism is just like death and taxes, it's gonna catch up to you one day. But that's a minor thing compared to all the foolishness I see in them. Shoplifting. Selling their body and not asking for nearly enough money. Putting sparkling objects on their priority list, but the rent check is bouncing. The list is plenty.

But I think the biggest misconception they got is with love. It's always love this, love that. And don't get me wrong, I'm not saying there is anything wrong with love. Isn't it our love that got us into this whole mess in the first place? The misfortune of being born with too much love for the people that society says we can't love.

The issue I see, and when I see it, it makes me sad. It's that these young queens—well, it's not just the fem realness queens. It's the banjee boys too, and the butch queens, and the lesbians. They think that love is going to save them. I know, doesn't that sound nice? How biblical. So they get out on the streets, skinny as shit because they aren't eating, and then they want to maintain that because they want to be fuckable. Because they think in order to find love, you first have to be fuckable. So they go out into the world think-ing that if they find someone who will love them—because their mother couldn't, because their father couldn't, because their god couldn't—if they go out and finally find someone who *can*, then everything is going to be set right. So they starve so they can look good, and they steal so they can look good, and they don't realize that all along, it don't matter who you find to love you, that love isn't going to make you feel anything more for yourself than you don't already got.

It is about love, but a different kind. A kind that you can only find and not substitute for. And I think it's hard for them to real-ize. So they go out to the balls for all the wrong reasons. Not all of them, but most of them. They go out seeking an audience of ador-ing fans who aren't gonna hurl shade. And they go out looking for their Adam or their Eve, their other half, the other pea in the pod, or whatever you want to imagine it as.

I just want to shake all of those darlings. Love is great, it is. But it's also so brief. Didn't these kids ever learn that even in the Garden of Eden, someone betrayed the other?

DANIEL

As the man drove up, he pointed to the monument and asked Dan-iel who was buried in Grant's Tomb, as if Daniel was supposed to know who the fuck was buried in a giant tomb. Daniel sat on his hands and chomped on his gum and looked out the window. The tomb was down a walkway, surrounded by trees, and anyways, it was too dark to see shit. "I don't know," he told the man, "who?"

The man laughed at him. "Are you fucking kidding me?"

"You drove me all the way up here to ask me about some tomb?" he said. "Don't waste my time, dude. If you're gonna be wishy-washy, you can just take me on back to the piers."

They were sitting in the back seat of the man's black Benz, parked somewhere between Riverside and Broadway. He wiped the sweat from his palms on his jeans and popped a big-ass bubble with his chicle.

"I'm not paying you to give me attitude," the man said. "I'm gonna fuck you. I'm sure as hell gonna fuck you, but first I want to know who you think is buried in Grant's Tomb."

"Yeah, I heard the question," he said. "But how the fuck is a boy supposed to know if you don't tell him first? I mean, really."

The man put his hands up to his face and Daniel could see the sliver of gold from his watch. It was a shiny thing, must've cost him a lot. Daniel shrugged and popped another bubble.

"It's Grant," the man said. "Grant. Grant is buried in Grant's tomb. Seriously, at least you're kind of pretty, otherwise—"

"So why the hell did you ask me if you already knew the answer?" Daniel said. "Fuck you, dude, don't laugh at me. Was this some kind of joke?"

"Oh, for Christ's sake."

"You're wasting my time, man. Making me feel stupid, which I don't appreciate."

The man told him to take off his pants. Daniel didn't know his name, he didn't know if he even wanted to know. Sometimes he would ask these men for their names, and sometimes they would tell him. They never asked for his name though.

"I'm not taking my pants off," he said. "I already told you last week that I ain't letting you fuck me. I don't get fucked."

"Well what good are you?" the man said under his breath.

"I fuckin' heard that," Daniel said. "I'm not Helen Keller over here. I got ears that work. You said you just wanted a blow job."

It was true that the man had said he wanted a blow job when he rolled up his car to where Daniel had been standing near the piers, leaning up against the corner. The man wanted to go to some abandoned warehouse that sat near the Hudson, a place that he said had couches and tables, which made Daniel think it didn't sound that bad. Pero when they walked in, half the windows were broken to shards that looked like cartoon-explosive stars. There were only four couches, and they were already occupied by a group of guys having an orgy fuckfest. "Fags," Daniel remembered the man had said, huffing under his breath, as if the man weren't one himself. Daniel watched the men fuck each other with their shirts on and jeans down by their knees, and then the man had grabbed him by the wrist and lead him back out from where they came—out the door, back to the car.

So the man insisted that they drive uptown, west side, to a place he knew that was dark and free. Now they were there, near the tomb. The man reached into the inside pocket of his jacket and took out a fifty. It looked so flat, so untouched, that Daniel had to touch it to believe that it wasn't a fake. He held it in front of Daniel as if it weren't even a question. "It won't hurt," the man said. "I promise."

"I want your watch too," Daniel said.

The man laughed and rolled up his sleeve to look at the watch as if he had forgotten it was even there. Daniel stared at the pelitos that were a hot diggity mess on the man's arm. Someone needed to tell him to trim, but Daniel wasn't about to throw shade.

"You want this?" the man said, but he sounded angry now. "You want my Rolex? Are you wasting my time now?" He was yelling and Daniel wanted to say, Whoa, whoa, whoa, chill out. It was just a joke, but he didn't mean it as a joke at first. Like so many things he had seen and wanted, he wanted that watch. He wanted to see it on his wrist, so chunky with gold that it would weigh his wrist down everywhere he went.

"It just looks nice, is all," Daniel said. "And I never had a watch before, that's why I—"

His head flew back into the headrest of the seat as the man flung his arm into Daniel's face. It was backhanded and if Daniel had been smiling, the watch would've smacked him square in the teeth.

"Shut the fuck up," the man said. "Take the fifty or get out of my fucking car."

Daniel took off his jeans and positioned himself on his knees. He wasn't doing it because he felt scared. If that were the case, he could always take out the blade from his pocket and wave it around, causing hell. He moved, ass up and head looking down at the speckles of dirt on the beige rug of the car. He did it because he wanted the fifty.

He didn't want to see the man as he fucked him. He sprawled his fingers straight out on the camel-colored leather that was so buttery, the sweat from his palms made his hand slip. The initial thrust was quicker and smoother than Daniel had expected. Pero sigue, sigue, sigue, sigue, and the man was more cariñoso than Daniel thought he would be. Tender—maybe that was the word.

There was a moment at the end when the man sped up and Daniel thought, No, no, I don't want this anymore. I want it to stop. But the man's cold watch rubbed up against his right shoulder blade, like the man was leaning his elbows on top of him as if Daniel were a table. And Daniel kept looking down and he thought of the two watches he could buy with that fifty dollars. No Rolexes, but still watches. Watches that could tell time, at any time, day or night. For himself and for Juanito. Matching.

The man came inside him and Daniel squeezed his eyes shut. He didn't want to focus on the wet, full feeling, so he forced himself to think about the way a crisp bill smells. He thought about whether anyone would pass by the car and see what was being done, or wonder, maybe, who was buried in that tomb over there behind the trees, as if anyone gave a fuck what was buried behind marble.

* * *

After the man dropped him back off at the piers, Daniel saw two more men and gave them handjobs that, even Daniel had to admit, just didn't live up to their usual razzle-dazzle. Daniel sat on a bench and smoked a cigarette, holding the smoke in for an extra second each time. He didn't know exactly what time it was, but just looking out and listening to the thinning crowds, he could tell the end of the night was coming. Lady Midnight had long climaxed and now she was ready for sleep.

It must have been somewhere in that sweet spot between four and

five in the morning, the night giving off a hint of purple-lighted surprise, the boom-booms settled con calma and those young queens
who sang along with Jody, about finding somebody new, looking
for a new love, baby, yeah, yeah, yeah—even *they* were tired now
and holding their tacones in their hand, barefoot walking, looking
to put their head down on something soft before sleep. The heel
clacks stopped clacking, the fingers stopped snapping, and the last
course of shade was served to all those starving ears looking for
sass. At least until the next day.

This was Daniel's favorite time in the whole damn city. River to
river, he couldn't think of another corner on the isla that vibrated
to their rhythms at that hour. It was a time when the performances
were over and the stage was empty, and Daniel could finally go back
uptown and fall asleep next to Juanito.

As he walked toward the 1 train on Christopher, he kept his head
down, hands tucked away in his pockets. Pero he still watched. He
watched those fierce things scurry over to the empty warehouses
along the West Side Highway, yearning for coke and a nice cock
to top it off. He watched the nenitas look out for free benches. He
watched the packs of banjee girls and banjee boys walking to the
club, or the after hours, where the realness would be on tip-top display and the nose candy was so smooth, it would take five or six
heavy rails to start a nosebleed. Heaven's to Dorothy, the queens
claimed, even the nosebleeds could be elegant.

He never needed a watch to know that that time of night was
coming, but he thought, *Wouldn't it be nice to have something glittery
for my wrist?* And it could tell him the time of day, goodness, like a
double whammy. He could know exactly when to pack it up, instead
of reading the energy of the streets for the go-home time. *Reading
the streets,* he thought, *is something more than intuition.* It was more
of tapping into an awareness of patterns. He couldn't read the stars
or the placement of the moon way up there in the sky, but damn,
wouldn't it be nice to twist his wrist and see a digital display telling
him where exactly in the night he was standing?

Sure, time could masquerade herself beyond any kind of recognition, just like an ugly queen could douse herself in a gallon of Drakkar Noir and paint her face like some pendeja—beyond total recognition, *be-yond*. *But a watch would change that,* he thought. As he approached the subway station, he pinched the subway token in his pocket and pressed his fingers into the groove in the center of it so hard that it would leave a dent on his fingers. He did this every night he was riding the subway back up to home. He loved the gentle pain on the tips of his fingers, and he loved to watch, después, his body working to push the skin back to its normal place. It only took a couple of seconds, and what magic, he thought, what magic our bodies could do.

He stood by himself on the subway platform and stared at a hobo who was wearing three jackets, head back and mouth open and snoring loud. Daniel decided then that he would buy a set of watches for both himself and Juanito. In the car, it was just a thought, but now it was a plan. He would buy it and surprise Juanito and then when they weren't together, at least they could arrange to look at their watches at the same time, like midnight on the dot, every night, look up at the moon, and think of each other. For the first time in days, he felt excited.

* * *

It felt like ages since they last cleaned the apartment, even though in reality, it had only been a week. When Daniel returned from the consignment shop with the two watches tucked away in a yellow plastic bag, Angel was working her shift at Pathmark and Juanito was taking a nap in his bedroom. Venus was sweeping the floor and using the broom as a dance prop for the music that must've been playing in her head, because the house was, otherwise, silent.

Daniel hid the watches under the sofa pillow and laughed at Venus, who he knew was trying to get a rise out of him. She overexaggerated her lip-syncing mouth movements, as if the end of the broom was a mic. She did a one-two-three salsa motion. She grinded up against Daniel's leg like she was dancing some kind of bachata. Daniel took the other broom and started sweeping with her, telling her shh-shh, Juanito is trying to get some *z*'s.

"What's gotten into you?" he asked her. "You take a triple shot of Café Bustelo or something? That shit is like liquid crack."

Venus shook her head no and pouted out her bright pink lips.

"You pumped about that new Revlon shade you got working on those labios?"

"Tampoco." She shook her head again and swept under the table.

Daniel held the broom closer to his body, as if he were grabbing on tight to the subway bar during a quick zoom through an express train tunnel. He looked at her head to toe to see if he could do a thorough read.

He saw it. The bracelet: chain-linked silver that made a boy want to scream, ¡Qué plateada!

"Oh, I see, I see," he said. "You're working a new bracelet. I see it on you, practically making that wrist come *alive* with the sound of music."

Venus singsonged her thank-you, bent down to brush the dust pile into the scooper. "Nena, you know this shit is Tiffany's."

"Damn, girl," he said. "You gotta have been saving up a pretty penny for that thing."

She gave him a side-look as she pressed the toe of her red patent pump to the basura so the lid would pop open. She let the dust fall in. "Whatchoo trying to say? You don't think I bought it?" she asked. "You don't think I could afford Tiffany's on my own?"

"I didn't say that." He stopped sweeping to look at her from across the room. "Oh please, Vee, you're the only girl I know who sweeps a floor in stilettos—"

"They're pumps."

"Whatever," he said. "They're big enough to make me sprain three ankles if I ever wore them. What I'm saying is, I know you're fabulous and I know you probably worked hard to get the bracelet. I'm not insinuating anything."

She squinted at him and pursed her lips.

"You squint any harder," he sassed her, "and you're gonna need a pair of bifocals."

"Oh hush," she said and laughed.

They kept sweeping until no more dust was coming up. Before they could prepare the mop to make the parquet sparkle, they broke out into a silent vogue fest. Venus started near the window and Daniel started near the door, but they faced each other. Then they walked, walked, walked to the center of the room.

Daniel focused on his movements, which he was still trying to get used to. He knew that Venus had years more experience than he did, and he felt like he was stumbling to hit the movements in single beats. *Lines*, he thought, *Egyptian hieroglyphic lines*. One, two, left foot in front of right. He tried to whip his arms around, but he was worried it would look too much like a damn windmill. Venus walked around him with her hands on her hips, looking straight ahead as if she were balancing a trophy on top of her head. Then they popped and dipped, careful to make sure their arms and legs didn't touch the other's body. Daniel laughed. He could only imagine how, without music to accompany them, it must've looked like a game of Twister. When they both popped back up off the floor, Venus balanced on her left leg and boom—did a Machiavellian suicide dip like schwam, bam, thank you, ma'am.

Daniel held out his hand for Venus to grab hold of to bring her back up to her feet. "You bested me, Vee," he said. "I got a lot to learn still. These movements are rough, yo."

She winked and smiled. "Like most things," she said, "it just takes time."

Once they finished mopping and they were waiting for the floor to dry, they sat cross-legged on the couch and Daniel told her he wanted to show her the matching watches he had just bought.

"Casio digitals," he said as he hurried to take the boxes out of the plastic bag. "So we don't gotta read the two hands. Did you know those Movados don't even have numbers or nothing?"

"Yeah," she said. "I seen one once with just a glitter dot at the midnight point."

"Exactly," he said. Now the box was in his hand but he didn't open it yet. "They're too expensive anyway. I didn't even realize, but I guess it makes sense. I just don't get how you can look at the time if there ain't no numbers."

"Rich people don't need to know the time," she said. "If they're late for an appointment by an hour because they read their time wrong, nobody's gonna yell at them, sabes?"

Daniel opened the box and he watched as Venus touched the gold links that made up the wrist band. "Pero don't you blab to Juanito about the gift," he said. "I want it to be a surprise."

"A gift?" she said, pinching the Tiffany on her wrist. "What're you implying?"

"Girl, what's bugging you?" he said. "I'm not implying nothing and this is the second time you're bugging today."

"Jesus, fine," she said. "I'll tell you. Just don't tell Angel. Do you think she already knows? Do you think she doesn't believe when I told her that I bought it myself?"

"Knows what? What the fuck are you talking about?"

"She would lose her shit if she knew I took it as a gift because sometimes gifts mean we're indebted to them?"

"Them?" he said. "Are you saying I shouldn't give Juanito the watch?"

Venus sighed and closed her eyes.

"You're acting loca and speaking all redondo," he said. "Can you explain to me what you mean?"

Venus told him about the Staten Island guy, the hotel room, the car, the gift, the show tickets. "He just gave it to me," she said, "I didn't even ask for nothing. I don't want to talk about it. Did you know that jellicle cats are queens of the night? Singing at astronomical heights?"

"What the fuck does jellicle mean?" Daniel said. "I don't see what the big deal is, if you didn't even ask for it. Are you singing *Cats* showtunes at me? You know I haven't seen it—"

Venus took the watch out and handed it to Daniel. "Well this is jazzy," she said. "Put it on your jellicle wrist so I can get a good, jellicle look-see."

Daniel unlatched the clasp and slipped it on his wrist. He jiggled his wrist once, then twice, to get the face in a position that comforted him.

"Oooooh, girl," Venus said, rushing her hands to the sides of her face. "All the yeses on that."

"You like it?" Daniel said. "Don't say jellicle again, I'm serious. You think he'll like it?"

"What do *you* think?" Venus said. "It's a much better gift than going to the Winter Garden, I'll tell you that much."

Daniel laughed as he took the watch off and put it back into the box. "Sí," he said, "but did you like the show anyway?"

"It was wacktastic," she said. "Who the hell needs to see life-size cats prancing onstage? The *actual* fuck?"

Then Venus let out a scream that could bend a stop sign. Daniel jumped up to his feet faster than fast. Venus took a deep breath, then she giggled. She looked at the middle of the sofa and pointed. It was just a spider.

"Fuck, yo," Daniel said. "You can't scream like that. That's so not cool. I almost shit myself just now. You want me to kill it for you?"

Venus said, "No, don't you dare! She probably spent a whole lot of energy building up that fanciful web she got spun up." She stood up next to Daniel and pushed the couch from against the wall. "Yeah," she said, leaning over. "Look at that. Looks just like silk, damn. I think I see some leftover glitter bits back here from the last shindig we threw for Angel's birthday. I'll be damned—looks like it's been some time since we swept back behind here."

She took off her heels and let them rest on the sofa, then she tiptoed to the cocina to get the broom. "Ave María," she said. "Looks like that little araña got herself a secret little lair back here too. I think one of my wig hairs is all up in her web."

* * *

Grand Central Station at two o'clock on a Tuesday afternoon was chaos, but it was also the only place a person could go during the day to look up and see the stars. That was why Daniel chose it as the spot for their midday date, and even though the central room was all hustle and bustle, coats and briefcases in a hurry, and people who were so intent on their destinations that they forgot to look up, Daniel still felt he and Juanito were all alone there. Just the two of them.

Daniel had the watches in his backpack. The idea was to present the watches to Juanito after they had traced the lines of the constellations that were painted on the sky-roof. The main terminal always made Daniel feel like he was walking into the age of oil men with monocles and so much money they could use it for toilet paper and it wouldn't be no matter. Now, as he walked through the main terminal, holding Juanito's hand, the main room was lit with yellow light and old-fashioned bulbs. The yellow was so soft, it made the air in the room feel like melting gold.

"There's something I wanna show you," Daniel said. "One of the Grand Central secrets. Do you know about it?"

"Secrets?" Juanito said. "What secrets?"

"The whispering corners," he said. "You ever hear of it?"

Juanito shook his head no and Daniel squeezed his hand and led the way to the side hallways. The vaulted ceilings had zigzagged brick inlays and at the top, there were two arrows to guide people. To the left, OYSTER BAR. To the right, TO TRAINS.

"If I stand over there," Daniel said, pointing, "and you stand a little ways over there, and I whisper some words, it'll secretly travel the sound over to you."

"No lo creo," Juanito gasped. "But wait, how does that even work?" His eyes were squeezing with thought.

"Because of science," Daniel said, "but I dunno the exact details. You wanna try it out?"

Juanito was already skipping over to the wall. He looked at Daniel and raised his eyebrows to ask if he was ready. Once he faced the wall, Daniel whispered, "I've got a sorpresa for someone, and that someone is you."

Daniel turned around to see Juanito, but Juanito was still facing the wall. Juanito turned around but looked at Daniel and shrugged. Daniel moved his hands to communicate, Okay, turn around again.

When Juanito was facing the wall again, Daniel whispered, "I bought you something real cute and I want to give it to you." He spun around real quick to see if Juanito caught any of it in his ears.

Juanito turned around, shook his head, and made a face that seemed to say, No words. So Daniel gave up. "Maybe we were standing in the wrong spot," he told Juanito as they walked back out to the main concourse. "I know I heard somewhere that there was a spot here, but maybe we were off by a couple of feet."

"It don't really matter," Juanito said. "The idea of it is cool anyway, but just look at that ceiling. I think I see a crab in that corner over there."

Daniel looked up to where Juanito was pointing. He thought he saw it, but he couldn't be sure. "Looks like they need to clean the ceiling un poco and refresh the paint lines, verdad?"

They walked over to the marble steps so they could sit down and look up. A woman in a white fur coat and earmuffs glided past them. "She's so fabulous," Juanito said as he sat down.

"She looked like a cotton ball in that fur," Daniel laughed.

"Totalmente," Juanito said, "but a fabulous cotton ball, no less."

Daniel put his arm around Juanito and they looked up at the ceiling and didn't say nada. Just took it all in, swallowing it with their eyes, feeling the warmth of the building and wondering how a room could feel so quiet and so loud at the same time. A couple minutes went by like that and Daniel couldn't bring himself to reach into his backpack for the watches. His stomach was all butterflies.

"You two," a voice said. Daniel looked to his right. It was a cop. His moustache was bushy and his sideburns were thick rails that came down to his jawbone. "What do you two think you're doing?"

Daniel took his arm off Juanito's shoulder and grabbed one of his backpack's straps. "We was just looking up, officer," Daniel said.

"You two can't do that here," the cop said. "You're blocking traffic."

"Who are we blocking?" Juanito said. "—officer," he added.

The cop crossed his arms and looked down at them.

"We're leaving," Daniel said. He rushed up to his feet and put his backpack on.

When they stepped outside, Daniel reached out his hand to hold onto Juanito's, but Juanito put his hands in his pockets. "No sé, Daniel," Juanito said. "Why'd you give up so easy?"

"Porque he knew we were gay," Daniel said.

"¿Y qué?"

"You wanna get your ass kicked by the police?"

"I'm just pissed off," Juanito huffed. "They never see us unless we're blocking someone's way."

* * *

Back at the house, they had things to themselves. The lights were off, the heat too, so Juanito spread a large piece of fabric over the table in the cocina while Daniel filled the biggest pot with water and put it on the stove to boil. He added two drops of lavender oil so the goal was two: as the water vapor filled the room, it would feel warmer and smell damn good.

They both lay under the table next to each other, staring at the beams of wood that kept the table standing. Daniel eyed-in on one rough edge that looked like if touched, it would give off a mean splinter. The fabric was so long, it flowed down and rubbed up against the floor and kept all the light out. "This feels comfy," he said, but Juanito laughed.

"No sé if my back feels comfy against the floor," Juanito said, "but it feels nice. It feels—safe."

Daniel moved to lean on his right elbow so that he could face Juanito. He glided his left fingers against Juanito's cheek and leaned in for a little besito.

Their clothes came off quickly, but nothing felt too rushed. Daniel didn't say any words. Neither did Juanito. Daniel just gazed into Juanito's eyes with each big movement as if to ask, Is this okay? And Juanito held his gaze, as if to say, Yes.

It was their first time together, but it wasn't as earth-shattering, soul-spinning, ground-shaking as people said it would be. There were no candles. No música. The only sound was the water gently boiling on the stove and the clapping sounds of their bodies in motion with, and against, each other.

When Daniel was on top of Juanito—Juanito's legs rested on Daniel's shoulders—Daniel looked down. His palms were sweaty and he was trying to lay enough force against the floor so that he wouldn't slip. He looked down at Juanito's face, but his eyes were squeezed shut and his head was to the side. Daniel stopped.

"You okay, papo?" Daniel asked. "Am I hurting you?"

Juanito rolled his head so that his face was looking up, but his eyes were still closed and he bit his lower labio. "Sí, I'm fine," Juanito said, "I'll get used to the pain."

"Am I hurting you?" he asked again.

"But the pain is what makes it," Juanito said, "—makes it feel intense."

Daniel didn't know if intense was good or bad. He didn't know if he should stop or go, so he went. He kept at it. He tried to focus on himself, not because he was being selfish, but because he figured that if he focused on the pleasure, he'd cum faster and the pain would stop for Juanito. His movements were slow, but deep, and right before he came, he leaned down so his mouth was close to Juanito's ear. Juanito's eyes were still closed and Daniel bit his earlobe and announced that he would cum, and then he did.

Daniel pulled out slowly and focused on Juanito's face. Juanito was wincing. Once Daniel was out, Juanito opened his eyes and sighed. When their gaze met, Juanito giggled.

"¿Qué?" Daniel said. "What's giving you the giggles?"

"Nothin'," Juanito said. "It's just that you drip-dropped a lot of sweat on me."

Daniel apologized and offered to get a towel.

"No, no," Juanito said. "It's okay. I like it. Makes me feel closer to you."

* * *

The difference between two types of fabric was lost on Daniel, who couldn't say if silk chiffon or georgette or ivory damask—words that Juanito said so often, he could recite them in his sleep—were stronger, prettier, or however else fabrics were judged against each other. Así, Daniel just laughed at himself when Juanito ran his fingers up and down the fabric that was on the table and said, "¿Esto? This is just *cotton*."

Daniel was in his undies now, sitting on the sofa with his legs bent so that he could hug his knees close to his chest. Juanito stood in front of the table, still naked, pretending to do a presenter's voice. "Ladies and gentlemen," Juanito said, two octaves lower than usual. "Tonight, Magician Juanito will do the trick of the century."

"The trick of the century, century, century," Daniel echoed from the sala, where he had a direct view of Juanito.

Juanito cupped his hands around his mouth and blew into them, then rubbed them together slowly and dramatically. "These magical fingers will remove—yes, remove!—this cotton fabric, from this table."

"Ay, Dios mío," Daniel cried, placing the back of his hand to his forehead like a vieja about to faint.

And then whoosh. The table cloth was whipped off in one swoop. He held the cloth in his hands like a bullfighter enticing a toro. He bowed for his audience and Daniel clapped, then moved into a standing ovation before they laughed so hard, it brought them to their knees and they were leaning on each other for support.

Then Juanito stopped laughing and Daniel asked him what was wrong. Juanito reached out and grabbed something that was on the floor near the leg of the table. "Didn't see this before," Juanito said.

"What is it?" Daniel asked. He looked at the piece of newspaper in his hand. "Gotta be a scrap of garbage, verdad?"

"No," Juanito said. "No, I don't think so—"

Juanito handed it to him and Daniel saw for himself: it was an announcement for a model search at Bloomingdale's.

"You think it belongs to Venus?" Daniel asked.

"Probably," Juanito said. He shrugged. "She never said a word. Not a peep."

"Nobody says a peep around here," Daniel said. "This shit is starting to feel like a house of damn secrets and I don't understand why."

"Secrets, secrets," Juanito said. "You keeping anything from me?"

Daniel tugged on the cotton that Juanito was holding still so that he could cover his toes with the end of it. "No," Daniel said.

Juanito stared at him and Daniel saw his left eyebrow twitch ever so daintily.

"You shouldn't play poker ever," Daniel said. "That face of yours can't hide a thing."

"What do you think I'm hiding?" Juanito said. "I asked *you*."

"You don't believe me when I said no," Daniel said. "And that's cause you're right. I do got a tiny secret that I got from you."

Maybe Daniel had misread the eyebrow twitch though. Juanito's eyes got big and Daniel thought he was going to cry. He got up quick to get his backpack and gave Juanito the box with the watch inside. "Open it up," he told Juanito. Juanito had some trouble with the tape on the side that kept it shut. "Just rip it open, no pasa nada. The box isn't the important part. It's what's inside that is."

When Juanito took it out and put it on his wrist, Daniel told him about all the ideas he had about it. How they could wear them every night—hell, every day even—but specially when they weren't together, like at the piers, and they could pick a time to look up at the sky and think of each other. "Like connected," Daniel said. "Or I dunno, maybe it's just corny and shit. Like Del Monte–level corny—"

"Shh," Juanito said and put his finger up to Daniel's mouth. Juanito held his finger there for a hot second and leaned in to kiss on top of it. "It's not corny," he told Daniel. "I like it a lot."

"I just don't want there to be any secrets," Daniel said, "between us. Let's play a game where we tell each other secrets, back and forth. To let them out in the open."

"Okay, I got one," Juanito said. "One time, cuando era joven, I stole a Charleston Chew. Didn't even have the sense to steal a better candy bar, like, the fuck did I choose a Charleston Chew for?" He laughed.

"Last week, I walked down the street and this homeless guy was asking for change," Daniel said. They both lay down together and bunched up the cotton fabric to use as a head rest. They were talking to each other, but looking at and directing their words to the ceiling, as if words had the same properties as air—heat rising above the rest. "—and he was jangling his cup and I walked past even though I had some change in my pocket."

"That's okay, papo," Juanito said. "Don't beat yourself up over it."

"I knew he was hungry, but I kept going."

"Everybody's hungry, Dani," Juanito said.

"Your turn," Daniel said. He kept looking up at the ceiling as he waited for Juanito's words. But nothing came.

"My papi—" Juanito said, "when I was a little boy, my papi—"

Daniel knew better than to turn around to face Juanito in that moment. The apartment was so still, Daniel feared that one movement would affect it all like a tiny pebble in a pool of water. The silence made Daniel feel on edge, so he said, "It's okay, I'll go again if you don't want to."

"Por favor," Juanito said.

Daniel could feel Juanito nod slowly against his shoulder. "When I was in middle school, like maybe twelve or eleven, or maybe it was ten—not the point, the point is that some little macho in training thought it would be cute to punch me in the face in the locker room."

The story wasn't true. He was shocked that he had just told such a flaming lie. He wanted to fill the silence and make Juanito feel more comfortable before he told his story about his father—whatever that story was. But Daniel could have picked a better story, one that wasn't a lie.

Juanito turned his face into Daniel's shoulder-armpit area and sobbed. "Sorry," he kept repeating, "I'm sorry. I'm getting mocos all up on your T-shirt."

"No digas sorry," Daniel said. He didn't know what else to say to comfort Juanito. He didn't need Juanito's apologies. He could wash the mocos off his shirt at the landromat.

"I don't want to play this game anymore."

"Maybe we should go take a nap," Daniel said. Juanito nodded so Daniel unclasped the watch on his wrist, then did the same to the watch on Juanito's wrist, and let them both rest on the table next to each other. Then he picked up Juanito, who was clutching the cotton fabric. "No more secrets then," Daniel said. "We shouldn't have made it a game in the first place."

JUANITO

When he was seven, he already had a routine down pat. When he came home from school, he'd watch *Sesame Street* on the television for a little bit. Then he'd go to his room and take the Barbie doll from her secret hiding spot—in the drawer where his sweatpants were, in the very back corner—and play with her.

"Guess what, guess what," he told Barbie one night. "When it's summertime, I'm gonna go see my father in Puerto Rico, can you *believe* it?"

He fashioned a comb out of five paper clips that he bent into a new shape. It didn't really look like a comb, but it had the prongs and kind of worked. As long as her hair looked fabulous, he was perfectly content.

He felt like Barbie was the only one who could listen to him. And she always had that pearly white sonrisa, even if he told her the sad stuff. He felt like his mother was always out of the house, working at the Jacobs' apartment on Park Avenue, too busy being a mommy to those two blonde girls who were so pretty. So much prettier than Juanito thought he could ever be. When he went to visit his mother one afternoon at work, and the two girls told him he couldn't play with their Barbies because he was a boy, he thought, *Oh yeah? I'll show you*. And he stole one of the Barbies just to spite them.

One day at school, a boy named Steven came up to Juanito and said he heard that Juanito was gonna go meet his papi on the island, and was it true? Juanito nodded his head yes. Steven shrugged and said he was hoping to see his primos on the island too. Then he told Juanito to go up to Catalina and push her into the wall when they were walking down the hallway. Their school had red tape on the ground in a line, and the teachers always told them to stay on that red line or things would get combobulated. Juanito kept his head down and stared at the line as they walked back from gym class to Mrs. Caruso's second grade room. Mrs. Caruso was not simpática, ever since she called Marisela a monster because she ate a crayon. And Marisela cried quietly for the rest of the day, too scared to show Mrs. Caruso her tears.

As they walked down the hallways, Catalina was in front of him and Steven was behind him. Juanito could hear Steven making throat noises. He even felt Steven nudging his shoulder at one point when they marched past the bathrooms. Juanito looked down at the red line, looked over at Catalina's black Mary Janes. "You better do it, Juan," Steven said. "Or else."

Juanito wanted to scream, What for? Why do I gotta do this? Why does it need to be done in the first place? He wanted to scream, You're being a bully, Steven, and leave me alone.

The perfect moment came when they were lined up outside Mrs. Caruso's door, waiting to go in. Catalina leaned against the wall and Juanito had the perfect chance to push her. But he couldn't do it. He couldn't hurt her. He didn't see the point.

So later that day, Juanito came home with a fresh bruise at the back of his head and he told Barbie all about it. "He pushed me," he said to Barbie, guiding the paper-clip comb through her hair. "And my head hit the wall and everyone laughed at me. Even Catalina laughed at me."

There was Barbie's happy face, with her flowing blond pelo, the little white studded earrings. "He called me a pansy wimp," he told her. "I don't understand why they don't like me, Barbie."

A week later, Steven took a pair of scissors from the arts and crafts box. When they were taking a spelling test, Steven grabbed a small chunk of Juanito's hair and chopped it off. Mrs. Caruso was angry and sent Steven to the principal and brought Juanito out to the hallway to talk to him.

"He's a little beast," she told Juanito in the hallway. "Don't worry, Juan. Your hair will grow back."

Juanito sniffled a little, and then blew his nose when Mrs. Caruso gave him a tissue from the tissue box.

When he got home that afternoon, as he was telling Barbie about his missing piece of hair, he could smell the lentil-and-potato soup that his mother was making for dinner. It was his favorite kind of soup, and the air was always thick with it on the nights that she made it. He liked to close his eyes and imagine he was swimming in a sea of lentils and friendly sharks made of potato chunks.

He grabbed his pair of safety scissors from his pencil box, and pinched Barbie's hair between his index and middle fingers. He cut. He snipped. Until Barbie's blond pelos were scattered on the floor. "Don't worry, Barbie," he told her. "I'm not a monster. I just want us to match more. When my hair grows back, so will yours."

It only took a week for the little patch of hair to grow back on the back of Juanito's head. And then another week passed, and he would talk to Barbie and cry about the boys at school. How now it wasn't just Steven, but more of them. Then another week passed and he talked to Barbie and realized that her beautiful blond hair wasn't going to grow back. Not that week, not ever. What had he done, he thought, *I'm a monster.*

* * *

A month after Steven had snipped off a chunk of his hair, Juanito walked into the cocina and saw Mr. Jacobs standing in front of the nevera, talking to his mother. "Say hi to Mr. Jacobs, Juanito," his mother told him. He could tell by her tone that she wasn't happy.

He said hi to Mr. Jacobs and Mr. Jacobs said hi back. It was Juanito's worst nightmare. Surely Mr. Jacobs was there because the girls realized that Juanito had stolen their Barbie doll and had come to demand that Juanito give her back. But that couldn't happen, Juanito thought. The girls wouldn't want a half-bald Barbie doll, and then Juanito would be in trouble. Unless, of course, the girls could be tricked into believing that her hair had always been that way. Pero that was a risk. He didn't know how much the girls knew about hair. Besides, it didn't even matter because he was going to go to PR and his hair would grow back and it's not like things like that mattered in PR. Papi would be so cool, it wouldn't matter.

Juanito turned back and started walking toward his bedroom. "Where are you going so fast?" Mr. Jacobs asked him. He was smiling. "Where are you running to, Mr. Juanito?"

Juanito lied and said he forgot a cup in his bedroom. He went back into his room, shut the door, and locked it. He grabbed Barbie by the waist and shoved her back into the sweatpants drawer. There, he thought. Even if Mr. Jacobs came for her, he wouldn't know where to look.

When he walked back into the cocina, Juanito heard his mother say, "I can't believe you didn't have the decency to come while he was at school?"

"What do you want from me, Marisol?" Mr. Jacobs said. "Why does everything have to be hidden?"

His mother gestured at Juanito with her chin. Mr. Jacobs turned around.

"I wasn't hiding anything," Juanito said, "I just didn't have a cup in there. But I thought I did."

"Here, baby," his mother said. "Why don't you get Mommy a scratch lotto ticket from the bodega?" She glanced back at Mr. Jacobs.

"Yes, Juan," Mr. Jacobs said. "Here's five dollars. Get two tickets and a candy bar for yourself."

"Don't go into the bedroom," Juanito said. "You can only go into my bedroom when I'm home, okay?"

"That sounds fair to me," Mr. Jacobs said.

He didn't know how long it took him, probably about the length of one cartoon program and a half, but when Juanito came back home, Mr. Jacobs was gone and his mother was in the shower. He came back with two scratchy tickets and a Kit Kat and stood at the door of the bathroom with the candy in one hand and the tickets en la otra. The water stopped a minute later and he could hear his mother's feet stepping out of the tub. As the door opened, a nube of steam burst out into the hallway. His mother had one towel wrapped around her body, another wrapped around her pelo, balanced on top of her head.

At first, she didn't see him. She stood in the door and leaned against the side. She sniffled and wiped her eyes.

"Ma," Juanito said and she jumped. "Here are the tickets. What will we do with five whole thousand dollars?"

"Jesus, Juanito," she screamed. "Don't sneak around. I mean, don't sneak up on me. I didn't see you there."

She walked into her bedroom and shut the door before he could follow her. Before he could knock, she opened the door again. "Where did this come from?" she asked. "Did you put that there?"

"I'm sorry," he sobbed, "I thought it would grow back."

"¿Qué dices, m'ijo?" she said. "Grow what back? I just want to know where did that money come from?" She was pointing at the fifty-dollar bill that was on top of her bright red drawer.

Juanito shook his head and held out the lotto tickets in his hand. "Did we already win some money from the tickets?"

"I can't fucking believe that man," she said. "Does he think I'm some kind of whore?"

"A what?"

"Nothing, papi," she said, picking up the bill and giving it to Juanito. "Hold on to this while mommy gets dressed. We're going to the diner to get some eggs and hash browns."

"Are we going with Mr. Jacobs?" Juanito asked.

"No, Juanito," she said. "I'll be damned if we use this money for anything other than food."

*   *   *

Papi had to cancel that summer, and the next, and then the next. But then he called the apartment and spoke to his mother and it finally seemed like it was going to happen for real this time.

At first, Mami was all objections and no-no-no's. She said she didn't understand where Juanito's father had pulled the money from. "Surely he must've pulled it out of someone's ass," she said one night after dinner.

Juanito begged her, please, please, and then in Spanish, por favor, por favor. As if begging held different weight depending on the language.

Mami still said no, nunca. She called his father That Pendejo Desagracia'o. She said that he had bailed three summers in a row, after an entire childhood of bailing, and she was worried that the bastard was setting them both up for disappointment.

But then she got to talking to some of her girlfriends and her tune changed along the lines of: "Well, he's your father," and "Who am I to say no?" and "Me cago en la leche de la puta that gave birth to his sorry ass, but that man is your father and you should go meet him, but only if you want to."

* * *

Juanito wasn't thinking, really, when he decided to watch *Jaws* for the first time only a month before heading to PR. He'd watched it at a sleepover and now the thought of being in the middle of an island, surrounded by nothing but water, potentially shark-infested water, was enough to give him churra pains. He didn't want no tiburón feasting on his bony legs!

He packed enough clothes to last two months, even though he knew he was only going to be there for a month. He had waited so many summers for this! He wanted to make sure he had outfits for all kinds of occasions—and he didn't know what types of things Papi would want to do. There were so many possibilities: like did San Juan have a McDonald's? Were they planning on going swimming? Pool or beach? He'd need comfy shorts for treks through El Yunque. One towel or two? Maybe three? In order to fit everything into the maleta real good, he had to roll up his calzoncillos and socks and put them along the outer edges of all the bigger clothes. That way he could tuck Barbie in one of the side pockets.

He grabbed her by the waist and held her out in front of him. *Uf*—her hair was so messy, it was borderline sinful. She still had some strands left from the Haircut Incident, but things were looking a little patchy. He should've had the sense to shave her head bald and make the claim she was just being fashion forward.

He would do that when he came back home. There was no need in worrying about her hair before the vacation. It's not like he was actually going to *show* his father that he had a doll. Absolutely not. He just wanted her to be there, tucked away as a safety precaution. Barbie was a good luck charm, a listener, and most of all, a secret.

* * *

In the fotos that Juanito had seen of his father, the man was always holding his mother around the shoulder. His mother looked so crazy happy, as if her smiles were caused by a never-ending surge of electricity and the plug was somewhere outside of the picture's view. His father was smiling también. Even though Papi didn't show teeth in any of the fotos, his thick moustache seemed to widen out and take up more of his face when he was smiling.

In Juanito's favorite foto, Papi is looking buff as anything on the Wildwood boardwalk. The Ferris wheel is in the background with its glitter lights and the sun is in the pink phase of setting. Mami is in a bikini looking like Miss Teen Taina Boricua 1968 with her big gold hoops and Papi is wearing a tight white T-shirt and red short-shorts showing off his hairy legs.

"Ay, carajo," Mami had once said when she fumbled on that foto. She told him that she didn't even remember the day it was taken. "If I didn't see it before my very eyes," she said, "I wouldn't even believe it happened. I must be losing my ever-living mind."

Nah, Juanito thought, sitting next to her as she went through the shoe box that held all the fotos, he couldn't believe what she said. He didn't understand how a person could just forget something like that, like, without even trying.

*   *   *

It was the first week of July and thank god the plane had thingies that blew air conditioning on his body. He was nervous the entire plane ride over, even though the nice stewardess with blond hair and red lipstick made sure he was comfy. She gave him so many bags of peanuts, he had to drink three entire bottles of water. He had a window seat and his stomach turned and tumbled as he looked out over the water, wiping the salt from the peanuts onto the sides of his shorts.

Once he got his maleta from the claim, he walked to Arrivals and looked for a sign with his name on it. In theory, he would be able to recognize the man behind the sign as his own father, but Juanito had never met him before and how was he supposed to recognize a person, even if they shared blood, if they had never met? There was a part of him that thought maybe, just maybe, there would be some kind of click-connection when they were face-to-face. Pero when he looked up, searching, he didn't see his name on any signs. He didn't see any men he knew. There was no click-connection tampoco.

A beautiful man who was probably old enough to drink but not old enough to be his father came up to him and spoke to him in a quick rush of Spanish. It was so fast that all the *r*'s became *d*'s and the ends of his words were eaten up. Juanito couldn't understand a word, so he just looked at the man's face with a look that was surely dumbfounded.

"English?" the beautiful man said. His eyes were the color of creamy espresso. He had a mole on his right cheek. "You only English? Me, no."

"I'm sorry," Juanito said, holding his arms up slowly in a shrug. He could get by on some Spanglish, but there was no way he could keep up an entire fluent conversation with someone speaking so fast.

He stood there alone, watching men and women and families buzz past him, some speaking English, most speaking Spanish. A little girl with pigtails and a yellow sundress was holding on to her father's hand. She was skipping, but getting ahead of herself because her father was walking too slow. Her arm was tugging at his, like come on, slowpoke. He crouched down and tugged on her pigtail and whispered something that made her giggle.

When Juanito watched the girl and her father walk out the door, he felt a loneliness creep up inside him. He looked around for another family for his eyes to hold on to, but no one caught his attention. He was all by himself and the idea finally hit him. He had no idea what he would do if his father didn't come to get him. He had his return ticket dated one month from now, but he didn't know where he would go.

He heard someone call his name behind him and he turned. There he was, his father. He looked skinnier now than in those

Wildwood fotos. His moustache was pencil-thin above his upper lip. A cigarette dangled on the tip of his lips, as if one sudden move could make it fall to the ground and leave a burn mark.

"That's you, verdad?" Papi said, reaching for Juanito's maleta. "Coño, you got your mother's face, I can't believe it. Spitting images, I tell you."

There he finally was, standing next to Juanito, after all those years. Juanito wanted to jump up and down, but he didn't want to seem like some baby who couldn't control his excitement. He also didn't want to yell at Papi for being a little late. None of that mattered anymore. Juanito was in Puerto Rico and it was going to be a good month.

"Damn, what'd you put in this thing?" Papi said, taking the maleta. "It's so heavy. How'd you carry that around with you everywhere?"

Juanito shrugged.

"My man," Papi said, play-punching the side of Juanito's arm. "You must got crazy strength in those arms. ¡Tan fuerte! Maybe you could be a ball player one day, my little Mickey Mantle or some shit."

"It was nothing," Juanito said, blushing. "Really."

* * *

The house was a cement cube painted pastel blue. There were bars on all the windows that Papi said kept out the people with sticky fingers. Papi had a plastic recliner chair on the back porch, but when Juanito went to adjust the back, it was too rusted to open further. So Juanito sat inside, in front of the fan in the sala that blew the warm air around, and took a nap.

The next morning, Papi told him to unpack his swim trunks because they were going to a surprise place, but then once they were in the car for ten minutes or so, they were lost and driving in circles.

"Do you know where we're going?" Juanito said.

"You know what my father always used to say," Papi said, looking over his left shoulder to make sure no other car was coming so he could turn right. "He used to say that patience is a virtue."

A few minutes later, they were at the same intersection again, with Papi looking over his left shoulder to make sure they were in the clear for the turn.

"Pa," Juanito said, trying to sound nice and not like a giant nag. "We were just here. You sure we know where we're going?"

"Ya, sin duda, I know," Papi snapped. Then, "I didn't mean to yell and shit. But if you ask me the same questions over and over again, you're gonna get me angry and I'm gonna yell."

Papi pulled over and asked a woman for directions. She told them to get on the highway until he saw the mountain, but not the first mountain, because that wasn't a mountain, it was just a hill, but then the second mountain, that was a *mountain,* couldn't miss it. Take the exit after that mountain, then make a right at the Texaco station and then it was only a few minutes more from there.

Dang, Juanito thought, where in god's word were they going to end up?

*　*　*

He had to give it to her—the woman was right about the mountain. It was very clear, once they were up front and driving, that *that* was the mountain. But the Texaco station? Wrong. It was an Esso station, and they were supposed to make a left, not a right.

"You ready to go swimming?" Papi asked when they finally made it. He perked up in the driver's seat so he could scan for a parking spot.

"I'm ready to sit on a towel and soak up the sun," Juanito said.

"Yeah?" Papi said. "But I got this reservation thing, on a boat, no te preocupes, I got it paid for, my man. Cut my cigar habit a little, bought some cheaper vodka to pay for it, so you don't gotta put anything in."

Juanito didn't understand how he'd be able to put something in, even if he wanted to, without some kind of allowance. Which he didn't have.

"But, Papi—"

"What? You don't know how to swim?" Papi asked. "Your mother didn't get you lessons at the Y?"

"It's not that," Juanito said.

"You're right, you're right, they got ese, ese salvavidas, what's that in English?"

"Life vests?"

"Yeah, the swimmy things. Eso," Papi said.

Juanito wanted to throw a tantrum, but he knew that wouldn't work. He still had an entire month living with Papi in the campo. He didn't want to ruin nothing by refusing the tickets, or refusing to swim, or even worse—looking like a sissy if he told the truth about his fear of boy-eating sharks. And, dang, Papi had paid for those tickets too. He had to go in.

They shared the boat with two couples. The first were newly-weds. He knew this because they announced it to everyone as soon as they stepped foot on the boat. At any given moment, they were either sucking face or holding hands or, in some way, attaching their bodies to each other. The other pareja were middle age. "They," the middle-aged woman said to her husband, eyeing the honeymooners during a heavy make-out session, "certainly look like they're having a good time."

"Hush," the man said, "they will hear you."

Juanito watched as the woman perfected her side-glare eyebrow freeze. "Do I honestly," the woman whispered, but still loud enough for Juanito to hear, "look like I give a single, solitary fuck if they hear me?"

Who was this woman, Juanito thought, and how could he become friends with her? He wanted to grow up to be like her, or if not that, he wanted to grow up and be surrounded by women just like her.

"Can you please, please, please not," the man said.

Juanito stared at them and they saw him. The man squeezed his face into a painful smile and the woman said, "Isn't he just adorable? ¿Hablas inglés, niño?" she asked, louder now, as if she were talking to a deaf-mute.

Juanito said yes.

"Mmm," the woman said, taking a sip of her lemonade with a straw. "Yes, this is just so nice. The views, the water. Lovely."

"Yes," the man said. "Just lovely. The views are something else."

* * *

He thought he knew what it must feel like to drown, not because he'd ever drowned in real life, but because it had happened in dreams. He called them the quicksand dreams, called them this to no one in particular other than himself. In these dreams, he walked in a forest and then the ground beneath him would turn to quicksand and he slowly sank down into it, knowing that soon he wouldn't be able to breathe. Then he'd actually go under and hold his breath until he couldn't take it anymore, gasping for air as he jolted awake.

It was always like this and there was nothing he could do to stop it. Whenever the dream started and he was in that familiar jungle, he knew exactly how it would play out, and his body would lay tense in bed until it was over.

* * *

"You're not coming in?" Juanito asked, holding his life vest like the restraints on an upside-down rollercoaster. He bobbed up and down with the olas in the water.

"Dame un momento," Papi said. All the others had come in: the newlyweds, the older couple, the captain. "I'm just working on my thirst."

The water was warmer than he expected. It almost felt like a bath, which wasn't like any other playa he ever experienced before. Certainly not like Jones Beach. He could actually *see* his toes in these waters. He looked back toward the land, at the food stands that dotted the sand. Instead of hot dog stands like at Coney Island, there were little setups selling pastelitos in napkins so soaked in grease, they looked yellow and damp. They even had piraguas in white paper cones.

Half an hour in, Juanito was dolphin-kicking like a real-life merboy. He splashed the water in the air so that the droplets looked like glitter hitting the sun rays. He did this thing where he pointed out his toes as much as he could, like a ballerina floating in the water. He swam on his back. He swam the breaststroke. He even swam on his side. But then, when he was treading water and moving his arms like he was making a snow angel, he was pretty sure he felt a bump on his toe.

It was his worst fear come to life. It was a shark—it *had* to be. What else could it be in those waters? It was a shark and it had come to devour him alive.

"Jaws," he screamed. "Tiburón, tiburón, help." Pero he had swam out too far from the boat for anyone to hear him. He switched from Spanish to English faster than a dice man in the South Bronx. "Help me, ayúdame, por favor, help."

He flailed about so much that he started to go down a few inches. He flailed some more and then he was starting to go under. Water was in his mouth. He could feel the saltiness burn the back of his throat.

He pretended he was the strongest merman known to the sea and he kicked and swam back to the boat where Papi was asleep with a Coronita bottle cradled against his chest. Juanito screamed at Papi to help him back up.

Papi startle-jumped awake and the bottle fell in the water. He reached out an arm and with that, Juanito was back up on the boat. He lay sprawled at Papi's feet, all dramatic, like an actor playing dead in a crime movie when the police are putting the yellow tape around the cuerpo. "Where were you all this time?" he said. "I almost died out there."

"What in sense're you talking about?" Papi said.

"I was being attacked by a shark and you didn't do nothing to come get me," Juanito said. "You stupid pendejo desgraciado."

Papi slapped him. "No digas eso," Papi said. "You speak to me like that again and I'll beat you into tomorrow and yesterday at the same time."

* * *

Two mornings later, Juanito put the espresso pot on the stove and was waiting for the gurgle-sigh to let him know when to turn down the heat. Papi was showing him how to make it the way he liked it. Papi showed him where the coffee grinds were and how to carefully spoon them into the pot, pack them in, then twist it shut so that no steam could get out.

"You wanna trap the air in," Papi said, "or else the liquid flies everywhere and shit."

His instructions were clear: in order to drink coffee like a man, it needed to be strong and black, sin azúcar.

"Hey," Papi said, slapping Juanito's hand as he scooped the coffee dust into the chamber and packed it down with the back of the spoon. "What'd I say about that pinky?"

"I'm sorry," Juanito said.

"No," Papi said. "What'd I say about that pinky?"

"You said to keep the pinky down," Juanito said. "I'm sorry."

"Coffee gotta have strong hands, sabes?" Papi said. "Nothing in a hand being delicada o algo así, nothing with a pinky up, coño."

Juanito let the spoon back down on the counter and watched the pot on the stove. In two minutes, the water would boil and bubble up into the pot. Then he would pour it into Papi's mug. No sugar.

"Shit," Papi said, under his breath, "don't need no fuckin' princesas up in here, ya tú sabes." He took a sip of his glass of OJ, clicked his tongue, and opened the cabinet under the sink to grab a big plastic bottle of vodka. He added a splash more into the OJ.

"What do you think my boys at the shop'll think if they saw my flesh and blood scooping grinds out así, con la mano así?"

It didn't sound like a question that Papi wanted answered in the moment, so Juanito didn't say anything.

He practiced for every morning, preparing espresso for Papi just the way he wanted it. A week passed and he felt like he was starting to master it. Or at least he was trying to make sure that he didn't mess it up. Porque if he messed up, even if it was just once, he was afraid that Papi would get tired of him, send him back, scream THIS IS THE LAST STRAW ON THE COÑO'S BACK, and never want to see him again. It was simple, really. He just wanted Papi to love him.

So after a week of practicing, he wanted to surprise Papi with an afternoon cup of coffee. Like a wake-me-up refresher for when Papi got up from his midday nap, smelling like the thick-smoke cigars he smoked. He focused hard on the pinky, how to summon the energy to keep it down. Whenever he washed his hands under the faucet, he clenched and unclenched his hands, thinking that if biceps curls could make an arm bigger, hand clenches could make the hands stronger. And stronger would be manlier. And manlier would be better.

The flame was steady under the pot, and now the espresso was gurgling. Juanito switched the heat off and grabbed the pot handle, careful to pour two cups without making a mess. He could hear Papi's chanclas dragging on the floor in the hallway. He liked to imagine it was like the cartoons, where the curlicue was a squiggle of steam that latched on to the character's nose and reeled him into the cocina.

Juanito grabbed the mugs and rushed them to the table. He set them down before the heat burned his palms. He never understood why he didn't grab the handles. That's what handles were there for—for grabbing on to—but he never did because he liked the burn. He liked to see how long he could hold on before he couldn't hold on no more.

He sat down as Papi's footsteps got closer. He added a spoonful of sugar and cream to his own mug before Papi could see him do it.

"You prissy little bitch," Papi said, standing in the doorway.

"No," Juanito said. "It was just one spoonful of sugar. Just to make it less amargo, less, less—"

"What is this bullshit?" Papi said and in his thick hand, Juanito saw Barbie in all her balding glory.

He was caught and he knew there was no way around it. There wasn't no lie in the entire book of lies that could save him now, so he did what his gut and his heart were both telling him to do: defend.

"She's not bullshit," he said, reaching out a loving hand to take her. Once he said it, he knew he couldn't take it back. "I brought her with me 'cause she's like a good luck charm and I was worried about the plane ride."

"Ave María," Papi said, over and over again, like he couldn't believe it. "What're people gonna think?"

"I was nervous," Juanito said, careful to hold back his tears because he knew that crying in front of Papi, especially now, would make him seem even more like some maricón-bitch.

"The fuck happened to her head, con ese, ese—her scalp," Papi said.

Juanito didn't say anything. He didn't know how to say everything that needed to be said. He didn't know how to explain to Papi that he had shaved her head in a misguided act of solidarity, or that it was a boy at school who had snipped off a piece of Juanito's hair in the first place, and that deep down, he was getting this feeling that he was different from all the other boys, softer, gentler, and that this was not seen as a good thing. He didn't know what to say, so he didn't say anything and when Papi stared back at him and shook his head like, are you deaf too, Juanito said he was sorry.

"You're sorry?" Papi said. "Dime: did that fucking bitch give you this shit?" Even though he didn't refer to her by name, Juanito knew that he was talking about his mother. There was no one else it could be. She was the only person they both had in common.

Juanito said no.

"What do you mean no?" Papi said. "She trying to turn my son into some maricón cocksucker? She think that's good revenge on me, huh?"

Juanito wanted to crawl under the table so he didn't have to look at his papi as he yelled. He looked at the two empty chairs, waiting to be sat in. He looked at the cups of espresso, getting cold. "I'm sorry," he said.

"Enough with the sorry," Papi yelled. "Sorry this, sorry that." He punched him in the face and Juanito fell back and onto the floor. He watched as Papi lifted the garbage can lid and threw Barbie inside. He couldn't hold his tears in anymore, and all he could sob was, "No, don't do that to her, please."

"You tell her that I never got nothing done to me," Papi said. "I was always on top, always the man."

Juanito crawled over to the basura to try to grab Barbie back out, but Papi put his foot on top of the lid.

"I'm not ready," Juanito said, "to throw her away like that. I know her hair is a little busted but she's my favorite thing in the whole wide world. Por favor."

Papi didn't move and Juanito was tired of begging. He wanted to say something mean. He wanted to hurt him.

"You shouldn't've gone through my maleta," Juanito said. "You're a sorry excuse for a father."

Papi grabbed him by his hair and dragged him like that to the sofa. Juanito lay there, too scared to move, too scared to even listen to his own breathing. Papi took off his belt, pulled down Juanito's pants, and whipped him, saying, "If you wanna act like some maricón, then act like one, pero you know I gotta beat some sense into you to make you a man," and he whipped him and lashed him until the skin on his culo opened and he bled.

VENUS

Every Friday during the early afternoons, Venus and Angel went somewhere in the city all dressed up to the nines-tens-elevens. Each week they picked a different place in order to keep things new and fresh. They even called themselves the Ladies Who Lunch, and girl, lunch they did. This week was Angel's choice and Venus found her little self sitting across from homegirl at Lindy's in Midtown. Angel used the side of her fork to slice into a chunk of strawberry cheesecake.

"I am salivating so hard over this," Angel talked through a glob of cheesecake, "it's not even funny. If only cheesecake weren't so fattening, I'd eat it every day."

"Gross," Venus said. She sipped on her lemon water.

Angel put her fork down and stared at Venus. "What do you mean gross?" Angel said.

"I mean that cheesecake is gross," Venus said. "It's too thick, I don't know."

"What can I say?" Angel said, bringing the fork to her mouth and only taking a small nibble of the cheesecake on the edge of it. "I like my men like I like my cheesecake: thick, creamy, and covered in strawberry sauce." She threw her head back to let out what sounded like half laugh, half snort.

Venus rolled her eyes. Angel always had the audacity to compare the men she liked to pieces of food. "Of all the foods," Venus said, "you're gonna pick this shit?"

"Excuse me," Angel said. She dabbed the napkin at her mouth. "Ladies Who Lunch don't speak so mal hablada, with shit-this and gross-that. Use your words. Use your mouth."

"Oh, I'll use my mouth alright," Venus said, "on that fine-ass waiter over there. Did you see that bulge?"

"Mmm girl," Angel said with another glob of cheesecake in her mouth, "did I ever? Like a marble sculpture coming to life. Makes me dream of a restaurant-themed porno with us as the three estrellas."

They cackled together.

"I wish," Venus said.

"Ahh, my porn name would be Feliz Taylor," Angel said. "What do you think?"

"You're not gonna believe this," Venus said, "but my grand-mother used to dress me up as Elizabeth Taylor, back when I was a youth."

Angel scream-laughed, saying, "Stop-stop-stop, you're killing me."

"Yes, I know. I wish I still had the photographs to prove it," Venus said, yawning. "Don't get too excited though. I think your delicious meal of a man is straight."

"Ay, nena," Angel said. "They always are, right? One of the biggest shames in the whole world—so much for the eyes to see, but so little we can touch."

* * *

An hour later, when Angel asked for the check, Venus could see that she made a point to linger her eyes on the waiter's bulge. Angel stared so long at it before handing over the bills in her hand, that the waiter looked down to see if he had a stain or something wrong on his pants. "No, no," Angel said. "Nothing's wrong. Everything about it is so right."

"We're just admiring, honey," Venus said. "Must be hard carrying that bad boy around with you everywhere." The man blushed and laughed. "You must be new to the city, huh?"

"How'd you know?" the waiter asked, making eyes with Venus. She took in his blue eyes and thought, *Damn, that is a face made for the movie screens.*

"We're brujas," Angel said. "You speak Spanish? Where you coming here from?"

"Iowa," he said. He fidgeted with the pen in his hand until the cap fell down and he had to bend over to pick it up.

"Oh, girl," Venus said. "I don't even know where that is, but sounds exotic. Eye-oh-wah." She played with the vowels on her lips.

"Excuse my friend over here," Angel said, shifting in her seat to face the waiter. "She can read a man, but she can't read a map." Angel winked at her and Venus play-huffed. "I know Iowa. Don't even get me started on corn, darling. It's my absolute favorite vegetable."

Venus laughed and finished the rest of her water, letting an ice cube glide onto her tongue so she could feel it slowly melt. "Corn?" Venus said. "Be honest, mama. You only like corn because it feels good to hold a thick cob in those delicate hands."

The waiter boy looked like he was watching a truck explode in slow motion. As if he didn't know how to stop watching. "Don't mind us, darling," Angel said. "I came for some cheesecake. I was just hungry."

"She gets cravings every now and then," Venus said. "For cheese-cake, imagine!"

He looked like he wanted to bounce back to the kitchen, but that was what made this game so fun. She got to rile them up and then see them figure out how to peel themselves away.

"And this one over here," Angel said, pointing a limp finger at Venus, "didn't have any cheesecake today. You could just imagine how starved she is."

"I'm so hungry for a good, meaty man," she said, playing her ace card and revealing the whole point of the game, "that someone needs to alert Sally Struthers to my cause."

"Uh," he said. "Excuse me, but I need to get back to—serving."

He spun around and walked to the table across the way, to two men in business suits and Angel said under her breath, "Well he could serve me any day."

She and Angel played this game every week and whoever could make the straight boy blush first won all the points. Venus always liked to win, but she had to admit that this time, Angel had got the best of the situation.

"Maybe he wasn't straight," Angel said. Venus could hear the sound of hope in that tone.

"I wouldn't bet on it," Venus said.

"Hush, nena," Angel said. "Don't break your mother's heart."

They walked from Times Square to Fifth with struts so fierce, it was a hot shame that Donna Summer wasn't there to give them theme music. "Bad girls, uh uh, talkin' 'bout those sad girls, uh uh."

Angel led her into Saks and told her there was someone she wanted to introduce to Venus.

Now Venus got all excited, thinking that she was gonna meet somebody new. But once they got upstairs, Angel led her this way and that and pointed to a rack of Chanel suits. "Allow me to introduce you," Angel said. "Isn't she just a marvel?"

The suit was still hanging on the rack as Angel held it by the sleeves, like she was holding out its hands and asking it to get on the dance floor from off the sidelines.

It was a beautiful Chanel. How crazy she had been to think she was about to meet a new person on the floor and in the middle of racks of the softest cashmere and silk.

"I think that when I buy her," Angel said, "I'm going to name her CoCo. Doesn't that sound smooth?"

Venus was doing cartwheels in her mind just thinking about Angel strutting down the street in a Chanel suit. It was black-and-white herringbone, and the buttons looked like they were so sewn into place, they'd never pop off. Venus took the hanger off the rack and put the suit up to Angel's chest. Angel put her hands on her hips and gave a sharp turn to her head.

"Give me a straight-up *Vogue* shot," Venus said. "Cover girl, yes, cover girl, pose for me, lady."

Then Venus saw the price tag dangling near the neckline. Angel must've seen Venus's eyes pop when the price registered in her mind.

"I know, I know," Angel said. She covered her eyes like a little girl about to play peekaboo. "Don't remind me of the numbers. I already know."

"Whoa, girl," Venus said. "Now that's a pretty price to pay if there ever was one."

"It's gonna take some time for me to save up," Angel said. "Maybe ten months if I do it proper. Pero I think I can do it."

"That's right, mama," Venus said. "You got this. And what a dazzle you will be."

"It's gonna fit like a glove right over my heart," Angel said. "I can just feel it."

Venus hummed and put Ms. CoCo back on the rack. "Do they even do layaway here?"

Angel said her plan was to just save up and get whichever style was most classic when she had enough saved to buy one. "I don't know if I ever told you this," Angel said, "but back when I first met Hector, he took me here."

No, Venus thought, *I haven't heard this story.*

"And I tried on this beautiful black-and-white herringbone suit," Angel said. "I swear on all the shoes in the world that I was giving off some Princess Diana realness."

Venus squealed and clapped her hands.

"I fell in love that day," she said. "I knew that one day, I would return to get my Chanel," Angel said, sighing. "I miss Hector real hard, nena. That man was my true love."

"Yes, mama," Venus said. "I totally feel you. And the only way to keep him around is to remember him. You know, to keep him with you always."

"I do," Angel said, reaching out her fingers to the shoulder of the suit, then gliding them down the sleeve. "I really do."

"I know you do," Venus said, grabbing hold of the other sleeve. "Men come and go, I always say that. Maybe love is shorter than it should be, but hot diggity damn, Chanel is fuckin' forever."

* * *

If guilt were something that weighed an ounce, she'd have so much of it that she'd be running marathons to shed the extra pounds. Venus and Angel had always been tight. Like, wasn't that their thing? They could go through the thick and thin, call themselves the Ladies Who Lunch, and tease the straight boys who were so clearly from other places, so clearly so new to New York that they were too polite to talk back to the two sassy Latin boys in drag pumping up the sass machine right in front of their very eyes. Yes, girlfriend, that was their *thing*.

Angel had told Venus all her secrets, but Venus felt like she hadn't returned the favor. That day, as they left Saks, Angel told Venus about the Bloomingdale's Model Search. Had even invited Venus to join her, saying, "Come on, nena. Let's show them how a real woman can look on a magazine page. Come with?"

But Venus said no. Not because she didn't want to see her face taped up on a billboard or tucked somewhere in between the perfume ads of *Vogue*, but because she didn't want to compete against her own house mother. She totally believed that Angel deserved more of the attention than she did anyway.

When they left Saks for the afternoon and walked up to the southeast corner of Central Park near the Plaza and the Paris and the horses with carriages, Angel bought them both hot dogs with a mound of sauerkraut on top. They sat on the benches on the outer rim of Central Park so their feet could stop pounding.

"For you, darling," Angel said, handing Venus one of the hot dogs. "Just don't have too much fun with it. It's meant for eating, you know."

Venus rolled her eyes. "And why do you think I'm always about to do something sexy-nasty all the time?"

"Porque you *do*," Angel said. She took her first bite and dabbed her mouth with the napkin. "You're the dictionary definition of unpredictable."

Venus moved her neck back so her hair could move itself out of her face. "Dictionary?" she said, eyes wide. "Oh no, don't you read me, mami. We don't even own a dictionary, so there."

"That's 'cause I don't need one to know how to read a girl like you," Angel said.

Venus laughed and took a bite of her hot dog. After she swallowed, she said, "I know you're playing, but hush it down before you hurt my feelings."

Angel had finished her hot dog by now. The damn girl could inhale her food quicker than a city rat could in its fastest dreams. "I wanna know about this man you're seeing," Angel said.

"What man?" Venus said. "You know I been seeing a few down at the piers."

"No," Angel said. "You know what I mean, nena. That man you're seeing, dímelo todo."

Venus sighed. She knew Angel was referring to the Staten Island man, and she wondered how she had gotten word. "And how," Venus said, "did you find out?"

"I got eyes on the back of my head and all around the corners of this city," Angel said, but Venus could call her bluff. Angel may know a lot more than appears to her own beautiful eyes, but Venus knew that this game was a game of postures. Angel didn't know that much, but she needed to pretend to in order to find out more.

"He got me tickets to see *Cats: The Musical* and then we had sex in a hotel room," Venus said. "And that's it, I swear on Saint Fendi and Saint Laurent, and that's all I wanna talk about."

"*Cats*?" Angel said. "Who the fuck is about to see life-size cat-people doing a jig on stage, spinning on garbage cans?"

"That's what *I* said," Venus screamed. They both threw their hands high and laughed. "See, our minds are on the same wavelength."

Angel gave her a double air-kiss. "Pero don't you make me worry about you, Venus," she said, "porque I don't like to worry and I know you're unpredictable as all fuck. Excuse my French, but I worry. I do worry about you, boo-boo."

* * *

Venus worried about Angel too. It wasn't like that street was one-way. She worried that Angel would never find a new love, or even some other kind of almost-love that a girl could use to move on and see life afresh. Maybe Venus was hiding this whole Staten Island situation from Angel because she knew she had broken the rules—at least two rules, if she had to think about it—but it was deeper than that. Venus didn't know how to talk to Angel about her affection for men anymore because she was afraid of hurting Angel. She didn't want to talk about a topic that she knew was slowly eating away at Angel. Angel pined for Hector, that much was apparent to everyone. Who could blame the girl? Hector was a suave-ass chulo whose death was enough to make even the hardest and coldest of queens cry. Not that Angel was hard or cold, but Venus knew that Angel's heart was too warm, too open, and too sensitive to move past Hector. Forever, maybe. And it's for that reason that Venus couldn't tell Angel about the men from the streets she was feeling the hots and colds for. She couldn't bear to see that look in Angel's eyes—the one that pretended strength when, really, she wanted to collapse.

* * *

Charles had promised her many things. A semiprivate gym membership where she could watch him lifting weights and then venture into the sauna to sweat out whatever she wanted to sweat out. An in-ground swimming pool in his backyard, which she had never stuck a toe in, but she still liked the idea of it being there whenever she wanted to make use of it. Access to all the food in the fridge, especially the kiwis and cantaloupe and thin strips of beef brisket, all foods that seemed so exotic because they were never foods she could find at home. She spent two days out of the week there now. As she took off her shoes to let her toes glide against the pearly off-white shag rug, she couldn't help but think that she was finally living the daydream she had always set for herself, the one where she was a princess sharing a suburban castle with her man.

But of course, this all came at a price. What he was able to give her with his money, she would have to give him with her body. She had no control over when he would want it, or where. It didn't bother her because she always argued that shit like this didn't make a woman into a whore, like people said. She always distrusted when society tried to tell her how she should feel. Because wasn't it a double standard piece of bullshit that pretty young women could marry rich dudes and get these same luxuries? So where was the difference, she wanted to know.

The nice days were when they both wanted to fuck at the same time. She could lean back and run her fingers through the patch of hairs on his chest, growing out of his heart. But then there were the not-nice days, when she just wasn't in the mood, or she was sore from the time before, but she still took him because she feared she couldn't say no. If she said no, she thought he would just go back on the streets and find someone else who would say yes.

Just a week after her Saks venture with Angel, he had promised her a picnic with a strawberry dessert at the end. They were there, the strawberries were there, even the blanket was spread out on the grass in the backyard, but then his pager went off. Venus could already tell from the frown that something was up.

"I'm so, so sorry," he told her as he zipped his pants and tightened his leather-braided belt. "I need to get this testimony. From a client's witness. For a case. And fuck," he said. "I'll be back as soon as possible. I'll practically fly through traffic to get back to you."

She spent the two hours sprawled on the sofa downstairs eating purple and green grapes, filling the time with episodes of *Guiding Light* and *The Price Is Right*. She wished Angel were with her, sitting on that couch, so they could talk shit about the man who had been offered the showcase full of dining room furniture, when she could really tell he wanted the lavish getaway to Paris. Or she wished Juanito were there, feeding his sewing machine with the gobble-gobble sound filling the quiet room. Or Daniel, whose energy always felt calming and assured, even when she pinched his biceps and squealed in glee. She'd ask them all the important question of the hour: "Ladies," she imagined herself saying, "how the hell is it possible for a microphone like the one that Bob Barker is holding to be so fuckin' pencil-thin, but then *I* gotta watch my meals to keep my figure?"

* * *

She was taking a little disco nap in a pair of Charles's roomy sweatpants and an XL white T-shirt. When the front door slammed, she startled awake. On the TV, *General Hospital* was running. She dragged her feet to the kitchen to wash the bowl of strawberries so they could cut them up and go outside to have their picnic date.

When she turned on the sink water, she heard a pile of papers fall to the ground behind her. Venus spun around and saw a woman standing in the doorway that connected the dining room to the cocina. "Oh, Jesus Lord and Mary," the woman said. She was wearing a work-suit combo: khaki-colored blazer and matching skirt paired with navy tights that made Venus want to say, No, honey.

Venus grabbed the short knife from the counter. She had planned to chop up the strawberries with it, but now she was going to handle the situation in front of her. "What the fuck are you doing in my house?" Venus said.

"*Your* house?" the woman said.

Venus held the knife out in front of her and this woman looked at it, rolled her eyes, and leaned down to grab the last of the fallen papers. In any other situation, Venus would've complimented her on the fabulous shade of red on her nails, but this woman was creeping up on her territory, so there would be no room or time for compliments.

"Oh Jesus, Charles," the woman said, rolling her eyes. "I see he hasn't learned a thing."

"Excuse you, he has learned many things," Venus said. "But it would not be proper to discuss the formalities of such learned things with you, so excuse me, bitch, can you kindly walk your khaki skirt and navy tight combo out of this goddamn kitchen before I find the strength to slash you for trespassing."

The woman laughed. "Trespassing? Oh, give me a break," she said. "God, this is so fucked I don't even know whether to laugh or cry. Un-be-lie-va-ble." She walked over to the phone and dialed a number. "Hi—yes hi, this is Linda," she spoke into the receiver. "Could you please tell Charles to get home, it's urgent—no, it's absolutely urgent. Okay, wonderful, thank you."

Venus put the knife down and turned the water off.

"Put down the knife," Linda said.

"I'm not even holding it?"

"We'll get this whole mess sorted out once Charles gets back." She walked over to the sink and grabbed a strawberry by the grassy stem area. Venus wasn't wearing her heels, so when Linda stood next to her near the sink, Linda had a few inches on her. Venus looked up at Linda's gaze.

"God," Linda said. Venus was so close, she could see the globs of mascara at the tips of Linda's short eyelashes. "Do I even want to know how old you are?" she asked. She bit into the strawberry. "No, don't tell me," Linda said. "I don't want to know."

Venus had no idea what the fuck was going on and she was feeling a whirlwind of feelings. They stood on either side of the kitchen's island in total silence, staring at each other as if they could both use laser beams to turn the other into a puddle of ashes.

"So," Venus said, "you come prancing all up in here and you're still not going to introduce your rude ass to me."

"Oh, hello, my name is Linda," she said, overly chipper. "That's L-i-n-d-a. Did Charles ever mention Linda to you before? Does the name Linda ring a bell?"

Venus traced the fronts of her teeth with her tongue. She shook her head, like, obviously he hadn't. She hadn't asked for a serving of sarcasm.

"No? Of course not. How about the word *ex-wife*, does that ring a bell?" Linda said. "Soon-to-be, I should clarify. We still have to sign on the dotted line."

"How was I supposed to know?" Venus said. Her first instinct was to say sorry, but then she figured fuck it. She wasn't at fault, so she wasn't going to apologize for something that wasn't her doing.

"You let him fuck you?" Linda said. "No, wait. I don't even want to know." She walked past Venus to the living room. She rummaged through her purse, then patted the pockets of her blazer. She asked if Venus had seen her cigarettes.

"Yeah, I let him fuck me," Venus said. "And no, I didn't see your ciggies."

"You better be using prophylactics," Linda said.

"The fuck does that mean?"

"Condoms," Linda said. "Rubbers. I watch the news. I see what's happening."

"Fuck you," Venus said. "I don't got the virus."

They had been using condoms, most of the time, but that wasn't any of Linda's business so she could back that truck up. Venus turned around and grabbed the strawberries by the handful and laid them on the counter. She wondered when was the last time Linda and Charles had fucked. She wondered if Linda were the type of woman to use the phrase *make love*.

Venus took the largest butcher knife in the wooden knife block and started slicing them like she was trying to slice a finger off a body.

"Careful, bitch," Linda said, "you will scratch the counter that way."

Venus grabbed the knife with both hands like it was an ax. She sliced the strawberries into the tiniest pieces she could do. Cut in half, then half again, then half again. Until all the little halves and their seeds were swimming on top of their own red juice.

"Oh, who the hell am I kidding?" Linda said. "He's keeping the house, so you could take a machete to the walls and I'd stand here next to you and offer a hand."

Who the fuck did this Linda woman think she was, coming into this house and being so sassy with her? Venus couldn't tell if they were on the same team or not. She couldn't tell who it was that should be blamed. If Linda wasn't the ex-wife, Venus probably would've taken to her. When the front door opened and slammed shut, both their heads turned toward the front of the house.

Linda spotted her box of Virginias on the kitchen counter near the microwave. She lit a long, slim cigarette and stood at the edge of the living room, where the off-white carpet met the off-white kitchen tile.

Venus turned around with the butcher knife in her hand. A little half-half of a strawberry slid down the edge of the blade, onto the floor. The kitchen counter had knife marks that looked like she was keeping tally.

Charles appeared in the hallway right in the middle of them. "Oh god," he said when he saw them both. "This was not supposed to happen."

Linda dragged on her slim cigarette and gave him a look like, No shit, Sherlock. She crossed her nonsmoking arm across her chest and scrunched her face into a sarcastic smile. "Not like it's the first time," she said, then exhaled the rest of the smoke she had been keeping in. "You just can't keep it in your pants, can you, you piece of shit?"

"Could you please not smoke in the house?" Charles said. "You know I don't like it when people smoke in the house."

"Are you fucking kidding me, you selfish son-of-a-bitch bastard," Linda said, and god, did Venus want to put that knife down and clap her hands. Maybe they could tag team and take him down together.

"No, Linda," he said, "I'm not fucking kidding you. I don't like cigarette smoke—"

"And I don't like it when you bring low-class whores into our house," Linda said. "Because until we sign those papers, this house is still partly mine."

"Hey now, bitch," Venus said. It felt like everyone was turning on everyone now. There was no way she'd take a liking to this bitch now. "Who're you calling low-class?"

Linda shot a look at Venus, then at Charles. "Really, Charles? Really?"

Charles shook his head and looked down at the tile. "I'm so sorry that this happened," he said, "to the both of you."

"If you're going to waste the money," Linda said, "you couldn't even get a nice-looking one?"

Venus slammed the knife in the sink. Who did this bitch think she was? "Bitch," Venus said, "you're wearing rhinestone earrings during the day and you're gonna call me ugly?"

"Charles," Linda said. "Can you please get your plaything out of my kitchen?"

"Linda—" Charles said.

"Don't Linda me," Linda said. "I'm going outside to get some air, and when I come back, I want him out of here."

"Don't *him* me," Venus said, "with your misshapen face and crow's-feet. At least I look like more of a woman than you."

As Linda walked past Venus to go outside, Venus rolled her neck. Her hair flipped back behind her shoulders.

"Venus," Charles said. It was just the two of them now and the way that Charles had said her name made her want to take the knife and stab herself in the tummy. His tone wasn't exactly like he was talking to a child, and it wasn't a scolding tone either, but he stretched out the vowels like something bad was gonna come. "I'm sorry, we had this whole picnic planned, but—"

"It happens," Venus said, waving her right hand in the air and letting her wrist go limp. "This too shall pass, isn't that what they say?"

"Well, Venus—" Charles said.

"I don't like when you say my name like that," she said. "Like all sad and shit."

"I need you to go home," he said. "We can't have our picnic. I'm sorry."

"If it's because I overcut the strawberries, I totally get you," she said. "I cut them up too small. I mean, look at them." She grabbed a handful of the teeny-tiny strawberry bits. "I got carried away, whoopsies, you know? I'll just run to the supermarket and get another batch. I'll use a smaller knife next time."

Charles sighed. "I'll give you some money so that you can take a cab home, okay?" He stepped toward her, but she was already leaning against the counter. She couldn't go back anymore without hitting a wall. She wished that she could take it all back. If she could, she would Krazy Glue all the strawberries back into whole pieces.

She looked at his face and knew that it was over. She took the pieces that remained in her hands and threw them at him. The strawberry came undone midair, then plopped on the tile floor. Even her throw couldn't reach him.

He took out all the cash in his wallet, balled it together with a rubber band he pulled from his pocket, and held it out to her.

At first she didn't believe it was there. She slowly reached out to take hold, as if too fast a move would trigger it to come alive and bite her. "Am I gonna see you again?" she said. She was scared to say it, so the words came out slowly.

His laugh sounded pained. "Damn, Venus," he said. "Is that your way of asking for more money?"

She wanted to say no. She just wanted to keep seeing him and she was confused about what was happening. If she could, she would tell him that she really liked him, liked spending time with him, that he wasn't like the other guys, that she felt safer with him, but she was too scared. So she just looked at his lips, closed her eyes, and said yes.

"Wow," he said. "You're all the same. Get out. You have enough to take a cab and last you a week."

"I didn't mean it like that."

"I don't see how else you could've meant it," he said.

He slumped down in a chair at the kitchen table and held his head in his hands so that she couldn't even get a final glimpse of his face as she walked down the hallway, to the front door. When she stepped outside, Linda was on the front steps smoking another ciga-rette. Linda stared at her. She asked Linda where she could get a cab.

"You know," Linda said, "we have a daughter."

"And the cab?"

"The fuck do I know?" Linda said. "I drive everywhere."

ANGEL

When the day finally came, she didn't want to leave anything up to chance. Chance could be more fickle than the sale price of a gallon of gas during hard times. When she woke up, she had a choice to make: dress conservatively or go all out. She walked to the closet door where she had two outfit choices on hangers that she selected the night before. On the left, the pink one-piece jumpsuit. Low back, exposed sternum. She could pair it with a large gold chain. On the right, gray wide-leg suit pants with a power-executive blazer. Very Annie Hall with those shoulder pads, looking like a Latina version of Diane Keaton. The two choices couldn't be more opposite.

She turned to the right and chose the more conservative option. The suit. Well, it was more like a suit as seen through the lens of a woman who had an inner wild side, someone who could deal with the fact that pants that flared weren't just for the dance floor. And no, she told herself, she wouldn't second-guess her choice. She knew all about the power of first impressions. She knew that the judges would look at her and, in the span of five seconds, their minds would be made up. There would be nothing she could say that could add or subtract from an already made-up mind. She didn't want to run the risk of—por ejemplo—wearing the pink one-piece jumpsuit. She'd walk up to them and they'd see her as a Latina first. And then the jumpsuit? If they were all white, they'd never take her serious. She knew that she had to work a hundred times harder just to get a normal ounce of respect. That's because as a proud Boricua, she had to work ten times harder. As a gay person, five times harder. And then double all of that shit because she was a pre-op transsexual woman. And because of math, that there is a hundred.

She got naked and shaved again—even though she shaved the night before, she couldn't take any risks. She taped it all back. She put on her makeup. She did her hair right. She just wanted to make sure that the outfit was a proper representation of who she was as a person. That's why she didn't want to go all out, dressed like a pendeja or some shit. When the suit was finally on, she turned in front of the mirror and mouthed the words, "You got this, mama."

All she wanted was for that outfit to scream in subtle tones: refined, elegant, woman.

* * *

Bloomies during the day wasn't anything to be messed with. The front facade—black marble with BLOOMINGDALE'S in big, art deco letters—looked like she was about to enter a fancy, seven-star hotel. She got out of the cab, one leg at a time like all the white women in movies did, and her heels never felt realer as she walked to the door. Lexington Avenue was wild behind her with cars and cabs and people and the anticipation she always felt when she went into these stores—Saks, Bloomies, Bergdorf, Ferragamo, Dior, Fiorucci—that as soon as she could make it past the front doors, she would be surrounded on all sides by Beauty with a capital *B*.

She lit up a cigarette and walked around the outside blocks of the store, prepping herself with nicotine before her big moment. There, from across the street, she dragged on her Newport 100 and stared at a pair of big-ass, gold cowboy boots in the Fiorucci window. God! Live mannequins in the window. Oh, to even dream of it all!

When she finished her smoke, she walked through the Lexington Ave entrance and went up the escalator and saw the line. Not only was it long, but the floor-to-wall mirrors in the place made it look like there were an infinity's worth of people waiting to be seen. It reminded her of the time she went to Six Flags in Jersey with Hector. They had waited three-and-a-half damn hours to go on the Scream Machine. Now that was love, she told herself, to wait on line for an upside-down loop coaster all because her man was so excited to go on it. Oh, she remembered his face that day. He looked like a boy waiting for Santa Claus with *all* the presents. She had waited with him and they split a funnel cake that had so much sugar, it felt like the fried dough grease was pumping through her veins afterward. When they finally went on the roller coaster, the speeds and drops banged her head against the restraint thing and fucked her up big time: she had a migraine all the next day. But that was what she did in the name of love. Now she took a few steps forward in line and wondered what he would say if he was there next to her. Would he say she was beautiful?

No, she didn't want to think about it. She took a wad of tissue out of her purse and dabbed her eyes so that nothing would smudge. There was a time and a place, and this was neither. She would think about him later, when she could be alone with her thoughts. When she could smoke a cigarette and cry at the unfairness of it all. Now she looked out at the sea of blond hair, thin bodies, aerosoled perms, hoops, purses, heels, gowns—denim? Yes, some of them were wearing denim. Bless!

To pass the time, she tried to figure out who were the girls that had beach houses in the Hamptons, the ones who referred to the Catskills as "the country" and the beaches in Jersey as "the shore." She thought that girl, that girl, and that one over there with the Chanel bag could probably afford to fly first class, and those five way over there probably couldn't even afford coach. She sighed. White skin, blue eyes, hair that could probably be straightened without a hot iron. There was the occasional morena, some dark-dark, some high-yellow. And the occasional Latina, from the pale Boricuas to the darker Dominicanas. If there were other drag queens, God Bless Them and God Bless America because they were passing so hard, even *she* couldn't spot them. She took a few steps forward and wondered for how long she would be waiting there. And yet, these girls had come dressed in different outfits, to different degrees, hoping that it was their face, or their body, or their whatever that would get them spotted. What was it about life that made beauty feel so important? She didn't know, but she felt drawn into it too. Just like everyone else in line, she only wanted someone to look at her and tell her she was beautiful. She thought that maybe, just maybe, if she was beautiful, things would get better.

* * *

As the line got shorter, it was easier to see the judges. There were four of them at the table: two men and two women. The two men looked dapper in their navy suits. They struck Angel as the type of eligible bachelors who were in their early forties, but deflated their age whenever the question came up at a gay bar or backyard soiree. The younger woman was the model who won last year. Her suit was cream-colored with big shoulder pads that made the entire ensemble look festive. The older woman was Wilhelmina herself, donning a herringbone top and a long pearl necklace that was double-wrapped around her neck.

A news reporter was off to the right, just after the table, asking some of the girls for comments about the process. "But where does this square with women's lib?" he kept saying. Angel knew there was no such thing as a bad question, but sometimes she wondered.

As she looked out at all the beauty around her, she asked herself— when beauty was something everyone strived for and wanted to em- body, when she was surrounded by so much of it, in such extreme amounts—why did it make her feel so sad to be around?

Her heart sank, as if gravity had finally found its way into her and was pulling her heart to the center of the Earth. She knew when she looked at that beautiful model who was last year's winner— her white, shining smile; her luscious hair fit for a TV commer- cial; her supple earlobes; her chin that was rounded just so without any surgery—she knew that she had no chance. She thought about leaving the line, cutting her losses, and going home where she would tell no one about what had happened and what she had been foolish enough to dream of. But it was too late, she was already at the table.

"Hi," the young woman greeted her and they shook hands. "Well don't you look wonderful today? What's your name?"

Angel had no illusions about her friendliness. She had heard her say the same exact line to the girl in front of her, and the girl in front of that girl. Angel smiled and told her what her name was.

The woman asked for her headshot.

"What do you mean?" Angel said. She froze. Of course she knew what the woman meant, but she didn't have a headshot with her. She didn't think she needed one.

"A photograph? With your face?" the woman said. She said

it nice enough to Angel. Even smiled as she said it. Did she really think that Angel was too stupid to know what a headshot was?

"The classified ad didn't say nothing about a headshot," Angel said, trying to be as polite as possible. She didn't want to ruin her shot by being rude.

"Oh? Well," the woman said. "I suppose it doesn't matter. We can jot down your information here and Robert down there can take a quick shot. Thanks for stopping by!"

Thanks for stopping by? Was this just a stopping by kind of thing? After waiting in line for how long, Angel was surprised to realize that yes, it was. It was just a drive-by. Smile and nod, keep your chin up, abs sucked in to give a bustier effect.

She walked down the table and the two men smiled and gave her a simple one-nod-and-done of the head. Finally, she was in front of Wilhelmina, whose pearl earrings made her earlobes drag down a little bit. Angel smiled as their eyes met.

"You are beautiful," Wilhelmina said and Angel thought, *Pinch me now.* "Thank you for stopping by today."

It was a relief that Angel didn't faint right then and there. She felt light-headed though, so when the words came out, she didn't realize how abrupt she may have come across. "Is that it?" Angel said. "What more do I need to do? Do I need to put my contact information down anywhere?"

"Oh, no dear," Wilhelmina said with a smile. "We received your headshot and shall find you if we have a need. Thank you again. You look beautiful."

Angel could tell that the words, though impersonal, were sincere. She tried to imagine how many women had to hear those same disappointing words, and how many times Wilhelmina would have to say them in just one day. She lost count.

She thanked Wilhelmina and walked away. She didn't have the heart to tell Wilhelmina that she had been suffering from a case of the gran pendejas and didn't think to come with a headshot. But she had no illusions about anything. She knew they didn't want her, and that was that. *C'est la vie.*

* * *

She didn't have any change, so she had to call Miguel collect. She stood on Fifty-Ninth with an unlit cigarette in her right hand. She tilted her head to the side so that the phone booth receiver was wedged between her ear and her shoulder. When she heard his voice, she was glad she hadn't got a busy tone, or worse, her mother.

"Mira, just listen to me," she said. She told him to meet her at Barbary Coast on Seventh near Fourteenth Street in an hour and a half. He asked if everything was alright, and she said yes, she just needed a whiskey sour and a shoulder. "I have had *a day,*" she said. She told him she was going to go shopping now. She used the words *retail therapy* and said that she would see him at the bar.

She went immediately across the street, into the Fiorucci store, and picked out an entire outfit of gold lamé. It was head to toe, even those damn cowboy boots. Once she was in the dressing room, a cute young butch queen opened the fitting room for her and she took off the Annie Hall flared pantsuit as fast as she could. She put the gold lamé pieces on, and even though they were all about one half size too small, the spandex or lycra or whatever it was stretched around her. She looked ridiculous, like a toddler wrapped in gold, with two gold-sprayed hot dogs for legs, and those damn cowboy boots. She stared at herself in the mirror and wished Hector were there to hold her. She started to cry until there was a quick tapping at the door.

"Honey," the young boy attendant sang. "You okay in there?"

Angel opened the door and when she saw the boy's look of shock and awe, she could only imagine what her mascara situation was like.

"You look horrible," the boy said.

Angel whimpered.

"Oh no," the boy said. "That sounded harsh. I just meant to say that your makeup was running. What is the deal? That outfit is so fresh. The gold lamé was a *choice* and a *decision*, but you are working it. I'll say."

"You really think so?" she said. She dug through her purse to look for her tissues so she could wipe at her face and blow the mocos out of her nose.

"I'm gonna tell you what my mother tells me," the boy said. "She sits me down and says, Xavier, no one should ever cry when they're wearing lamé."

Angel was about to blow her nose when she laughed. "It's my party," Angel said, "and I'll cry if I want to."

"Oh, okay, Lesley Gore," the boy said, dripping in sarcasm. He held on to a bunch of hangers, hip out to the side and elbow leaning on the door.

"You'd cry if it happened to you too," Angel said.

"No, please," the boy said. "I hate sing-alongs—unless it's 'It's Raining Men,' and then *only* for a bridge and chorus—so let's not do this."

Angel took a seat on top of her original outfit that lay on the dressing room bench. Well this one was being a sassy little thing. Angel didn't have the energy to argue with him. She didn't even have the energy to ask him to let her be in peace. "Humidity is rising," she said. "Barometer's getting low."

"Ugh," he said, rolling his eyes. "According to all sources, the street's the place to go."

"Tall, blonde, dark, and lean."

"Okay now you're going out of order and testing my patience."

Angel's laugh turned into a sob.

"Gosh, I hate seeing people cry," the boy said. He dropped a hanger and left it there. "So, let me tell you a story about lamé."

"You have a story about lamé?"

"Yes?" the boy said. "Have you ever in your life seen a butch queen with a nine-inch-plus cock wearing lamé pants on a dance floor?"

Angel didn't know if she was supposed to answer yes or no. The answer was no, she thought, though it was certainly possible she *had,* but had not thought to pause, stare, take it all in, store it to memory, etcetera.

"That wasn't a story," she said. "That was a question."

"Because," the boy continued, "I have. And I'll never forget how close I came to the divine that night."

"How old are you?" Angel said.

"That is irrelevent," the boy snapped. "Your eyes haven't really seen anything until they've seen that."

Angel really had no idea what to say. She just wanted to take a nap. "Could you imagine if it really did start to rain men one day?" she said. "It would be deadly, like cannonballs. Everyone would have to run for cover—"

"I wouldn't think too much into it," the boy said. "So, do you want the lamé or not? Because if you're not gonna take it, I need to put it back on hangers and get it back on the floor."

"Yeah, sure," Angel said, "I guess I'll take it."

"Oh, I knew it," the boy said. "I knew you would."

* * *

Removing any chance of returning the outfit later, she decided to snip the tags at the register and wear it out of the store. Because who could stop her from wearing nothing but gold lamé if that's what she wanted? It certainly wasn't the most outrageous outfit she had ever seen on the streets of Manhattan. In New York, a bitch could wear cellophane and nobody would blink twice. She loved that about her city, how even the most outrageous people could have a home in it.

She took the 6 and then the L. When she walked into Barbary Coast, Miguel was sitting alone at the bar, picking at some peanuts. She scurried over to him, put her hands on his shoulder, and kissed his cheek.

"Qué jodienda," he said, looking at her outfit. "What the fuck are you wearing gold aluminum foil for?"

"It's not foil, it's lamé," she said, seizing the moment as an educational experience. It wasn't even four yet, so the bar was nearly empty. There were two flacos with platinum-blond hair, and a viejo in a bowtie sitting alone with a martini glass. She waved down the bartender and ordered two whiskey sours.

"You made it seem like this was an emergency," he said. "I rushed the fuck out of the house to get here, for what? To see you dressed for the clubs?" He sighed as she sat down next to him.

"I just had an entire day of disappointment," she said. "Is it too much to ask you to squeeze a little pena out of your heart?" She explained everything that had happened with the model search: the other women, the unbearable amounts of beauty, the outfits, the line, the implied rejection.

"Damn, Angel, that's so fucked-up," he said. "How're you dealing?"

"Well, I just bought this outfit as an impulse purchase," she said. "So that's pretty much how I'm dealing."

He smiled and winked at her. "So you're making it alright, verdad?" he said. "Never seen a girl wrapped in gold that wasn't some kind of alright."

Their drinks arrived and she lay down a twenty to cover the both of them. She smacked his hand as he reached for his wallet. "My treat this time," she said. "The least I could do for making you trek to a gay bar in the middle of the day."

"There I was," he said, "thinking you were gonna lay some shitty news on me, like you had got the virus or some shit."

His words took her back. She drank an extra-big sip from her glass so she could feel the whiskey's bite in the back of her throat. "Don't joke about that," she said. She tried not to sound too angry. She didn't want him to get defensive about it. The thing that bothered her was that Miguel had known Hector. He knew how Hector died.

Miguel apologized and Angel felt bad. She was sad that no matter what, their experiences of life were still going to be so different, she'd have to explain how and why certain things hurt her. She didn't feel like getting into it today. Sitting in a bar explaining virus anxiety to her straight brother while downing the last drops of a whiskey sour in an outfit of gold lamé. This was not how she imagined it would go. She had called him on the payphone so that she could see a familiar face, to hug someone she loved, and feel alright about the world.

"Why don't you ever come around to see me?" she said.

"You never invite me," he said. "It's always bar this, lunch that, I'm on a payphone, Miguel, and we gotta meet now."

"Qué porquería," she said, but she had an inkling that he was right. "You know you don't need to RSVP to come to my house."

"Just say when," he said. "You know I got shit to do in the evenings and nights, but maybe one day, you know, early and shit."

"You're still dealing?" she said, holding the empty glass up for the bartender's attention.

"Yeah, but it's no biggie."

She asked him what he was dealing these days, was it still weed or had he moved on to higher sights.

"Smack," he said.

She got closer to his ear so she could hush. "Dealing manteca, are you fucking kidding?" she said. "And how do you feel when those kids overdose? How do you let that sit in your heart at night?"

"Jesus," he said. "I don't wanna talk about this shit with you."

"Fuck that," she said.

"Yeah, fuck that," he said. "Just lay off it. You want me and Mami to starve? I'm just doing what I gotta do, alright?"

* * *

Before she left the bar, she went to the bathroom to change back into her suit. When she got home, Venus was waiting by the stove, Juanito was sewing something at the kitchen table, and Daniel was laying on the sofa. She walked in and they all greeted her. "Ay, Dios mío," Juanito shouted out, putting a momentary pause on his sewing. "You look like a million buckaroos. Where were you at?"

"Oh my," Venus said, scurrying over to kiss her on the cheek. "I spy with my little eye: a shopping bag from Fiorucci."

"Open it," Daniel said from the couch. "Show us what's dazzlin'."

Angel turned the bag upside down and the gold lamé outfit plopped out into a puddle of itself. "Double ay Dios mío," Juanito said. He gasped in a bunch of air. "So much fabric. All lamé?"

"All *gold* lamé," Venus corrected. "Well," she continued, fingers pinched around the pants like a claw in an arcade game, "this is certainly a statement."

"You know how she is when she has a bad day," Angel said, "she goes shopping." She hoped that would settle it and the conversation would be over.

"Hmm, well I do love some lamé," Venus said, tiptoeing her way back to the stove so she could stir her oatmeal. She unlidded the small pot and the steam came up like a little fog machine.

After Angel went into her room, folded the new lamé, and put it away in the drawer, she decided that she didn't want to keep the secret from them all. She marched back out of her room and stood at a point in the living room where she could see all three of her children. "I just want to tell you," she said, "that I went on a model search and they didn't like me enough to want to pursue me. And I'm okay with it. I've dealt with worse and I'll move on. I didn't want to keep it from you."

There was silence for a second. Venus dropped her spoon in the oatmeal and came over to give her a hug.

"You mean," Daniel said, "the Bloomingdale's Model Search?"

"How'd you know?" she said.

She watched as Daniel and Juanito locked eyes.

"We found the newspaper clipping by accident," Juanito said. "We thought maybe it belonged to Venus since she keeps the most secrets from all of us."

Venus undid her arms from the hug so she could turn toward Juanito. "Excuse you!"

"¿Y qué?" Juanito said.

"C'mon, girl," Daniel said. "You know it's true."

Venus marched back to her oatmeal and took a spoonful. "Don't be hateful."

Angel watched Juanito and Daniel roll their eyes. She knew what she could do to lighten the mood. She went back into her room, took out the lamé, and changed into it. She put a tape in the boom box and put some Whitney on blast and marched out with her arms up. "Come on, nenas," she said to them all. "Dance with me."

"Now see," Juanito said. "Those judges must've been downright locas to not see what they're missing out on with you."

"Tha's riiiight," Venus said, clapping her hands and ready to pump it up. "How Will I Know" was on, and they all gathered by Angel's side to dance. Out the window, the sunset looked like it could be placed smack on the side of a butter container.

"I suppose it's important to remember, in times like this," Angel said above the music, "that we simply cannot blame the straight world for their lack of imagination."

THREE

DORIAN

The goal, of course, is to pass as fully as possible. If I'm a man but I feel like a woman, and I can dress like a woman, and wear makeup like a woman, the more I *look* like a woman, then the better I can pass. You see, passing has always been the key to banjee realness. If I wanted to pass as a straight macho dude—which I personally would never want to do, I'd rather burn off my eyebrows and jump into the Hudson River in December—but let's say that I *did* want to pass as a straight macho dude and I come to the ball dressed looking like someone who could rob you with a knife and call you a fag and punch you in the face for no reason, well then hooray for me—that's passing. And the judges will reward me with a trophy and applause.

Passing is an art form, darling. It's a craft. And just like any craft, the artistic ideal is always impossible to achieve. We can try and try and try as hard as possible to pass as a woman, but if I'm a biological man, I can only go up to a certain point. The rest is all imagination. But just because it's impossible doesn't mean that should stop someone. We shoot to come as close to that perfection as we possibly can. I think Angel and Venus were impossible beauties—anyone could look at them and think, *Now she is a* woman.

But I think the larger issue is what it means to have this impossible beauty outside of the ball scene. It's not like the world is going to look at you and say, Yes, honeys, you've worked so hard for this and we love you for it. No, that shit is not going to happen and we've got to be real about it. I'm interested in what happens when the balls are over and everybody's gotta go home. Because you've got queens who come here and feel on top of the world because we've given them a trophy, but then what? They go home and get the shit beat out of them for being a faggot? Please. That's less than ideal, obviously.

I like to think, darling, that we all need to face the fact that the whole world isn't a giant ball. I mean, I think it would be wonderful if it was. Maybe there'd be less war and more glitter, less bloodshed and more fabulous. You know what I'm saying? But we've got to face the reality of the situation before us. And that reality is a harsher one.

My friend Keith used to tell me that I was just being a critical queen, and why did I have to say all of those things. I'd snap back that I'm just being realistic, and could he not? What can I say? It was a difficult time. People were dropping left and right, not from violence or bashing, but from that virus. Gosh. It was atrocious. Of course we were all scared, all mortified, for heaven's sake.

I remember one summer, Fire Island was relatively quiet. People were just scared rigid and all the beautiful Chelsea bunnies were disappearing, and by disappearing, I mean dropping dead, honey. Excuse my bluntness, but facts are facts. So Keith and I were sipping mai tais by the pool, no one was swimming at five in the morning because that's hangover hour, but Keith and I were always the early birds. I was trying to get him to come to this ACT UP protest. We were going to do a stage-in at the cathedral in Midtown, and Keith was saying no, no, he couldn't go because the police were already on his ass for graffiti on the subway. I just couldn't believe that, not because I thought he was lying. I knew he was telling the truth, but it's just the nerve of some people! Not Keith, but the police. Can it only pass as art when it's on a canvas? Can no one see art when it's right under their nose? No, apparently not. Why am I surprised? Why am I still *always* surprised?

The first time I saw his art—well, first let me say that he painted these bloated stick figures who look like they always want to dance together. So I saw it and thought, Yes, queen, I'm on board with this. So the first time I saw this one specific piece of his, it had a black stick figure being choked by a sperm. So this sperm, on one end, was a noose. And the other end, it had a mouth and was eating the other stick figure. I said, Keith, darling, this is horrid. So dark. Where is the beauty in this? And he said, Dorian, if you say that, you're telling me that I need to turn this virus into something beautiful?

Two years after Keith died, I was walking in a museum exhibit of his work. I was just beside myself with grief, to see his work on the walls as if they belonged to some time that had passed us by, even though we were still in the thick of it. I saw this canvas with two stick figure men holding up a giant heart. You can tell they're struggling because they're bent on their knees and pushing up against the ground. And this heart is bigger than them—bigger than the both of them combined—and there are shining ray-lines coming out of the heart, and I thought, *Damn, Keith.* Even in the grave he was pulling stunts. I cried right there in the middle of the museum, and there are few things I hate more than crying inside, around other people. I always say, if you need to cry, go outside, bitch. But there I was, being a fat old blubbery mess and some young man put his arm around me and held me. I had never seen this man before, and never saw him again. He didn't say anything to me, he just held me as I cried and it was a moment that's just impossible to describe the full effect of.

I'm still figuring out how to process all of that, all of *this*, darling. I'm not sure I ever will.

JUANITO

Nerves were getting the best of him. He knew how vicious the ball crowd could be. Sometimes the shade just felt like downright ice. But he wasn't a kid anymore. He could handle this. He walked to the mirror that was duct-taped to his closet door so he could see what he looked like in the purple dress. The dress he had made for himself over how many months? Five months, sewn by those very fingers on his hands. He looked up and saw: marvelous. He was simply mar-vel-ous.

He didn't tell the others about the ball. He wanted to go to make his debut all alone. His plan was to pretend to be like the Puerto Rican Cinderella, staying out on the town until the clock ticked midnight and the subway turned into a pastelito and he lost his chancla running down some stairs. Oh, could anyone imagine? That would be downright silly.

He didn't tell them because it was more of a relief not to have them around for his very first walk. The nerves were eating him alive! Sure, he loved them dearly, but now without them there, he felt less pressure. He could trip, or lose, or throw unwitty shade, and they wouldn't see. Bottom line: If they weren't there, there was no way for him to disappoint them.

Juanito showed up at the Lodge with some time to spare, so he walked into the bathroom behind the main room. There were queens, young and old, going in and out of the men's and women's doors. Juanito didn't have to do his business, he just wanted to stare at himself in the mirror to make sure his makeup was done up right and that the subway ride didn't add any wrinkles to his dress. He wanted to pass the time without sitting alone waiting for the show to start.

When he walked into the men's room, two queens were having it out in front of one of the broken sinks. When the door closed behind Juanito, the queens turned their heads and stared at him. Juanito pretended not to notice their stares. He walked to the other sink to see if he needed to put more lipstick on. He reached into the purse he had borrwed from Venus to get the tube of lipstick.

"I can't take it off, mama," the younger queen said to the older one. "You can't take off a vest. It's a vest!"

Juanito kissed out his lips in the mirror, but ran his eyes to the side to see if he could watch them argue.

"You need to take that shit off," the older one said. "Nobody in they right mind wears a vest to a ball. You ain't walking in SCHOOL or BANJEE GIRL REALNESS. Girl, you are walking in TOWN & COUNTRY. You ever seen a white lady in *Town & Country* wear a goddamn vest?"

The younger one sighed. "But if I take it off," she said, "then people are going to see my flabby stomach." She took off the vest as if that would be proof.

Juanito took a step back from the mirror and fluffed his hair in the air to try to add some volume. He usually kept it back in a short ponytail, but now he needed to let it down. He swooped his head back and forth to let the hair fall naturally.

"I said," the older one said, "not nobody wears a vest to a ball. I'm helping you from making a mistake. Look at Juanito Xtravaganza over here, look at that fabulous dress he is working tonight."

Juanito turned his head, like who me? He looked at the older queen and immediately knew her face. The first time he had met Pepper LaBeija, she was screaming at Paris Dupree. "You can tell her that I am the legendary mother, and if she has a problem, she can take it up with me," Pepper had said without an ounce of irony. "I will tell her to look at my face—no lines, no wrinkles, no bags. She can stare at my youth—and suffer."

Now Pepper smiled at Juanito. He could see the eyetooth that was missing on her right side.

"Hello prettiness," Pepper said. She held her hand up and wiggled her fingers instead of waving. "I heard about Angel's woes. The poor thing. My oh my. Sometimes it feels like the universe is pulling a giant stunt on that one."

"I'll tell her you send your love," Juanito said.

"Please do," Pepper said. The young LaBeija stomped past Juanito and stormed out of the bathroom. Pepper shouted out to her, "I know you're gonna take that damn vest off, Dynasty."

Juanito smiled and Pepper saw.

"Oh, boy-child," Pepper said, "your eyebrows are looking sharp. Wax or pluck?"

Juanito said pluck.

"You lucky bitch," Pepper said. "I can't ever pluck mine right so I went to my girl Janise at the waxing place—and she was talking the whole time, eating up the minutes, telling me it was about to change my life. I told her, Girl, whatchoo talkin' about change my life?—just wax my damn eyebrows and lip already—"

"Pepper," Juanito said. "You think I look alright tonight? It's my first ball, I don't know if you know that, and I'm just worrying all inside."

"Well," Pepper said, "you're not wearing a vest, so that's a start. But, my oh my, you do look wonderful. The trick is all in the confidence."

"And what if I ain't got the confidence?"

"You gotta pretend then," Pepper said. "I've seen countless queens—I'm talkin' real ugly bitches—win trophies because they were confident. If you got the energy and the *umph,* the judges are gonna see it in the outfit. And the crowd will go wild and eat you up."

Juanito sighed.

"And you already got a leg up," Pepper said. "Cuz you ain't got an ugly bone in that body. Angel always picks the cute ones. The Xtravaganzas are fabulous—not as fabulous as the LaBeijas, honey, let's be real—but you'll be just fine."

* * *

He was missing an accessory. That was all that was spinning around his head as he walked to a corner table and sat alone watching the queens settle into place with their groups and families, as he watched the judges take to the stage with their placards that read eight, nine, ten, as the emcees hooked up the mic and made sure the trophies were arranged in size order on the side table behind the judges. Someone turned on the large fan in the corner and, from the mezzanine, someone dumped down a large box of the little Styrofoam nuggets that people put in boxes when they shipped gifts. It was like white chunks of confetti hailing down on the group, getting stuck in people's perms and jheri curls.

And he was missing a damn accessory. How had he forgotten? He was so swept up in making the dress—from scratch, mind you. And altering it. And resewing it. He scratched the back of his scalp and looked out at all the kids who hadn't been stupid enough to forget their accessories. He looked at all the outfits that popped and dazzled the floor and he came up with a list of reasons why he wouldn't win and take home a trophy. He just wished Daniel were there, to hold him, maybe, or simply tell him that he was overthinking the situation and that he needed to take a chill pill.

Across the way, he saw a red faux-snakeskin dress, cut off just above the knee, rising just below the cleavage point. It was body tight, with matching red gloves that went up to the boy's elbows. He was smoking a cigarette and dishing shade with some chica in a silver lamé tube top, hair that was overly permed and hairsprayed, with an emerald-encrusted brooch in the middle of her flat chest. Juanito could see the outline of her hardened nips through the tight lamé. Then a few tables down, he saw a black queen with a completely shaven head and a box hat angled just above his right ear. Juanito had no idea how it was staying on top of his head without sliding off. *Maybe tape,* he thought, *certainly not glue,* but he couldn't be sure. He wouldn't put it past a queen to hot glue some shit to her head. Another boy, this time to Juanito's left, was wearing eyelashes that must've been four inches long. How the hell could someone even blink in those?

There were dresses so long and so fitted, they looked like mermaid tails made of silk, made of polyester, made of nylon and acrylic, organza, tulle, rayon for heaven's sake. There were dresses so short and so flowy, one gust of the fan could give a girl a peek of some ass cheeks à la Marilyn Monroe.

Pero there he was, a flaco boy alone, donning a fitted dress of purple silk. With no accessory. With no family. He reached into his bag to grab Venus's compact mirror so that he could look at his lipstick situation again.

"Child," a voice said behind him. He turned and saw Pepper. "Don't tell me you're going to sit by your damn self all night long."

"Dani's gonna come for the second half," Juanito lied.

"And what about the first half?" Pepper said, "that's what I'm talking about."

"You already know they're all at the funeral," Juanito said. "Dorian's friend. They performed at Sally's together, or something."

"People dropping left and right," Pepper said. "And it's always close to home, ain't it? But that don't mean you should ever be sitting by your lonesome."

Pepper grabbed him by the wrist and practically dragged his ass all the way to the table in the right back corner where all the other LaBeija children were sitting.

"Pepper," Juanito said. "I'm the only Xtravaganza here."

"Just because you're sitting with us don't mean you're a LaBeija," Pepper said. "Even though bitches would die in order to be reborn as a LaBeija."

"Yes, honey," one of the LaBeija children said, enunciating each word, "tell it like it is."

Someone came up behind Pepper and put a real-life snake around her neck as if it were a scarf. The creature must've been three or four feet long, and it just lay there doing a 360 with its head to catch a glimpse with its black sequin eyes.

Juanito gasped and put his hand up to his heart.

"Oh, this?" Pepper said and laughed. "What can I say? I prefer my boas to have scales, not feathers. We call her Lana Turner because she's a fabulous addition to any neck."

Alright, Juanito thought, *it has been confirmed: these bitches were cray-ʒee.* If only Angel could see, she'd have a coronary and be shocked back to life in the span of two heartbeats. Venus would probably shriek and run away in her heels. Maybe Daniel would laugh, and that thought made Juanito wish that Dani were there to witness this charade with him.

"I forgot to bring an accessory," Juanito said. "Maybe forgot ain't the right word. I never had one in the first place. You can't really forget something you never had."

"Oh, child," Pepper said while scratch-petting Lana Turner with her pinky finger—the only fingernail that was longer than the rest. "Everybody needs an accessory."

"Hell yasss," said the young LaBeija who had put Lana Turner on Pepper's neck. He was a flaming black fem queen with gold eye shadow on. He must've been no older than fourteen. "My body is my accessory." He pulled his tank top down to flash Juanito his nipple, which was pierced with a gold ring.

"Hush, JayJay," Pepper said. Lana Turner hissed. "Does Miss Juanito look like he's got time for some foolishness right about now?"

JayJay shook his head.

"Here," Pepper said. "I already came loaded with four accessories— y'all know me." Pepper rolled her head back to make eyes with all her children around the table. "I am the reigning queen of accessories."

"Yes," said the young LaBeija, "tell it like it is."

Pepper grabbed Lana Turner with both hands and put her on Juanito's neck. Juanito froze, as if even one inch of a body movement would be enough to get his little ass choked to death.

"Pepper, no," Juanito whispered so softly, even he could barely hear the words come out of his mouth.

"I am feeling this," Pepper said, clapping her hands. "From this angle, I'm seeing *Ziegfeld Girl,* but from this angle—" Pepper moved to the other side of Juanito, but he was too scared to shift his neck to follow her "—I'm seeing *The Bad and the Beautiful.*"

Lana Turner didn't feel like what Juanito would've expected. She didn't feel wet or gross, pero more like a leather bag or a garden hose wrapped in a satin swatch. Lana Turner was all muscle, he thought, and as he focused on this, he breathed and relaxed his shoulders. Maybe he could rock Miss Turner for the catwalk. Wouldn't that be daring? Hell fucking yes, and then he'd have a story that would make Daniel say, Daaaamn girl.

"What do you think, Miss Thang?" Pepper said. She got close to Juanito's ear, close enough that Lana could've licked Pepper's golden hoop earring that made her earlobe sag down. "Sorry to pull a stunt like this in front of all the children. If you don't wanna wear her, I'll take her off and there'll be no tea and no shade about it."

Juanito turned to face Pepper, whose face was studying his. Pepper's face was worn and he wondered how many years she had been here, walking these same balls, constantly coming up with new outfits and accessories. How many years had it taken her to figure out that a snake could be worn like a scarf? Juanito wanted to know how many children Pepper had taken off the streets, how many had walked in balls, how many had run away, how many had the virus, how many had died, and, most of all, how Pepper could take it all on. It was just like when he started to think of all the things that Angel had done for him and for their house. He wanted to know what kind of impulse made a young queen want to take in her own kind and help them through. He wondered if, one day, he would be like them.

"I'll do it," he told Pepper.

"You sure now?"

Juanito said yes, and stuck out his fingers to pet Lana Turner.

"Only with your nails," Pepper said. "She only likes to be scratched with one finger at a time."

* * *

The category was FEM REALNESS QUEEN: FIRST TIME IN DRAGS AT A BALL, ONE THROUGH SEVENTEEN. Though Juanito took this all very seriously, the name of the category always made him giggle because the age bracket was like some kind of kiddie gymnastics competition. He tried to imagine a four-year-old queen walking down the runway in a baptism dress, slaying baby bitches with a bottle in hand, maybe a clean diaper, throwing so much shade, she could mop the floor with it. Imagine! Their parents would simply die of shock.

He stood at the back of the room and faced the judges. As "You Give Good Love" by Whitney Houston came over the speakers, he slowly stepped forward. Whitney was his cue. Unlike the other categories, which required house beats and freestyle turntables, Juanito wanted to make his debut with something slower than usual—at least at first. He walked out with Lana Turner on his damn neck—Yes, queens, he wanted to shout, she's a real snake—his arms out to the sides, fingers splayed out fresh. He kept his eyes on the judges table and on the golden glints of the trophies behind them. What a dream.

But then bam, just as Juanito had instructed the DJ turning the tunes, Whitney morphed into Rochelle's "Love Me Tonight" and the crowd lost their shit. *I'm not here to dance, I'm here for romance.* "Is that bitch wearing a *snake*?" someone screamed from the mezzanine. "Yes, mamacita, take that floor," another screamed. *I want you to love me, ooo-aaah.* He walked one foot in front of the other, like there was an invisible line and he was walking in Paris or Milan. He matched the rhythms of the song to his body—with each one-two, with each whoa-whoa, he rocked his hips and shoulders in opposing directions so that his body could look like an *S* in motion. Right before the steps up to the stage, he grabbed Lana Turner with both his hands, and lifted her above his head like a weight lifter making a final display of fuerza with the bar. And then, por fin, with Lana above his head, he shimmied his ass down to the floor and popped back up, walked up the stairs to be face-to-face with the judges who had looks like wow. And he was doing it all in heels, imagine.

Now it was a matter of silent communication, that was what a good vogue was all about. He put Lana Turner back on his neck.

He glided his right hand over his left arm, like he was applying lotion over his skin. *Smooth, look how smooth my skin is.* He made eye contact with the judges. He winked. *Confidence.* He rolled his head back as if he were reaching orgasm and ruffled his hair with his right hand. The queens at the tables and on the mezzanine were losing it fast, practically convulsing with oohs and ahhs and screams of yessss-bitch-get-it. *I'm not here to dance . . . I just need to believe.* And then he snapped his fingers and turned around in one single, solitary beat.

Then the problem came, and it all went down just as quickly as it had come up. On the third step down, he overstepped and fell forward until his chest was flat on the floor. The music kept playing, but he froze. Lana Turner slid off his neck and slithered on the floor next to him. He put his palms down and pushed himself up, and as soon as he stood and wiped off the dust from the front and back of his silk dress, Pepper was standing in front of him.

Pepper picked up Lana Turner and held her out in front of her own body. Pepper started dancing around Juanito in a square formation. At first, Juanito didn't know what was happening, but the song was about to end and he had ruined his chances. Pero then he figured it out. Pepper was offering him a save. Pepper's hand was stretched out, and Juanito grabbed on. Pepper pulled him up. Juanito went with it: he mirrored Pepper's movements, so it looked like they were doing a duet. He wondered how it would look to the crowd.

People must've been feeling forgiving that night because everyone was standing and stomping and it felt like the walls were vibrating and if they weren't careful the entire building would collapse into a pretty little puddle of wooden beams and when everyone who walked in FEM REALNESS QUEEN: FIRST TIME IN DRAGS AT A BALL, ONE THROUGH SEVENTEEN got up there in a line waiting for the trophies to be announced and they said *and the runner up is* and the name wasn't his name and that meant that he had *won* and he was crying then and holding his hands up to his eyes because he didn't want anyone to see him cry and Pepper came up from behind him and held out the big trophy and the thing was huge he didn't know how he would lug it home in one piece and Pepper hugged him and the whole room was love love love love love.

VENUS

The first time she walked a ball, she walked in RUNWAY. She wanted to win so badly, she would've made someone bleed if she had to. But she didn't like to admit that to many people because she didn't want to come across as too vicious.

Her accessory was a large silver ball that was the size of a globe. It was as reflective as a goddamn mirror, so when she first saw it, she knew she had to walk with it. She spent an entire fucking hour cleaning it to make sure that shit sparkled. It was autumn, so she wore a form-fitting camel-colored wool dress with a turtleneck. Sleeveless, of course. She wanted to be hot, but not too hot. That was the quandary. That was *always* the quandry with autumn. One had to follow the weather forecasts with an extra eye out, like a smooth cat watching for rain.

She didn't just win that night. She swept the floor with those bitches. When Paris Dupree called out her name, it took both arms for her to lift the silver ball above her head in triumph. The bitch next to her passed out from heat exhaustion—the poor thing—and to think, in hindsight, maybe Venus should've taken a pause to help the damsel up to her feet. But whatever. The past was in the past. Maybe the damsel shouldn't've worn sleeves. It was a hot shame that time machines didn't exist. Even with the best intentions, she couldn't change what was already done.

So when Juanito came home that evening and wrapped his arms around Venus and announced that he had walked in a ball without them knowing, and then won his category, Venus sprang out of the chair and screamed like she was being murdered. The little puto didn't even let them go see him walk! Yes, she was upset for a hot second that Juanito had kept it secret from them, but then she let that feeling pass. Angel reached out for the trophy and was all smiles. Venus turned to look at Daniel, who looked shocked and frozen. It seemed like he was trying to cover his upsetness, opening his mouth with an *umm, ahh,* every couple of seconds. Who could blame the poor thing, being kept out of the loop. But maybe Venus was reading him wrong.

She knew it wasn't her place to control whether Juanito wanted them around or not. When it came to love and support, the small stuff like that did not matter. Juanito had the trophy now and Venus was happy for him. She could just imagine the happiness that must've been buzzing inside Juanito.

Angel was holding the trophy now, shining it with a baby wipe. Venus reached out to grab it. She wanted to take hold of it in her arms to feel that it was real.

When Angel passed it over to her, Venus reached out her neck and planted a wet kiss on Juanito's cheek. It was like the rush was spreading from Juanito to Venus—and what a rush it was. Venus could search an entire lifetime for rushes like that. She never wanted the feeling, the buzz, the light, to ever fade away. Whatever law of the universe that said all highs must come to an end was a damn shame. If they came to end, well they wouldn't be highs, would they?

* * *

It wasn't an easy sell at first, but Venus told Juanito that she wanted to take him away so they could celebrate, just the two of them. She pegged it as a nice vacay, a time for the two of them to bond. She even busted out into a Go-Go's tune about how this was their vacation, all they ever wanted, vacation, time to get away. She told Juanito that the place would be a lovely, beachside hotel. There'd be nothing tacky about it, the boys would be sexy as all fuck, the women would be fashion icons, and the salt water taffy would be fresh. As it turned out, the hotel was actually a motel, the two full beds had damp floral-print comforters that were dotted in brown-rimmed cigarette burns, the men were brutos, and the girls pulled their bubble gum with their fingers. Venus wanted to scream out to them, "Don't you realize that's how you get *germs*?" But she didn't. She just sat on the wooden bench with her eyes looking out at the Jersey ocean, fuming.

The thing about Wildwood was that it was popping during the summer—chulos and chulas every-freakin'-where on the pier with the rides. But in October? Less so. At least there was a haunted pirate ship on the pier that they could go to. Halloween was a week away, so the crowd was kind of thin. No one out in costumes, but it was whatever. The goal was to have a weekend getaway with the newest reigning queen of their house. She could only hope that Juanito was going to enjoy himself. They couldn't go out and swim, unless they wanted to freeze their toesies off. But Wildwood in early October was like her favorite secret in all of New Jersey: the hotels were cheap, the restaurants were looking to pack, the weather was still fairly warm, the beaches free to stand on.

When they checked into the motel, got the keys, and walked into the room, Juanito put his bag down on the bed and plopped down right next to it like he was going to make a snow angel on top of the sheets. "It feels so nice," he said, "to lie down and rest."

"Yes, papo," Venus said. "I hear you." She just wanted to sit in the chair, take off her heels, and press her thumb into her foot as hard as she could.

"We're gonna have the best time," Juanito said.

"From your mouth to the queen's ears," Venus said.

She walked into the bathroom and emptied an entire can of disinfectant all over the floor, the shower, and the sink. It was a trick that Angel had shown her. She popped her head back into the bedroom and was about to ask Juanito what they should wear that night, but she saw that his head was buried in the pillow. Aw, he looked so peaceful when he was napping.

She tiptoed closer to the bed and put the blanket over Juanito's body, so he wouldn't be cold if he woke up during the night. Even though she had never known Juanito when he was a little boy, and even though she had never seen pictures of him from that time, whenever she saw him napping, it was like she could envision a younger Juanito was right there, in front of her very eyes.

* * *

"Oh," Juanito said the next morning. He was smoking out on the balcony with the sliding door open. "You wanna go out there like *that*?"

"Like what, darling?" Venus said, trying her hardest not to gasp. Was he insulting her outfit? It wasn't that outlandish: a lime green blouse with a gold chain belt set high on the waist with tight white pants and red espadrilles. She was pretty sure she had worn it before and Juanito had seen her wear it out on the town.

Juanito dragged on his cigarette and rested his knee on the sliding glass door. Venus could feel the cool air coming in off the beach, even though she couldn't see the sand because the boardwalk buildings were blocking their view. "I didn't mean it like that," Juanito said. "It's just that we're in—New Jersey."

"So what?" Venus said.

"Look," Juanito said. "I know you're all about passing. But I'm not all out-and-about like you. A boy can flirt with drag sometimes, or spend the day browsing a fabric store, and still want to live as a man."

She stood in the middle of the room and she felt like maybe the outfit was all wrong. "I suppose," she said. "But where's the fun in that?" She didn't know what to do with her hands.

"I'm just worried that all the machos are gonna see us," Juanito said, "and we'll get bashed. We're not home right now. We are not in Kansas anymore. And I didn't pack much in the fem department, if you know what I mean."

"You don't think we can pass?" Venus said, watching as Juanito stubbed out his cig and looked for an area where he could throw it out over the balcony.

"I think you can pass fine," Juanito said, "but not me. Or maybe, I don't know. It's going to be bright out with the sun. It's not like when we go around late at night at the piers or inside at the balls."

Juanito had a point. The sun could be the most unforgiving type of light. The question was whether they had the confidence to do it anyway. If anything, they could turn their outfits into *conversation pieces*.

"I'm okay with it," Venus said. "And if they mess with us, we'll just kick their asses."

"You make it sound so easy," Juanito said.

"It really shouldn't be that hard."

"Passing?" Juanito said. "Or kicking their asses?"

Maybe she was wrong about it all. Maybe they should take the safer route and dress more masc, not push any buttons or push their luck too far.

"Both," she said, thinking, *Fuck it*. She didn't come to New Jersey to hide from anyone, not even herself. "I think we could take on whatever comes our way."

Juanito took a deep breath and stepped inside the motel room again. "Okay, nena," he said, sliding the glass door shut again. "I trust you."

* * *

They made a list of rides they wanted to go on: roller coaster, spinny teacups, Ferris wheel, slingshot. Maybe they'd play one or two games, but not the game where the balloons fill up until they pop, because they both hated the sound of balloons popping. If Venus couldn't tell when the balloon was going to explode, she didn't know when to expect to flinch. She hated that her body didn't know when and how to protect itself when the pop came.

As they got ready to leave the room, Juanito's outfit was simple. Good thing Venus had packed some extra clothes, even if they were a little tight on Juanito: white-washed denim poom-poom shorts with sneakers, a bright orange cami that made his olive skin look like a deep-set tan. He had brought his own fake-gold nameplate necklace that said JUANA, because that was the closest they could find to JUANITO when they were buying jewelry last month on 125th Street. Homeboy was going the fem route, indeed.

Venus double-checked her pockets to make sure they weren't leaving anything behind and then she closed and locked the door. They had the passes, the ride tickets, a bottle of water, and keys. No sooner did they walk halfway down the hallway when she heard someone say, "Oh, my god, Janice."

"What?" the other girl said.

"Would you look at them?" the first girl said.

"Oh, my god, Karen," the other girl said. "Did you see that belt?"

"Es'cuse me." The first girl popped her head out of the room. Their door was wide open and there were several other teens lying on the bed and the floor. "Where'd you get that friggin' gold belt?" She was looking straight at Venus.

"Oh, thanks," Venus said, wanting to call her darling, but thinking better of it. "I bought it somewhere in Manhattan."

"Right on," the other girl said. She was chomping on her gum like if she didn't, her teeth would fall out of her mouth.

Venus could see into their entire room. The bathroom door was open and the tub was full of ice and handles of booze. These girls looked high school age and the room looked ready for a party alright. Juanito cleared his throat.

"Well, thanks," Venus said to the girls. She waved at them with her fingers.

Once they were down the hall, Juanito said, "I can't put a finger on why, but there's something off about those girls."

"Watch yourself," Venus said, "because they could probably say the same thing about us. Judgments, judgments are no fun."

"Unless you share with everyone?"

"I don't see what the big deal is," Venus said. "They seemed like perfect dolls if you ask me."

"You just think that because they complimented your belt," he said, holding the front door open for her. They both stepped outside and put on their sunglasses to walk to the boardwalk, but not before they both exclaimed, "Blinding!"

"Well, what can I do if they have good taste?" Venus said, and laughed. "Not like it's a crime to give someone a compliment."

"I think they were——" Juanito paused. "Oh, never mind."

"No," Venus said. "Just say whatever you were going to say."

They had to stop at the crosswalk to wait for a car to pass before they could cross. Venus could feel the wind nipping at her ankles. "I think they were mocking you," Juanito said. "I'm sorry, and I'm not certain about it, but that's just how it seemed to me."

Venus laughed. "You're just being paranoid because you're not used to walking out like this."

"Oh, you don't think I can handle walking out like this?"

As soon as Venus said it, she wanted to take it back. "Oh fuck," she said. "I didn't mean it like that."

"No," Juanito said. "No, you're right." He stopped walking and reached into the bag and pulled out the bar passes without looking Venus in the eye. "Here you go," he said, cold as anything. "Just pin it to your blouse."

"I'm sorry, Juanito," Venus said, but Juanito still didn't say anything. "I'll hold on to it," she said, the pass in her hand. "I don't want to puncture any holes into the fabric."

"You know what your problem is?" Juanito said. "You're too trusting, Venus."

She squeezed the pass and shrugged. Maybe he was right. Maybe she was too trusting. He was reading her harder than a medical book written in German. She didn't want to fight. She just wanted to drink a nice glass of white wine and close her eyes in the autumn breeze.

"My trust," Venus said, "is all I got, girl. Where do you wanna sit?"

Juanito pointed to an open table behind the bar.

"Good choice," she said. "Just in case we need quick refills."

And at that, she kicked back her head toward the sky to laugh and kiki while Juanito walked over to the table, alone.

* * *

She loved to close her eyes on the roller coaster because then she couldn't anticipate what was going to happen before it happened. She couldn't stand the unexpected when it came to balloons popping, but a roller coaster was a different story. It was like a full-body experience: she was locked in tight, she was sitting next to her sister, she could throw her hands up in the air and scream all loud. Like she knew that shit was gonna drop, that she'd be thrust to the left and the right, like it was a roller coaster and that's what people expected, right? But if she had her eyes closed and everything was dark, the twists and turns, ups and downs, all came as a surprise. So, when she sat there next to Juanito, squeezing his hand, saying, "Are you ready, nena? Are you fucking ready?" even though they were only going up, slowly, with the metal *tick tick tick tick tick tick* of the track, it was all in anticipation of the weightless feeling of her stomach going to mush in her very body. And when they went over that curve at the top and gravity took over, she let out a scream that bitches could hear on the farthest moon from the sun. She didn't care if the wind fucked up her hair—the knots would be so unbelievable, it would for sure take a full hour to comb them out—but she didn't care because this felt worth it. She squeezed Juanito's hand as the coaster did a sharp right curve and Juanito's body pressed up against hers. How could that boy not scream? Not even a peep out of him. Whatever, though, because she could scream loud enough for the two of them, and when the ride came to an end and there was no one in line behind them, the cute attendent boy with the delicious booty told them they could go on again, and that's what they did, but this time she was all out of wind and instead of screaming, she just breathed in and out and felt the air against her neck. This was a rush she never wanted to stop, never ever.

* * *

That night, when Juanito asked what they were going to get for dinner, Venus rushed to her luggage and pulled out her final surprise: a little baggie of coke. "Who needs dinner," she told him, "when you can have cocaine-dinner?"

"Oh, Venus," he said. "You didn't."

"My treat, darling."

Juanito said he was famished and needed to eat something before, so while she was cutting up lines on top of the TV, Juanito plopped himself on the chair in the corner and bit into an apple. Venus used a razer blade that was no longer than her pinky finger. It wasn't that sharp—it must've been old and dulled out from various uses, all of which she didn't want to know about—but it was perfect for cutting up the lines. She tried to be all mathematical about it: two thick rails, four lines, and two bumps. She rolled up a dollar bill and handed it out to Juanito. "A good ol' George Washington for you," she said and curtsied. Juanito laughed.

"Thank you, ma'am." He looked at the dollar bill straw and said, "Hello, Georgie boy."

When Juanito blew through his first rail, she clapped her hands and bounced on her toes. "I'm so proud of you," she said, reaching out for George.

"For blowing a rail?" Juanito said.

"No, silly." Venus walked over to the TV and leaned over to blow through her rail. When she popped back up, she pressed her nostrils with her fingers to put pressure on her septum. "I'm proud of you for winning your category. For walking the ball. That shit takes balls, you know what I mean." She felt the rush in her head, in that sweet spot behind the eyeballs. The coke was starting to hit her. "I'm proud of you for being you, for doing you, for walking—"

Juanito wiped up some residue from where his rail was and rubbed it on his top gums and passed his tongue over his teeth. He nodded his head, yes, yes, yes.

"But let me just say," Venus said, holding out her hands like there was a large audience in front of her and she needed them to shush. "First—I need to stand for this—" She stood and started to pace around the room, hands out like she was in need of some balance. "Let me just say that it was kind of fucked-up—no, it was a little more than fucked-up—that you didn't tell us about it beforehand, because you knew we wanted to be there for you, especially me, I wanted to bethereforyou—"

Juanito blew through half of the next line and tried to say something, but Venus held out her hand.

"No," she said. "Let me finish. What I was saying was that you knew we would've loved to have seen you out there, walking, strutting, doing your thing, and we would've cheered you on, watched you slay bitches, given you words of encouragements." She had paced all the way to the closet door, so now she marched her little booty back to the TV to do her next line.

"I know, I know," Juanito said. He put his head in his hand, like he was going to rub Vaseline on his forehead. It was a pose that the telenovela stars did when they were expressing woe. Then he bolted up and stood on the bed, right in the middle. "Don't cry for me, Argentina," he said, one hand over his heart, the other reaching out.

"The truth is"—Venus grabbed her comb and used it as a microphone—"I never left you. All through my wild days, my—"

"Venus!" Juanito said and snapped his fingers to attention. "I was *saying*—It's just that I was so scared. I was scared that if I had everyone there, and if I fucked it up, it would be like I was letting you down. Jesus, this blow is strong." He reached his handsies up to the popcorn ceiling to feel the texture of it. It looked like stubble.

"Ay, nena," she said. "You shouldn't've feeled that way."

"I know," he said, bringing his hands into fists and bringing them to his chest. "But I did, and you know we can't control how we feel. We just feel."

"I feel ev-er-y-thing," Venus said. She was tapping all ten of her fingers against her waist. She pulled out a stick of gum from her purse and started chomping on it. And, yes, she did know what Juanito was saying. She nodded and now her lips and teeth were all numb and the gum was there. Juanito said he couldn't feel the back of his throat and he started snorting a little, like he was going to hawk a wad of spit, but he didn't actually spit anything out, which made her laugh and she told him not to worry, that it was just the coke in action.

"I wish Daniel were here right now," he said. "You think he's mad that I didn't tell him about the ball? You know, when I was up there on the stage doing my thing, I had a regret. Like I wished that I had told all of you about it. I thought maybe I made a mistake."

All that was left for them to do were the two little bumps and she wanted to save those for when they needed a pick-me-up. She looked up at Juanito who was an electric pulse of energy right there on the bed, he looked like a kid about to start jumping up and down from a sugar rush. He was their newest, reigning queen, the sweetest most gentlest boy she knew, and he was in love. "Ay, nena," she said, leaning against the bathroom door. "You really love him something hard, don't you?"

"That's it," he screamed, as if he were realizing this thought for the first time. "I do. I really do. That's what this feeling is. I should call him and tell him that I love him right this very moment."

"Oh, no, no," she said, walking over to the bed to grab him by the ankles. She told him to sit down next to her and she put his hands in hers. "That's not a very good idea. You're so coked out of your mind—and I'm not saying you don't love him, because that much is true, nena—but you're gonna dial that phone and all the words are gonna come out in a coke rush and he's gonna be, like, What the fuck are you saying?—You feel me, nena?"

He nodded and now they fell back to lay on the comforter. He sighed. "You know I was thinking the other day—you know me when I get in a mood and I'm alone with my *thoughts*," he said. "I was thinking that I want kids."

Venus hummed and nodded. She blew her gum into a tiny bubble and devoured it in one, toothy bite. "You gonna leave us and start your own house, already?" she said.

"Nah," he said. "I was thinking that I want kids with Daniel. And it's a hot damn shame that the two of us can't have kids together. Like how we're taught that when two people are in love, they get together and live in a house and make a baby. Well, us two are in love and we live in a house and it makes me sad to think that we can't make a baby that is half-part him and half-part me."

She had never thought of it that way. She had never thought of herself as being capable of being a mother. It was as if being born in a trapped body made that out of the question, as if she was bound to spend her whole life trying to make her soul and her body parts match up, and because of that, she couldn't even wrap her mind around having kids. All she could imagine from her life right now was having fun, finding her future husband, and getting her sex change. Then one day, if all of those things added up, she would think about taking on the responsibility of children.

"Ay, nena," she said, putting her hand over Juanito's heart. "You're just setting yourself up for heartbreak with that thought."

"I know," he said. "But I still wish it could happen. Maybe one day, with science?"

"Ay, Dios," she said. "Science can do many things, but now I think you're asking for a bit much. How do you expect science to make it possible for two boys to make a baby?"

"You think what all the haters say is true?" Juanito said. "Like how it's unnatural for us to even be together because nature makes it impossible for us to make kids?"

"Oh, don't even get me started on that brand of bullshit," Venus said, sitting up again to take the last bump of coke. "The natural world is more fucking complicated than the smartest motherfucker can make sense of," she said. "So who the hell are they to tell us shit?"

Juanito slow clapped.

"Get your ass up here," she said, holding out the rolled-up

George straw. "You're a reigning queen. You're in love. And honey, we got some bumps to do."

* * *

Well past midnight, Venus scurried into the bathroom to blow a rail of coke. Before leaving the room, she checked to make sure that Juanito was asleep. She adjusted the blanket so that it wasn't covering his face. She wanted to make sure that he had fresh air to breathe while she stepped out.

In her chest, she could feel her heart doing the hustle. She walked out into the night's cold breeze. The telephone booth stood alone at the edge of the parking lot, under the orange glow of a streetlight. She lit a cigarette and adored the way the nicotine meshed with the blow. It felt like a crank of electricity was lit in the back of her head. She could go on like that for hours, days, however long it would decide to last. She slipped the coins in and dialed his number from memory.

"Hello?" Linda said. "Who is this? Is everything okay?"

She waited, flicking the cigarette so it would ash, even though there wasn't anything left on the end of it to ash.

"Hello?" Linda said again.

She dragged on the cig and hung up. After a pause, she fed more coins in and dialed again. She hoped that he would pick up this time.

"Is there an emergency?" Linda said.

Yes, she thought, *there is*. She didn't say this though. Instead, she took the phone and bashed it against the metal box. *Bam, bam, bam*. A tinge of remorse bubbled inside her, but it was beat out by the rush of the blow. She let go of the receiver and let it dangle by its metal wire. Then she picked it up with two fingers and hung it up formally.

She finished the cig and killed it under her shoe. She put the last of her change into the phone and dialed one last time.

"If you don't tell me who this is," Linda said, "I will disconnect this phone, so help me god."

"Put him on the phone," she said. "You know who this is."

Silence. She could hear Linda's voice telling him something, but she couldn't make out the words. That meant she was sleeping next to him. Not only was she still in the same house, but she was sleeping in the same bed. "Listen to me," Linda said. "He's going downstairs to take this call so I can go back to sleep. But if you think we have time for your *Fatal Attraction* bullshit, you are mistaken."

"I'm on the other end," Charles said. "I'll take it from here."

The sound of his voice made Venus's heart sink. He sounded tired, so she cleared her throat and said, "Sorry to wake you like this, but I just wanted to say—"

"You called my house," he hissed the last word, "at this hour because you *just wanted to say?*"

"I thought you two were getting divorced," she said. She lit another cig and held in the smoke an extra heartbeat.

He sighed. "Things are complicated," he said.

"I know," she said. "I'm feeling a lot of complications too. I miss seeing you. I miss hearing your voice."

"Hang up the fucking phone," Linda screamed.

"I said I will handle this," Charles said. "Look, Venus. We have a daughter. I'm trying my best to figure out what I'm doing, and I really, really need for you to leave me be so that I can do that."

"Okay, yeah," she said. "Sure."

"Can you do that for me, please?"

"No," she said. "I don't get it. What does that bitch have that I don't got?"

He sighed and she leaned her head back against the booth's plexiglass.

"I'm sorry," he said. "I'm going to hang up now."

"No, don't do it. Don't hang up on me," she said, but it was too late.

*   *   *

Two days later, when she and Juanito got back to the city, she walked to the corner alone to hail a cab. She had the cabbie drop her off right in front of the salon, and when she told her girl Leilah to buzz it all off and Leilah said to the three other clients in the place, "Now this girl has lost her damn mind," Venus thought that maybe she would regret shaving it all off, but she didn't care.

"Just do it please," Venus said.

Venus stared at herself in the mirror as Leilah passed her fingers through Venus's hair. It felt good to feel another person connect with her body in a way that felt gentle. "Yes," Venus said, "Absolutely. I want a crew cut like the military men."

"Okay, baby," Leilah said. "But I still think you're crazy. How long did it take you to grow this all out?"

Venus closed her eyes and tried to count the months. It was like she hadn't thought of the time in strict days, or weeks, or months. Time had passed in monumental moments, starting with the car, then the first time she had gone to Charles's house, *Cats*, the hotel room, the days at the gym watching him sweat—she couldn't bear to go on. She opened her eyes and looked at Leilah's reflection in the mirror. "Months," Venus said. "Not sure exactly how many, but yeah, months."

"You want me to give you a number two all around?"

Venus nodded yes and felt the area in the back of her head where Leilah's fingers were pinching hold at some of her hair.

Leilah worked her fingers and scissors. First, she pinched bunches of hair and snipped them away with the scissors. They fell to the sides of the chair and lay there all alone, scattered against the linoleum. Once it was short enough, Leilah used a mechanical taper that buzzed against Venus's scalp and the vibrations soothed her. She closed her eyes and felt her entire head humming along with the clipper machine.

Leilah had shaved off the left side of her head and was moving the long black cord to the other side of the chair. Venus opened her eyes and stared at her head in the mirror. She saw herself cut in two by her own hairline. As if half of her head was trapped in the past, and the other side was rushing into the future.

Hurry, she thought, *please hurry.* She didn't know how long she could stand to look at the half-finished product that was staring right back at her in that mirror.

This will be a new me, she thought. *A new goddamn me.*

When Leilah had finished up and swept up all the hairs around the chair, Venus saw someone who looked like herself in the mirror, but not quite. Without the big hair on top of her head, she looked younger. She looked like the boy that used to stare at her in the mirror when she was eight, nine, ten. It was that same face. She was older now, but that face still had the same quality. She started to cry.

"Now see," Leilah said as she swept what remained of the hair into a dust pan. "Didn't I tell you?"

"I love it," Venus lied. "I cry all the time. Even when I love something."

She didn't feel like explaining it all to Leilah, who had been so kind to take her in without an appointment. It was just the two of them now. Venus wanted to rush her ass out of there before Leilah's next appointment came in. She didn't want anyone to see her having a moment.

"Look, girl," Leilah said as Venus spread her fingers out and rubbed the peach fuzz on top of her head with the palms of her hands. "You know you've been my homegirl for some time now. I got you. You grow that hair back out a little, then you come back to me when it's grown and I'll see if we can get a good weave for you."

"But I do love it," Venus said, still in tears. She took out her wad of money and handed over three bills that would cover the cut and tip. She asked Leilah for some tissues so she could blow the boogies in her nose and wipe away the tears that were still flowing hard.

As she headed out that door to walk those ten blocks back home, she wished that she could take a time machine into the past. Maybe she wouldn't call Charles. Maybe she wouldn't even have met Charles in the first place. Maybe she wouldn't have gone to Wildwood, or walked in balls, or ran away from Serenity, or left New Jersey. Maybe she would've kept her hair. If only she could have the power to change things, she thought. But then again, she knew it was a waste of energy to dream about a power that she could never have.

ANGEL

Oooh, aaah, baby. Angel was dancing herself in circles in the middle of the sala, feeling the beat within her heart, that beat in her heart, that beat, as Lisa Lisa sang her anthem on the radio—and nena, every time that tune came on, her heart did double-beats and triple-booms and she wanted to shout out, Yes I can, Yes I *can* feel that beat in my heart.

She had the apartment all to herself and she was trying to plan out her outfit for the weekend. She made a bangin' grilled cheese for lunch that day and danced around in her underwear like no one was watching. She glided her way between her open closet and the sofa in the sala, dangling hangers from her pinky fingers, laying pieces together so she could plan an outfit that dazzled. She took a deep breath, lit a cigarette, and opened up her bedroom window so she could blow the smoke into the wind.

She leaned against the window frame so that she could face her closet. She was eyeing a hot pink one-piece jumpsuit with a drop back that lay on the hanger all the way to the right. She dragged on the cigarette and held it in for a sec before exhaling. She just needed to find the right accessory to pair it with. Something like a costume necklace that would draw the eye to her neckline, or maybe a simple bracelet to make her wrist pop. Or maybe she was just in need of a good clutch.

She pressed the tip of the cigarette against one of the bricks that held the window frame together and the flame went out. She flicked the butt as far as she could. How many times had she replayed this fantasy in her head? Oh, countless, yes, it would be almost foolish to even try to put a number on it. Each time, the daydream ended with her in front of a camera flash, next to a handsome papi chulo with a microphone asking her how she felt. Divine, she'd say to this dream-man. Absolutamente divina. Then, for whatever reason, they were holding champagne flutes and she screamed into the dream-camera: Don't you just love when the bubbles tickle the back of your throat!

The building buzzer went off and Angel screamed her coño carajos and jumped so fast that she almost fell down on the floor next to her tacones. She pressed the button to speak and said into the intercom: "Yes, darling. Speak to me."

When she pressed the listen button, all she heard was air and a little bit of static. She pressed the speak button again: "I said, speak to me, tell me your name, slay me with your words." Her wit just tickled her. Again, she pressed for listen and got nothing but air.

She shrugged and raised the volume on the radio and screamed a hot daaaamn into the air when Rochelle took it over with a version of "Love Me Tonight." She couldn't *not* dance to this song. That would be physically impossible. It felt like the tune set itself in her body. A pulse of electricidad. She rolled her neck and then jiggled her shoulders back and forth. She shimmied hard and shaked her culo. She picked up her jumpsuit and glided over to the full-length mirror in the hallway so she could dance in front of it.

The buzzer went off again. She pushed her hair behind her ears and walked over to the intercom again. She pressed the button with the tip of her red nail and spoke: "Yes? Make thyself known to the queen of this castle?"

Nada. Like speaking to a damn wall.

"Speak to me, child," she screamed. "If you're looking for Toya, she's 5A, not 4A, darling. And if you're in need of Marcus, well Lord help you, nena, because you need prayers. He's 3A, not 4A, but think about that rock before you melt it and prick your pretty little arms."

Just when she lifted her finger from the listen button, it buzzed a-damn-gain. She huffed and pressed to speak one last time: "Listen you damn crackhead, stop buzzing in on my peace. Go buzz someone else to death if you don't got anything better to do. I'm trying to put together an outfit that would make even the good Lord Jesus

wanna let down his hair and have a damn kiki and you are getting
in my way."

* * *

The thing about pink was that it could be such a disarming color.
There were so many different intensities. If a girl didn't align all the
shades correctly in one outfit, she'd run the risk of looking like she
didn't know what the hell she was doing. Angel had three different
shades of lipstick and she was trying to find one that could match
best with the hotness of the jumpsuit. She twisted each tube out and
looked back and forth between it and the dress.

After her lips were all done up right, she decided it would be best
to live a little in the outfit to see if it was comfortable enough. One
of the biggest ways an outfit could fail was if someone put it on and
then the fabric, the accessories, the makeup held the true self back
from showing. That would be bad. So she walked over to the sink to
wash the dishes when she saw Venus standing in the hallway.

Angel hadn't seen or heard Venus enter. She let out a blood-
curdling scream, as if she had seen a cockroach the size of Alaska.
Then Venus screamed, either out of shock or just to join the chorus.

"Ay, nena, when did you get here?" Angel said, catching her
breath. "Scared me so bad, I'm not gonna sleep for a week—pero
qué pasó with that head of yours? Where's your hair?"

Venus did a deep inhale and raised her chin high, all dignified. "I
was going for something radical," Venus said. "I love it, just so you
know. It's a new me."

Angel didn't quite believe that, but she tried to make sure her lips
weren't pressed or her eyebrows didn't raise. She didn't want Venus
to sense any shade.

"And where," Venus said, "are you going dressed to the nines
like that?"

Angel turned the sink water off. "Can't your mother want to
dress nice for the day?"

"You're not working today," Venus said.

"I said, can't a woman dress nice for the day?"

"To do dishes?"

Now Venus was the one giving sass. Wasn't that a shit? Angel put the plate that she had been rinsing into the drying rack and Venus started to cry.

"Well, damn," Angel said. "I didn't think it was *that* bad—"

"No, don't say nothin', mama," Venus said. She brought her hands up to her face to cover her eyes, just like she did whenever she cried in front of Angel. Angel wondered why Venus had to cover herself whenever she cried in front of other people. Hadn't they known each other for long enough that she wouldn't need to cover up in front of her?

"You look fly as hell and I—" Venus said, wiping at her eyes. "I just simply love my new haircut."

She started bawling again and Angel looked at her, like, Oh, really now. She crossed her arms. "Why are you crying over something that you say you love?" Angel said. "You think I'm some kind of purebred tonta that don't got eyes to see? You think I don't know your heart is hurting?"

Venus made a move down the hallway for her room. "No," Angel said to her, firm but con calma. "Get over here and talk to me. You've been keeping all kinds of mysteries from me and now you're gonna have to speak to me."

"He doesn't wanna see me again," Venus said.

"Mr. *Cats* Man?" Angel said.

Venus nodded and walked all dazed to the sofa. She collapsed on top of the pillows. Angel scurried over to her and sat next to her, giving some side-hug comfort. Angel tried to think of some words to help the poor nenita. She tried with a light broma first, to evaluate the severity of the hurt: "Ay, you shouldn't give any light of day to a man who enjoyed *Cats*. I mean, what an atrocity of the imagination—"

"He has a wife," Venus sobbed. "He has a daughter."

"¡Qué hijo de puta!" Angel said. A daughter! The piece of shit.

It was worse than she thought. "I swear, why in the world would you even mess with a situation like that?"

"I didn't know," Venus said. "How was I supposed to know?"

"You went back to his house?" Angel said. She placed her index finger on Venus's cheek and turned Venus's face to her own. "Look at me," she said. "You telling me that you went to his house when you know what I say about that?"

Venus couldn't even look into her eyes, but what Angel saw made her heart want to break into sharp little pieces. Venus was her girl and here she was a crying shame. Venus looked so damn young when she cried. If Angel could be like an esponja and absorb all the pain in her house, she would do it faster than half a heartbeat. But she knew pain wasn't like a liquid spill that could be cleaned up so easy.

"I'm taking your silence," Angel said, "as a yes ma'am, you did, in fact, go to his house."

Venus nodded.

"Did the pendejo rape you?" Angel said. "Do we need to go over there and kick his bruto ass together?"

"No," Venus said. "He didn't fuck with me like that. He was nice."

"Nice?" Angel said. The word sounded like acid rain hitting summer cement with a sizzle. "Nice? They are never nice. We don't work for the nice ones."

"But he *was* nice," Venus said.

"Ay, Dios mío, again with the nice," Angel said.

"We were supposed to have a strawberry picnic," Venus said. She started sobbing again.

"A strawberry picnic?" Angel was all shock and awe. "Ay, why not add some blackberries and blueberries and some mothafuckin' sorbet and champagne to that, nena? What kind of damn movie-world do you think we live in?"

Angel stood up to get her girl some tissues. What was she gonna do with her, this wildflower child of the streets? If love wasn't gonna kill that one, heartbreak could place a close second.

"Mira," Angel said, now across the room near the closet. "I got an old wig we could use if you want some hair realness."

Venus nodded.

"I'm not mad," Angel said. "You know that, verdad?"

"I know," Venus said. "I know."

"I'm just—" Angel said, "astonished with you, girl. You think this world is all glitter and cotton candy and love?"

She reached onto the high shelf of the closet and grabbed the wig with all five fingers, like she was mushing a mound of plátanos for a mofongo with nothing but the fingers on her hands.

"You're saying," Venus said, "I'm stupid for believing that I can go out there and try to find love? At least I go out there and try to search for something that's real. You're just throwing your shit at me because you can't face the fact that Hector ain't coming back from the dead."

Angel stood in the corner of the room with the wig in her hand and the urge to throw it at Venus. She inhaled. "Here you go," Angel said. She let the wig fall into Venus's lap. "If you want to take it, here it is, take it from me."

"Angie," Venus said, so damn soft that Angel almost didn't hear it. "I'm sorry. I didn't mean that."

"I know you didn't," Angel said. "It just came out with all the feelings. I know how it is, nena."

*　*　*

Venus walked out of the bathroom, balancing the wig on her head like Lucille Ball balancing a headdress. Angel didn't dare say a word. Pobrecita. That peluca was way too big on that little body of hers.

"Ay, nena," Angel said, biting her lip as if that could send some kind of telepathic power to the top of Venus's head to keep that wig from falling. "You look beautiful, like hermosa total. I swear."

"Now don't lie to me, mama," Venus said. She walked to the mirror slowly so she could keep it all on balance. Those curls were like Marie Antoinette–level shit. Angel watched as Venus looked at her reflection. Venus screamed a loud string of sounds that sounded so incomprehensible, Angel couldn't tell if there were words somewhere in there.

"Don't scream, nena. You're rockin' that look like Iris Chacón," Angel said. "Just own it. Make like it's all an extension of you."

"Iris Chacón?" Venus gasped. "Why don't you just kill me now? I don't got the ass or the bust to even pretend at that."

"Mira, que *preciosa* eres," Angel said. "Like you're going to break out into a rendition of 'El Cumbanchero' on the Letterman show."

Venus sobbed.

"Ay, Venus," Angel said. She walked over to place a gentle wrist on her daughter's shoulder. "If you're gonna cry, at least let it all out. There's no point in choking it all in."

"I don't wanna look like Iris Chacón," Venus said. She sobbed again. "I just wanna look like Venus Xtravaganza."

Venus choked back another sob. Her face was going beet.

"Well, who else you planning on looking like?" Angel said. "There's only one of you in this whole world, for better or worse." She hugged Venus and could feel her girl shaking. She told her to sit down on the sofa while she got her a glass of water.

"Mira," Angel said. "Nobody told you to chop off your pelo like that. Be a big girl and take life by the balls, you hear me? We'll get through this if you just take a little chill pill."

Venus stood up, one leg at a time. Angel held her hand through it all. "Fine, but just for the record," Venus said, "I hate this wig. It is too big for a human head."

"You don't gotta wear it," Angel said. "Nobody is forcing you." She watched Venus put the wig back on and the curls engulfed her face. It was a pulpo trying to latch onto her brain with all eight of its curled tentacles. Venus stared at herself in the mirror again and whimpered.

"But I can't *not* wear something," Venus said. "I look ugly with no hair."

"Ay, nena, you—"

The buzzer rang. Venus was close to the intercom so she pressed the button to listen. Angel watched her as she had trouble moving the synthetic pelos out of the way so she could put her ear up to the speaker. Like before, there was nobody on the other end.

"Maybe it's broke," Venus said, but Angel couldn't see her face behind all the hair.

"It's not broke. I swear on the santos, y the gatos, y todos los patos," Angel said, "these crackheads are something else today. They've been buzzing my head off ever since noontime came around."

The buzzer lit up again so Angel stuck her head out the window to see if she could get a look at who it was. From where her head was at, she couldn't get a good angle at the building's vestibule.

Just then, the apartment door swung open. It was Daniel, huffing and puffing like he was gonna blow the house down.

"What's got you in a knot?" Venus said. She stepped away from the door and stared at Daniel through the wall of wig hair.

Angel gave Venus a look to hush. "Where's little Juanito?" she asked.

"He's fine, pero—" Daniel was catching his breath. Poor nene must've run up the four flights of stairs faster than Wile E. Coyote on a dynamite mission.

The buzzer went off again, pero this time, it was only for a blip. Daniel shot a look up at Venus. "What's with the ginormous wig?" Daniel said.

"This doesn't look like a time to talk about wigs, Dani," Angel said, waving hands in the air. She grabbed Daniel's earlobe to drag him to the sofa. "What's with all the huff and puff? You sound like you just ran the Olympics."

"It's your mom," Daniel said. He wasn't looking at no one in particular, so Angel didn't know whose mom was in question.

"Who?" Venus said.

"Damn yo, Venus," Daniel said. "I can't take you seriously with that wig on—"

"Dani, calla already with the damn peluca," Angel said. "Her head's shaved. Now whose mother is where, you said?"

"Yours." Daniel made eyes straight at Angel. "She's here and she's looking busted as all hell. Juanito's downstairs holding her back. She's practically foaming from the mouth like fuckin' Cujo."

"Juanito is holding her back?" Venus said. "But he can't hold back a fly."

"Don't underestimate him," Daniel said. "Sometimes he's got this inner He-Man strength that comes out to play whenever he senses trouble."

"Wait, wait, wait," Angel said. "I'm trying to follow all your words." She fanned out all ten fingers and pushed out her hands all fierce in front of her body. It was a look that said, Stop in the Name of Love, Before You Break My Heart. "My mother is here? You sure you got the right mother in mind?"

"She said she was your mother." Daniel shrugged. "I guess I never met her so I don't really know. All I had to go on was her word."

Angel stood up from the sofa without using her arms for support. She just rose with her hands still stretched out on either side of her body, fingers out like she was walking a tightrope in some fucked-up circus act and she needed her arms out to keep her from falling over. She walked over to the intercom and pressed the talk button.

"Juanito," she said. "You down there, nene?" She held down the button with two nails instead of one, just to be sure. "If you're really there with my mother, it's all good. You can bring her up here." Then she turned around and said to no one in particular, "I'll believe it when I see it with my own damn eyes."

* * *

Nothing could fool the eyes. Whenever she needed proof, she just needed to see in order to believe. Like when she wanted to remind herself that humans were, at their root, good and loving beings, all she needed to see was a giggling baby. When she needed to see the wonders of creation, she went to the public library, like Hector did, and watched fast-forward videos of trees and flowers in bloom. When she needed to accept that Hector was gone, she just needed to see his body there, on the hospital bed, when the nurse said she was so sorry and Angel screamed out that she didn't want her sorry.

So now there was her mother, standing before Angel's eyes, looking like the hot mess that Daniel had pegged her to be. Everyone stood up because no one knew what to do. Angel looked at Venus, at that wig that was consuming her face, then at Daniel and Juanito, who had their arms resting on each other's shoulder. Angel imagined what this scene must look like from her mother's eyes. For a hot second, she wanted to close her eyes and imagine that none of this faggotry was happening. She imagined that no one was in the room, that she wasn't wearing a hot pink jumpsuit with silver stilettos like it was just another night at the Roxy, or the Garage, or Studio 54, or the Saint, or the Pyramid, or god forbid, the Mineshaft.

She took a deep breath and pushed back her shoulders. "Venus," Angel said, "could you close the door. Juanito, could you pour a glass of water for my mother."

Venus and Juanito moved quick without saying a word.

"You look shell-shocked, Ma," Angel said. "It's okay. None of us are gonna bite you."

Mami stood there looking like all the color had been drained from her face. The woman had hardly aged. Well, if she was going to be shady, she would point out that maybe Mami looked a little dehydrated and tired (but who wasn't, really?). And it wasn't like Angel was going to dish some ingenuine compliment for her. Angel had figured out years ago that Mami was not the type of woman who knew how to take a compliment—she never said thank you.

When Juanito came back with the glass of water, Mami refused it. Angel offered her some pineapple soda, but that was all she could offer, she said, porque they didn't have anything else in the fridge at the moment.

"I didn't come to drink," Mami said. "Why don't you answer your phone?"

"I'm sorry that we don't keep rum stocked in my house," Angel said.

"Damn, Angel," Daniel said under his breath, but it was loud enough that Angel and everyone else could hear it.

"I was calling all morning, but there was nothing." Mami's slow words were like lashes. "Y entonces I come to ring the bell, and it ringsringsrings, cada hora, pero you don't let me in."

Juanito was still holding the glass of water out for Mami to take hold. It looked like he didn't know what to do with it, or with himself, standing in the middle of them, so Angel took the glass and downed the water in what felt like one gulp. "I thought you were a crackhead going to town on my buzzer," Angel said. "The phone company must've stopped service for a little blip, you know how it can get sometimes—"

"Miguel is dead," Mami said.

Time checked itself, like someone was mixing a house record and put their hand on the vinyl to slow down the spin. "That's not even funny," Angel said. "You're just being malicious now."

"It's true," Mami said, "my son is dead. They killed him."

What kind of cruel trick was she trying to pull now? Angel always knew that her mother was something cruel, but she didn't think that she had the cojones to march up into Angel's own house and mess with her like this. She had to have known that Angel loved Miguel like something fierce. She knew that Miguel and Angel kept in contact, and now Mami was manipulating strings just to make her feel bad.

"I just talked to him—" Angel said. She tried to think of exactly when it had been. Before the last ball, on the pay phone, like always, but she had gotten lunch with him a week ago. Now she wasn't sure. Maybe it was two weeks ago? Three? It was odd how remembering worked, how tricky it could be when trying to pin something down exactly. The mind was like a trapeze artist playing tricks in the air.

"Who killed him?" Daniel asked. Angel shot her head toward Daniel and Juanito. She had forgotten they were standing there.

"She said *they*," Venus said, and Angel shot her head to the other side to look at her nena. "I think we're all just wondering who did it, verdad?"

Angel looked back at her mother who seemed more concerned with Angel's outfit than the question. Maybe the jumpsuit and stilettos weren't right for this situation, but did her mother need to *glare* at her? How dare she throw shade on her outfit at a time like this?

"They," Mami said. "Nobody know shit. Nobody tell me what happen. Pero esto es lo que pasó: they shoot him in his car. Esos-hijos-de-puta."

"He had a car?" Angel said. The fact that she didn't know this detail about her brother's life was what stung her first. How was it that she could live with her brother for nineteen years, get lunch with him and listen to his life, but then at the end of things, realize that she had not known him at all?

Venus took off the wig and started to fan her face with the copy of *Cosmo* that was on the coffee table. Mami glared at the wig. "Creo que I made a mistake," Mami said. "I come here at a bad time."

Angel felt light-headed and the room was spinny. When it came to all these things about Miguel's life, she wondered if he withheld from her because of all the shit she gave him about the weed. Motherfucking guilt was a bitter feeling. She held out the glass and told Venus to get her the pineapple soda this time. Maybe the sugar would help make the dots in her vision settle down. The last thing she needed to do was collapse in front of her mother, who already thought she was weak.

"Mira con esa peluca," Mami said, pointing at Venus's head. "Y tú, Angel, con that tackiness you're wearing. I come to tell you that my son is shot and dead and you're over here playing dress-up."

The way that Mami referred to Miguel as her son pissed Angel off like she had no idea. It was a complicated emotion for her to feel. She felt like Mami was completely erasing Angel from the picture by making it seem like she had only one son. Angel knew that Mami had one son and one daughter (Angel, clearly), but she knew that Mami didn't think this way. Not once had Mami ever referred to Angel as her daughter. Not once had she acknowledged Angel's womanhood, and that hurt her beyond comprehension.

Angel took a step toward her mother. Angel was full of rage, and she knew that in order to be the better woman, she would have to take the high road. But she didn't have the map to the high road. How like Mami to be a critical mess. Angel took another step closer, not because she wanted to be near Mami, but because she wanted to be near the door so that when she swung it open and told her to get the fuck out, it could all happen in one swoop.

"Mira," Angel said. "You know what kind of life I live, and I'm proud of that life, so I don't know what you were expecting to see when you marched your critical ass up into my house."

"Eh, eh, eh—"

"Don't you interrupt me," Angel said. "I won't stand your ignorant ass coming into my own damn house, telling me I'm playing dress-up. I bought this dress at Bloomingdale's, do you have any idea what it means to me that I selected and paid for this dress all by my damn self? No, you don't because good, high-quality fashion wouldn't bite *you* in the ass. I don't have to—and I don't want to—legitimize my own damn clothes, or the wigs that I own, or my own damn body to you. Even if you are my mother."

Venus came back with the pineapple soda. Juanito and Daniel stood on both sides of Angel now, like her army of children ready to protect her. Or if they couldn't protect, por lo menos, they would be right by her side. Mira, Angel wanted to say, look at my family now. Look at all this love we got for each other.

"You can walk out any time you want," Angel said. "The door is right behind you."

Now Mami cried. Angel couldn't tell if they were crocodile tears or real ones. She could feel the muscles in her back tense up at the immediate feeling of distrust. Qué horrible—to think that someone could cry for the sole purpose of making her feel bad about herself.

Mami wiped the mocos from her nose, gave Angel a one-up, and said, "It should have you been you."

"Bitch," Venus said, "what're you saying about my mother?"

Angel held out her arm to block Venus from attacking Mami. Angel told Daniel to hold Venus back. Angel looked at Juanito's eyes and saw that he was searching her for something. It was a look that Angel hadn't ever seen, but she must have been aware of that gaze all along. He was looking up to Angel to see how she would handle the situation. It made her feel nervous and safe at the same time.

"How can you be a mother," Angel said, as dignified as she could muster, "when you act so cruel to your daughter? How can you say someone should've died over another? You think my life got no value. Well, look around you and see that it does."

Angel shot out her hands and spun around slowly. This, Angel could say, is my house and even though it may not look like much to you, I've built this thing from the ground up and filled it with people who love me. Mami kept crying.

"Maybe if you weren't such a horrible mother," Angel said, "you wouldn't have driven Papi to jump off that building and the drug dealers on the streets wouldn't have gone to shoot up your son." It was harsh, she knew that, very harsh. And maybe if she had more time to think about what she wanted to say, she wouldn't have used those words. But she did, she said them and there was no taking them back. "Maybe you should," she continued, "call the santera lady you got on the hookup at the botánica and she can kill a chicken so nothing bad happens again."

Mami was sobbing mad hard now. Angel had gone in for the jugular and it worked. Por supuesto, Angel didn't believe anything about the santera lady's voodoo powers, but she knew that words were like a knife and the most artful kind of shade could lacerate.

Mami walked up to Angel so close that Angel could count the nose hairs sprouting out of Mami's nostrils. She stared at her mother's puffy eyes, the blue-purple crow's-feet, the red tree-branched vessels in her eyeballs. "Angel," Mami said, bringing her hand up to touch Angel's cheek. "I'm sorry, I said it all out of anger. I came here, no? Porque even if you abandoned me and refused to come back home when we asked, I knew that you two were getting lunch and speaking all the time. I know that you had love for him."

Before she heard the words again, stated so matter-of-factly, this had all been another in a long series of power struggles with Mami. As if Angel didn't even know what they were fighting for. Pero now it hit her like a brick—Miguel was dead. He wasn't coming back. Somebody, or somebodies, had shot him. And they, whoever they were, would probably never be found, because that's just how that bad episode of crime TV went in their neighborhood.

Now Angel cried. She cried so hard that she grabbed onto her mother with both arms. They held onto each other and sobbed so hard, they had to get their knees onto the ground so they didn't fall over. They stayed there, together, having a moment to themselves as all the others watched in silence.

DANIEL

There were preparations that needed to be made. There were clothes that needed to be ironed, ties that needed to be transformed into Windsor knots, shoes that needed polish, teeth that needed flossing, pimples that needed *something* because cover-up would be a no-no, hair that needed to be uncurled, flat-ironed, held back into clips that looked masculine. That was the key, masculinity. It was, essentially, the problem. Not for Daniel, but for the others. Angel's mother made it clear: if anyone came to Miguel's wake dressed in drag, she would drag them out by the hairs on their chinny-chin-chin.

"Ugh," Venus said, "how'm I gonna pass as straight?"

Juanito laughed and clapped his hands over his mouth.

"It's not funny," Venus said. She was tying the laces on her black shoes. "God, I haven't worn flats in ages."

"Your arches will love you," Juanito said.

"Today is a serious day," Venus said. "Don't make light of it."

"I think what he means," Daniel said to Venus, "is that the idea of you—*you*—passing as straight is kind of funny."

"The ironic thing is this," Venus said. "She says she doesn't want anyone dressed in drag. But if she asks me to dress like a man, it's *basically* like she is asking me to show up in drag. I don't even know how to act like a man anymore."

"Well, for starters," Juanito said, slapping Venus's limp wrist. "You'll need to work on body language. Wrists, hips, neck."

"Ugh," Venus said. "What a burden. What if someone talks to me? What do straight guys even talk about?"

"Baseball, booze, and pussy," Daniel said.

"Oh, well then forget it," Venus said, throwing her hands up and walking into the bathroom. "I'm just gonna chain-smoke outside and when someone talks to me, I'll pretend that I don't speak English." She closed the bathroom door and Daniel could hear the hairspray can going off.

When they all had their thrift-store funeral suits on, Angel came out of her bedroom and walked up to Daniel with her hands on the untied tie around her neck. She whispered his name. "I need your help," she said, holding the two silk ends.

"Come here," Daniel said. It was a blood-red tie with a repeated white rose pattern. He grabbed hold of the ends and lifted the longer side over, then under, then near the neck and through the hole he had formed. When the knot was done, he told Angel to straighten her neck so he could make it snug around her, fitted and fine.

* * *

When they arrived, a group of people around the casket were talking about how much of a marvel it was that the funeral home could do an open casket, how auténtico the body looked, especially considering Miguel had been shot in the neck, twice, pero nobody could see the hole on the side or nothing. One woman, whom the others referred to as Titi Adalita, said the body looked very fresh. Had anyone ever seen a body so fresh? She told the group that when she dies, she could only hope to look that fresh.

Fresh, yes so fresh, everyone hummed in agreement. Qué fresco está este cuerpo, an old woman with no teeth said. Daniel looked down at the body in the casket, surrounded by flowers and crucifix palmas. Fresh? Daniel didn't know if he agreed about that, but what did he know?

He shrugged and turned to face Angel. "You doing alright, Mami?" he whispered.

"Hush," Angel said. She didn't take her eyes off her brother. "Don't call me that here."

Daniel blushed.

"Ugh," Venus whispered. "Rip this tie off my throat, por favor."

Angel gently slapped the side of Venus's arm. "Would you behave yourself, please?" Angel said.

Venus stopped fidgeting and stood still. When they kneeled down to pray around Miguel's body, Daniel peeked out of the corners of his eyes and saw Venus wrap her pinky finger around Angel's pinky finger, and it made Daniel want to cry.

* * *

Juanito wanted a cigarette, so they both went outside to light up. "This is horrible," Juanito said. "If I hear one more person say the word *fresh*, I'm going to scream."

"I know, right?" Daniel said. "As if he was a plate of berries in the nevera or something."

"Please, promise me," Juanito said, "that when I die, you're just gonna cremate my body. I don't ever want people crowding around my body and saying shit."

"Oh god, don't say that."

"What?" Juanito said, flicking one butt to the ground so he could chain up the next one. "I just want to spread out into the wind," he said, after lighting the next cig. "Just pick somewhere nice."

What took Daniel back was not the assumption that Juanito was making about them being together until the day they died, but that Juanito was jumping to the conclusion that he would die first. "Can we not do this right now?" Daniel said.

"Yeah, you're right," Juanito said. "I'm sorry."

Daniel closed his eyes and leaned his head back against the cement building. There were few things he loved more than savoring the calmness in his brain when the nicotine was settling in. He exhaled and Juanito gasped.

"What?" Daniel said, eyes still closed.

"Oh, you are not going to believe this," Juanito said. "This is real bad."

Daniel opened his eyes and Juanito put his hand on Daniel's arm, as if the image would go away—just a mirage!—if they held on to each other.

She was approaching, dressed in full drag—black elegant dress, a wig big enough to cover her large head, and a diamond necklace that Daniel was pretty sure was nothing more than cubic zirconia. She was smoking her cig through an Audrey Hepburn cig holder, like she was about to get breakfast at Tiffany's instead of going to a funeral. Daniel took a final drag of his cig and dropped it on the ground so he could step it out.

"Dorian," Daniel said, as Dorian gave them both double air-kisses. "Didn't Angel tell you about the dress code?"

"Darlings," Dorian said. "There's no such thing as a dress code—only dress suggestions."

"Ay, Dios mío," Juanito said. "You're certainly going to push some buttons when you walk in there."

"Dorian, please think this over," Daniel said. "You're gonna start something."

"I know, little darling," Dorian said. "And I tried. Believe me, I tried. But I don't own any menswear that would be appropriate for the occasion. If I came in denim, I'd have to go home and shoot myself for the shame of it all."

"Angel's gonna die when she sees you," Juanito said.

Dorian let her head back and laughed. "Well," she said. "I'm already dressed for a funeral."

"Please," Daniel said.

"I'm a human being," Dorian said. "I've got a soul. I've got a mouth. I will walk in there to pray for their loss, so help me god."

* * *

Daniel knew that there was no telling Dorian what to do. Dorian marched to her own fucking tune. So he knew that shit was going to fly when Dorian walked in. He held on to Juanito's hand and they waited a few heartbeats before following Dorian in. They didn't want Angel's mother to think they were connected at all. They didn't want to feel her wrath.

Dorian walked in there, head high. Daniel and Juanito stood at the edge of the doorway so they were far enough to feel outside of the situation, but close enough to see everything. Dorian marched all up in there like she was Jackie O at a gala in a long black dress with rhinestones. (Rhinestones! During the day!) She had one of those lace veils over her face. French manicure. The man was pure class.

When she walked in, Angel looked like she wanted to drop dead right then and there. And her mother? Don't even get a bitch started. She had on her falcon eyes, just watching Dorian who went to kneel down in front of the casket to pray the rosary.

All of the old women were silent, trying hard not to stare, but staring anyway. No one talked or made a hush. Angel's mother walked over to the priest. Daniel couldn't hear what she said, but she must've said *something*.

The priest walked over to Dorian, whose head was angled down into her praying hands. He tapped her on the shoulder and whispered into her ear. She looked at him and said, "How dare you? You call yourself a servant of the Lord?"

He didn't say anything back to her.

"How dare you ask me to leave?" Dorian stood up and looked out at the crowd of people gawking at her. "Yes, I know I'm beautiful," she said to everyone. "But it's rude to stare."

Juanito snorted and Daniel wanted to laugh and snap his fingers in solidarity. Oh, the hug they would give her when everything was over.

Once they were outside, they walked a block away so they could congregate without worrying about what Angel's family would think if they saw them all together.

Angel ran out to join them on the corner, but she didn't hug Dorian. "What was that?" Angel said. "What were you pulling in there? Dressed like that? I told you not to."

Dorian dished out a smirk. "I knew I had to come, darling," she said. "I wanted to be here for you."

"But I told you—"

"And, darling," Dorian said, "I'm telling you something now." Angel hushed her mouth and blushed a little, like a child being scolded. It was an odd feeling for Daniel to see their mother being told what's what. "After all I've done for you, you just stood there silent while I had to stand there, alone, as if I was some kind of freak show."

"I—"

"You," Dorian said, taking over the floor again, making no hesitation to show that Angel would have her time to speak, but now was not that time. "You know who I am, Angel. And you know I'm not going to change or play dress-up just so that I can fit into some fucked-up version of the world those people think we should be trapped in. I'm disappointed in you."

Angel's eyes began to water and Daniel put his arm around his mother.

"That's enough," Daniel said to Dorian. "You made your point."

Dorian looked at Daniel, up and down, and then she walked away from them as Angel cried.

FOUR

DORIAN

Life is a ferocious motherfucker, that's what I always say. And it's not death that you need to worry about. He always comes, and he's usually quiet about it. But life, boy. She is loud and fast and—vicious.

Back before Hector died, I remember talking to him. Oh gosh, he was so young then. One of the LaBeijas, I think it was Crystal, told Hector that he was a slut. Now, of course, as he was telling me this I was thinking, *And? Isn't that a compliment?*

No, he told me, it wasn't a compliment.

Well, you can always take it as one, I said. Now *that* had him thinking. I asked him what he was so afraid of. So what, she called him a slut? Can't a queen make her own decisions and decide who and when and how she wants to quench that sexual thirst? Because god knows we get thirsty.

So I'll tell you what I told him. I said, we fags are gonna hurl the same shade that the straight people toss at us, except they don't call it shade and we do. And when she calls you a slut, you can't call her a slut back because that would be a lazy read. Like, honestly. But you find another flaw in her and bring it out. Make it larger than life and toss it right back into her misshapen face and have a good kiki about it.

And Hector said to me, Yo, Dorian, what're you afraid of if you ain't afraid of words?

I had to think about what to tell him because I know what I'm afraid of, but I wasn't about to vocalize it. Especially to him. He was so young then, and if being called a slut could hurt him, I didn't want to set anything else into that mind of his that would make him worry. So I told him I was a fearless motherfucker and did he not know that already about me?

Ha! And he laughed and I laughed and we all laughed and kiki'd together until he forgot about the question or was too afraid to ask me twice.

What I was, and still am, afraid of was much harder. You know, back when I was a—young queen. OK . . . , I wasn't that young, but I was young*er*—I had some friends down in New Orleans. This was in the seventies. They were preparing for pride festivities at the UpStairs in the French Quarter. And then somebody came in, doused the place with gasoline, and lit a match. Yes, lit a goddamn match and torched the place with all those pretty people inside it. In our safe place. What more can I ever say? To this day, whenever I perform, I refuse to wear flammable fabrics. I just can't shake that fear. I can't.

But I couldn't tell all of that to Hector baby. He'd never come back stage to take off my wigs after that! He'd be scared as straight as a mascara wand. So I told him something to try to reassure him. I told him what I always say when someone tries to take away the power that I have over my own damn body by calling me a slut. I told him that I wish I could just take out my compact mirror and turn it around on the other person. Because unless you're a nun, you shouldn't be hypocrite enough to talk down to someone for being slutty. Like damn.

So I always say that when the world calls you a slut, just kick back your legs and fuck and enjoy it. Because if life don't call you a slut, she's gonna find something else to call you.

And life is too short to be a Puritan. Who wants that anyway? That would be no fun at all.

VENUS

The biggest shame in the whole world was that coke wasn't a vegetable. If it was, she would be chock-full of vitamins and minerals. When she was blowing through lines, she didn't have to think about how she felt. She was too blown to give a fuck. That's what she loved about coke. It made her whole body tingle. Her mind felt sharp, alive. More than anything else, it made her feel confident.

That winter, she fell into a kind of habit. She wasn't addicted. It was just a habit, nothing more. She started off doing bumps of blow on the tips of keys, every now and then. Then she started doing her bumps after having a little cafecito in the morning at the bodega. Then she graduated to lines on top of the metal boxes that house the toilet paper rolls in the public bathrooms. When the mood was right and she had a good wad of cash on her, after pulling some tricks, she'd get a fresh baggie and celebrate with a big fat rail. But that was only when she had the money. She didn't want to blow through all her money and run out of stuff. That would put her in a pickle.

In an ideal world, she would cut lines with the edge of a charge card. But she didn't have any charge cards. Instead, she used the next best thing: a dull razor blade about the length of her pinky finger. Damn, sometimes even a glance at the refined powder made her think of powdered sugar, and she'd have the urge to take a pinch of the coke in her fingers and sprinkle it on top of a muffin or a slice of lemon pound cake.

But she would never! That would be wasteful, and she didn't want to be wasteful with her coke. Snorting it was always the better experience than rubbing it on her gums or tongue. She'd rather feel the brain do twirls than have her mouth go numb, though she had to admit, the thought of putting it on lemon cake made her wonder if maybe her throat would go numb in the process.

She was already coked out of her mind when she got to Washington Square Park. It was the middle of the day and the sky was so blue and bright, not a cloud to be heard of. She sat on a bench and dug a key into her coke baggie, brought the scoop up to her nose, and inhaled it gently. She licked the tip of the key and pinched her nose so that the inside of her nostrils could absorb what needed to be absorbed. She turned to look at the young dude—probably an NYU kid—who was taking a nap next to her on the bench. She wished he wasn't napping because she would kill for a good convo. Oh yes, she wanted to talk and talk and talk. And she had interesting things to say, so maybe that guy would listen to her and be charmed.

"Why, hello, I didn't see you there," she said, even though she had been sitting on the bench for a couple of minutes and *had* seen him there. He probably didn't notice. She waited for him to wake up and she could feel the coke gears in her mind clicking into place. The sky was getting even brighter now, so she reached into her backpack and put on her sunglasses. "Hello?" she said, hunching over him to see his face. She wanted to see if he was handsome, and she couldn't tell because his arm was covering half of his head, but his bone structure looked sturdy.

"Gosh," she said to him, "you have the loveliest eyebrows. You know, I got this theory that if your eyebrows are done on point, then everything else in your life just falls into place. Just falls right into place, I tell you. Isn't that a great theory?"

Still no reply.

"Well," she continued, "I guess I can ask you to confirm or deny it, but I really hope that you confirm it, because if you don't, it would send my life into a tailspin."

Still nothing.

"Okay," she said, "maybe I'm being dramatic. I know it's a lot to process. Wow, what a beautiful day. I love beautiful days, they just make me want to stand up and spread my arms."

She stood up and spread her arms up, up, up, and then she just had to sit back down. But not before rolling out her ankles a little. It was good to stretch a little bit.

Still no response from that one. She laughed and moved her hand to flip back her hair, but then she remembered that her hair wasn't long anymore. It was just out of habit. A natural reflex. How strange.

"Look," she said, "if you don't wanna talk to me, just tell me. I'm a big girl, I can handle it. Otherwise, I'll just keep talking because I love to talk, especially on beautiful days. Look, there isn't a cloud in sight. Amazing. I mean, you don't even know me, but I could talk an ear off. Ask anyone. I just talk and talk and talk and then, boom, you look down on the ground and there's your ear, the ear that was on your body, but there it is on the ground now. Fallen off." She took a deep sigh. "Do you have any gum? I'd really love to chew on a nice wad of bubble gum. Oh, damn now, you are a silent one. I mean, I do love a good silent man. So underrated, silence, you know? One time I let this guy fuck me and he was so loud, and the whole time I was thinking, *Can't you just be a couple notches more quiet, can't you learn something from the silent dudes, I mean shiiit.* Like, when he came, I thought he was having a stroke or some shit. Like he was dying, it was animal-like. But then I realized he was just enjoying himself and I thought, *Good for you.* And then I thought, *Good for him? No, good for* me.

"I mean, if you don't say nothing, I'm just gonna keep blabbing and when you go back to your dorm or whatever, you're gonna tell your friends, Oh, wow, I met this chick today and she could not keep a lid on it. You know, it's like when you give a girl an inch, she'll just want eight more."

Still no response. Not even a chuckle to her joke.

"Oh, come on, you are a tough crowd. That's what we call a joke. And it was a cute joke, if I might say so myself, shiiit. I always think my jokes are funny though, but I guess you're making me re-think that. But I guess when I think about it, everyone thinks their own jokes are funny, because, like, why would they say them if they didn't think they were funny?"

She looked over at him. Not a budge. He was out cold. Maybe he took something. Damn, she wanted whatever he was having. "Well you're no fun," she said. She put her arm on his side to shake him. She knew it'd be rude to startle him awake, but she wanted to talk and she wanted to listen. She was tired of being alone, but he still didn't move.

"Oh," she said. "Oh god."

He wasn't moving, she didn't know if he was even breathing. When she looked at his eyeballs, they looked like they were rolling back. "I'll be damned," she said. "You're one dead motherfucker, aren't you?"

She didn't know why she was asking him if he was dead, because that'd be some nonsensical bullshit. Like, duh, he wouldn't be able to respond. She needed to get out of there quick before the police found him—found *them*. She needed to find somewhere else to go.

* * *

She went to the subways because she loved the subways. She loved that every inch of the metal cars was covered in squiggly lined graffiti. She loved the ads for bagels and lox. She loved that the Equestris Restaurant had taken out an ad calling itself the most exciting restaurant in New York, as if anyone would ever want to trek to the outer edges of Queens to eat a meal at a horse track. She loved the mix of outfits and people—that anyone who got on the train was instantly an equal in those minutes or hours, however long it would take a person to get to wherever they were going. That afternoon, she sat down on the seat below the words Pelham Bay and Brooklyn Bridge. Venus was sandwiched between an older white lady in stockings and a wool skirt, and a middle-aged white dude who was holding up a newspaper above his knees. She wanted to compliment the man on his red tie, which she could swear was a Dior, but she knew she couldn't do that. She wouldn't dare break the unspoken rule of the subway: this was not a place for talking to strangers. NEWPORTS: ALIVE WITH PLEASURE! She loved that, there, underground, she could feel alone in a car full of people. And damn, she would kill for a good menthol cigarette.

Somewhere below Midtown Manhattan, the train was full but not too full, which meant that some people were standing because there were no more seats, but it wasn't like they were a packed can of sardines. Venus had her legs crossed and was delving into her copy of *Myra Breckinridge*, which she loved to crack open after doing some lines. She was at the part where Miss Myra's in the infirmary after attending her Posture class and Rusty is being friendly with her (ever since their dinner at the Cock and Bull), when all out of the blue, a man in a suit stepped on Venus's foot. She looked up from *Myra* in order to read him: he was wearing gold wire-rimmed glasses and had a tie that was striped horizontally. He'd probably be bald before the decade ended. He didn't apologize for stepping on her toesies, so she glared at him.

She watched as he avoided looking at her. He held onto the bar above her and scratched his salt-and-pepper sideburns with his free hand. But after the doors closed and the train started moving on toward the next stop, the man unzipped his pants and plopped his dick right in the middle of her book.

Now she had seen some shit before, and of course she knew that a person could never predict the level of New York Crazy they would witness on the street or the subway at any given time, on any given day, but this was taking it over the line somewhere. She was too shocked to even scream. A dick on her book? *The absolute nerve,* she thought, as she looked at it. Uncut, oddly veiny, but not in a hot way. It was like an anteater nose, and could he beg her pardon if she informed him that his dick was in need of some aloe vera lotion. It wasn't a pretty penis, though she didn't know if that would've made any difference. A beautiful penis could still be shocking, but perhaps for different reasons.

But what got her riled up was that as she continued to gape at him, he wasn't even looking down at her. It was like he had gone and done this weird-ass thing, but then didn't want to see her reaction, or didn't want to even acknowledge that she was sitting there, behind that book that now held his dick. Like she was fucking invisible. And what the fuck did he think she was going to do? Stick out a finger and stroke it as if it was a newborn puppy too young to even open its eyes, and say to him, Aw, would you look at this cute little penis laying in my book?

No! She would rather not. The train kept going because, now she realized, they were in an express tunnel. *Wondrous,* she thought, *that's just my luck.* Like some kind of fucked-up version of Murphy's Law. She looked to her left, where the man kept staring at his newspaper, then to her right, at the older white lady who was spending 100 percent of her energy and attention on smoothing out the wrinkles in her wool skirt. She looked out at the other people around her on the train—the white woman with knee-high patent leather boots, plus her skinny boyfriend who was resting his head on her shoulder, the woman with her grocery cart full of plastic bags, the young muscular black dude in the red beret near the sliding doors. They all looked around at anything and anyone but her, but the man, but his ugly dick. No one was helping her.

"I beg your absolute pardon," she said, loud enough for everyone to hear, "but could you please let me read my book?"

He ignored her and she was ready to rage out at him. His dick was still there, blocking words, being a nuisance. She knew what she had to do—clearly what Myra herself, that bad bitch, would do in that moment too—but she had to wait in order to time it right. She stared down at the guy's dick. She stared at the thick vein in the middle and watched as the man was becoming harder, like it was a balloon slowly being inflated. This was some fucked-up bullshit and she couldn't even wrap her mind around it. She knew that New Yorkers could get down with some kinky shit—how could she not, she had met enough of them down at the piers—but she had never thought someone would have the balls to do this to her in the middle of the damn public.

When the train slid into the next station and stopped, right before the doors opened, she placed her open palms on each side of the hardcover book, and then she slammed it shut, squeezing his dick inside the book as hard as she could.

He didn't scream but she could tell from the wince on his face that he was pained.

"I asked you nicely," she yelled. "If you don't bruise, I hope you at least got a paper cut so bad, it'll sting for a week."

He put it back in his pants and zipped up. "You fucking tranny bitch," he said, running off before the doors slid back closed.

"Oh dear," the old lady next to her said. She put a hand on Venus's thigh. "Are you alright?"

The man to her left put down his newspaper and looked at Venus and nodded his head, but for what? To acknowledge her presence? Venus had no idea, and what good would that do anyway?

The rest of the people in the car kept on staring at whatever they were focused on. Like nothing had happened. It made Venus even wonder if what she had just experienced was real, or if she had just imagined it all up. Surely her coke was good, but it wasn't good enough to make her hallucinate an entire situation like that.

"Yes," Venus said to the lady. "I'm fine, thank you for asking."

But what she really wanted to do was stand up and rage against each and every person on the train who knew what was happening and chose to not say or do nothing. She didn't do that though. She just sat there and opened her book back up where she left off: Myra was talking about postponing something, but Venus had already forgotten what needed to be postponed. She felt tired now, all of a sudden, wondering if she could make it through a single goddamn day without having a dick thrown into her face.

She needed another line. The train kept zooming through the tunnel and she looked out the window at the shadows against the tunnel walls. She needed to get off that train and find a bathroom. She reached into her pocket to feel the small baggy of coke and she closed her eyes to daydream of how light her mind would feel when she took her next sniff.

* * *

She spent the afternoon on a bench at the piers reading Vidal. She spent the evening at the Gray's Papaya, eating sauerkraut with her fingers out of those little plastic cuppies because there was no way she could stomach a hot dog after all the coke she had blown through. Then, once night hit, she went to a bar in the West Village and listened to a group of older queens attempt to work their way through some sad show tunes. Songs about hopes and dreams and futures that seemed bleak, at best. After an especially depressing rendition of "One Hand, One Heart" from *West Side Story*, the man singing fell to his knees only halfway through and had to be carried off stage by two lesbians who cooed, It's alright, it's alright. And when they were outside smoking a cigarette, whispers began: the gossip was that the man's partner had been checked into St. Vincent's, which was a shock to everyone because he had looked fine just the week before on Fire Island.

That was Venus's cue to leave. She could watch or hear no more of that. In the bathroom, she reached into her pocket to see how much coke she had left. Nothing, just residue, and the crash was creeping up on her something hard. The pressure in her temples felt like metal nails were digging in slowly, making their way to her eyeballs. She reached into her backpack and glided her hand along the bottom to see if she had any loose bills or spare change. Her fingers hit some coins, but when she added it all up, she had about three dollars' worth of quarters, which definitely wasn't enough to get a belly-button-size bump of coke. She wasn't even sure it'd be enough to get her a bump's worth of baking soda, if she had to be real about it.

She walked up to Times Square to see if she could pop into one of the peep shows with the side booths. To take a nap. A couple of quarters could buy her—maybe an hour's worth in the little booths?

It took her forty minutes to walk from the Village to Times Square. The whole time she walked, she had this fantasy that Myra Breckinridge would come to life, offer her a silver platter full of rails and tight tubes of C-notes to use as nose straws. It would be fabulousness.

She saw the first peep show sign right around the corner from Sally's, where some of the ball children did their drag shows for the bridge-and-tunnel crowd. Dorian had always talked about her own forays at Sally's, dancing with her titties out for the closeted husbands who'd take the LIRR or NJ Transit back to their boring-ass ticky-tacky homes where they pursued their lives as breeders. All Dorian's words, not hers.

She walked inside the tiny booth, sat down on the stool, took off her heels, and inserted her twenty-five cents. When the curtain rose, a young girl was in silk lingerie, pushing her big breasts together behind the plexiglass. Now, if Venus had any interest in actually viewing the show, she would've asked for a boy dancer, but she wasn't delusional—she knew there was no such thing as a boy dancer in one of these kinds of peep shows. No demand for such. And Venus was tired, so she didn't want to watch shit. So, while the girl played with herself, Venus gave herself a little foot massage because her arches were killing her after all those hours trekking in heels.

She didn't know how quickly it had taken her to fall asleep, but when she heard the tap-tap-tapping against the plexiglass, she startled awake. The girl was on the other side, looking pissed as hell. Venus knew that the girl couldn't see her because the viewing room where she was sitting was dark. They were designed so that the performers couldn't see the viewers. The girl's face was all WHAT THE FUCK ARE YOU DOING, IT'S TIME FOR MORE QUARTERS.

Venus picked up the phone that was in the booth so she could talk to the girl. The phone was such an old, gross, sticky thing that Venus didn't even want to bring it completely to her ear.

"You're such a doll, honey," Venus said, yawning. "Just looking at your chest is making me jealous."

"Excuse me?" the girl said.

"Oh yes, right, maybe I should clarify," Venus said. "I'm not your average customer. I'm a flaming homosexual, honey. Just my presence alone could flame this building down." She was being witty and it tickled her, but she was getting off message. She was broke and tired and gay. She needed to communicate that. "Well the thing is," she continued, "I had a few quarters on me and I was just trying to take a nap."

The girl looked like she wanted to cry. And Venus could only imagine: being young and performing at a place like that, and then your clientele just wants to nap while you shove two wet fingers up your pussy? Horrid. Probably better to be stuck between a rock and a hard-hard place.

The girl flicked the light switch and Venus's booth lit up with fluorescent lighting. Venus hated fluorescent lighting. *The road to hell*, she always thought, *wasn't paved with good intentions. It was paved with fluorescent lights*. "Dear," Venus screamed, covering her eyes. "It's too much."

"You can't take a nap here," the girl screamed into the telephone. "Get a room for that. Don't you see I'm trying to work?"

"And you *are* working," Venus said. She could certainly empathize. She knew how it was, when things were rough and she needed to get some cash. But what could a girl do? She was out of money and energy. She had no more coke.

The rush of nausea hit her. She swallowed two or three times quickly to keep from vomiting. "Please, honey," Venus said, her voice so soft that it almost embarrassed her. Just the thought of seeming weak in front of a stranger made her self-conscious. "Please, I've had a day, I'm sure you can relate. Can I please just sleep here for a hot second?"

By now, her eyes were adjusting to the lighting and she could look up at the girl, who was kneeling on the ground of the plexiglass-encased room. There was a red velvet curtain all around, and the girl looked right back at Venus. "You really don't," the girl said, "have anything more to give?"

The girl's fingernails were bright blue acrylic press-ons that were too wide for her thin hands and small nail beds. "No," Venus said. "Maybe, hold on." She wondered if the girl was too new at this to get the proper size press-ons, or if she had just made a mistake and selected the wrong size.

Venus reached into her backpack and took out the empty coke baggie. It looked like a Ziploc bag made for a Barbie doll. She slid it in the small tray where dollar bills were supposed to go for making special requests of the performers.

The girl took the baggie with two fingers and ripped it open by the sides. She put it on her tongue and she sucked on it for a hot moment, then spit it out so it hit the glass and slid down. "Haven't had any of that since I first came to the city," the girl said, "if you can believe it."

The curtain on the other side of the cube swung open and Venus could see the outlines of a man in the other booth. The girl moved over to the other side and smushed her tits together as a signal that the next show would begin.

Venus saw a cockroach near her feet, but she was too tired to flinch or scream. She grabbed her heels and tried to swat at it. It scurried away and Venus looked up one last time at the girl, wondering if the shadowed man in that other box could see Venus with the bright white lights on. And if he could, she wondered what it was, exactly, that he could see.

* * *

She smoked cigarette after cigarette wondering where to go. She couldn't go back home that night, not in her current state of affairs. Angel would positively kill her if she saw her like that, especially if her nose started to act up with a nosebleed. Being in that house made her realize how much she missed Charles. She found it painful to watch Daniel and Juanito be so cariñosos with each other. Whenever she looked at Angel, she saw a mirror of her own pain too. Like Charles was not even on the same level as Hector was, but she still felt the absence of him. She wanted to stay away from all that. She wanted more blow.

There was no way she'd be able to score some coke in the Bronx. She'd have much better luck doing that in Manhattan because the farther uptown she went, the more rocky the powder became. And she didn't want crack.

Then there was the issue of the piers. No, she didn't want to go back down there. She didn't feel like getting into cars, or sitting alone near a boom box watching other people have their fun. She didn't have the energy or the absolute patience to be around groups of people. That left her with two options, she thought, as she waited at the crosswalk. She looked to see if there were any cars or trucks zooming by so that she could step out into the street and jaywalk.

She could go to one of the rundown hotels or movie theatres in the area, the ones that catered to the Port Authority crowd—the pimps, the girls in poom-poom shorts, the visitors arriving by bus, looking to score.

Some hotels had rules and some did not. Not written rules though. Not like the hotels in the beach towns she would visit with Angel back in their heyday when they were barely twenty-one, sipping margaritas with too much salt, staring at the Jersey boys, figuring out how to get a ride from Long Branch to Sandy Hook's nudie beach. Those beachside motels had rules about shirts and shoes, which was always meant to say, you had to wear them or get out. Wear sandals by the pool, or get out. Wear a shirt and shorts at the pizza joint, or get out. Everybody was caught up in a list of rules. The hotels in New York were the same.

She always had a love-hate fascination with these hotels, ever since she had first come to the city, fresh from Port Authority, and trekked up to Central Park. Gosh, it was disorienting to think of how many years had passed. She wondered what she would say to her younger self, if it were possible to send a message in a bottle back through time. What would she say that night, right before he took her to the Plaza and fucked her on that bed? Would she even say anything at all, even if she could?

It was so useless to think about, she almost hated herself for trying. She waited at the crosswalk still. It was unbelievable how quickly time swept by in the grand scheme of things, yet how long it could take for a fucking crosswalk signal to change. How was it that it could only take a handful of months, or just a teeny-tiny sliver of years, for certain aspects of herself to become unrecognizable? Now, as she prepared to cross that street, among the neon signs shining for the peep shows and the pimps and the prosties in knee-highs, she just wanted another line of coke and she didn't care what she had to do to get it.

Another ciggie went into her mouth, but her book of matches was all out of lights. This would not do, not at all. She needed this smoke. She needed a fuck too. She needed a bag of coke, a wink of sleep, some morsel of happiness would be nice too. A man to say he loved her and it didn't matter how old she got, he would always be there by her side. How much was that to ask for?

"'Scuse me," she said to the next man who passed her by. He kept walking and she said, "I said, Excuse me. I just need a light."

He turned around and flicked a book of matches at her. But it fell short and the book landed on the sidewalk. She had to crouch down to pick it up. He kept walking and she wanted to give him the finger for being so rude, but he had given her what she wanted, hadn't he? She kept the finger to herself and lit her cigarette.

"'Scuse me, darling," she said to the next woman who passed by. She looked outrageous in her orange jacket. It was a confusing splash of orange puffs and strings. *Probably one of the FIT students*, she thought. "I'm just wondering," Venus said, "if you could tell me what day we're on?"

"What?" the woman said.

"What's the day today?" Venus said, and then before the woman could respond, she blurted out, "Honey, you're giving me *Sesame Street* realness in that jacket."

"What," the woman said, "the fuck is that supposed to mean?"

"It's a compliment," Venus said, "trust me. You know where I can score some coke?"

The woman eyed Venus hard. Her eyes were purposefully smeared with bright blue eye shadow. Très edgy, Venus wanted to say, but she kept it to herself.

"I'm not some cop," Venus said. "Just a flaming queen in need of some lines."

The woman looked torn, like she didn't know if she wanted to keep walking the street or if she wanted to give Venus the hookup.

"At least tell me what day of the week it is, darling," Venus said. "Cat got your tongue?"

"Thursday morning," the woman said, "and I am way too fucking drunk for this right now. Who *are* you?" When she put her hands inside her pocket, Venus thought she looked like a life-size orange lint ball that somehow sprouted a head and legs. Venus was enthralled by her and wanted to know where she was going. This woman was so chic, there was no way she didn't know where to score some coke.

The woman pulled her hands out of her jacket and looked left and right. She reached out her hands to offer Venus a little bump off her pinky nail.

"Fabulous, radiant, yes," Venus said. "You're such a doll." She pinched her nose so the lining of her nostril could eat it all up for breakfast. "And it's Thursday," she said, throwing her hands up in the air. "And we've got the whole weekend ahead of us, right, honey?"

With that, the woman turned her back to Venus and threw up all over her damn self. It didn't matter though, because Venus was feeling good, feeling fly, feeling all of her feelings. A little vomit here or there wouldn't stop her from enjoying her high.

JUANITO

He and Daniel were in charge of decorating the tree while Angel made her bomb-ass chicken noodle. He was looking forward to that soup more than anything else that day.

They didn't have any stringy lights, so they decided to dress the tree with whatever party streamers and tinsel that Angel had in a cardboard box in the closet. "Ay, Dios mío," he said, pulling out a long cord of silver tinsel from the box. "If I could, I would make a sweater out of this shit."

Daniel laughed. "That'd be one helluva itchy sweater."

Juanito clicked his teeth. "Pues," he said, "I guess you wouldn't get one then, now would you? Not with that kind of mentality." He lifted his shoulder and play-huffed in Daniel's direction.

Daniel rolled his eyes. "Qué drama," he said.

The tree that Angel had been kind enough to select for them, but which she absolutely refused to help them carry down the block and up the stairs, was three feet tall. It made the tree in Rockefeller Center look ginormous, but Juanito still thought it was cute. Like they had their own baby tree right there in the sala. Daniel held the end of the party streamer between his teeth while he tried to squeeze into the corner of the room. He was trying to get the streamer around the tree. He couldn't reach all the way, so he had to go around.

Angel was in the cocina, stirring the pot. She asked if Venus had called. The soup, she shouted out, was almost ready for the taking.

"Nah," Daniel said. "Haven't heard a thing from her in hours."

"Days," Juanito added.

"Ay, what am I going to do with that one?" Angel said. "Supongo que I'll leave an extra bowl out for her, pero damn, Miss Free Spirit over there must be feeling the Christmas cheer."

"She's probably waiting in line at Macy's," Juanito said. "Waiting to sit on Santa's lap."

"You're certainly feeling feisty today," Daniel said.

Juanito blew him an air-kiss and grabbed one of the tinsel ropes and wrapped it around Daniel's neck so he could pull him in for a kiss. Then he pranced over to the cocina and wrapped another tinsel rope around Angel's neck and said, "Come on, mami, ven acá."

"Ay, Juanito," Angel said. "You know I'm a little busy over here with this food situation."

"Yeah, yeah," Juanito said. "I see it all, but you can always take a little break and dance with me for a hot second." He rolled his shoulders up and down and shimmied his chest while pouting out his lips. He was trying to channel a silly energy, and it must've worked, because Angel laughed so quick and hard, she hiccuped.

"Yo," Daniel shouted from the sala.

"You don't gotta yell," Juanito said. "We can hear you loud and clear. It's not like we're on Mars. We're just in the cocina."

"Hardy har," Daniel said. "Yo, Angel? I don't see no star or angel muñequita in the box. What do we put on top of this thing?"

Juanito flipped the left side of his tinsel-boa over his right shoulder just like a scarf. "Goddamn," he said. "We are workin' this tinsel like it's tinsel-fuckin'-town."

Angel smiled at him while she rolled her eyes. "Ay, Juanito, tinsel is tacky," she said.

Juanito let out an exaggerated gasp. He pretended to whip his hair back. "How could you say that, darling," Juanito said. "I can't even look at you."

"Juanito, could you please," Daniel said. "I'm trying to finish up the tree. We need to put something on the top of it."

"We could make a star out of construction paper," Angel said.

"Ugh," Juanito said. "And you said tinsel was tacky?"

Daniel laughed. Angel told Juanito to stir the soup.

"How about we put Venus's giant dildo at the top?" Juanito said.

"And then, when her wandering ass finally comes back home, she'll have to climb the tree to get it."

"The tree is only three feet high," Daniel said.

"We are not putting a penis on top of our Christmas tree, Juanito," Angel said. Her arms were crossed like she meant business.

¿Por qué tan seria? Juanito thought, wanting to push her buttons even more. "Well what about if we put it in the nativity scene then?"

"¡Ay, Dios mío!" Angel said, doing the sign of the cross. "You are being a sucia, Juanito. We can just use one of my tacones for the tree. The higher the heel the better, don'tcha think?"

Juanito stirred the soup and then tasted just a drop from the wooden spoon. It burned his tongue.

"I think I got a red one," Angel said, "and Venus has an emerald one. Then it'd be Christmas colors so it could feel matchy-matchy."

* * *

By the time the soup was eaten and the two tacones were placed on top of the Christmas tree, Venus still wasn't back. Daniel was flipping through a magazine and Juanito was sitting next to him on the sofa filing his fingernails. Juanito could hear Angel in the cocina, slamming drawers and opening cabinets only to shut them right after.

"Dani," Juanito whispered. "Could you do something? She's about to lose her shit if Venus don't walk through this door in a second."

Daniel looked up from the magazine and sighed. "I know," he said. "Pero I don't know what to do."

"Y yo tampoco," Juanito said. "Pero you're better at soothing words than I am."

Daniel shut the magazine and called out to Angel. "'Ey, mama," he said. "Why don't you come settle down over here with us and we can paint your nails."

"Good idea," Juanito said, gently slapping him on the side of his chest. He didn't know why he didn't think of the idea first.

Angel said she couldn't. She was too busy putting Venus's left-over bowl of soup in a Tupperware. "And then, I don't know what she's gonna do. She's gonna have to reheat it on the stove or some-thing," she said aloud.

"There's worse things, right, mama?" Juanito said. "Por lo menos, she'll have some soup waiting for her when she gets back."

"That's not all she'll have waiting for her," Angel said, "porque I'm gonna give her a piece of my mind *and* my mouth when she struts in here. Can you believe the nerve of that girl?"

"Oooh, look at you," Daniel said. "Being all bad over there."

"Hush," Angel said, waving her hand like she was gonna swat a fly.

"You love her too much to give her a scolding," Daniel said.

Juanito nudged him with his elbow, like, you better quiet down and not mess with Angel when she's feeling like a fire-breathing dragon.

"Don't make me give you a piece of my words too," Angel said, popping her head out of the cocina so she could make eyes with Daniel. Daniel rolled his neck back and sighed.

Juanito walked over to where Angel was, right in front of the stove. He put his hand on her arm to get her to stop moving. "She'll be fine," Juanito said. "You know she'll be fine."

"Who says I know she'll be fine?" Angel said. "Who says I know anything? The more I think I know, the more I learn that I'm wrong."

"Mira, mami," Daniel shouted from the sala. "Let's take you to Unique Boutique tomorrow to get your mind off things. Noth-ing like a new pair of shoes to make a nena forget her problems, right?"

"Yeaaah," Juanito said. "There ain't never a bad time for a new pair of shoes. And plus, she's gonna come in here eventually and have some good stories to tell us," Juanito said.

"It's been two days," Angel said. "She's never done this before. If she's gone for a while, at least she calls."

"So she'll call," Juanito said, but as he stared at the chunks of carrots and pollo that sunk to the bottom of the Tupperware, he started to have dudas about it too. "You should put a lid on that," he said, pointing to the Tupperware.

"I can't find it," Angel said. She scanned all around the counter-top and then crouched down to check the cabinet where the other Tupperwares were.

"It's right there," Juanito said, "behind the sugar jar."

"Ay, Juanito," Angel said. "What would I do without you?"

* * *

The next day, shoe shopping with Angel was like pulling teeth. Homegirl couldn't get excited about anything—patent leather pumps, a pair of yellow kitten heels, not even the ballerina flats in bright purple. Juanito knew something was really, totally off, when he found a pair of second-hand Guccis that didn't make Angel bat an eyelash.

"The Guccis were on markdown," Juanito told Daniel later that night, "and she still wouldn't crack a smile."

"Jesus," was all Daniel could say.

On the subway ride home, Angel kept talking about how worried she was. It was all she talked about all day. "Mother's intuition," she said, "mother's intuition is always right and this feeling that I got is all kinds of wrong."

Before they got back to the apartment, Daniel picked up three bottles of red wine. As soon as they were home, Juanito uncorked them and practically fed them to Angel like she was a baby in need of formula. "Toma," Juanito said, "you gonna get some real good sleep tonight, okay?"

Angel nodded her head and drank.

Once Daniel carried Angel to her cama for sleep time, he and Daniel cuddled on the sofa with the TV on. The nightly news was about to finish up and the sports guy was blabbing. They kept the TV on so it could give them some background noise.

"I think she might be right," Daniel said.

"Ay, no, not you too."

"Pero listen, Juanito," Daniel said. "Each and every one of us ran away from home, like why do you even think we're here right now in this fucking apartment?"

"You think she ran away from us?"

"I'm saying," Daniel said, "that it sure as hell is a possibility. And Angel knows that."

"She wouldn't leave us," Juanito said.

"Oh, come on, you and I both know that she wanted to be in a big old fancy house," Daniel said, "and she found that guy from Staten Island."

Juanito sighed. Daniel was right. He had to be. Venus had always said that was her dream: money and a house and a white dude who could give her things.

"But that guy was an asshole," Juanito said. "Ese pendejo was still married. Don't you remember?"

"¿Y qué?" Daniel said. "That don't mean shit. You don't think she'd go back to him? Of course she would. In a heartbeat or a second, whichever came faster."

Juanito turned his head. He was trying to think it all over. He couldn't believe it and he couldn't bear to see the TV screen or the side of Daniel's face.

"Maybe she had another man," Daniel said softly.

"Ay, Dios mío," Juanito said. "Pero she could have called or said something. What did she think we were going to do? Lock her in the apartment and refuse to let her out?"

It was a pointless question. He knew that Venus wouldn't ever think they would lock her in or hold her back. Pero ahora, the answer that Juanito didn't want to face was much harder to deal with— the thought that maybe Venus loved them so much that she couldn't bear to say goodbye to them at all.

He rested his head on Daniel's shoulder and, even though they had nothing more to say to each other, they stayed up for another hour, watching infomercials for the amazing Ginsu knife. The last image Juanito could remember before he passed out was of a free-floating hand slicing the shit out of a watermlon—right down the middle.

* * *

That night, his dreams haunted him. He dreamed of vagabond wigs that jumped off heads and walked away. He dreamed of wigs in heels, dancing on the tops of cars with cigarettes dangling from their lips. He saw wigs that sprouted legs and danced "Thriller" faster than Michael did. In his last dream, he saw Venus sitting on a revolving circular bed of wig hair, eating a piece of cheesecake with her hands. Nada happened except she finished the cheesecake and said, "Damn, I was really having a moment there."

He jerked awake and he was still on the couch next to Daniel. *Good Morning America* was on TV and he shook Daniel awake to tell him about the dream. Daniel yawned. "What're you talking about?" Daniel mumbled. "She hates cheesecake."

* * *

Five days later, Angel got a call from the police department. He and Daniel didn't know that Angel had filed a missing person's report until the phone rang right before lunchtime. Daniel had just finished preparing some rice and beans and Juanito was putting forks on the table. They looked at each other from across the room as Angel hung up. Juanito could see the panic in Daniel's eyes.

"Pues," Juanito said. "What did they say?"

Angel said that she needed to go over there and they would talk about it when she came back.

Once Angel left, he was too nervioso to eat. "You should really eat something," Daniel said.

"But my whole body is bugging out," Juanito said.

"Por eso," Daniel said. "Food'll coat the lining of your stomach and help calm you down."

Juanito looked at the steaming mounds of rice that were still too hot to touch. He really wasn't hungry and he knew it would burn his tongue. "I can't," Juanito said. "I just don't understand why she didn't ring us."

"There's the leftover soup in the nevera if you want me to heat it up for you," Daniel offered.

"No," Juanito said. "I'm not eating Venus's soup."

"Pero—"

"Pero nothing," Juanito said. "I'm not eating Venus's soup, and that's it."

"You're right," Daniel said, pressing the mound of rice down with the back of his fork. "I don't think I can eat neither."

They waited for three hours like that—chain-smoking and staring at the TV as *The Price Is Right,* the news, and *All My Children* started and ended. Juanito didn't even notice what color dress Susan Lucci was wearing that day.

When he heard the key turning in the door, he stood up and watched Angel walk in. She closed the door slowly. It wasn't until she looked at them that she began to cry. Daniel ran over to her and helped her walk to the dining room table without falling over.

"¿Qué pasó?" Daniel said, even though Juanito didn't want to know what happened, but rather, *where* she was.

Angel said that Venus was dead. Some heartless motherfucker must've strangled her throat. Her body was found under the bed of some Times Square motel with wounds around her neck that probably meant strangulation. Angel said that's what the cops told her. She said she had to identify the body in the morgue. The woman cop told her that Angel was lucky to have filed a missing persons report, because the body was waiting there and they were already drawing up plans to ship her to Potter's Field.

"And I said to her, how could you just send someone to Potter's

Field without seeing if someone comes by?" Angel said. "And she said to me, because usually nobody does come by."

Juanito looked at Daniel. His face was whiter than a pearl earring. Juanito put his head on the table and sobbed. He could feel Daniel's fingers running through his hair, massaging his scalp.

No one said a word, porque what could they even say? Until finally, Daniel asked the question they must've all been thinking, "What the fuck do we do now?"

ANGEL

When Hector died, she had to sign the papers that said City Burial. Not because she wanted to, but because she had no other choice. They didn't have enough money to give him a private funeral, the kind with a box and flower wreaths and a priest who could come in to say some words. People kept saying that it was only the good who died young, but this pissed Angel off to no end. She didn't care if it was the good or the evil or anything in between. She wanted to tell everyone to shut the fuck up, because unless they could raise Hector from the dead, she didn't want to hear shit.

What a city burial meant, she didn't know. Once the papers were signed, she spoke to several people on the phone and someone gave her the contact information for the Hart Island Project. If she wanted to visit Hector's grave, they told her she could take a ferry from City Island's Fordham Street pier. There was only one ferry a day, so she couldn't miss it. She kept the phone number taped to the nevera door and she saw it every time she got up to get a glass of milk or fry an egg, but she didn't call the number. She didn't want to go see the site. She was fine in her mind knowing that at least the city had been nice enough to bury him on an island, and even though she knew it wasn't going to be some kind of tropical beach island, it could always be worse.

For months she had dreams that he was still alive. These were the cruelest dreams because when she woke up, there were two or three seconds where she thought that he actually was still alive. Then the realization hit her like a brick wall—that no, he was dead, still dead, ain't coming back to her. How many times did her waking mind have to play this trick on her? It just wasn't fair.

One day just after lunch, she was listening to the local news on the AM stations, all static, sparkle, and hiss. The man said a crack baby was born and died in a toilet bowl somewhere off the Bowery. No mother came forward and the baby didn't have a speck of dust for family. So the city was sending the baby to Potter's Field on Hart Island.

Hart Island? Her ears perked up, but the man was already on to the next news cycle. *That's the shit about the news, isn't it?* she thought. They couldn't even stop to mourn for a loss after each story. No, it was always on to the next thing, then the next.

The next day, she went on down to the New York Public Library to read about Hart Island because she was confused as to why Hector and an abandoned crack baby were sharing space.

She was dumbstruck by the first thing she learned: that it wasn't spelled Heart. Here she had thought, all along, that Hector was buried on an island named after the heart. She had imagined it as a place of love surrounded by water. But no. She learned that it was the Rikers inmates who did all the digging: two rows of pine coffins, three high and more than twenty across. All for the pay of less than a dollar an hour. Each plot marked by a single block of concrete. Abandoned people, the homeless, victims of murders, those too poor to pay, on and on.

Then another book said that the island was first used as a Civil War prison camp, an institution for locos, a sanatorium for TB patients so their coughing wouldn't spread. This meant little to her, though, because she didn't think she knew anyone on Rikers, the Civil War felt so far away that it wasn't packing any emotional punches, and she didn't want to know more about TB patients.

She found a microfilm of a newspaper article that was only dated from a couple months back. First baby to die of AIDS in NYC, buried in the only single grave on the island. She tried to imagine this baby's tiny fingers, tiny toes, how many inmates it'd take to dig a hole the size of a shoe box. She wondered if those inmate dudes knew what they were digging for that day, staring at a hole so small. Concrete marker, the article read, SC B1 1985: Special Child, Baby 1, 1985.

She couldn't read anymore. She went to the bathroom and threw up. She went home and, that night, she dreamed of a small island in the shape of a heart with a giant hole in the middle. The hole was full of amputated arms and legs, all waiting for their other matching limb. Hector was at the bottom of the pile, staring up at her, waving with both arms, and even though she saw him down there, her voice refused to work and she couldn't get out any sound.

* * *

She'd be damned if she let the same thing happen to Venus's body. So that morning, she spritzed her Chanel No. 5 on both wrists and got on the train en route to the funeral home in Chelsea that was— word on the street—friendly with the community. Only place, in the beginning years of the crisis, that wasn't wrapping boys in black garbage bags and sealing their coffins.

When she arrived, she was almost kicked to her ass from the overload smell of flowers. Carnations, the ugliest of flowers, were everywhere. There were two wakes in progress and she didn't need to pop her head in to confirm what she already knew. They were probably young, they were probably gay, and the biological families were probably absent.

Once she was in the director's office and had explained what had happened, the topic turned to the small details. The pricing estimate, which was a bullet list of points.

"Why are you charging me for nail polish?" she asked James, the parlor's sales guy. "This much for nail polish?"

"It's not just the polish," he said, as if he had said it five hundred times before. "In that fee, you're also paying for the specific type of polish used and for the expertise of the embalmer who knows how to safely curate the body."

She didn't know what to say, so she just shook her head.

"You said your friend didn't—" he said, "didn't have the virus."

"Not that we know of," Angel said. "She was strangled to death."

"Right, right," he said. "This makes things easier, as I'm sure you can tell."

"Could I save that money by painting the nails myself?" she asked. "I think I have just enough expertise in that department."

He told her no. Unfortunately, it would be a safety hazard to have a non-embalmer near the body. And what did she know? She hadn't done any of this before. It amazed her that even the people who worked in Death could turn it all into a business. There was money to be milked everywhere, even if you weren't alive. Who knew? She didn't. Hector was buried on Hart's Island, for fuck's sake. She had promised herself that no one else she knew and loved would get the funeral of an abandoned crack baby. Not if she could help it.

* * *

When she opened the door and stared into the closet, she knew that she would have to do some reaching. She used both hands to part the clothes that were dangling by their hangers. She got to her knees in the dark of night so Juanito and Daniel wouldn't see what she was doing. She took out the memory box that she kept in the back corner. There was the envelope. It was thick now with bills that she had been saving. She held the one marked *Dreams* in her hands, then she turned it upside down so the money could fall to the floor beside her.

She organized the bills into piles of ones and fives and tens and higher. She counted and recounted to make sure the number wasn't wrong. She got the same number three times and knew there was no way it could be off. That should be enough, she told herself.

She put the bills back in the envelope from smallest to biggest. She picked up the picture of her and Hector from the Coney Island photo booth. (It was the photos that made the memory box the hardest to open.) On her absolute life and soul, she couldn't believe how young she looked in those pictures. If she could go back to that time, she'd tell herself to enjoy things more, to not worry so much. What a babyface she had, letting the foto rest on her bedside table. Time was something else entirely.

She thought about the Chanel suit that she was so close to buying. She refused to accept that it would never be hers. Sure, she was emptying her savings, but that didn't mean Chanel was out of reach. It would just take longer. She didn't know how she would be able to go up to that Saks counter without Venus or Hector by her side, to say, Yes, Mama, Wear That Chanel, but she'd take those steps when she came to them. Now, she was back to square one.

The next morning, she returned to the funeral parlor exactly when they opened. It was strange to see James come up to the door to unlock it. Just like when she was young and in school, she imagined that all her teachers lived under their desks and never left the building. It was the same with James and the funeral parlor. She couldn't even imagine what his life was like outside of this place.

"You're a little short," he said, blushing. "Let me recount. Maybe I made a mistake."

"No," she said, inhaling deeply. "I counted three times at home. Count again. I'm positive it's right."

He thumbed through the stack again, then another time. She sat straighter in her chair. *Posture*, she thought, *posture, posture*.

"I'm so sorry," he said, "you are indeed short. By four hundred fifty."

What she would do for a goddamn cigarette. She would draw the nicotine in and hold it in her lungs until she passed out. "But I don't have four hundred fifty more," she said. "I just don't have it."

He looked at her and sighed. He looked back down at the money that was there and she wished for the magical ability to make more appear.

She'd have to come up with some other plan. And quickly. She spun her mind to think of options: Go back on the streets? Pick up another job? Even if she did both, there was no way she could come up with almost five hundred in that short of a time span. She tried to think of who could lend her money. Dorian? No, that wouldn't work. Dorian had her own struggles.

"What about," she said, "a city burial?"

The words made her want to cry, but what could she do? She had no options. The money she had saved wasn't enough. She had failed.

"A city burial?" James said. "You mean Potter's Field? That's always an option, but—"

She said yes, and said we, she meant I, a few years ago, um—her lover died three years back and she couldn't afford a pot to piss in at the time. She didn't really remember what the process was like for city burials and she wanted to know if he could help her fill out the paperwork.

"Your lover is buried on Hart Island?"

She had to sit on her hands so that she didn't have to feel them shaking anymore. She couldn't look at him because she was so ashamed, so she looked down and nodded her head.

"Oh, Christ," he said. "I can't let you do this right before Christmas." He brought his hands onto the desk and put his forehead into his hands. "Okay, I'll figure something out. We can make this work."

"What?" she said. "What do you mean?"

"Don't worry about it," he said. "We'll cover the rest of it. That look on your face is breaking my heart and it's been a hard year. I've never had to bury so many young people. Every week. I don't understand what's going on."

"Thank you," she said. Now they were both crying, but she knew they were crying for different things. She couldn't ever say why another person was crying at any given time, because she couldn't read minds. That seemed to her one of the most heartbreaking things about being human.

She wasn't just crying for the friend that she would never get back, the friend that she had failed to help, even though she didn't know how she could've helped her in the first place. She was crying because if it weren't for James's offer, she didn't know what she would have done. Yes, she was grateful for all of that, but she was also sad that she wasn't lucky enough to have the kind of life where she didn't need to depend on the kindess of strangers.

* * *

As soon as she got back to the apartment, she wanted to collapse into a ball. It was dark and Daniel and Juanito had beat her to the sleep game. They must've fallen asleep together on the couch on accident. She watched them snuggling, arms intertwined. She walked, careful not to clack her heels so that the sound wouldn't stir them awake. She adjusted the cotton blanket over them to make sure that when they eventually woke up, they wouldn't find themselves cold.

Tomorrow, she thought, tomorrow we will plan this service together. She went to her room and everything was throwing shadows. She left the lights off and looked at everything sitting in the light that poured in from the street lamps. There, standing alone on her dresser, were her trophies from all the balls she had won. So many that the one shelf couldn't hold them all and they spilled over to the floor. Golden plastic statuettes of winged women with hands reaching up in the air, holding torches above their heads, all perched on fake marble bases. They each had the name of the ball they belonged to and the year of the event. She kept them in time order, from the early years to present. She loved to see the sizes grow as her talent had grown.

She turned around and peeked into Venus's room across the hall. She looked at her collection of trophies from the same balls. Oh, how they had laughed and kiki'd when they won shit together, like they were gonna take over the world with their sass, charm, charisma, beauty.

Angel walked over to the bed, which Venus had left unmade before venturing out. There was a purple camiseta on the edge—

perfectly ironed and waiting for somebody to snatch it up, put it on. She picked it up and brought it to her nose and inhaled the spritz of Jungle Gardenia that Venus always sprayed on her trigger points. "Porque," she could hear Venus saying, "those are the points on the body that make the perfume come up off the skin. Makes a girl smell like a thousand bucks."

More than anything, Angel needed several large gulps of white wine and something to eat. When she walked back out to the cocina and opened the nevera door, the yellow light spilled into the room. Pero there wasn't nothing inside: no wine, no food, only a little tub of butter that Angel thought may have been expired. Even if it wasn't, she wasn't about to eat butter straight with a spoon. She was too tired to run back downstairs to get something from the bodega. She closed the nevera door and the light went out again.

Around the wall, she peeked out at Daniel and Juanito. She wanted to wake them up so she wouldn't be all alone, but she figured she would let them be. They were tired and she knew how that went. She was tired, too, damn it. She went to the closet and pulled out an extra blanket, spread it out on the floor next to the sofa where they lay still, and curled up on the floor right next to them. She closed her eyes and wished Hector were still around to hold her through all of this. Pero she knew that was an impossible dream, so as she focused on sleep; she thought, *Tomorrow, tomorrow we will get back up together and figure out what the hell to do next.*

PART THREE ·

THE SKY VIEW

(1991–1992)

The moon is always rising above your house. The houses of your neighbors look dull and lacking moonlight. But he is always going away from you. Inside his head there is always something more beautiful.

—Sarah Ruhl, *Eurydice*

DANIEL

Better believe that every part of his life had a soundtrack: a set of tunes so fine or so feeling, all it took was an un-dos-tres ritmo to get the soundboards of his mind spinning and shaking their cassette tape memorias. When he thought of his days with Juanito, he saw them in quick bursts of images with no sound. Some in color, some without, pero con sound? Nunca.

Like, one: there they were at the door, bags in hand, re-learning how to whisper. They needed to decide whether or not to kiss Angel goodbye. He was scared that one of them, or maybe the both of them, was gonna die on those streets, pulling tricks with those sketch-ass johns. Once Venus was dead and gone, he felt like he was seeing the potential for death everywhere.

He knew they couldn't say goodbye to Angel. (Ya, Dani—Juanito said to him—ya tú sabes que she'll kill us, fucking scratch our eyes out, if we don't say goodbye.) He knew Juanito was right, but he also knew that they couldn't say goodbye because, if they did, they never would've actually left.

Y dos: rickety subway ride alone on a Wednesday night, graffiti up the wazoo, watching some nena with permed out hair hurl vomit all over the plastic orange seats. Dos-dos: heading down to the pier and thinking, *Damn, how did we get to this?*

At least it was May, which meant not too warm, not too cold. He slept on the bench with one arm under his shoulder for support, y el otro with the switchblade—porque he knew that Juanito wasn't capable of—even if they were in danger—hurting any small thing.

Tres: on to the shelters, on to the job interviews in oversize suit jackets from Salvation, on to the nights when things got so bad, he wondered if they were going to wind up starving like the bums who were lined up on the Bowery. It didn't matter the time of day or night, there was always one dead that they'd have to tiptoe over, always careful not to disturb a body or else their soul'd find them and haunt their ass until kingdom come.

There they were, he and Juanito. Ain't nothing had nothing on them. They were louder than love. Louder than love, because damn, love ain't no low drumbeat. Love was so loud, they couldn't even hear it. Only see it, like light—flashing forward and giving not a single fuck for what stood in its way. There they were, he and his man, hand in hand, so loud you could only see them flash.

* * *

It took them a year on the streets plus two years in and out of shelters before they got their own place. With their old days and ways behind them, the apartment was a total matchbox on Driggs. They had a bed (taken from the street), but no frame. They had a TV, but no sofa, a VHS player, but no cable, an oven, but no microwave. They loved it anyway because they were only looking up to see if they had a roof—and they did.

In their first few weeks there, they developed certain rituals. They picked up plates and cheap utensils at the thrift store, and they washed and rewashed them. "Ay, Dani," Juanito said. "Look at how this fork *sparkles*. Just like brand new."

They would shower and walk around the living-dining room completely naked, just because they could. He would whistle at

Juanito and tell him how beautiful he was and that he should work, work, work that room like he owned it. He took it all in: the way that Juanito's calves flexed as he took each step, the way his abs *v*'d down to his patch of pelitos, the way his tiny pecs were defined *just enough,* and how his lower back muscles pinched in and accentuated his beautiful little culo.

After they bought their barely working TV—a bulky thing with antenna ears from god knows what year—at the used-electronics store, they started to rent scary movies from Blockbuster. They set up a bunch of blankets on the sala floor each week and held each other while the most fucked-up shit happened to the other people on the pantalla.

"Ay, por favor," Juanito would say whenever shit was going down. He rose in tone and intensity each time: "por favor, por *favor,* por fa-*vorr,*" as if each please would make the action stop. Like Carrie was just gonna stop midstab and be all, I forgive you bitches, let me just excuse myself and go home to eat Twizzlers and play with my cat.

Daniel wasn't quite sure why Juanito liked those pelis so much, because they seemed to scare him shitless. But he liked the routine of it. Maybe that was what Juanito loved about it too. They had finally become the type of people who fell into a routine, who were able to live out and express their love for each other by agreeing to lay together each Friday night and stare at a pantalla.

He would lay there with Juanito each week, holding his love in his arms and feeling Juanito's body tense up. He loved that Juanito could still be a total sass machine, even when he was scared shitless: about *The Exorcist* (ay, now that is one fucked-up little chica with a nasty vocabulary), Freddy Krueger (pues, por supuesto, if Johnny Depp was in my bed, I'd want to eat him to death también), Chuckie (uff, por favor, that creepy little muñeco es feísimo), *Carrie* (oh hell to the no).

Sometimes Daniel glanced over and watched the blue TV light against Juanito's face. He took in the way Juanito's body fit with his like a llave, and just at the moment when he felt like all was right with the world (he had always said it wouldn't take much to make him a happy man), he had mental flashes of the stories that Juanito shared with him about his childhood. He imagined Juanito as a little boy in pain, naked as his father beat the shit out of him for being too much of a damn princesa. In those moments, he looked at the pantalla to watch people die deaths with one hell of a lot of blood. Always blood: squirting, spraying, oozing. But couldn't a person just die from being hit to the head one too many times? The images on the screen seemed, somehow, better than imagining Juanito's young pain because, por lo menos, Daniel knew that shit in the peli was all fake. It was all death and blood and white girls screaming on a set somewhere in the past, and when the credits rolled and the room was black and the TV was turned off, it was all over.

During *Jaws,* Juanito caught him staring. "¿Qué?" Juanito asked. "What's wrong with my face?"

"—it's nothing," he said. "You just have an eyelash on your cheek." Juanito's long eyelashes were his prettiest feature, Daniel always believed. They curled upward naturally, for sure making every chica jealous of the way it made his eyes look real fem. (Once, a morena in Duane Reade had asked Juanito if he wore mascara, and he watched as Juanito smiled and said, "Girl, whatchoo think?") He picked off the eyelash between two fingers and told Juanito to make a wish.

Daniel felt Juanito's shoulders tense up and he pulled Juanito in closer. "Ese tiburón," Juanito said as Jaws rushed out of the ocean. "I don't understand why he's gotta eat all those innocent people when there are other things he can eat in the ocean." A body went under and the water foam went red. "Ay, por favor. Enough, Jaws! We get it."

"Dunna, dunna, dunna-dunnadunnadunna, ahhh!" Daniel hummed, and softly bit into Juanito's neck. Juanito flinched back as he laughed. "Yeah, but without Jaws," Daniel said, "it would be like, family goes to beach, family enjoys beach, family goes home with all their limbs."

"Exacto," Juanito said. "Why can't I just see a nice happy family story? That's all I'm sayin' I want."

Daniel pulled the blanket over their eyes and kissed Juanito on the tip of his nose, then on his lips. "You know what?" Daniel said. "You've got the prettiest eyes I've ever landed on. We're about to make our own happy family story." This was his dream, after all: no more hustling, then maybe one day they'd have their picket fence.

"Ay, you know how to make a boy feel like a princess."

"Ya tú sabes."

"I never want these movies to end," Juanito said. "Even if they're fucked-up and shit."

"¿Por qué? You wanna see more people get eaten by a killer shark?"

"I just hate endings, that's all," Juanito said, snuggling his head into Daniel's shoulder. "I just never want anything to end."

* * *

He worked at a furniture store to make the rent. Sometimes fancy-rich customers would push his buttons. They could be so demanding, he wanted to quit on the spot. But then he'd think about the rent, and swallow whatever anger the customers had provoked.

That day, what the vieja in front of the counter didn't understand was that she couldn't get the sofa delivered overnight. Even if she paid extra—Daniel lied—there was no way that it could be done.

"But I live on Eighty-Sixth and Park," she said, putting her hand up to her neckline so she could take each of her pearls between her fingers and roll them back and forth.

"I understand, ma'am," he said, staring at the bones in her hand. He always thought that the hands were the most intimate part of the body. All the face-lifts in the world, but the hands? Ain't nothing the doctors could do to the hands. "But there's still no way."

The woman leaned over the counter and huffed. "Listen, young man," she said, "there is no need to take a tone with me."

It always shocked him when white people felt they could reprimand him. He didn't realize that he had dished over any kind of tone. At least not any worth noting. The irony of the situation was that *she* was taking a tone with him. He took a deep breath and thought, *This too shall pass.*

"I apologize if you're hearing a tone," he said. Customers were a daily struggle.

But she was technically right. There was something he could do for her delivery, but he didn't feel like doing it. It's not like he thought of himself as a blazing mentiroso who told lies for no reason. He preferred the white lies, they were the harmless ones. He relished the sweet kind of power he felt when he told them. He couldn't deny someone a couch or a table or a thousand-dollar glass vase—if they were loca enough to buy one—but he could certainly delay their shipment if they were rude to him.

"But I don't think you are *understanding* what I am telling you," the woman said. "We are on the same island. It's only a matter of blocks. Which is a few miles away. What could it take a truck? Twenty minutes?" She spoke to him, he felt, as if he were a child: slow and steady, so the words could soak themselves in all good. "For goodness sake," she continued, enraging herself as she kept talking. "There is a near-empty truck outside that you could put the sofa in if you wanted to. But you simply don't want to."

He smiled, which was maybe the wrong thing to do. He reminded her—for the third time—that shipments only went out once a week, and that it took two days to process the orders. "And you haven't technically placed your order yet until we carbon copy your charge card," he said. "You haven't even *decided* on a model."

"Even if I *do* select a model, I would really like it delivered tonight. May I speak with the manager?"

"She's at lunch," he said. "I'm sorry, it's just not possible to deliver today."

Of course anything was possible if she was willing to pay big bucks, and over the course of five months working at Black & White

Decor, he had quickly learned that anyone north of Seventy-Second Street was willing to pay, as long as they felt that their demands were being met.

If he had to be real about it, he wanted that sofa for himself. For nearly two months, he'd been lusting after it in a way that was borderline weird to be lusting after a piece of furniture—how it would look in their empty room, how buttery soft the leather would feel against their skin as they watched their pelis, how shocked Juanito would be to see that he'd saved the money and actually gotten the damn thing. And it was (would be!) all theirs. No more piles of blankets no more.

It was a white leather Maurice Villency, completely flat with no back to rest on, as if it were a daybed, with two long tube-shaped pillows on the ends. "You gotta come see this sofa." He had called Juanito during his lunch break when it had first arrived two months earlier. "I can just see Lorraine Bracco walking into our apartment, clapping her hands twice, and saying, *The furniture's all Maurice Villen-ci-a.*"

"Stop it, you are joking."

He could hear Juanito's adorable giggle over the line. "Well, yeah, I'm joking. But only kind of. We're gonna buy this sofa, Juanito. We need to."

"No me tomes el pelo," Juanito said. "And with what money?"

"I don't even know," he said. "I'm still salivating over it."

"You know we can't afford it, babe."

He knew they couldn't afford it. When he had got back on the floor, he checked the tag. Two grand. Two *whole* grand. For a sofa. So he had spent the course of those two months—eight weeks and three days, to be exact—saving pocket change and picking from his paycheck, which came in the form of an envelope of cash at the end of each week.

Now, the woman slipped her bony fingers away from the necklace and squeezed her black leather wallet like it was a nutcracker and she was trying to break the world's meanest chestnut. "Well,

I suppose we could wait until next week," she said. The words sounded like they were paining every cell in her body. "I suppose we just have no choice, do we?"

"I'm sorry, ma'am."

"What do you think of the sofa anyway?" she said.

"Oh," he said. "I think there are other options—to save money. We have some new arrivals toward the front of the store that are a little cheaper—"

"Goodness," she said, "money isn't the issue. Neither is *function*. I'm referring to the style. What do you think of that style? I suppose I'm just a tad worried that my husband will see it and think it looks a bit too faggy."

It didn't bother him that she had used that word—even though the word itself was also fucked-up—but that she had said it to him in a whisper, as if it had been a joke shared between them and no one around them was meant to hear it.

"I'm not quite sure what you mean," he said. The words felt stiff in his mouth. Nothing had ever made him more aware of who he was—and how damn different he was—than being forced to interact with customers who spent thousands of dollars on muebles. He would take their words and phrases, try them on for size, see how comfortable they felt in his mouth, as if he were sitting down in a recliner to judge how comfy the cushions were. *Not quite sure what you mean:* the words felt like an antique wooden chair, hard with an unreclinable back. What he really wanted to say: every palabrota he had ever heard, even the ones he never had the cojones to say to rich viejas. He wanted to go full Evangelina from *Cadenas de amargura* on her old ass.

She must have noticed the look on his face—what that look was, he had no idea, but surely there had been some sign of rage, because she said, "Oh dear, I'm terribly sorry. I didn't mean to offend you."

"It's not a problem."

"I had no idea." She got closer to his face and whispered. "Plenty of my friends are homosexuals. My intention wasn't to be gauche. I do think it's a lovely couch."

*　*　*

That night, he and Juanito downed some beers on the roof of their building and he asked Juanito what he thought the woman had meant by the word.

"She was just acting a fool," Juanito said. "I don't think you should get too worked up about it."

"I'm not getting all worked up," he said. "I'm just trying to make sense of it. And she even knew that I was offended by it, but I didn't say nothing about nothing."

"Well, were you fucking some other guy on the couch?" Juanito said, laughing. "Then it would make some kinda sense for it to be a fag couch."

"Faggy, she said faggy."

"Es igual, ¿no?" Juanito rolled his eyes and took a swig.

"I guess," he said. He thought about what it was that people saw and made them realize he was gay. Or not gay. And when. He didn't understand how a person in the straight world could know these things. Sure, there came a moment when two men, walking a straight line down the street, eyes peeled to the ground, could look up and *see* and recognize another maricón walking down the street. The eyes might linger for a moment, drop down to check out the cuerpo, por un poco, then move on. No need for words. But with straight people? The idea that a straight person either could or couldn't tell made Daniel feel unsafe, not because he didn't want them knowing, but because he wanted to know *when* they knew so that he could feel safer in his own body.

With Juanito, who was as fem as the sequins on a Vegas show-girl bodice, there wasn't much to look past. But Daniel had always thought he was more about the banjee effect with his own masculinity. But banjee was just that: an effect, nothing more. "Do you really think I'd be fucking some other guy?"

"Claro que no, Dani," Juanito said. "Ay, you're really hot and bothered by it, huh? I think you're just angry because she took the sofa from you."

"Bueeeno, it was never ours in the first place," he said. "And we knew it'd never be ours."

"Ain't that the truth," Juanito said, sipping from the beer's bottle neck with his pinky up, all delicado.

It had taken all the strength he could muster, and then some, to fight the urge to take out a Sharpie in the stockroom and scribble all over the white leather so that, a week later, when it was rolled away and shipped out, she'd be in for quite the little sorpresa. He didn't know why he was being such a baby about it, but it was really bothering him.

Yet when he weighed the options and imagined how the scene would go, he decided against it. He imagined that the woman would call the store and complain to his manager, Charlene, the no-nonsense closeted lesbiana who had taken a chance on hiring him despite his being, as she said, *a little rough around the edges,* like he was some kind of cardboard cutout that hadn't been traced carefully enough. So there were his options: revenge or food? So he didn't pick up the Sharpie—didn't even look at it.

Juanito asked him if he wanted the last beer.

"No," Daniel said. "It's all yours for the taking."

He admired how Juanito didn't care about these incidents that he took so personally, like straight to the corazón. Pero, there was Juanito who didn't seem to give one single, flying fuck about how others perceived him. Must've learned that from Venus. When Juanito was doing the ball circuit years ago, one of the Duprees threatened to cut a bitch because Juanito had worn the same leopard-print leotard that one of their queens had worn at the last ball. "So what?" Venus had yelled, "like we're some kind of sacrificial-fucking-lamb. You bitches can eat my ass!" And when they called Juanito a copycatted, uninspired, little spic, Juanito didn't lose his shit like Venus had. He had simply held up her three fingers and said, "Read between the lines, that is, if you *can read,* you ignorant little cunts." He must've learned that from Angel. Yes, Juanito was cool-calm-collected in the way that Angel was: they could both call someone an ignorant little cunt and still sound as classy as the Queen of motherfucking England.

Then there was the time when they had first moved to Williamsburg. They were holding hands on their way to the bodega to get some cold cuts and chips. When an older Hasidic man wearing an oversize suit and black felt hat walked in the middle of them—like it was some kind of fucked-up game of Red Rover—grabbed each of their wrists and threw their hands apart, Daniel had been so enraged. The man had just kept on walking like it was nothing. Daniel wanted to turn around and punch the man in the face, but Juanito grabbed Daniel's arm and said, "Don't do it, papi. It's not worth it. I'm tellin' ya." Of course Juanito had been right, but it made Daniel wonder why he was no longer the reliably calm one in the relationship.

He finished off the last of his beer and let the glass bottle roll down the tilted cement surface of the roof. "I wanted that sofa," he said, "and she took it away from me."

"Pero mi amor," Juanito said. "It wasn't yours in the first place."

What was worse was that the sofa would sit there for a week, taunting him, with a white piece of paper that said SOLD in order to warn the others to back off, that shit was already taken.

"You know what she did when I imprinted her Amex?" he said. "When I handed her the pen to sign the slip form, our hands touched for, like, a second. And she fucking froze and looked at her hand like I had just given her leprosy."

"Ay, por *fa*-vor," Juanito waved his hand in the air.

"Like she thinks that just because I'm gay that I'm infected with the virus? Look at these hands." He threw his hands up, fingers out. "Okay, they're a little dry and I gotta clip my uñas, pero mira—no marks, no bruises, no sarcoma shit. No fuckin' virus."

"Daniel, ya, already."

"But for real, babe. For once, why couldn't that sofa just be mine," he said, looking out at the way the dark clouds over Manhattan moved in front of the needle at the top of the Empire State. It was a building that he had never visited in his entire life, but one that he noticed maybe every day. *The view from the top,* he thought, *must be one hell of a fucking view.* The park, the water, the puentes, and that edge on the horizon where the sky meets the land. That view, he imagined, you could probably see it all and then some.

* * *

The plan was simple: when Juanito was taking a shower, he would play the *Psycho* music in the cassette player with the volume on blast, and as the bathroom was filling with steam, he'd take the BBQ rib and pretend it was the knife, and then he'd pull back the shower curtain, and then the practical joke would be over and they'd laugh and kiki.

He got home from work in the evening, and Juanito was getting ready for a deejaying gig at the dance joint Lalalandia. "Ay, Dios mío," Juanito had said, "you should see those crazy white people letting loose." Since Juanito was never one to be really into the music scene, whenever he said things like that, Daniel thought maybe Juanito was really digging the job, or at least, the people-watching opportunities it afforded him. One time he told Daniel that a woman came dressed in an Easter Bunny costume, except instead of wearing the bunny head, she had painted her face paper-white and had a mop head as a wig. "And it wasn't like one those moño-weaves, but more like, dangly. You know? Fatal with a capital *F.*"

Now he had the rib in his hand and the bathroom was filling with steam because Juanito liked his showers to burn so hard, the skin on his legs would turn red. Daniel played the tape and when he pulled the curtain, Juanito screamed like the moon and the sky had merged midair.

"Why would you do that!" Juanito screamed, hitting Daniel on the arm.

Daniel laughed. Water was getting all over the floor. "I was just trying to be funny," he said. "Wait, are you crying? Ay, Juanito— I thought you'd find it funny."

"Ay-con-el-funny," Juanito said. His skinny body was covered in soapsuds. His hair was slicked back with conditioner. "And it will be *mad* funny when I get some rabid dog from Bay Ridge to come play Cujo with your prankster ass, right?"

"Oh, psh," he tried to joke. "I can take Cujo any day. I'm sorry, babe. I didn't mean to start something."

* * *

Cujo. Now that was one fucked-up little doggy. (Little? Not quite, but still.) That dog was something vicious entirely.

Daniel loved dogs. He loved how they were always happy to see their owners and greet other humans. He loved their sloppy-tongue hellos. When he was a kid, over the summertimes, he liked to watch the doggies who fell asleep outside the pool club across the street from his building. Since no dogs were allowed inside the club, people had to tie them up so they wouldn't run away. Daniel was always bothered by this. He didn't understand how someone could say they loved a dog and then want to tie them up to a pole. So, when his mother was out of the house or taking a nap, he'd go down and pet them and watch them sleep and feed them saltine crackers. He watched the way some of them twitched and moved the tips of their nose as they slept, as if they were dreaming of sniffing and running and being wild-wild in their sleep.

This is what Juanito's nightmares reminded him of, except más fuerte.

On the good nights, Juanito would just twitch and move slightly in Daniel's arms. It wasn't a big deal, but it was noticeable enough to wake Daniel up. It seemed like they were getting worse every week. Sweat absorbed into sheets, skin that was hot to the touch. Daniel wondered if maybe they were watching too many scary movies. Or maybe it was the practical jokes. He knew night sweats were a symptom of the virus but that would be impossible—they had just been tested. There was just no way. Even so, that wouldn't explain the night terrors. They couldn't afford a doctor's visit, but maybe they were gonna have to splurge. Oh, he really didn't know what to think, so he did what he always did: he blamed himself.

What baffled him even more was that Juanito always woke up and pretended like everything was okay. Daniel didn't want to make things awkward or embarrassing by bringing it up—he figured that eventually, if things got bad *enough,* Juanito would bring it up himself. But then there were the bad nights. Those nights scared Daniel the most.

During one fit, Juanito jolted straight up in bed like he was possessed by some dolor sin sentido. He watched as Juanito's mouth opened as if to scream like living hell, but not a single sound came out of his mouth.

"¿Qué pasa?" he begged Juanito. "What's happening, what's going wrong?"

Juanito's mouth stayed open and Daniel put his hand on Juanito's shoulder to try to get him to snap out of it. But he wasn't snapping out of nothing. Several seconds passed until Juanito's face went back to always and he fell back down to the pillow and started snoring.

"You're having nightmares," Daniel said the next morning while waiting for the toast to pop.

"Oh?" Juanito said. "It's nothing. No te preocupes."

But Daniel could sense that this was a mentira, maybe the kind of mentira that people who were in love told each other to help save feelings and avoid anxieties. And he believed Juanito, who said that everything was alright, because that's what he wanted to believe in the first place.

Two weeks later or so, Daniel found the glass pipe and the mini-blowtorch in the back of Juanito's sock drawer.

And what the fuck? All he needed was a pair of socks—his were all in the laundry—and Juanito was out on a run to the bodega to get some bread and cinnamon for their Sunday morning French toast. It's not like he had been *searching* for it.

He thought about opening the bedroom window and throwing the pipe out of it and watching it crash into a gazillion little pieces. He'd go downstairs and stomp on them with bare feet and when Juanito came back home with the bread and the cinnamon, he'd look him in the eyes and say, When you hurt, I hurt too, and he'd walk around a few steps and Juanito would see his bloody footprints and finally realize what he was doing.

No, he wouldn't do that. He put the pipe back in the drawer, as if he had never seen anything. He took the blowtorch and put it at the bottom of the cabinet in the bathroom, behind the rolls of extra toilet paper. When he heard the front door click and Juanito do his best Ricky-from-*I-Love-Lucy* impression—honey, I'm hooooome!—he walked out of the bedroom without socks, kissed Juanito on the cheek, looked at the bags, and said, "Do you need any help?"

JUANITO

His boss, Paul, asked Juanito to help pick up a new speaker from a friend's place on Greene. Juanito smoked a cigarette while Paul pressed the buzzer, then banged on the door, then cursed out the friend who had apparently forgotten about the ordeal. It was night, so all the stores on the street were closed. As they walked, Paul pouted. "I can't believe that jackass," Paul said, "isn't home right now."

"Maybe his buzzer is broken?" Juanito was feeling generous, though he was also annoyed that they had made the trek all the way to SoHo for nothing. Since they were in the area, Juanito asked, could they walk by the furniture store so he could get a glimpse of the famous sofa.

"Sure, why the hell not," Paul said. "Might as well do something so the journey isn't a complete waste."

When they arrived and looked through the glass window, he saw what Daniel was talking about. Folded in two, there was a small piece of paper that read SOLD. "Fuck," he said. "It really is too late."

"Don't worry," Paul said, patting a new soft pack of cigarettes on the inside of his wrist so the tobacco would tighten. "There's a shit-ton of other couches in the city." He put one between his lips and lit it.

"There are also tons of other speakers in the city," Juanito said.

"Don't," Paul said. "Fresh wound." He drew in so hard that the pleasure was evident on his face. It made Juanito crave one too. Paul blew out the smoke through his nostrils.

"Yeah," Juanito said. "But not this one. This is the one that he wanted."

But did he actually think he could've snatched it up before it was shipped out to its new owner? He had two hundred in his wallet, the little thing that he had made with duct tape and an X-Acto blade. What had Daniel said the other night up on the roof, was it two thousand? He thought maybe the store people could've given him credit, or some kind of payment plan option. He had heard somewhere that shit like that was possible.

"You'll find another, kid," Paul said. Juanito nodded. He hated when Paul called him kid. Claro, Paul was his boss and he could say whatever he wanted. Juanito couldn't even imagine the kind of money that it took to open up a joint like Lalalandia. The constant flow of bills—all in cash—for the iced-down drinks they served in small plastic cups. Pero, shit, did he have to call him kid?

Juanito looked back through the window at the darkened store. It was just about ten o'clock, after closing time in that sweet spot when the stores were shut and the clubs weren't full yet. He imagined that Daniel was at home sitting on the floor wrapped in a set of blankets, watching one of the scary pics that Juanito had turned him on to, until Juanito would walk in after his deejay set at three in the morning and find him passed out on the floor, waiting for him, all cute and shit, before going into their cama together. "I can't sleep in the bed without you," Daniel had once told him. "It would feel all wrong and lopsided."

It was cute when Daniel waited for him, but Juanito couldn't help but feel like it was time for Daniel to get out of the house sometimes, make friends, do something. When he told this to Daniel, his only response was that he was scared to. A little bit of fear was okay, Juanito could understand. Their area of Brooklyn was not like the Village. Their neighbors weren't fabulous queens. There were no gay bars. It was hard to meet new people if they didn't have a house to belong to, or balls to attend.

"C'mon," Paul said. "Let's hit it. The club's gonna be at full in just about an hour and you're on set."

Juanito shot another glance at the couch before they walked to the subway. "What do you think?" he asked Paul.

"About?"

"The couch," Juanito said. "What else?"

"Oh," Paul said. Juanito was two steps behind Paul and needed to catch up. Juanito could already feel the summer heat rushing up the steps like the infierno of piss smell that permeated the subway during the humid months. "To be honest with you," Paul continued, "I think it's not very practical. It doesn't really have a back, so you can't recline on it. It just looks like an oversize footrest."

"Sure, but Daniel is in love with it."

"And it's white," Paul said. "Sure, white is elegant. Especially in that ivory-bone slash silk-damask kind of way. But don't forget that white stains so easy. There's no getting around that fact."

Juanito shrugged. They were at the top of the stairs and Juanito watched as Paul fiddled with the gold hoop that was in his earlobe. He had been complaining earlier that the hole was infected and it was itching him like that one time in college when he got crabs. Except the itch was inside the lobe, not on his junk.

"Then scout out a similar one," Paul said. "I dunno what to tell you. That one got away."

"Yeah," Juanito said. He held onto the railing as they walked down to the station.

Qué extraño for objects to be placed in a window and put up for sale. And then for people to be lusting over them. When he was young, he thought that having enough money to buy an object—to own it and make it yours—was a sign that a person had made it alright in the world. That a place of security and comfort could exist out there, and that place was furnished to the nines and tens with objects of different sizes and shapes. But that sofa? That damn sofa. He could see what Daniel saw. It was different. It was *striking*.

He knew what he had to do. He had to convince Paul to give him a little bit of a raise. Or maybe a bonus. He leaned back on the subway column and turned to Paul. "I need you to pay me more," he said.

Paul raised his eyebrows and then looked past Juanito to see if the train's lights were down the tube and ready to pull up to the platform. Paul sighed, "I dunno, kid."

"Don't be buggin'. I see how much cash you got flowing at Lala," Juanito said. "It's just until I find a couch that matches. Think of it like a bonus for extra time. Then I can go back to regular once I got the couch."

Paul was standing too close to the edge as the train was whooshing up to the station. Juanito grabbed Paul's arm and pulled him closer to the column. "You trying to get yourself hit?" Juanito said.

"I wasn't going to fall," Paul said.

The doors opened to an empty car and Juanito said, "There's gotta be something I can do."

They stepped forward together and plopped down on two empty, orange seats. Paul turned to Juanito and smiled alarmingly. "You're right, kid," Paul said. "I'm sure I can figure out something for you to do."

* * *

The club was closed on Tuesday nights. It was usually his only free night of the week, so he took the train to the piers to see if he could get a glimpse of Angel. But homegirl wasn't walking around that night. Or if she was, Juanito couldn't find her. He took the long route home: walking east on Houston, through SoHo. He wanted to see if the sofa was still there.

But it wasn't. Gone, like poof. As if the shit had just sprouted piernas and walked it on out of there like Nancy Sinatra's boots made for walking. In its place, there was a dining room table. The sign said AUTHENTIC MAHOGANY. Giving vibes that it was the kind of table that could carry a ton of weight without even cracking a smidge. He imagined someone taking an ax to it, but failing to break it in two. That made him want it even more, knowing that it would never be his, that unbreakable table.

An hour later, he walked into the apartment and gave Daniel a kiss. "So the sofa's gone?" he asked Daniel.

"Sí," Daniel said. "How'd you know?" He was frying some chuletas on the stove. It was so hot in the cocina—windows open to the summer humedad, the little fan struggling in the corner to give any kind of wind. "We shipped it out today," Daniel said, using a fork to flip over the meat.

"Ay, bendito," Juanito said. He moved in front of the fan and un-stuck the T-shirt that was sticking to his chest. The fan was a little piece of shit—hardly blew nada—but Juanito loved it because it al-ways sounded like it was trying its best to keep them cool. He liked to joke around by calling it The Little Fan That Could. He twisted the knob to the highest setting.

Juanito set the table and, when he was done, he sat down on the uneven chair so that Daniel could have the sturdier one. He watched Daniel plop the chuletas on the plates and pour the leftover oil down the sink. Daniel said he was sorry that dinner was so small because he didn't have enough cash to get stuff for a mixed salad.

Juanito told him not to worry about it. "Ay, Daniel," he said.

"You're too sweet to be cooking every night. I don't deserve this."

He thought about bringing it up again: telling Daniel to get out of the apartment, to go make friends. At least Juanito had Lala and the space and coworkers that came with it.

"¿Estás loco?" Daniel said. "Of course you deserve this."

"I just want to do more, sabes?" Juanito said. "And you should be doing less, going out, meeting people."

Daniel smiled and looked down at his chuleta as he was cutting it with one of their knives. The knives they had were too dull. Daniel sighed and said, "We've already talked about this."

"I know that. I'm just saying," Juanito said. "It's been how many years?"

"I'm not ready to go out there and meet new people yet," Daniel said. His tone was not to be messed with.

Juanito wondered if they were ever going to have a conversation about Venus and Angel and their past. Or if their plan was to just keep all of the pain buried away, deal with the present, and hope that eventually things would be better.

"You know I love you," Daniel said. But Juanito didn't even think it was a matter of love. It was about Daniel saying they needed to leave Angel, and Juanito feeling like he had to make a choice. He couldn't understand how Daniel didn't understand that, but he didn't have the energy to push the issue.

"I love you too," Juanito said and they ate their meal together as the fan tried its best to give them air.

* * *

Paul had a patio with a little garden that was all dirt and no flowers. Juanito hadn't expected for Paul to invite him and some coworkers to his apartment for drinks after the club closed, but there they were, sipping on some drink. Juanito looked in the flowerpots to see if he could find any flowers, but he didn't see any. Paul probably saw Juanito looking because then he started telling the group about how he was trying to grow mint leaves so that he could add a little something authentic to his juleps and mojitos.

"Right, Juanito?" Paul said. "A mojito simply has to have the right mint leaves?"

"Sure," Juanito said, shrugging. He chuckled. He couldn't even remember the last time he had ordered a mojito.

It was almost five in the morning and Juanito felt like he needed to take a shower. It felt like an entire day's worth of city grime, plus an entire night's worth of club sweat, were caked onto his skin. He was sitting on the back patio of the Chelsea brownstone that had been turned into apartments. Heidi and Robert and Paul all went inside to refill their drinks.

He could see the sky starting to get lighter already. He imagined Daniel at home sleeping on the floor, and he felt bad. He really hoped that Daniel wasn't being a cabezota and sleeping on the floor just because he wasn't there to give him the cuddles. He hoped he was in bed with all the covers on him keeping him tight. Someone called him back inside. It was Robert.

"You want a G-and-T?" Robert asked.

Juanito said yes, that he would lend a hand.

"And a tongue," Robert said, cackling. "*God,* I'm being a nasty bitch. I'm just pulling your leg, Juanito."

Ever since he met Robert, Juanito was fascinated by him. He was a young Parsons student who hated Parsons, but loved New York City. Robert once invited Juanito to one of his performance art pieces that was at a gallery in Chelsea. Juanito brought Daniel and they stood there and watched as Robert kneeled on a giant plastic tarp as his boyfriend stood over him and cracked huevos over his naked body. The yolk dripped down and got all sticky-sticky over him as he just waited there with his lengua all out. The drip-drops of huevo dangled like long wads of phlegm.

"Ave María," Daniel had said to Juanito después. "I just don't understand why—"

"Se rompió los huevos," Juanito said, laughing. Broken eggs, broken balls. Robert had announced that it was a comment on masculinity. Juanito didn't really know how. He didn't know what to tell Daniel. He's from New Hampshire, Juanito had wanted to say, as if that would explain the locura. Pero he wasn't quite sure where New Hampshire was exactly, though he knew the general area. Not that New Hampshire really had anything to do with it—he knew that, claro—but whenever he saw Robert, so jovencito, he felt like Robert was the kind of kid who came to New York with the idea, somehow, that life would be like those movies where the white people come to the city in order to find themselves.

Now Robert was holding a bottle, waiting to pour. "How much tonic do you want?" Robert said. "Tell me when to stop."

He imagined that New York, for Robert, was a city of dreams. A city where a blond boy from New England could come with his sweater-vests and chinos and pay full price for an art school that he hated, just so that he could soak up the streets of Manhattan. Robert probably thought that the Bronx and Brooklyn and Queens and Staten Island were just afterthoughts, like jealous primas that were somehow related to Manhattan, but not really. He watched the tonic fill the glass half-full and said stop.

"You want a lime too?"

Juanito sliced the lime himself and dropped it in the drink and swirled the glass because there were no spoons on the counter. He watched Robert stir his drink with his finger and then lick it after, like he was a kid making a cake and he didn't want any icing to go to waste.

Robert was nineteen or twenty—he had never asked, or if he had, he didn't remember. Juanito was convinced that Paul only hired Robert because he was on a quest to fuck the boy.

When they walked into the sala, Heidi was on the couch telling Paul about her most recent acid trip. "I swear on my mother's grave," she said, "that I could see the corner of the room breathing. I was in this time-warp wonderland. It was incredible."

Paul was nodding his head viciously as Robert and Juanito sat on the other couch across from them. "I totally feel that," Paul said. Juanito watched as Heidi kept yapping—homegirl always had trouble keeping a lid on it, but the customers liked that about her and rewarded her with piles of tips. Plus, she was pretty and the straight boys went crazy for her eyes. They were so damn blue, Juanito felt like he'd turn to stone every time they made eye contact.

"What about you?" She turned to Juanito. "You got any piercings? Any that we *can't* see?"

Juanito laughed. "No," he said. It wasn't like he had any that they *could* see, anyway. He stared at Heidi's double nose rings and the string of hoops that went down both ears. He wanted to know if there was a story behind those piercings. If there was any pain involved. "Sorry to disappoint."

"Juanito would look good with his cock pierced," Paul said, getting up to fill his glass with more gin.

"Ay, por favor," Juanito said. "I would *never*. I can't take that kind of pain."

Robert swirled around his glass so that the ice cubes were clanking. "I've got both my nips done," he offered.

"Of course you do, sweetie," Paul shouted from the cocina. "I bet your boy toy really digs them."

"Excuse *me*," Robert said, hand out like he was a Supreme about to tell Paul to stop in the name of love. "But I am *his* boy toy."

"Oh, keep tellin' yourself that," Paul said, but Juanito agreed with Robert. Robert's boyfriend was at least fifteen years older than Robert—so then that would make him the boy toy, no?

Robert told them about the time he went to Punta Cana to get his nips pierced. He was in the back room of some bar called BAR and the guy who was piercing him wanted to fuck him, or at least that's what Robert said. Coulda been a lie, but Juanito didn't think of Robert as some kind of mentiroso who would indulge in a story like that.

"You think everyone wants to fuck you," Paul said, still in the kitchen.

Juanito chuckled.

"Hey!" Robert said.

"Oh god," Heidi said, chewing on an ice cube. "In a third world country. I'd never get my tits done in Mexico."

Juanito laughed and made eyes with Robert. "Dearie," Robert said, pointing a gentle finger up in the air. "Punta Cana is in the Dominican Republic."

"Same shit," Heidi said back.

Paul walked back in and sat down on the couch and crossed his legs. He was eating yogurt out of a martini glass.

"I hear the men there," Heidi said, "are hung as hell."

"I wouldn't know," Robert said in a singsong. He held his chin up, then raised his glass up in a toast. Pinky up, as if he were toasting to his own purity.

"Oh, please," Paul said. "The only reason that kid learned the metric system is because he needed to know how many centimeters the back of his throat could handle before gagging."

Heidi busted out a laugh and stuck out a hand to play with Robert's earlobe. Robert frowned and stared at his drink.

"You're a shady cunt, Paul," Robert said and Juanito was scandalized that Robert was taking such a tone with the man who employed him. "I'll get you back one day. When you least expect it."

"I somehow doubt that, Robert," Paul said. "But it's cute of you to think so." He blew Robert an air-kiss.

"Well if you're gonna be so nasty to me," Robert said, "can you at least bring Tina out to play to ease the salt wounds?"

Paul and Heidi laughed.

"Who the hell is Tina?" Juanito said.

Everyone laughed again, pero it wasn't no joke.

"You really want me to get Tina?" Paul said. Juanito stared at a fly that was buzzing up near the ceiling. He wanted to cup it in his hands and bring it outside so it could fly away.

Heidi poured a round of shots and Paul came back with the pipe and said, "Are we really about to do shots of gin, honey?"

"If that's all you've got," Heidi said, "then yes. Times is dire, boo-boo."

They all knocked their heads back and shot the gin. Juanito had to finish his in two swallows even though his shot glass wasn't that full. He could feel the pine taste opening up his sinuses.

"I really shouldn't," Heidi said, taking the glass pipe. "But you don't have to ask me twice."

"That a girl," Robert said, slow-clapping like a fem queen at a golf course. "Pass it over here." He lit the lighter and held it under the end of the glass, which was shaped like a little ball. It was meth, por supuesto. Juanito's inability to know a slang word when he heard it made him feel like, duh. Tina—like who the fuck did he think was gonna show up? Tina fucking Turner? (As if.) Ay, Dios mío—he wanted to smack himself silly. He wanted to be at home with Daniel, curled in a ball with Daniel's arm over his body. He wanted to sleep.

Robert twirled the flame under the glass and sucked the smoke out like a little boy sipping the last drops from a juice cuppie. It sounded like it was bubbling. When Robert was done, he held out the pipe for Juanito to take hold. "No," Juanito said. Not after Venus. What would Angel say? "I can't," he told Robert.

Robert shrugged and gave him a look like he was a dumbass for passing up what was free. Pero Juanito didn't care. He didn't want none of it, free or otherwise.

"Are you sure, Juanito?" Paul said. "My treat."

Juanito got up from the sofa and wiped his hands on his pants to get the sweat off. He told them he was gonna go to the bodega to get M&M's. As soon as it came out of his mouth, he wanted to take it all back in. M&M's? Was he fucking joking? They would see right through the lie.

"God," Heidi said. She held the smoke in her lungs and then coughed it out. "The thought of food right now makes me want to projectile vomit."

Robert rolled his eyes, but Juanito could tell Robert wasn't interested in anything Juanito was gonna say or do. Robert was just a young case of the benditos who wanted his damn hands on that pipe. Juanito watched as Robert tapped his thumb all frantic against the side of his leg. Robert was eyeing the pipe razor sharp. Paul threw him a key and said, "Don't get lost on your way back."

* * *

He didn't want M&M's. He didn't want anything to eat, for that matter. He had wanted to bust out of that apartment to get home, but now he had the key. He would *have* to go back or Paul would be pissed, and a pissed Paul was not what Juanito needed at the moment. Not until he got his raise, saved some money, and had that sofa.

Fuck, he thought as he walked to the bodega on the corner of Eighth Avenue. The sun was already up and people were doing their morning treks to work. It reminded him of the mornings at the piers, after Daniel and he had been walking all night, bending down to look in car windows to see if the money would flow. They'd finish just about the time when people were going to work—not because they wanted to, but because not nobody was looking to buy a piece of culo at nine in the fucking morning. Johns were sucio motherfuckers, but they also had jobs and families and lives to lead.

Daniel used to take him to the diner on Tenth Avenue and they'd order breakfast before heading back to the Bronx. Eggs with white toast smeared with mantequilla that looked so yellow, it had to be fake. The waitress would slam the plates down as if her presence were just a favor, and if they had a problem with her attitude, they could go fuck themselves.

Now, he stood there at the counter of the bodega and decided he wanted a coffee.

"You want sugar, sugar?" the man asked with a smirk. The man was feo in a sad way, Juanito thought. He imagined him as the type of guy whose bathroom was covered in wet pelitos and grime. Juanito envisioned a three-story walk-up with no windows and moldy wallpaper. He wasn't judging. It just made him feel sad.

"Not today," Juanito said. "No milk, no sugar."

"You sure?"

"Positive," Juanito said. "Just black."

Maybe a couple of years ago he would've gone to the bodega's backroom and sucked the poor dude off for a twenty and the thrill of it. Maybe he would've tried that pipe and his face would flush red just like Heidi's and Robert's and Paul's and he'd ramble on and on about whatever the fuck came to mind. But not today. Not this year. He was in love, damn it. He deserved better than that fucked-up shit.

* * *

"I came back to give you the key," Juanito said, hovering near the door.

Paul was walking around the sala, rearranging the picture frames he had on all the side tables, like they were girasoles that couldn't bend toward the sunlight on their own. "I thought you bounced out for good," Paul said. Heidi and Robert had already left. In the one frame Paul was holding onto, there was a woman in a graduation cap. Her smile was ear to ear. "No M&M's?" Paul said.

"I changed my mind," Juanito said. He held up the coffee cup higher as proof. "Why'd they leave already?"

Paul said that Robert had a studio class to go to in the morning. "I can't even fathom it," Paul said. "I would just *explode* if I had to go to a class like that at nine with my mind jumping around like this."

And Heidi? Paul said he didn't know. She left when Robert left. "Maybe they're fucking," Paul said.

"Ay, por favor," Juanito said. "Robert is *gay*."

"And Elton John was married," Paul said, "to a woman, no less." He moved the stained-glass Tiffany lamp from one side table to la otra. Juanito loved the tiny purple circles on the lamp. They looked like grapes crowned in the surrounding yellow glass bits.

Paul moved the lamp back to the original table but he stared back at the other table, as if maybe that was actually where it belonged. "Fuck, I'm just not sure what feels right," Paul said. "The lamp clearly needs to feel like it's on the right table. I just need to figure out which one is the right table."

"I don't know," Juanito said. "But also, back to that other point. Elton John is gay. And Robert is also gay, so—"

"Okay, you're right. They're probably not fucking," Paul said. "I've already moved on from that theory."

"Right," Juanito said. "I should maybe go home now."

"Oh, don't go yet." Paul was staring at the lamp as if it had grown a set of tetas. "Where do you think it belongs, kid?"

Juanito sighed. He tried to control his face so that he didn't give a side-eye or a glare. "Does it really matter?" he said.

"Of course it fucking matters," Paul said. "I need the feng shui to be in balance."

"The what?"

"Feng shui. Ever hear of it?" Paul said. "I swear, Juanito. Sometimes you're just like a child."

Juanito took a sip of coffee and it burned the back of his throat. He regretted not getting the sugar. The flavor was too damn amargo for his liking. But ordering coffee black was in the same field as ordering a drink on the rocks in his mind. He didn't like either, but the sound of the order sounded classy and maduro.

"Do you think I should move the sofa so it's facing that wall?" Paul said. "I should really move it so it's facing the wall. Shouldn't I? I just don't know."

"You know, Paul," he said. "I fucking hate it when you call me a kid. I'm not some dumbass kid. I'm nineteen, so talk to me like I'm a grown-ass adult."

Paul took his hands off the lamp and looked at Juanito's face. His eyes moved down to Juanito's chest, and Juanito did nothing but stare back at Paul, who was either chewing a piece of gum or just moving his tongue around his mouth like a spin cycle. It dawned on him: Paul was still really, really high.

"But you *are* a kid," Paul said. "Look at me, I'm forty-two. Okay, fuck. I'm forty-six. But that's not the point. The point is that everyone is a damn kid to me. You and Robert are both children."

Daaamn. He had just lumped him in the same category as Robert. Ay, Dios mío, this man was tripping balls. Could he even imagine. There he was, forty-six years old, loaded on Tina, dressed in a kimono with a lamp in his hand at god knows what hour. "What about Heidi?" Juanito said.

"Oh, she's a woman," Paul said, shooing his hand in the air. "She's irrelevant." Paul laughed, but Juanito walked into the cocina to dump out the coffee. He didn't want it anymore. He just wanted to go home.

"I feel younger when I'm around you," he heard Paul say from the other room. Juanito lifted his foot off the basura and the metal lid clanged down on the empty garbage.

"I really need to get home," Juanito said as he walked back into the sala. "Daniel's probably up and wondering where I am."

Paul was lighting the pipe again. He squinted as he held the smoke in. Head back, he blew the smoke up toward the ceiling. "You're gonna tell me that you aren't a kid, but you won't even try some Tina, like you're part of some gym assembly, antidrug campaign?"

"Ouch, Paul," Juanito said. "Would you fucking quit it."

Paul dropped the pipe down on the carpet and walked over to Juanito. His hands felt like hielo to the touch. He brought Juanito's fingers up to his chest. "Squeeze them," he told Juanito. "Squeeze my nipples."

"Paul—"

"Shh," Paul said, his voice down to a whisper.

Juanito had a choice to make. He was scared that if he walked out the door, Paul would fire him or say no to the raise. He wanted that sofa for Daniel. He closed his eyes and pinched Paul's nipples. He shouldn't've come to the party. He shouldn't've returned to drop off the key. He just should've gotten the M&M's, something sweet. Paul said harder, so Juanito clamped down harder, so hard that he was afraid that he would rip them off of Paul's body. Paul moaned. "God," he said. "You have no idea how good it feels."

* * *

The pipe was on the coffee table when Paul went to the bathroom and Juanito thought, *Maybe. What could one hit do?* Heidi and Robert did it. They all seemed perfectly fine. Okay, maybe they had their hot mess moments, but they still led normal lives. He wanted to know what that kind of feeling would do to him.

He picked it up with both hands because he was worried that he would drop it and the glass would shatter. He put his lips to the end of the pipe and lit the little rock in the glass bowl at the end. He flicked the lighter on and the flame danced under the glass and the rock sizzled a little. The tube filled with smoke and he inhaled it like he was taking a little sippy of weed.

It didn't take long to hit him. Then he was vibrating to a rhythm that felt like it always existed outside of himself, and that he was finally tapping into now. He had to stand up. He took another hit and kept it in. Paul was in the bathroom, and he had to stand up, so he stood. He needed to find Paul. He needed Paul to fuck him. That's all he could feel that he wanted. The world felt like harmony, and this harmony was buzzing inside him. A rush of horniness was grabbing at him. If he didn't have a cock inside him, he'd explode.

He undressed, took another hit, and lay on the sofa. He squiggled back and forth like a worm and started jerking himself off.

"What the fuck is happening right now?" Paul said. He was standing in the door frame of the bathroom. Because Juanito's head leaned off the edge of the couch, everything looked upside down.

"I took three hits," he said. "This shit is amazing."

"Three hits just now?" Paul said. "Oh, my god, you must be in a different dimension."

Juanito stood up and put his hand on Paul's bulge and felt it growing, pulsing. Paul closed his eyes. He told Paul that he needed to get fucked. Right now.

Paul pushed him on the sofa, unzipped his pants, took out a condom, and fucked him so hard, the sofa moved up against the wall.

He closed his eyes and imagined he could get fucked for the rest of time. He clenched his ass cheeks as Paul fucked him. He could feel Paul's pubes hitting up against him with each thrust. When Paul sped up, he knew the cum shot was coming and then it would be over. Paul held him down by his neck and moaned.

When Paul was done, he collapsed onto Juanito's back. He could feel Paul's sweat. "I can't believe we just did that," Paul said.

"Shh," Juanito said. He shifted his body so that he could face Paul. He put his finger up to Paul's lips. "Now I need you to promise me something."

"What is it?"

"I said *shh*," Juanito said. "I need you to promise me that you're going to get me that sofa, okay?"

"You really are a whore," Paul said.

"What did you just say?"

"Nothing," Paul said.

Juanito put his hand up to the side of Paul's face. He played with Paul's earlobe and leaned in to whisper. "If we keep doing this," he said, "there's no emotion involved. Don't you *ever* tell me that you love me."

DANIEL

He tried to trace the events of their lives together to find the point in time when things turned—when he could say, at this point in time, en este momento, Juanito turned to drugs. But when he thought about it, he realized that he couldn't find any one moment, and the idea that maybe Juanito's progression was slow and gradual was something that pained him more.

Maybe it was Daniel's fault. Maybe it was all of the horror movies. Maybe it was the fact that they hadn't actually talked about Angel and Venus and the Xtravaganzas since they left. Was Juanito holding it against him that they hadn't said goodbye to Angel? It wasn't that Daniel didn't want to talk about the past—or rather, their past together in that house—but now that things were on the up-turn in the grand, fucked-up montaña rusa that was their life, he preferred to treat the past like it was a quilt: they would add on squares for each momentito in their life, and then they could fold it up neatly and place it into a box, and then put that box under their bed. What he didn't realize, and was rather learning in the moment, was that those types of quilts couldn't be boxed away. They'd keep on growing until they needed to be cut.

Over the course of the next two weeks, Daniel convinced himself that the pipe and the blowtorch didn't actually belong to Juanito, that it must have been some kind of mistake, or Juanito was holding them for a friend at work. He knew how the club scene could get, and maybe Juanito was helping a coworker hooked on roca. It was just easier to think of it in these terms, and easy felt safer. And, as if to prove this thought process absolutely correct, when Daniel walked in from work one evening, Juanito was sitting on a couch in the sala with a cupcake in his hand. "Surprise!" Juanito said. There was a candle stabbed in the icing.

"What kinda jodienda is this?" he said. He had no possible clue how Juanito could get a sofa and buy drugs at the same time. He looked at the candlelight bouncing orange shades off Juanito's face and he wanted to say: Mira, my love, what is happening to your face? You're so thin, I could cut myself on your cheekbones.

Juanito lit the candle and began singing a made-up song called "I Bought a Couch For You" to the tune of "Happy Birthday." When Juanito was done, he looked at Daniel with eyes that were so big with expectation that it made Daniel's heart want to break.

"What is it?" Juanito said. "Don't you want to blow it out?"

In one quick puff, he blew out the candle and the orange light was gone.

When he flicked on the lights, he could see that the couch was white, like the Maurice Villency, except for the very obvious fact that it wasn't the Maurice Villency. But it was still beautiful and có-modo. "The only thing," Juanito said, "is that it's not leather."

"I love it," Daniel said, guiding his hand over the cloth. "It feels like jersey. We're going to take the best fucking naps on this thing."

He didn't understand why Juanito had done this, had gone through the trouble. Yes, they needed a couch, but he didn't need the surprise. He didn't need the secret.

"That ain't all we gonna do on it," Juanito said.

"Ay, babe," Daniel said. "You're so bad, I don't even know what you're thinking."

So maybe that was it. Maybe Juanito wasn't hitting la roca, or the manteca, or whatever it was that those pipes were for. Juanito was functional, he was working, he had saved up enough money to buy that couch—coño! But for the rest of the week, the nightmares continued.

A week later, when Daniel got home from work, Juanito didn't greet him at the door. Daniel shut the door with care not to be too loud or make a scene. He saw the telephone cord slithering its way under the bathroom door. He went up to the door and pressed his ear up to it. "Yeah?"—Daniel heard Juanito's voice—"Whatchoo gonna do with that thing, bad boy?"

It was enough. He didn't need to hear any more. He went to the sofa and pressed the side of his face to the cloth—how soft it was—and closed his eyes to sleep. He had learned long ago how to force back a cry, during a playground game that involved his classmate Marco slapping him across the face until he could feel his cheeks throbbing in the places where the fingers had marked him like fire. The slaps had hurt him so bad, he imagined that the stinging could take on its own life.

He woke up an hour later? A half hour later? He didn't know. It was dark out and Juanito had a hand on Daniel's shoulder. "How long've you been here?" Juanito asked.

Daniel hummed and mumbled something.

"When'd you get home?" Juanito asked.

"Not sure," he said. "Feels like I've been here for a while, but I think I just got here."

* * *

Maybe it would have been easier to bring it up. Just sit him down and tell him that he had found the pipe and he needed to know what the fuck was going on. But whenever Daniel entertained that thought, he turned straight to what he feared the most: that Juanito would deny it, turn his back, and walk out of their apartment for good. What could he say that could get Juanito to fess up? Would he have to use the ace of diamonds card and say: You wanna become just like Venus? Sucking dick just to get your next baggie of coke and then wind up strangled like a blow-up doll in some stank-ass hotel? Of course he didn't want to read him *that* hard, but he knew he needed to do something.

A couple of weeks passed. Then Juanito's manager, Paul, called one evening when Juanito was supposed to be at work. Paul was looking for Juanito. "What do you mean he's not there?" Daniel said.

He closed his eyes and let his head rest against the kitchen cabinet. *C'mon, Juanito,* he thought, *not now. Not after everything.* Daniel was about to start up the frying pans to prepare some food for them to have ready for the week. He even had Tupperwares set out.

"You don't know already?" Paul said.

"Know what?" Daniel said.

"Maybe you should ask what's going on," Paul said. "I'm calling to make sure he's okay."

Paul's story went like this: Juanito had shown up to work last night so fucked-up—and not just drunk, but *fucked-up*—took off all his clothes and ran around the place completely, bare-assed naked. Since he was supposed to be in the deejay's box, and no one was up there, the place went silent except for Juanito's shrill little cries as he spun around in circles with the club kids, who were all giving him eyes like, what the fuck is happening over here.

"Then he ran off to the bathroom," Paul said.

No, Juanito had not mentioned that earlier today. Sure, Daniel thought he looked hungover, but he thought that was just a result of working at a club until three in the morning.

Juanito came home that night and didn't say anything about it. Kissed him goodnight and as soon as his head hit the pillow, he was out.

The next night, Daniel ordered Chinese food just like they did every Friday because that's when Juanito worked the earlier shift. Eleven o'clock, Juanito still wasn't home. Twelve, still nothing. One, two. Fuck it, Daniel had to eat. The chicken lo mein was cold so he reheated it on the stove for a minute.

He popped in the movie he rented for the night: *It: Part One*. That psycho Pennywise clown was on the TV creeping it up when Juanito finally walked in.

"Where were you?" Daniel said. "Date night—remember? Your lo mein is on the table."

"Ay, mierda," Juanito said, wiping his eyes with his hands rapidly. "Work called. Heidi couldn't do the door shift so I had to stay a couple hours extra."

"Your food's gonna be cold now."

Daniel looked at Juanito: he was still standing by the door, chewing his gum in a fever rush, looking like he had just seen a child get run over by a truck. "No tengo hambre, Dani."

"I asked them to throw in extra fortune cookies for you." He watched as Juanito walked toward the bag and slipped his hand in. "Your hands are shaking," he said. "You gotta eat, for real."

"I don't want to," Juanito snapped. "I really, really, really am not hungry."

Juanito checked the answering machine, went into the bedroom, came back out of the bedroom, into the bedroom again, and back out. Just watching Juanito go back and forth made Daniel dizzy.

"¿Qué coño haces?" Daniel asked, finally, when Juanito was on his knees in the kitchen, scrubbing the floor around the refrigerator with a large pink sponge.

"Everything is so sucio in here lately," he said, scrubbing so hard, Daniel was worried he was going to unpeel the top layer of the linoleum.

"I just cleaned the kitchen. Like two days ago."

"Ya sé, ya sé," Juanito said. "But I want all of the floors to sparkle. I really need them to sparkle."

"Juanito, this is fucked-up. I'm not asking you. Come to the table and eat something."

"I told you. I'm. Not. Hungry," he said, raising the blackened sponge so they could both see it. "Where did all of this grimy shit come from? Do you *see* it? How can you not see it?"

Daniel got up from the table and kneeled down next to Juanito. "Yes, I see it. Look at me," he said, but Juanito kept scrubbing. "Fucking look at me. Is everything okay?"

"No, everything isn't okay," Juanito said. "Look at all this dirt."

"Just come to the table," Daniel said.

"I'm-not-fucking-hungry!"

"Why are you yelling at me?" he said as Juanito threw the sponge down on the floor and slipped past him and out of the kitchen. "¿Qué haces? You already checked the answering machine. No one left you a message. Paul didn't call you today to leave a message."

Juanito stopped in front of the tele as Pennywise the Clown said *Aw, come on bucko. Don't you want a balloon?* and they stared at each other in the darkness. "I'm so sorry, Daniel."

"What're you apologizing for?"

"Because I don't feel like eating and because I don't understand why we let this apartment get so sucio."

"I cleaned the kitchen two days ago, Juanito. Did you want me to scrub the edges with a toothbrush?"

"So you're saying it's all my fault?" Juanito said. He looked so damn skinny from where he stood.

Daniel wanted to grab him by the wrist and bring him to a mirror. He wanted to scream, How do you not see what is happening?

To your face? To your cheeks? You've got raccoon eyes, for fuck's sake, you're gonna die and then I'll be all alone without you.

He didn't say nothing. He didn't even grab his wrist.

"All I want," Juanito said, "is for the floors to sparkle."

Daniel held out his hand for Juanito to grab hold of. He guided Juanito back to the table while he chewed his gum and yapped on about the floor, how it should shine, how that Pine-Sol cleaner wasn't worth shit, how you could hardly smell the lemony fresh.

"Sí, you're right," Daniel said. "Pine-Sol ain't worth shit at all, and now you should sit down and eat something." He prepared a small plate of lo mein for Juanito with one of the small BBQ ribs with its bright red glaze. "Por favor, Juanito. When was the last time you ate?"

He watched as Juanito stared at the rib, at the noodles, then at the chopsticks, which were still connected. "Nothing's wrong," Juanito said, but that wasn't what the question was.

Nothing was wrong? *Bull to the shit,* he thought, as he walked to the drawer where they put random stuff, the things that were not quite garbage, but not quite useful: the thumbtacks and take-out menus, the Scotch tape and nails and business cards. He grabbed what he needed, walked over to the dining room table, and placed the object on the table in front of them. It was covered in a clean gray rag. "Toma," Daniel said. "Nothing's wrong? Open that."

As soon as Juanito took the rag off, he didn't seem to look at the thing as much as he looked *through* it. "What's that for?" Daniel asked. "I don't see you making no crème-fucking-brûlée around here."

Blowtorch in hand, Juanito's head slumped down. "Where'd you get this?" Juanito whispered.

"You know exactly where," he said. "So, nothing's wrong? I find *this* and then that pipe for god knows what. Crack? You smoking *crack*?"

"It's not crack—"

"I don't even want to know what it's for," he said, even though he did want to know. He was worried that he was going to throw up semidigested noodles all over the kitchen. "You shiver in bed almost every night, you're flaco as anything—skin and bones, really—and then every other day there is a message from some dude on the answering machine, and I have to listen to them telling you how many inches they've got, and how they're going to destroy your ass with it."

Juanito put his forehead on the table and started to cry.

"I know you haven't been going to work," Daniel said. "I spoke to Paul."

"No," Juanito said. He kept repeating it: no, no. The look he gave Daniel could have bent all the spoons in their sink. "He called here? What'd he say?"

"He's been looking for you, wondering why you're not showing up," Daniel said.

Juanito walked over to Daniel and edged in for a hug. He put his hands around Daniel's waist and rested his head on Daniel's right shoulder. Daniel could feel him sobbing ever so gently, but he just stood there with his arms to the sides, letting Juanito hold him. He hoped to dear god and all the saints that Juanito wasn't putting on a show.

"I'm sorry," Juanito whimpered. He kept repeating it, speaking into Daniel's neck as if it were Daniel's own skin that he was apologizing to. "Please don't leave me."

"And it's not like *we've* been having any sex," Daniel said.

"So this is all about sex?"

"Ay, Dios, Juanito. I didn't say that at all," he said. "I just want to know if everything is alright, and what the fuck am I supposed to think when all of *this*"—he waved his arm around, like *this* could be pointed to like a prize on *The Price Is Right*—"is going down?"

Daniel picked up the paper plates and shoved them in the brown bag. *If you don't want to eat, don't eat then.* He ripped the stapled take-out menu off and put it in the drawer of loose objects. He slammed it shut harder than he wanted to. When he turned around, Juanito was standing in front of him completely naked. His clothes were thrown into a pile on the floor next to the table. "You want it," Juanito said and Daniel could see the little groove of bone where his rib cage was meant to protect his heart. "You want to fuck? Then come, come and take it."

"Ya. Deja," Daniel said, swatting his hand.

"Come."

Daniel didn't want to look. He didn't want to see Juanito when he was pulling some shit. "Damn, Juanito," he said, crying now. "I'm not some trick. Why're you playing me like this?"

"Come on, I want you." Juanito walked over to him and placed his hand on Daniel's cheek. The inside of Juanito's palm felt dry and bumpy and Daniel could barely hear the words as they came out of Juanito's mouth. "Use my hole," Juanito said. "Just fuck me already, if that's what you want."

He felt Juanito's hand pulling him to the living room. "Push me down," Juanito told him. He could feel himself getting hard. His mind was telling him no, but his body was still capable of doing it. It terrified him, this lack of control, this drive to fuck Juanito as hard as all the johns who had fucked him in cars and in parks—had fucked the both of them when they were working on the streets. Juanito, who had helped train him to get into a car and suck a dick. Juanito, who had sobbed into his shoulder on some nights when the men were particularly mean. ("He told me he wanted to fuck me in half," he remembered Juanito had cried one night, years ago.)

"You're too gentle with me," Juanito said, now. "You think I'm just fragile. Like I'm one of those plates that you wash and wash and wash. Well push me down and just fucking take my ass already, if that's what you want."

Daniel felt his hard-on pressing against his pants, but he didn't want to fuck Juanito like that. He wiped the tears from his cheeks. He could never use, or take, or fuck, or not be gentle with him.

"Take it already, Dani."

Daniel thought of how, when they had first met in the Bronx, Juanito had told him one night, drunk off his ass, that the summer when he was twelve, his mother sent him to PR to visit the father that he hardly knew, and that when his father had put the pieces together—how had he known? Did his hips sway, were his wrists limp, did he linger too long on *S* sounds?—his father had raped him repeatedly over the course of the entire summer. "Cógeme, Dani." He remembered how Juanito had cried that night. Daniel had held him, Juanito's back facing him so they could both look out the window instead of at each other.

Now Juanito was rushing to unzip Daniel's pants. Daniel pushed him away. He didn't mean to push him as hard as he did, but Juanito fell backward onto the couch. For the first time that night, their eyes met and Daniel could see that sly twinkle in Juanito's eyes that meant he was longing for something.

"Push me again," Juanito said.

"Tell me something," Daniel said. "Are you fucking high right now?" Daniel didn't know if it would be better or worse if Juanito were loaded. He didn't want to think about it. The way the orange light from the street came in through the window, Daniel could barely see Juanito's face as he lay there on the sofa with his legs up, masturbating himself. Daniel barely recognized him.

"Don't be silly," Juanito said. Daniel stood next to the sofa and watched as Juanito placed two fingers in his mouth and sucked. Then Juanito brought his fingers from his mouth to his hole and started to fingerfuck himself, at first gently, and then so rough, Daniel almost had to ask him to stop because it was difficult to watch.

Juanito's head snapped back as he moaned. His back arched back. Daniel was fully hard now and he spit on Juanito's hole and thrust inside quickly. He wasn't going to take this slow, he wanted Juanito to feel everything. He pounded until Juanito's body jolted hard. Juanito winced. "Coño," Juanito said. "Oh fuck, pulloutpullout."

Daniel guided Juanito up and put a pillow behind his head. "¿Qué pasó?" Daniel asked, pulling out. "What? What went wrong?"

He didn't expect it to be as bad as it was. He flicked the lights on and Juanito covered his eyes with one hand and covered his ass with the other. There wasn't a lot of blood, but there was still blood. Juanito stared at the stain on the couch—about the size of a handprint—and he just stood there.

"You're bleeding," Daniel said. "You gotta take a shower or something, it's gonna start dripping down your leg."

"No," Juanito said, already halfway to the sink, reaching for a sponge. "I gotta clean the couch. It's gonna stain."

"Fuck it," Daniel said. "It's not gonna come out."

When Juanito was in the shower, Daniel could hear him crying. Whatever drug he was on was probably wearing off. He squatted on the floor near the sofa with a sponge in his hand, trying his best to do damage control on the stain with cold water and soap.

"I need you to be honest with me," Daniel said when Juanito was finally clean, laying next to him in bed. "And don't give me some bullshit, Juanito."

"I'm sorry, Dani."

"Coño, why're you bleeding so bad? That's not a normal amount of blood. Where'd you go tonight?" he asked. "Where're you going to all these afternoons and nights?"

"—"

"You got fucked? Is that it?"

"Promise you won't get mad?"

He looked at Juanito and then at the new couch. It looked bulky in the shadows of the streetlight, all alone in the middle of the empty room. Daniel covered his face with his hands and said, "Ay, Dios mío, Juanito. I can't fucking believe you right now."

* * *

The next morning, the crystal was worn off and Juanito sat dazed at the table. He held onto a glass of water as he explained the deal he had made with Paul. Daniel stood while he listened and watched Juanito take occasional sips, until there was only one ice cube left.

Paul had paid for the sofa, Juanito explained. And in return, Juanito paid off his debt with sex. Things got out of control. He never meant to get hooked.

Daniel winced. "I'm gonna fuck that bastard up so bad," he said. "He's not gonna know right from left."

"No," Juanito said, sliding the ice cube around the bottom of the glass. "We can't do that."

"Like hell I can't," Daniel said.

But Juanito explained why not. Paul had called earlier in the week, demanding for more, even though Juanito thought he was paid off. "He said, you still owe me two more fucks, don't think I lost count. Pero I think he was just tweaked out," Juanito said, "because I dunno where he got that math from."

Juanito said that when he had told Paul no, Paul got so pissed that he threatened to call Amex and claim that Juanito had stolen his charge card and bought the sofa with it.

"So what do I do?" Juanito said. "I did buy it with his card. It was me. But he was there with me, te lo juro. He said it was okay to buy it."

"You've gotta quit," Daniel said. "Are you kidding me? You can't stay working for him." He was walking in circles around the room. Juanito drank what was left of the melted ice cube. "Juanito? Tell me that you *can't*."

Juanito said that he thought if they had sex one last time, it would be over. "I don't wanna go to jail for fraud or whatever, like he was saying they'd do to me," Juanito said. "Maybe he can have his fill and then we can all move on."

"Have his fill? I can't believe this," Daniel said. He stopped pacing and threw his hands into the air. "Are you fucking *bugging* right now?" He couldn't stand it, so he walked out of the room.

"Where're you going?" Juanito's voice cracked. "Daniel, por favor, don't leave me."

Daniel walked into the bathroom and threw up into the toilet. The hurling was so strained, he felt the side of his abs burn. He could smell the vomit stuck in the back of his nose. He heard the door creak open, and when he turned his head to look, Juanito was standing in the doorway. Juanito told him that he was a mess and that Daniel should leave him and go find someone better, someone who didn't have issues, who wasn't an addict, who could love him.

"Are you telling me," Daniel said, "that you don't love me?" Neither of them were crying and Daniel felt like he needed to throw up again. Juanito's face was so stern that it made Daniel want to crack into pieces.

"I do love you," Juanito said.

"Then show me," Daniel said. "It's not supposed to be this hard." Juanito nodded.

"Leave his address on a piece of paper. But promise me this will be the end of it," Daniel said. He couldn't look at Juanito as he said it. "I gotta know where to find you."

"Okay."

"If I find you strangled under his bed like Venus was," he said. "I'll never forgive myself."

JUANITO

Two wine glasses were filled to the top with white wine. Paul poured too much in and now Juanito was worried they'd spill over. Paul had ice cubes in his wine and they clanked around every time he picked up his glass. Sade's "Your Love Is King" was blasting on loop, and by the time it played for a fourth time and Sade said, *This is no sad or sorry dream*, Juanito picked up his glass, closed his eyes, and took a gulp.

"Do you like it?" Paul asked. "It's a Riesling."

"A what?"

"Riesling," Paul said. "It's a type of white wine. It's sweet."

Juanito forced a smile. Maybe sweet was one word for it, but the sabor made his tongue squeeze like if he was eating a lemon raw. White wine was white wine. They all tasted the same.

"So," Paul said. He sighed. "Our last time together."

Juanito hadn't expected the fanfare. The apple-cinnamon candles that made the apartment smell like a fucking apple pie. Paul had even spread rose petals on the satin blanket that was on the rug in the middle of the room. What a sick fuck. Was still gonna fuck him on the damn floor, but thought the rose petals would make it more cariñoso. Por favor. He should just quit now. Make like the shit on Maury Povich and throw the glass in his face and scream, You are not the father. And I quit. Don't need that Lalalandia bullshit anymore.

"How nice," Juanito said instead. He sipped the wine slowly because he knew what would happen when the glass was empty. Juanito didn't see another bottle of wine.

"I do hope that one day," Paul said, "you'll see that I care for you."

Juanito didn't say anything. Just took another tiny sip.

"We should've never let the drugs get in the way of that," Paul said, and Juanito thought, *Exactly, dude.* "We should've just enjoyed the carnal aspect of it."

The *carnal* aspect? The fuck did he mean? Juanito didn't say anything. He knew he couldn't. Because when he thought about who had started it all, he knew that all roads led back to him.

"Say something, Juanito."

"What can I say?" Juanito said. "You're forcing me here to have sex with you because you threatened me? Is that what you want from me?"

"I think we just have a misunderstanding—"

"What's there to misunderstand?" Juanito said. "I didn't want to come. You backed me into this corner with your talk of fraud and Amex and whatever. So, if you've got me here to fuck me one last time, just fuck me already or let me go home."

"Oh, come on, Juanito."—*gotta crown me with your heart*—"You know that I love you. What else could I do? You were playing hard to get. You weren't coming back to me."

"Ay, Dios mío," Juanito said. He jolted off of the sofa. "I wasn't playing shit. Would you shut that damn tape off? If I hear this song one more time, I'm going to rip my leg hairs out my body and scream."

"Didn't you hear me?"

"Oh, I heard you," Juanito said. He thought about throwing the wine glass directly at Paul's cabezota. "You gotta listen to what I'm telling you."

Paul was up near the tape player, pulling out the tape and putting it back on the shelf.

"No, no, don't put in another tape," Juanito said. "Blow out the candles. Clean up the petals from the floor."

"But—"

"No, listen," Juanito said. "I don't love you. I love Daniel. I was only having sex with you because of the drugs and because I was trying to get Daniel that sofa."

Paul stood up straight. "So you led me on?" Paul said.

"Are you kidding me?" Juanito said. "Okay, I get it. I guess that makes me a horrible person, but I just wanted to make Daniel happy, and shit got out of hand." It reminded Juanito of the nightmares he had as a child: standing in an ordinary place, nothing out of whack, then the ground turns to quicksand and it sucks him under until he startles himself awake, gasping.

"You say I owe you one more session," Juanito said. "Do it and let's get it over with so that I can go back to my man, go back to my apartment and my regular life."

Paul stared at him and blinked. Juanito had never seen him cry before. It shocked him to see it happening, for some reason. It was like he didn't think Paul was the type of person who could cry in front of others. He didn't think someone who was cruel enough to threaten someone into having sex with them was capable of crying in front of that person.

Juanito tried to feel bad, he really did, but he couldn't squeeze any pena out of his heart, no matter how hard he tried. He couldn't even believe that Paul was in love with him. Like, *how* the hell did he think the way he was acting was an expression of love? Juanito, más que nunca, felt like he was walking around with a giant sign on his forehead that said, HEY, YOU PEOPLE, IF YOU LOVE ME, THEN PLEASE, BEAT THE SHIT OUT OF ME. Why did people think they could treat him like that? He wanted to know. But the other question he asked himself sometimes, the one he refused to entertain for more than a scalding-hot moment was: Why did he take that shit from them in the first place?

He didn't have an answer, or if he did, it was buried under years' worth of shit that he didn't feel strong enough to shovel through.

"Oh, my god, would you look at me," Paul said. He ran his fingers through his hair. "I've become exactly what I never wanted to become."

"What's that?" Juanito said. "A manipulative hijo de puta?"

"No," he said. "An old, bitter queen."

Juanito watched now as Paul placed his hands up to his face to cover himself as he sobbed. Juanito waited for the lágrimas to turn to violence. He waited for Paul to decide to punch him, to rip down his pants and fuck him anyway. He waited for Paul to take that Sade tape and whip it at his face from across the room. But then there was a knock at the door.

Probably the neighbors knocking to complain about the loud music. He looked at Paul to see who was going to answer it. Paul said he didn't want to answer the door in tears, and could Juanito see who was there. Juanito thought about saying no, making Paul open the door so the whole world could see him like that. But he didn't do that. Even though Juanito didn't feel any pity for the man in front of him, he didn't want to be cruel to him.

When Juanito opened the door and he saw Daniel standing there, his heart felt like it was levitating inside his body. "Why," Juanito said, "are you here?"

"Are you okay?" Daniel asked. Juanito stood in the doorway. He didn't want to open the door all of the way to let him in. He didn't want Daniel to come and play like he was some kind of knight in shining armor.

"Now?" Juanito said. "You came *now*? You don't think I can handle this on my own?"

"Who's there?" Paul called out. Juanito envisioned a room with a giant fan. Then piles of shit being thrown up at the blades like confetti.

"It's me," Daniel shouted out to him, "you fuckface."

"Daniel, por favor," Juanito said. He put his hand on Daniel's chest. He could feel the nervous beats of Daniel's heart. Daniel pushed the door open and walked down the hallway toward the sala.

"Candles?" Daniel said. "Rose petals?" He turned back to look at Juanito now, as if his eyes were asking Juanito what was going on.

"It's not what it looks like," Juanito said. His heart was beating loca-loca and he had to focus on his inhales to make sure he was breathing. He felt dizzy.

Juanito looked at them both standing there, the sofa separating the two. He threw up his hands. "I can't do this," Juanito said. "I just can't."

He bolted toward the bathroom with his hand up against the wall to make sure he didn't pass the hell out. Once inside, he locked himself in.

The cold water ran in the sink when he twisted the knob. He splashed some on his face and watched as the droplets slid down it. He stared at the dark circles under his eyes, like bruises in the shape of crescent moons. He could never understand why they were called circles when the shape itself wasn't complete. He forced a big smile and stared at the lines where the gum met the tooth. Why did teeth have roots? How could they just sit there all tight, so sturdy, and *function*?

When he walked backward and leaned back against the wall, he slid down until his nalgas were slapped up against the cold tile. Seashell-patterned tiles. A magazine rack that placed the fashion magazines before the pornos, so that visitors wouldn't be able to see the dirt that Paul was really into when he was alone in that room with nothing but himself and his hand. The thought of it made Juanito want to vomit. And he could do that. He could vomit into the little toilet seat, but no, he didn't feel like making more of a mess.

He could hear Daniel screaming at Paul, but he couldn't hear the exact words. Then the sound of glass breaking. He felt too tired to stand up and do something about it. That was it. Paul was going to call the charge card company and he would be sent to jail for a crime he didn't commit. No way was a jury gonna find his ass not guilty. Not after the shit the lawyers would pull up. And then he'd be gone for one, two, how many years? Without Daniel. He pushed his head back against the wall and looked up, like when the mujeres were in trouble in the telenovelas and they looked up as if Jesus himself was gonna come down to rescue their sorry asses.

And then he saw it. The pipe. In the corner, cuddling up against the side of the sink, behind the toilet. An odd place for a pipe. Either Paul had forgotten it there after dropping it, or he thought it was good for the feng shui.

Juanito held the pipe in his hand. He loved how smooth the glass felt, and when he closed his eyes, the feeling of his fingers wrapped around it made something tingle. If he really focused, he could almost imagine his lungs filling with that sweet rock. Just the fantasy alone was orgasmic.

He got up and rummaged through the cabinet across from the toilet. He knew that Paul kept his rock stash in a little plastic baggie wrapped inside of a toilet paper roll. He fished through the rolls, first ripping off the paper that encased them. By the time he got to the fourth roll, he found a smushed up plastic bag jammed into the center of the tube. He used his finger as a hook and pulled it out.

He could hear them fighting now. He heard Paul laughing. Juanito looked at the beautiful rock between his fingers. He placed it into the pipe. All he needed was a light.

"Come on, Juanito," Daniel called. "Let's get out of here."

No. You can't do this. Not now. Not anymore. Deja la rock.

There was a knock on the door. *I'm fine, Daniel. Just splashing water on my face.* Where was the torch? He needed the torch. Search under the sink. Razors, shaving cream, toilet cleaner, mounds of cotton balls, bags full of Q-tips. What could Paul possibly do with all those fucking Q-tips? Then, the torch. Silver. No.

Do not touch it. Not even a finger. Another knock. Water running.

But fuck, it's so clear like a salt rock. Water running and click the lighter up, fizzle-sizzle, that inhale all minty fresh. Yes.

When he finally opened the door, he was high and Daniel was leaning up against the wall. "Oh, thank god," Daniel said.

"What happened to your eyebrow?" Juanito asked. He put a hand up to Daniel's face as if touching the blood would answer the question. Maybe he could find a butterfly bandage somewhere.

"It's nothing," Daniel said. "Don't worry."

Juanito could feel the tingle spreading to two areas. From his toes up through his ankles and further up. And then his chin through his jawline and further down. The two tingles would meet halfway and everything would be ecstatic and charged.

"Look at me," Daniel said. Juanito looked at his lips. He looked at his ears. He moved his right hand up to the hair near Daniel's ears to push the longer strands back a little.

"You need," he told Daniel, "to get a haircut this weekend."

And there it was: the tingle, the merging. Oh yes, that fucking feeling. Yes.

"You don't have to do this," Daniel said. "We can leave right now if you want—"

Juanito ate Daniel's face with his eyes. Daniel really was so beautiful. The small beauty mark on his right cheek. The way his five o'clock shadow made his face look rugged. His dimples whenever he smiled. But Daniel wasn't smiling now.

He watched as Daniel's eyes glided over Juanito's shoulder. The pipe was still on the bathroom counter. Surely this is what made Daniel's mouth curl into itself. Juanito felt too high to give a damn what Daniel could see.

Juanito put his hand on Daniel's cheek and even though he felt like every particle in his body was charged with static electricity, he could tell that his own eyes were crying because his cheeks were wet. "I'm sorry," he said, looking straight at Daniel's neck.

"Fuck, Juanito—" Daniel said. "Again?"

"Goddamn," Juanito screamed, so much energy he was up on his tippy toes. "Don't you *feel* it?"

Daniel put his hand up to Juanito's cheek to wipe away the tears. "No," Daniel said. "I have no idea what you're feeling right now."

DANIEL

He only had two options: stay in the sala while it happened or watch. He chose to watch. The cama was so big, it felt like it was the only thing in the bedroom. Daniel could hear Angel's words in the back of his mind: *Never trust a man that only has a bed and a kitchen table because then you know that all they think about is their damn appetite.*

He brought a wooden chair from the cocina into the bedroom. Placed it next to the bed to make sure that Paul didn't pull some sick shit. Paul was just as high as Juanito. Daniel watched as Paul stripped the bed of its comforter and its sheets. Paul placed two brown towels in the middle of the bed, crisscrossed. As he leaned over the bed, he looked at Daniel, squeezed his own nipples, and smirked.

It was that smirk that made Daniel want to bash his face in, but he knew that would solve nobody's problems. He knew that if Paul called Amex, they would be fucked.

It broke his heart to know that Juanito was loaded and still wanted this. It was like there was some switch inside Juanito's mind that made him desire that kind of sex when he was high. Even though Daniel couldn't understand it, he could at least be there to make sure that Juanito didn't get too hurt in the process. Por lo menos, that was what Daniel told himself in order to comfort himself. In a fucked-up situation like this, he had to do all he could to convince himself that he was trying to be a good and loving boyfriend.

Paul held Juanito's hand as he led him in. They collapsed onto the bed together, Paul on top. Daniel watched Juanito's face burst into pleasure as Paul slid his cock inside Juanito's ass. Daniel shivered and closed his eyes.

He tried to think of happy things. He thought of freshly made tembleque, still cold from the nevera. He thought of the time they had taken the ferry to Sandy Hook so they could go to the nude beach. Juanito had been too shy to take his trunks off for the world to see, and it had made Daniel quietly sad to think that Juanito was unaware of his own body's beauty.

The room was hot and dark. Daniel didn't know why Paul kept his windows closed. A little air wouldn't kill anyone. Juanito's body was covered in sweat. So was Paul's. They slipped against each other like there wasn't any traction to be had.

The light from the sala glowed off the sides of Paul's arms, which he was using to support himself on top of Juanito. Juanito was on his stomach. Paul pushed his hands against Juanito's back to keep his body still. He slapped Juanito's ass. Juanito cried out so loud that when he inhaled, it sounded like a whoop.

Daniel thought of the time they went to the mermaid parade in Coney Island, got hot dogs and cheese fries at Nathan's, and Juanito had dabbed a bit of cheese sauce on the tip of his nose, crossing his eyes like a goofy clown, just because he wanted to make Daniel laugh. He thought of the time that Juanito had asked him in bed if he thought, and to be straight with him, if Juanito was beautiful and worthy of love. Daniel had turned Juanito over to face him in the dark, where he could see the city streetlights creating shadow patterns on Juanito's softly illuminated face and said, Yes of course, baby. Of course you are beautiful.

Now Paul stopped fucking Juanito and twisted him by the legs into a new position. Juanito was on his back, legs flailing in the air. Daniel thought about what would happen if Juanito suddenly changed his mind. What then?

Paul was fucking him so hard, hand over Juanito's mouth to muffle any screams or moans. Daniel could no longer watch. He thought about throwing his hands up, getting up, and walking out. But he knew he couldn't leave that room. He couldn't leave Juanito there, so he shut his eyes and his mind was filled with nothing but the smell of sweat and shit and the sounds of Paul's skin slapping against Juanito's culo.

Outside the room, Daniel could imagine the candles still burning, the empty glasses of wine, the tape player without sound, the rose petals stranded on the rug. Paul grunted and then stopped. Daniel watched Paul lay his entire weight on top of Juanito's wet body. Paul was crying.

"Why," Paul said, nuzzling Juanito's cheek with his chin. "Why don't you love me?"

Because you're a sick fuck, Daniel thought, *who has no idea how to express your love.*

"Why, Juanito?" Paul said, stretching his arms so that he wasn't leaning on Juanito no more. "Why why why why?" And with each why, he pounded harder until Juanito sobbed for the first time. Juanito looked directly at Daniel.

Paul didn't stop. He was fucking as hard as he could and Daniel watched as Juanito squeezed his eyes shut and sobbed. Daniel got out of the chair and knelt on the ground next to the bed. He reached for Juanito's hand, and held onto it for as long as it took for the session to finally come to an end.

* * *

When they had first stepped foot in their apartment in Williamsburg, it felt like they were gonna take Brooklyn by storm with their love. They had nothing in their hands except the bags they could carry and whatever hope was shining in their eyes. He let Juanito run up those stairs first. Juanito was so happy, he practically took those steps two at a time. Daniel was doing his best to keep up with him, following the jingle-jangle sounds of the keys up the stairs and to the door. Then they stood together like wow. Not believing their luck.

Of course the whole place was empty, but that made it feel even more magical. It was afternoon some time, and the light had lit the whole place. All the walls and the wooden floors.

"Ay, mira," Juanito said. "We got our very own nevera." He was swinging open the fridge door like he was Amish and ain't seen one before. Daniel thought it was the cutest motion. "I'm gonna buy all the yogurt thingies," Juanito said, "and keep them fresh in here for the both of us."

Daniel dropped his bags and walked from the sala to the bedroom with his arms wide open like that chica from *The Sound of Music* when she's on the mountain singing out to the world. La-la-la. They spun together in circles until they fell down on the floor into puddles of their own laughing selves.

And they held each other.

"Ay, mira over there," Juanito said to him, holding his hand all tight. "We got a window."

Daniel wanted to say, Of course we got a window. This ain't a jail cell. Even jail cells got little windows. But he was talking bigger. That window was bigger. He watched as Juanito looked up and out of it, at the blue up there with the clouds.

"Damn, what a view," Juanito said. "Hot damn." It felt like they had stumbled on the one place on Earth that was all theirs. "We got the sky view," Juanito continued. "I mean, damn, don't it feel like we got the whole sky just to ourselves?"

"Yeah," Daniel said. "It does."

And it did. It really, really did.

CODA

GOING

(1993)

In the dream Randy's leaping into
the future, and still here; Michael's holding him
and releasing at once. Just as Steve's

holding Jerry, though he's already gone,
Marie holding John, gone, Maggie holding
her John, gone, Carlos and Darren
holding another Michael, gone,

and I'm holding Wally, who's going.
Where isn't the question,
though we think it is;
we don't even know where the living are

—Mark Doty, *Atlantis*

ANGEL

Every Wednesday she took the subway. She woke in the morning, stood in front of the mirror, and put on the Chanel suit slowly. She needed to luxuriate in the process of putting it on, one arm at a time, like she was soaking in a bubble bath made of herringbone fabric.

Ever since she bought the suit, she loved to watch it drape on the hanger. She could do it for hours, just sit there and watch it. *Dios mío,* she thought every time she saw it, *this belongs to me.* And claro que sí, baby, delicate fabrics call for delicate hands and delicate grips. If only the whole world could've seen her then—walking to the subway like she was going to the biggest ball in all of New York.

This Wednesday was no different. She got tea from the bodega so that, just in case it spilled, it wouldn't stain. She took a deep inhale, double-checked to make sure it was buttoned proper. She had on a smooth wig (no curls, just waves), those beautiful patent leather cockroach-killer pumps that had been calling her name ever since she saw them on the rack, a cute little teardrop pillbox hat that cost four bucks at a cute thrifty dig in SoHo, and a cane to keep her upright. To top it all off, she wore a black knitted veil to cover up the purple spots. She wanted to channel Jackie O at John's funeral. For that matter, she wanted to take the funeral look to the subway underground. She looked at herself in the mirror now, took it *all* in, and adjusted her lapels with a quick pinch of the fingers.

As always, the 6 was empty when she got on at Castle Hill. It wasn't until Seventy-Seventh and Lex when things started to fill up. Rush hour—it was the only time of day to do it. She made sure to stand up in the middle of the car as the bodies filled in until everything was so tight. She loved the calentito energy that people gave off when they were standing right up against her—all warmth, especially in the summer. It was like the best example of what made a New Yorker a New Yorker: the ability to put up with anything—rats the size of cats, fucked-up subway cars that were less glamorous than a room at Rikers, the always-present humo of piss on the hottest days—and they all did it because that was Nueva fuckin' Yol, the city that felt alive and buzzing with energy. Whenever Angel saw the skyline at night, just after a fresh sunset, she'd think, I might be dying, but thank god I still got my eyes because is that not a sight to behold or what?

Suits surrounded her on all sides. She held in her breath. She closed her eyes and pretended, for a little hot second, that she was a real businesswoman who was en route to a real office, and there it was, because who could tell everyone around her that it wasn't the case? She was wearing Chanel, for fuck's sake! For all they knew, she was one of *them*.

There was the truth of it: she rode that train every Wednesday because she had the virus and she knew that nobody wanted to touch her. Once a week, she could put on her Chanel, get on that subway, and when the train cars were packed with people, she could feel human bodies all against her and feel their warmth.

DANIEL

He probably should have left the neighborhood and gone somewhere else. He had dreams of picking up and going somewhere he could take evening walks, somewhere he could slice watermelons and eat them straight to the rind, somewhere he could raise kids, and if not kids, a dog or maybe two. But they were just fantasies and nothing more. The thought of moving gave him churra pains. Everything it entailed sounded like a pain in the ass: packing shit up only to unpack it later, carrying boxes into a truck, labeling the things that needed to be carried.

He was horny all the time, but he didn't dare cruise around Williamsburg or Bushwick. He tried the parks in the West Village, but it only took a couple of blow jobs for him to get tired of getting sucked on a bench, in the dark, out in the semi-open. He tried the piers, but just being there brought back too many memories that he didn't want to think about. He walked into a porn shop in Times Square and, as soon as he stepped foot inside, he walked right back out.

Then he found the phone hotlines. All it took was a quick ring of the nine-hundred number and he could record his own message about what he was like and what he wanted to do. He could also listen to the recordings that other guys left. It took him a couple days of listening to figure out the gist of things about what kind of info he was supposed to leave: age, race, height, hung or not hung (exact inches optional, but preferred), HIV-status was a must, and then other details like kinks. Some of the messages were so fancy, but all he wanted to do was fuck. He didn't want to bottom. "Total top only," he said in his recording, "condom is a must, nonnegotiable."

It only took a week for him to learn that, somewhere in the five boroughs, at any given time, there was a thirsty bottom looking for a big-dicked top. The calls came back immediately. He had a string of guys who were down, but the only thing he had was their word. Who knew how cute they'd be? What if they lied about their age or height or whatever else?

The thing was: most guys didn't lie. There was Jason, Justin, Joshua. Ricardo, Preston, Frankie. Arthur, Kyle One, Kyle Two, Kyle Three. The more guys he fucked, the more he wanted to. He was gobbling them up like Pac-Man on a full board.

One night, after he fucked Preston, he lay in bed watching him get dressed to leave. He scratched his armpit hair with one hand and relaxed his head further in the pillow. Preston lingered by the door. "What's wrong?" Daniel asked.

"We've been doing this for a couple times now," Preston said, "and I was wondering—"

"I already told you," Daniel said. "I'm neg and not looking for anything serious."

"I'm not asking about that," Preston said. Daniel should've known. Preston was the worrier. "You say that you don't have a boyfriend, but whose stuff is all this? Like these pants folded over here?" He picked up Juanito's pants from the corner of the bedroom. "Whose are these?" he asked. "They look too small for you."

Daniel faked a laugh to make Preston realize he was being ridiculous. "Why're you being paranoid?" Daniel said.

It was a stupid question to ask. He knew why Preston was asking. It's not that Preston was looking for a boyfriend. Daniel knew that already. But Preston was more scared than the others of catching the virus. Daniel sighed. "I already told you, dude," Daniel said. "I don't have a boyfriend and I don't have the virus."

"Are you sure?" Preston said.

"Yes," he said.

It was a long story to explain and he never felt like telling any of them. How could he say to a stranger—because that was what these guys were, strangers—that the love of his life had killed himself? Two months earlier, he walked into the apartment and Juanito was in bed with a plastic bag duct-taped around his head. The suicide note was short: he had tested positive, he felt guilty, he couldn't handle this, he asked Daniel to forgive him, he didn't want to die a slow or painful death, that was it, signed, goodbye with love.

And now Preston was going to stand there and think that he knew what was going on? It was laughable, Daniel thought, because there was no way he could explain to any of these easy fucks what his life felt like now that everyone around him was gone. How he had to get tested every couple of months because he was scared that the negative results were hiding something. How there were no antibodies in his body that could be detected, but how could the tests really be sure? How could that even be the case if Juanito had seroconverted? It was easier to just shut down when guys like Preston pressed him. He felt so much rage.

"Get out," Daniel said. It wasn't like he was lying to Preston anyway. All the tests pointed toward negative. He used condoms.

"What?" Preston said.

"You need to leave," Daniel said. There it was: his heart had shrunk to three-sizes-too-small. He could hear the meanness in his voice.

"Why're you being so rude?" Preston said.

"Why're you still standing there?"

"You know," Preston said. "You seemed like a nice guy at first."

"Well," Daniel said. "I guess you were wrong about that."

* * *

But he knew that Preston wasn't wrong about that. That night, Daniel lay naked in bed, crying himself to sleep over the type of person he'd become. He hated sleeping alone, in the dark. He took one of the pillows and propped it between his knees so he could cuddle against something.

There was his apartment, full of shadows. He'd saved all of Juanito's things as if their home was some kind of museum or monument to their life together. It was useless and fucked-up.

The next afternoon, he stuffed Juanito's jeans into a black garbage bag and tied the string into a double-knot. He carried it over his shoulder to the edge of the street where the garbage would be collected later that night. When he walked down the street, he looked back at the bag, thinking maybe he would take it back. He could haul it upstairs, cut open the knot, put the jeans back into the drawer where they were supposed to go. Pero from down the block, all the black bags looked the same. All lumpy and ready to be taken away.

He opened all the drawers and created a pile of all of Juanito's things. Ties, shoes, tank tops, loose spools of fabric, the sewing box with a hundred needles stuck into pillows like they were voodoo dolls, button-downs, his comb, aerosol, the nameplate necklace that he had bought as a gag, books of matches from this place and that. He no longer remembered when they had gone to Boy Bar, but there was the matchbook as proof, ready to burn when struck.

The sewing machine was in the corner where Juanito had last used it to make an ascot from fabric he bought on markdown in the Garment District. No, he refused to throw away the thing. He didn't know how to sew anything together, but he would keep it.

When the apartment was emptied of all reminders, he lay in bed waiting for the sound of the garbage truck. Pero when he woke the next morning, he had no memory of hearing the sanitation crew come by. He peeked out the window and it was all gone. He went to brush his teeth, and he stared at the toothbrush all alone in the cup. Later, he told himself, he'd go to the pharmacy to get another toothbrush to balance things out. A cup should always have two, so the weight of one wouldn't knock the thing over.

He couldn't keep going like this. He knew he would have to bite the bullet. She was the one person who could help him through this loss, if she was willing to take him back.

* * *

"What the fuck does that mean?" he said on the phone. He was glad Dorian picked up. He didn't know what other options he had. His back was up against the counter, near the sink that held a week's worth of dishes. He didn't have any more clean spoons left.

"Encephalitis," Dorian said again, slower and louder, like he was talking to the deaf.

"I heard you the first time," he said. Bless her. "I still don't know what the fuck it means?"

"Darling, you disappear and reappear and you call to ask me this nonsense? You hear the word encephalitis and you ask me what that means? Are you sure you're a gay in this year of the Lord?" Dorian said.

"Damn, Dorian. I'm sorry. I didn't realize it was a gay thing."

"It's not a gay thing, darling. It's an AIDS thing," Dorian said. "It's like dementia. You'll be lucky if she still remembers you."

* * *

He had to sit on the stoop of her new building for two hours until he saw her walking down the street. "It's me," he told her when she walked toward the steps. She had one hand in her purse, fishing for keys. When she looked back up at him, her stare was dead-neutral. "Do you remember me?" he asked softly.

Angel pulled out her keys and reached for the lock. "Of course I remember," she said. "Where's Juanito?"

He didn't feel like talking about that yet so he shifted the conversation. "Are you wearing Chanel?"

"Why yes," she said, extending her arms out for a moment of dazzle. "Don't you love it?"

"Where were you going dressed so fancy?" he said, fearing that she might've been coming back from another funeral.

"Nowhere special. It's Wednesday," she said, as if that answered it. "Where's Juanito?" She had to push the door in order to unjam it.

He was quiet, thinking about where to start. He had never actually had to explain it aloud to anyone before. *Words*—he thought— *words could be so damn impossible sometimes.*

She held the door open for him, waiting for him to come up the steps and back into the house. "Oooh," she said. "No, don't tell me. I don't think I'm ready to hear this."

* * *

He had been so happy to see her, and so relieved that she remembered him, that he didn't even notice how fucked-up she looked. He noticed later that evening, when he heated up some leftover arroz con pollo that she had in a Tupperware. When she took off the Chanel and changed into gray pajamas, Daniel could see how flaca she was. He saw the purple sarcoma spots—one on her forehead, another on her left triceps. He didn't know where else they were and he didn't want to ask.

He was so hungry that he inhaled his food in a couple of minutes. Angel had only taken a couple bites. He watched as she moved the fork slowly down, missing the plate once, twice, again. She stabbed at the rim of the paper plate. It took her an entire minute—he knew because he counted the seconds in his head—for her to successfully take a spoonful of rice from the plate to her mouth.

"You okay, mama?" he asked. "You want me to help you?"

She chewed and shook her head.

"You sure?" he said.

"I said I got it fine," she said.

* * *

They lived like this for another few days: Angel moving at a glacial pace and Daniel wondering if she did, as she claimed, have everything under control. One afternoon, he walked out of the bathroom to find her on the floor, trying to shove a videotape into a cassette player.

"What is happening here?" he asked her.

"All I wanna do," she said, "is watch *Pretty Woman*."

* * *

Angel complained about a sore in her mouth and shooting pains that felt like needle pricks. He went with her to the hospital to have a CAT scan done so a doctor could tell them where the pain was shooting from. They gave her a shot of ethanol because the doc said it'd permanently kill the offending nerve.

"What's for dinner tonight?" Angel asked on the subway ride home. She rested her head on his shoulder.

"I think I'll make lasagna," he said.

"Oh yummy," she said. She yawned and he could feel her jaw-bone against his body. "What a treat."

An hour later, he was prepping the sauce and she asked, again, what he was making for dinner.

"Lasagna," he said, peeking his head out of the cocina to look at her collapsed on the couch. "We talked about this on the subway, remember?"

"Right, right," she said, scratching her arm.

A half hour later, she came into the cocina while he was stirring the sauce pot. He had the oven fan on to blow away any steam. She opened the cabinet where she kept her pills and took out the Vicodin. She popped one into her mouth and turned on the sink to gather water into her hand. She gulped the pill down. It was probably her fourth Vicodin that afternoon, if he was counting correctly.

"What're you making for dinner?" she said. "It smells really good."

"I'm making lasagna, Angel," he said. "Maybe if you didn't overdo it with the painkillers, you'd remember."

She put the orange pill bottle back into the cabinet and closed the door slowly. "Who do you think you're talking to like that? I'm in pain," she said. "I'm not Juanito. I'm not the one with the drug problem and I never have been."

He stopped stirring and grabbed the wooden spoon out of the pot. He watched her move back to the couch as if she hadn't just taken a sword and shoved it into his heart.

"How'd you know about that?" he said. He hadn't told her anything about Juanito's drug problem. They didn't keep in touch with anyone from the ball scene either, so he had no idea how the gossip train would've made it back to Angel's ears. "I asked you a question," he shouted and pointed the spoon at her. Tomato sauce dropped to the floor.

"He came here," she said. "He needed help."

He couldn't believe what he was hearing. He didn't know why Juanito would hide that from him, or for that matter, why Angel wouldn't've mentioned it when he first arrived on her steps. "You're lying," he said. "What jodienda bullshit are you passing off?"

Angel shrugged. "It's true," she said.

"It's not true," he screamed. He waved the spoon in the air and sauce flew everywhere. "You're mis-remembering. You're going loca. You can't even remember that we're having lasagna for dinner tonight and you're telling me that Juanito came here, to you, for help."

"Sí, claro." She was saying it so matter of fact. It was like he had asked her if it was raining and she looked out to see whether there was anything falling from the sky.

"If that's all true," he said, "then what happened?"

"I told him he needed to stop it with the drugs," she said, "but then I told him I couldn't do anything more for him and he needed to leave."

No. He couldn't wrap his mind around this. Angel had turned Juanito away. He wanted to know when this was: before or after the sofa, at what level of his addiction, before or after the clinic test.

"You turned him away?" he said. He didn't scream. He clenched his fists behind his back as hard as he could.

"Turned who away?" Angel said.

Daniel couldn't look at her anymore. He went back to the cocina to stare at the sauce. Their lasagna was almost ready, but he didn't have an appetite anymore.

*   *   *

"I don't think it tastes *that* bad," Angel said, slowly bringing the fork to her mouth. The lasagna piece fell back on the plate and she had to retry.

"You think my cooking tastes bad?" he said. He didn't have the energy to keep talking to her more that night.

"Es que, I just don't understand why you're crying into your food," she said. "It doesn't taste so bad that you gotta cry over it."

He looked up. Her face was mad puffy from the Prednisone. She had no clue. "I'm not crying because it's bad," he said. "I'm crying because you hurt my feelings? Before dinner?"

"I did?" she said. "Pues, maybe you should come with me tomorrow on the subways. It's Wednesday. We'll dress up nice and get cheesecake."

* * *

The suit, all buttoned up, gave Angel a jazzy look. By the time they hit Midtown, the car was packed and Daniel asked her if she wanted to move to a less crowded space. She swatted her hand at him to hush up. He couldn't see her eyes behind the black veil she wore. "Don't you feel it?" she said. Just where the veil cut off, he saw her lips. No lipstick, just purple lip liner.

"Feel what?" he said, fearing she was losing more than her memories.

She moved closer to his ear. "I love feeling everyone's body up against mine. I don't know how to explain it," she whispered as the train screeched to a stop so the doors could open. "I just love feeling all this life and blood pumping around me."

When they hit Union Square, people weren't packed as close to them anymore. People were staring but Daniel didn't know why. They were definitely staring. He looked at the floor, then at his hand on the pole. Angel was focusing on an ad like she wanted to memorize every possible aspect of it. Then he saw the problem.

There was a stream of brown coming down her leg. "Mama," he whispered into her ear, not wanting anyone else to hear, even though everyone around them seemed to know except Angel. When he had her attention, he said, "Your leg, mira."

Angel looked down at the shit running down her leg. Her breath went fast and deep. She fainted and Daniel had to remove his hand from the pole in order to catch her from falling straight out.

"Shh-shh," he said. He was carrying her now and the smell was everywhere. "I got you, mama. We're going back home."

* * *

He put the suit on a hanger while Angel napped. He ran some cold water and dabbed the stains with a sponge. He knew he'd have to take it to the dry cleaner's, but he was trying his best to do damage control before it got that far. He hoped it wasn't ruined forever. There must be something someone could do. Surely there must be a way to take a stain out of fabric.

He swept the dust and combined all the trash bags in the apartment and brought them to the Dumpster on the side street. When he came back up, Angel stood in the middle of the sala in her pajamas. "There you are," she said. Her face was puffy and she could barely open up her eyelids all the way. "Where'd you go?"

"Just getting rid of some stuff."

She walked over to him and wrapped her bony arms around his shoulders. "Ay, Hector," she said. "You should tell me when you're going out like that. You know I get scared when people just walk out like that without words before."

He swiped some hair out of her face. It was wet and sticking to her forehead. "I'm sorry," he said. He knew he had to play along.

"You know, Hector baby," she said. "I'm so excited to be a mother. I think I found a new girl at the piers to be our first Xtravaganza. Her name is Venus. Don't cry, babe. You got any sights on anyone who could be a good Xtravaganza?"

"Yeah," he said. "I'll go out there and do my best."

He had a flash of what his life would be like now, when Angel was gone: walking the streets and bringing the nenas and the banjees and the fierce fire sparkler kings and queens into their house. He didn't *want* this responsibility, but he had inherited it.

Angel unwrapped her arms from their hug. "Ay, mira," she said. "I knew you'd be the best father this house could ask for."

* * *

She wanted to go to the roof to dance. So that's what they did. The sun was setting pink on the horizon and the Manhattan scrapers looked like Lego pieces from where they danced in the Bronx. "I could do this everyday," she said, and Daniel hummed. He didn't want to cry in front of her again.

In one month, she would die in St. Vincent's, crying for her mother. Daniel wouldn't know how to find her mother. He didn't know her name or where she lived. In five months, Dorian would also die. Pepper LaBeija would call Daniel and they'd cry together on the line. A week afterward, Daniel would read Dorian's obit in the *New York Times* and think, *Of course this fabulous bitch is making headlines even from the grave!* Months later, Dorian's children would go through the closet and find the chest. And the mummy. A motherfucking mummified body, oh yes. Bullet wound, wrapped in imitation leather, because of course it was. Pinned to the body, a note: *This poor soul broke into my apartment and I was forced to shoot him.*

But now? Now it was just the two of them on the roof. "Hector baby," Angel said. "Hold me up while we spin."

They had the boom box, but they didn't need music then. The sun was setting and he held her skeletal body close to him. She hummed a song with a one-two-three beat that he didn't recognize, but they stepped one-two-three, one-two-three, she was guiding him forward, showing him where to go.

She released his hand and, without a word, started walking toward the staircase. "Wait," he called out to her. "Don't go yet. Let's dance one more time."

"Pero, Hector," she said and he wept. "I'm tired, baby."

ACKNOWLEDGMENTS

I am incredibly grateful to my large and complicated family for instilling in me a belief in the power of love and perseverance. I'm also thankful for the power of their storytelling. Special shout-out to my parents, Maurice and Nanette, as well as to my sister, Jenna.

A million thanks to my agents, Ellen Levine and Alexa Stark at Trident, for seeing the spark of something in my early pages and for being fierce advocates along the way. Thank you to Claire Roberts and the foreign rights team, for representing my work to the larger world, and to Rich Green and Will Watkins at ICM Partners, for doing the same in L.A.

Enormous thanks to my editor, Megan Lynch, for her encouragement, enthusiasm, and brilliance. Thanks also to everyone at Ecco, for their belief and support, especially Emma Dries and Martin Wilson. Another thanks goes to Juliet Mabey and everyone at Oneworld in the United Kingdom.

To the Iowa Writers' Workshop, for taking a chance on me. Thank you to Connie Brothers, Deb West, and Jan Zenisek. Thanks also to my brilliant peers there, especially Sorrel Westbook-Wilson, Shaun Hamill, Karen Parkman, Moira Casados Cassidy, Mgbechi Erondu, Magogodi Makhene, Derek Nnuro, Eskor Johnson, Melody Murray, Alex Madison, Maria Kuznetsova, Delaney Nolan, Sarah Frye, Lindsay Stern, Iracema Drew, Jason Hinojosa, and De'Shawn Winslow. All saw parts of this novel in various early forms, and encouraged me to finish.

Much love to the Fine Arts Work Center in Provincetown and to the jury who selected my sample out of the pile: Jeffery Renard Allen, Sarah Braunstein, Christa Fraser, Paul Harding, Porochista Khakpour, Paul Lisicky, Matthew Neill Null, and Joanna Scott.

Spending those seven months living on a sand dune at the end of the world, in paradise, was the experience of a lifetime. Special shout-out to Alison and John Ferring, for endowing my fellowship there.

To the teachers who inspired me along the way: In New Jersey—Jaime Vander Velde and Andi Mulshine. At Columbia—Karen Russell, Sonya Chung, Stacey D'Erasmo, Josh Bell, Amy Benson, and Jenny Davidson. At Iowa—Ethan Canin, Bennett Sims, Sam Chang, Margot Livesey, Marilynne Robinson, Paul Harding, and Ayana Mathis. For their wisdom and advice along the way, Andrea Barrrett, Yiyun Li, Edward P. Jones, and Michael Cunningham.

Though this book is not a factual history, I am indebted to Jennie Livingston and *Paris Is Burning* for the creative spark that led to these pages. To Dorian, Angel, Hector, and Venus, whose lives and consciousnesses I've spent countless hours thinking about. When I started this, I didn't think it would turn into a novel, but alas.

Finally, to all the gentle souls we lost to the virus, and to the brothers and sisters at Pulse who left us too soon. This book is for you.

JOSEPH CASSARA was born and raised in New Jersey. He holds degrees from Columbia University and the Iowa Writers' Workshop and has been a writing fellow at the Fine Arts Work Center in Provincetown, Massachusetts. *The House of Impossible Beauties* is his first novel. He lives in Iowa.